Trade Secrets

Holly Rozner

TRADE SECRETS
Copyright © 2012 by Holly Rozner. All rights reserved
Printed in the United States of America. No part of this book can
be used or reprinted in any manner whatsoever without written
permission except in the case of brief quotations embodied in critical
articles and reviews. For information, visit hollyrozner.com

Money Smart, Inc.
Glencoe, Illinois

ISBN-13:9780986016301

First Edition

This is a work of fiction. All names, places, characters and incidents are entirely imaginary, except for those historical events that are part of the public domain and have been published in newspapers or in court documents. Any resemblance to persons living or dead is coincidental.

Book Cover and Design
by adazing.com

For my father, Joseph Fleischman, who left his dreams and his books.

"It's what one does, and nothing else, that shows the stuff one's made of."
Jean-Paul Sartre, *No Exit*

"They threw you in and told you the rules and the first time they caught you off base they killed you...
Stay around and they would kill you."
Ernest Hemingway, *A Farewell to Arms*

Acknowledgements

It takes a village to raise a child or to write a book. I know this to be true because there were countless people involved in creating <u>TRADE SECRETS</u>. I want to thank my early readers, some who knew this book under a different title: Toby Aronstrom, Hal Gershowitz, Sophia Marcovitz and Myra Sanderman. Arthur Pine, the literary agent, was the first to put his professional endorsement on the novel. Rita Turow, whom I met at Off-Campus writer's workshop, provided editorial expertise; Teri Drake led me to the *Love Is Murder* conference; Marilyn Cohen invented the back-story. Lois Davis, Denise Chaimovitz, Sylvia Margolies, Judi Stone and Gail Jacobson offered critical insight that shaped the final copy. Enid Baron worked on the query letter. Darcie Chan, whom I never met, graciously sent me information so I could begin the self-publishing process. Carla Arnell added the finishing touch.

Most important, my family: my husband, Irwin, who gave me space to write and diligently proofed the book for last minute errors; and my daughters, Jory Strosberg and Elory Rozner, who were constant cheerleaders and lent their resources during this long, wonderful process.

chapter 1

Chicago, 1986

REMY MASTERMAN BREEZED through the gilded door of her apartment building and slid into a taxi the doorman had hailed.

"The Exchange," she announced.

The cab sped though Lincoln Park before turning on to Lake Shore Drive and then south on Michigan Avenue. A block past Water Tower as traffic slowed to a crawl, Remy's heart began to pound. She glanced at her watch. Her appointment at the Exchange was scheduled for 11:00. Only three months had passed since her father's fatal crash, the event that had prompted her to buy a membership at the Exchange to unearth answers to questions that plagued her. With the interview only minutes away, Remy worried that her emotions might prevent her from discovering the secrets she sought.

A bus blocked the intersection at Wacker Drive. Remy vaulted out of the cab and handed the driver ten dollars without waiting for change. Wearing a black skirt that revealed a dancer's legs, Remy tossed a jacket over her shoulder as she rushed towards the glass and steel building that housed the largest trading pits in the world. If her feet hurt, it didn't show on her face. Determination hardened those curious eyes as her high heels tapped along the marble foyer.

10:40. Still time to stop at the visitors' gallery before meeting the Committee in the West Tower. Remy rode an elevator to the third floor and followed the guard's directions.

There it was: a glass-enclosed room overlooking the vast trading floor. It had been so many years since she had stood here with her father who was able to interpret the commotion before her. With him the chaos made sense.

Amidst a burst of lollipop-colored jackets, hundreds of men hunched together. The rubber floorboards were strewn with paper: copies of discarded customer orders, gum wrappers, trading cards and Kleenex, as if confetti had fallen from the ceiling. Telephones lined the room, dotted with large banners from dozens of brokerage companies. Clerks in yellow and orange bounded through the maze of bodies to deliver an order while Remy searched the crowd for clues.

"Five on a 100," one man mouthed, his arms spread towards the ceiling. The pane that separated her from the deafening din silenced his voice, but his intention could be understood from a hand signal as he sprang to catch a trade. Though she couldn't decipher exactly what he was trying to say, she guessed he was a buyer.

"Sold," another motioned. A deal was consummated. A deal that could smash lives as it had her father's. Her body tensed. The bloody image of his accident haunted her as it did every day. The late night phone call. The sirens. The ambulance. Remy tried to understand how her father, who was one of the strongest men she had known, could have taken his own life. There had been a change in his behavior for several weeks before the accident. He had stopped going out and even lost interest in cooking, which had long been his hobby. When Remy asked what was wrong, he said it was nothing.

"Those bastards at the Exchange are assholes. Don't worry, darling. Everything will be OK."

Remy knew that something had happened, but there was no way to find what it was. After the accident she turned to her husband for emotional support, but Stuart Masterman was busy vying for partner at Sloan and Kirk, and casually dismissed her.

That was when she came up with her own plan. She told Stuart she intended to buy a seat in order to trade. He told her not to, that she would get herself into trouble. When he actually forbade her to do it, she walked out.

A small crowd was gathering near Remy in the gallery. Secretaries, lawyers, businessmen: people came from offices all over the Loop to make sense of the famous turmoil below. Remy wondered what they could understand. Even her father couldn't explain it all.

The trading floor was the size of a football field, a far cry from the tiny room where trading had started a hundred years earlier with a handful of men huddled around chalkboards used for reporting trades.

Today, hundreds crowded into various pits. There were very few women: occasionally sisters or wives of someone whose family had ties to the Exchange. Otherwise, women rarely ventured into this territory.

The neon boards along the wall flashed prices in half-second intervals. From this vantage point it was difficult to see what was traded in each quadrant, for there weren't signs for each pit.

The Trade building, the ultimate in modern technology, towered over the city's center as a shrine to its great god, Money. Volume on this exchange surpassed that at any other because of its chairman, Zachary Silverman, who presided like a Titan from his fortieth floor office at Crestwood Trading.

Now Zach Silverman was calling the shots and her father, Harry Saks, was dead. It took all of Remy's strength to hold back tears, wondering what Zach knew. He didn't even attend the funeral. Instead, he sent a note explaining that he had been in D.C. for meetings and had missed his connections.

Remy was nervous. Her plan was not well defined. Maybe this was a mistake. If she decided not to use the seat she had bought, she could lease it out to another trader and make some money on the rent. She didn't have to do this. Then she remembered visiting Zachary's office when she was sixteen and a wave of sadness washed over her. Remy checked her watch against the digital clock on the wall. Tucking a red briefcase under her arm, she took a deep breath. This was where her father's career began and where it ended. She had no idea what she would learn or how she would learn it, but nothing could stop her. Remy nodded politely to the security guard and waited quietly for an elevator.

On the eleventh floor she read the bulletin listing the day's meetings. When she found the one pertaining to her, she sat down on a leather sofa and retrieved a gold compact from her handbag. A touch of gloss to her lips and a hint of rouge to her cheeks. Then, wondering if those interviewing her would even notice how she looked, she zipped the bag.

"Miss Masterman?" A woman in uniform came to get her.

"I'm Remy Masterman," she answered, as she followed the messenger into the assigned room.

Trade Secrets

The moment she stepped inside and faced a dozen men seated around the mahogany table, her confidence faded. Each wore a badge on his jacket. At the far end was a microphone. The chairman of the Committee whose badge read MOUSE directed her to take a seat. Remy accepted an oversized chair, pulled the mike towards her and smiled weakly. Nobody returned the smile.

"Remy Masterman," MOUSE announced, leafing through her paperwork. His real name was carved in small letters under his acronym. Her father had once told her that only the letters on the badge were important; your real name meant nothing.

"Do you intend to trade?" he asked.

Remy nodded. She answered his questions in a businesslike manner: where she lived, whether she owned or rented her apartment and how many years she had worked as an accountant. She wondered if any of this information was pertinent as she caught one of the men glancing at his watch, clearly bored, not caring about her or ever imagining what she had come to learn.

Their eyes were riveted on her, as if they had never interviewed a woman before, certainly none that looked like this, her auburn hair cascading to her shoulders, her alabaster skin shimmering under the light. No one could guess her motive for being here.

Remy had practiced what she would say, expecting the interview to take hours. She assumed they would probe into her background and ask why she had chosen to trade. Instead, within fifteen minutes, without asking much, they accepted her check, granting her a license to trade.

In the hallway Remy relaxed. So far, so good.

Still the experience was unsettling. Were these interviews a charade? It seemed as if anyone but a convicted criminal could pass such an inspection. And though she knew that no one needed special connections to join the Exchange, that anyone with collateral could walk in off the street, fill out the application and buy or lease a seat, it surprised her that there was not more to it. At least she was confident that no one would know she was Harry Saks' daughter. Because of a legal technicality on a stock certificate she held jointly with her ex-husband, Remy had not changed her name back to Saks, something that would now mask her identity. Not even Zach Silverman would recognize her.

She was given a sheet of instructions, including orders to pick up her badge. She hurried through the packed hall until she found the room where she was fingerprinted and photographed. As she waited for her badge to be etched with her name, a flock of traders dashed through the corridor. Soon she would be one of them.

One week ago Remy had deposited the required money in a clearinghouse, the firm that would act as a broker for the purchase of her seat and guarantee her trades. That was behind her. At noon Remy was handed a badge, the emblem that would designate which Index she could trade. She cradled it in her hands and rubbed it for good luck, something her dad taught her. This ritual, like the one the family followed to sit in the living room before a trip, as if the interlude would ensure a safe trip, remained her tradition. As she clutched it in her hand, the conflict of being on her father's turf without his sanction nearly overcame her. She paused for a minute before hurrying through the hallway to meet her best friend, Lara, at the corner deli.

A man wearing a black trading jacket with bold silver stripes was rushing towards her. The large pin on his lapel flashed JAYJAY. So this is the legend! She met his gaze with wary eyes. Famous for the Excalibur he drove, license plate BIGINDEX, Jason was one of the traders her father had told her about. The society columns were full of stories about Jason Bramson, so it was no secret that he was one of Chicago's most eligible playboys.

"Sorry," he said, holding out his arm to keep her from falling as he bumped into her.

"It's all right."

"Are you OK?" he asked.

"I'm fine." He leaned over to pick up the *Tribune* that had slipped out of her hands. She brushed the hair from her face, as he twirled her around.

"Good. Gotta run, doll." Then off he went, followed by a retinue of clerks who hoped to hitch their star to his.

Remy watched him breeze through the crowd as if he were the only person on earth. He was exactly like the people her father described when he told stories about this reckless society. Traders would toss aside anyone who got in their way, grabbing what belonged to them, as if everything did. They hungered endlessly for more, showing off their treasures without any taste. Big Cars, Thick Wallets and NO TAXES! This universe drew attention and envy. To the outside world, standing in a pit seemed like a road to easy money. How could you not be right at least half the time? But trading wasn't just a guess. Her father explained why memberships at the Exchange were expensive: Being inside the pits gave traders an edge. He also warned that this all-male club was off-limits for a lady. Now circumstances made his restriction meaningless.

When Jason's entourage disappeared, Remy stood alone in the hallway, surprised at how much she had accomplished. The interview was behind her. This afternoon, her ID would be sent to the clearinghouse for processing and then, once she completed the orientation, she'd be good to go.

Holly Rozner

How her life had changed! An only child, Remy was raised to be an actress. The transition from theatre to trading would have been unthinkable for her mother, Lila Saks. Growing up, Remy immersed herself in Hollywood magazines as a distraction, going to movies Saturday afternoons with friends, sometimes sitting through a double feature, occasionally even watching the same one over so she could study a favorite scene and imitate the actresses in front of a mirror when she was alone. Remy wrote to the stars and joined their fan clubs. In college, she changed her name from Andrea to Remy, visualizing how nicely it would fit on a marquee.

Her mother, a dancer before she married Harry Saks, taught Remy the score to Broadway shows. By the time Remy was in kindergarten, she had memorized most of the lyrics to *Funny Girl*. She entertained at family functions, sometimes with her mom. When she was nine, she saw *Pippin* and she was hooked. She had to be on the stage! In 1976, after her mother died, her father took her to New York to see Ethel Merman and Mary Martin at Carnegie Hall. The following summer at the National Music Camp in Michigan, Remy began voice lessons. The songs of musical theater filled the terrible void of her mother's death and left a remnant of her mother to hold in her heart.

When Remy became a theatre major at Northwestern University, she was required to learn every aspect of a production, even how to build sets and light a proscenium stage. It was in her sophomore year, during rehearsals as the lead for *Kiss Me Kate,* that Remy met Alan Greenberg, a graduate student, five years older than she, living in a fourth floor walk-up, nothing like Remy's house in Wilmette. Alan seduced her with an intensity she had never known. Playing Kate to his Petruchio the summer of her junior year, Remy ignored all the obvious signs that he was the wrong guy. Brooding, sometimes depressed, Alan's detachment kept Remy on edge. Captivated by his occasional charm, she rationalized that his behavior was the sign of an artistic temperament. She imagined them traveling the world, performing in plays, accepting awards, maybe even raising a family. Remy assumed that Alan would propose after graduation. Instead, he married his childhood sweetheart without actually breaking up with her.

Remy was devastated. She missed final calls for the Wa-Mu show and lost interest in her classes. She couldn't memorize scripts, had trouble sleeping and stopped practicing her dance routines. She retreated from social events and made it clear to friends that she didn't want Alan's name brought up, though secretly she looked for him in coffee houses they had once frequented after rehearsals, and lingered near his apartment building, not knowing at all what she would have done had she confronted him.

Heartbroken, Remy became disenchanted with the theater. Her father didn't know how to help her, but eventually he suggested she change her major. He assured her that the study of economics would help establish an equal footing with men, that the concrete formulas would give her something to call her own. She followed his advice and eventually began to view actors who feigned to be someone else as simply adolescent.

The experience with Alan shattered her faith in men. For two years Remy refused to date. Then at a family party she met a lawyer, Stuart Masterman, exactly the kind of man her mother would have chosen for her had her mother been alive. Stuart took Remy to the opera and to see avant-garde films, eating at expensive French restaurants where he always managed to get a reservation. Remy tried to fit into his conservative life and for some time convinced herself that he was the right guy. When he presented her with a gorgeous diamond, she decided to give marriage a shot. Her job as an accountant was getting tedious. It was time to settle down.

Remy talked herself into believing that her first instincts were wrong and that Stuart was a terrific person, but when he couldn't stop impressing others with what he knew, love withered like tired grass. How could she have made another bad choice, she wondered as she quietly shared her disappointment with friends, only to learn that their marriages also had problems. However, when Stuart refused to support her after her father's accident and treated her like a glass doll he could control, Remy felt trapped. She needed a man who would take care about her. Stuart would always put himself first. In less than a year, the marriage was over.

Wearing a jacket and freshly laminated badge, Remy stared at herself in the ladies' room mirror. She was dressed like the others, but she was different. No one else had her reason for being here. She walked into the trading room and took a spot in the middle of the empty pit where orientation would begin.

The pit was a mini coliseum—an octagon, twelve feet wide with tiered steps surrounding the circumference. During business hours, traders stood in the center, the brokers on the rim. Now it was filled with just a dozen men who were assigned to her session. In the after-hours silence, the room barely resembled the scene she had witnessed from the gallery. The lights on the boards were dead, the phone lines hushed, the clerks gone. Paper littering the floor was the only proof of the earlier pandemonium. She was the sole woman. The men spoke among themselves as Remy tried to figure out what all of it meant. The session was scheduled to begin at 3:15. As she assembled the trading cards a clerk had handed her, Remy looked up and saw Jason Bramson examining his manicured nails. He wore khaki slacks and gym shoes. A tie was required for men on the trading floor. Some of these ties were the first ones ever worn by a trader on a lucky day, now nearly in shreds, but a symbol of good fortune. Jason's red, white and blue tie matched his navy jacket.

"Hi," she said. "Remember me?"

"Hi, honey," he crooned, looking her up and down.

"My name is not Honey," she shot back.

He studied the badge. "REM then," he bowed mouthing the letters.

"Remy."

"With an I or a Y?" he asked, smiling.

Her throat tightened.

"It sounds the same. R-E-M-Y," she whispered.

He moved closer.

"That honey thing—it means nothing." His eyes narrowed and she noticed the dimple in his chin. Then without asking, he grasped her elbow and steered her towards the others.

He was terribly handsome, his curly hair framing a round face. When he placed his hand against her back, she could feel her defenses crumble. So far the men in her life had turned out to be such jerks. The hard-to-resist look this guy wore was unnerving.

"Ever traded?" he asked gently.

"No. Never."

"Then let me show you how."

She stepped aside. He stood on the top step of the octagon pit and passed out more trading cards before assuming his position as their instructor.

"I took some already," she explained.

"Hold this in your hand," he commanded. "On one side of the card, you write down what you bought and who you bought it from; on the other side," he said, flipping his own trading card over, "you write down what you sold, how much you sold and who you sold it to. You do this immediately after you agree on a trade with another trader. Then you mark the time down so if there is a dispute there will be a record of what traded in that time frame."

Glowing self-confidently in the fame that was his, Jason moved about the small crowd. Remy presumed this was his payback to the Exchange, a small token for the mint he had made.

"As you can see, "seat" is a contradiction because traders are not allowed to sit down. Every day you will have to establish your spot." He shuffled down the stairs to the center of the pit, trying to help them visualize the pit during regular hours. "The brokers stand on the top step so clerks can reach the telephone banks and avoid wading through the "local" traders who stand in the center. You will not have a place assigned to you. Sometimes you may find that you are too far from the broker to be heard. That's why we often depend on hand signals. A hand on the forehead means one thing; a hand on the chin, something else. Words are seldom exchanged because you cannot hear across a pit. Yet billions trade with few mistakes."

Remy was intent on following every word. Her father taught her that if you listen carefully, you could avoid mistakes. How did his luck turn inside out if he knew so much about this place?

"Once a trade is made, it is time stamped by the machine on the desks nearby," he said, pointing to the bank of desks that surrounded the room, "and then sent back to the broker. It is confirmed by phone and the trade is complete. All this takes seconds."

Her eyes remained on him.

"An error between two traders is called an out-trade, a discrepancy. Should you write down one amount and the other trader writes another you are "out" the difference. Both parties must split the error. So reconfirm every trade made."

Then Jason divided the crowd into buyers and sellers. He stood on the top step of the pit and pretended to be the broker, yelling out an order while each practiced buying or selling against it. They learned where to record their trade and have it time stamped before it was put in a pile to be processed. The shouting continued with a blast of voices that made the words unintelligible. This simulated trading session lasted for only twenty minutes but left Remy's head spinning. The introduction certainly didn't prepare anyone for actual trading and the noise, with everyone screaming at the same time, made her shake. When the bell rang, it was evident that there would be a lot more to learn on the job.

Jason smiled at Remy. Without thinking, she ran her fingers through her hair, a habit she couldn't control; it was like the tell a player makes at a poker table, disclosing his closed hand. Her face flushed. This man, this Jason Bramson, had aroused her, something she didn't want him to know. She needed a quiet place to let the feelings subside. As he moved towards her, Remy grabbed her belongings and left without saying good-bye.

As she turned around, she caught the expression on his face. His head was cocked to one side and his big brown eyes had a look that said he was surprised she hadn't stuck around. She left, rode the escalator to the lobby, and then stood completely still. She had done it! Tomorrow she could start. So far everything had gone smoothly. The ease of it frightened her. She had half-expected the process to take weeks. Instead they were ready for her, and she wasn't sure she was ready for them.

Holly Rozner

Above her head the carved figure of Hermes adorned the entrance of the building. *The god of commerce and patron of thieves.* She remembered this from a Greek mythology class. Odd to find it here.

As the revolving doors and Remy reached the sunlight, she spotted Zachary Silverman's silver Bentley parked across the street. The number 100 on its license plate came with the landscape of Chicago politics, an obvious *quid pro quo* for jobs Zach provided to the Mayor's office.

Next to the car stood the man, yellow tie and signature kerchief in his breast pocket, looking more like a gangster than the Chairman of the Exchange. Zach also ran the largest clearing house in the building where orders were processed before they were taken to the trading floor. This inside information gave him an edge over trades before they were filled. Seeing him made Remy realize how daunting her task was. Single-handedly Zach had catapulted the Exchange into unparalleled dominance by inventing an Index, a basket of stocks that provided mutual funds a place to hedge their risk.

Remy's father, Harry Saks, and Zachary Silverman played on the same basketball team in Appleton, Wisconsin. When Harry took off for Chicago to be an accountant, Zach remained in Wisconsin building his real estate empire, buying land and selling it "on contract" without giving the purchaser a deed. He divided large parcels into small lots for individuals. When the buyer defaulted, he sold the lot again, boosting the price with each transaction. His customers discovered too late that they would never get the deed they were owed. Eventually the courts determined this practice was illegal and he was forced out of town. In 1961, Zach fled to Chicago. When he heard the trading pits were virtual money machines, he plopped down five hundred dollars to buy a seat, plucked Harry out of his cubicle and offered him a slice of the pie. Zach would stand in the pit handling orders telephoned to the floor and Harry would cover the backroom. For nearly twenty years they were a perfectly paired vaudeville team.

Zach siphoned off the first dollar of every trade for himself by filling orders for himself before he filled the customer's and then selling his order at a profit to the customer who would never know the difference. Harry didn't know what Zach was doing. As the money rolled in, Zach needed someone to work the floor with him, to make it harder to see how he was stealing money. He needed a bagman, his lawyer, Ivan Bloch, told him. Another trader he would sneak trades to, who would secretly split the profit with him.

"You will make a fortune," Zach pledged to Oscar Doheney when he hired him.

Oscar was just twenty-six, living with his mother in Zach's apartment building. Every year Mrs. Doheney invited Zach for Thanksgiving and Christmas. Her hospitality opened up Zach's eyes to a new world. In Wisconsin Zach stuck close to his Jewish roots. Afraid that he would fall in love with a Shiksa, Zach's parents kept the Gentile community away. Oscar and his mother welcomed Zach into their Irish family and Zach loved them. The young men understood each other and when Zach made it clear that Harry was never to know about their far-fetched schemes, Oscar just grinned.

Oscar was adept at bagging trades, but when the Bull Market began its run in 1982, they needed more help. No smart alecks. No independent thinkers. Someone who simply took orders. They would pay for his silence. That's when they picked Jason Bramson, a pretty boy with his eyes on big bucks: greedy enough not to ask embarrassing questions. The perfect bagman to add to their payroll.

Holly Rozner

The Bentley parked on the street was a tiny grain of Zach's fortune. A home on the lake in Highland Park, a villa in Boca, a lodge in Aspen. Zach reeked of success like the smell of disgusting cologne.

Remy watched Zach get into his car. She thought he looked younger than his fifty-eight years. He held a telephone in his hand while the chauffeur opened the door. Quote machines, women and cars; they thrilled Zachary Silverman.

As the stoplight changed, Remy crossed the street. A bus passing in the wrong direction jarred her. In an experiment to move traffic along, the Mayor had ordered buses on certain streets to be routed in the opposite direction. This confusion had caused an upheaval because Chicagoans didn't look right when they were stepping off a curb. The Mayor wouldn't budge. Remy watched as someone nearly missed the bus. She had considered walking up Michigan Avenue, but she was too tired and quickly hailed a taxi. Settling into the back seat, her thoughts drifted to Jason Bramson and the way his eyes probed hers, as if he were able to read her thoughts.

This was the wrong time to complicate her life, the wrong time to get involved. Jason reminded her of Stuart. She had walked away from that. For the moment she needed to meet the right people and ask pertinent questions or she would never find out about her dad. As the cab inched across the bridge, Remy forced Jason out of her mind so she could keep a level head and learn to trade.

There was no time for romance. Certainly no time for heartache. Not now. Maybe not for a very long time.

chapter 2

September, 1986

JOEY FORTUNATO LIVED on the third floor of a three-flat in Ravenswood. After four years in Chicago, it was still all he could afford. He had run away from New York and his mother's home-cooked oatmeal so he wouldn't end up like his dad, a barber, catering to customers who made appointments they didn't keep. Joey's chance to go to night school disappeared when he pocketed the tuition his folks gave him and bought a used car. That was 1982. Now there was no hope of learning a trade. No one in his family had ever inspired a turnaround. All his mother wanted was her son nearby, but that was not what Joey needed.

His father's shop was located on the lower level of one of the Twin Towers. At night his dad would brag about the money his customers made, describing how they dressed and detailing their vacations, as if their success were his. It was hard for Joey to listen. Fed up with his father's dreams, Joey decided to strike out on his own. He had heard that Chicago had a heart. That was where he would strike it rich.

During the day Joey worked at Chernins, a shoe store in the west Loop, and took real-estate classes at night. But when he flunked the exam, he lost confidence and gave that up.

One day Oscar Doheney wandered into the store, wearing a red trading jacket. Joey had read about these famous jackets and badges. He had watched traders on the "L" train and had begun to envy this inner circle. An article about the pits in the *Sun Times* had caught his eye, and he immediately began asking Oscar questions. As Oscar sputtered on about the pits, Joey was all ears. The money made on the trading floor was all Joey wanted for himself.

This was what Chicago was about. The pits were the most renowned in the world. Joey hadn't allowed himself to imagine it, but this is what he had hoped for when he left New York. It might not be Wall Street, but it was next best. He saw himself wearing of those jackets with JOEY emblazoned on a badge.

"Could I see the trading floor?" Joey pleaded.

Oscar looked him over carefully, assessing what was in this for him. Not likely to give anything away without making a trade for himself, Oscar replied, "Sure, kid. I'll take you on the floor."

"You mean it?"

"You'll come downtown one afternoon after 3:00. No one is allowed on the floor before we close." Then he asked, as if it were an afterthought, "What are you earning here?"

Joey looked away.

"Could you live on $100 a week?"

"Not easily."

"Too bad," said Oscar, "because I need a new clerk. If you could work for me and learn the business, maybe one day you could trade."

The image of money, buckets of it, seared Joey's mind.

"It's not like being a stock broker." Joey was afraid that Oscar could read his thoughts, hear his heart thumping. "A traders' life is not in an office—no pin- stripe suits or silk ties."

"It doesn't matter. I need more to live on," Joey said.

Oscar knew this. He wanted find out how cheaply he could get Joey. Every kid in Chicago wanted in on the action. The rich ones worked for nothing. The dream of wearing a trading jacket was as sexy as the major leagues.

"Come tomorrow. Maybe we can work something out."

Oscar Doheney was a goddamn fairy godmother.

The following afternoon, Joey rushed to the visitors' gallery and watched the frenzy. Those people were the luckiest guys on earth. When Oscar took him on the trading floor, Joey was spellbound, imagining himself in the middle of all of that madness.

Then Oscar invited him to meet Zachary Silverman. In the office on the fortieth floor, Joey could see a all the way to Lake Michigan. In the center of the room sat a large oval table made of stainless steel. In two corners were machines that displayed the price of stocks and commodities from all over the world. Twelve brown leather chairs surrounded the table. Joey sat in one of them, his hand running across the smooth leather, wishing he could sit back and relax the way he imagined Oscar and Zachary when they analyzed the markets.

His hands were cold. He could feel his heart beat. He folded his arms. What could he say that would make them like him, want him enough to hire him and let him into their exclusive, expensive world?

"Great view," he stammered, standing up when Zachary entered the room. Joey Fortunato had never heard of Zachary Silverman, but it took just a second for the young man to realize that he was standing in the presence of absolute authority. Zach's success infused the air as he strode confidently to the head of the table and inched his way into the chair, his eyes on Joey.

Oscar looked at Zach and Zach looked at Oscar. They had the right kid. Eager. Pliable. Hungry. He would follow their instructions.

"You would be clerking for Oscar," Zachary said, leaning forward so that his paunchy stomach indented as it poked the table. "Oscar runs the pit. But in a few years, the Exchange will start trading smaller stocks and Oscar will need someone to run that pit for him. We're interviewing people because it's such an important job. Eventually we will need someone to take over."

"Yes," Joey said as if he had been asked a question. Never did he stop to think why they might consider him. He just felt plain lucky.

Oscar narrowed his stare as if to photograph Joey. He spoke in a hushed tone to Zachary, loud enough for Joey to hear. "This is a boy we can depend on, Zach."

Joey leaned forward to say something. Zach didn't give him a chance. He placed his fat hand on Joey's shoulder and stood next to him. "We have our man," Zach said, squeezing Joey's shoulder. "Joey will do just fine." Joey looked up at him and nodded. Then Zach took his hand away, lit a cigar and walked out of the room without another word.

Joey was puzzled. These men knew nothing about him. How did they know they could trust him? What could they see in him that he couldn't see in himself? What difference did it make? If he could be part of their team, he would never ask for another thing. All he wanted was to wear the kind of clothes they wore, have his nails buffed like that. To breeze through a room and demand respect, not like his dad.

That day in the shoe store it looked like his prayers were answered. Now he could see that the fantasy had been a figment of his own imagination. He had heard what he wanted to hear. When he thought carefully about his conversations with Oscar, Joey couldn't even remember what Oscar had promised or how much he had invented.

Joey Fortunato became Oscar's clerk in the pit. The tips Oscar gave Joey were worth twice his salary at the shoe store and Oscar paid him cash so there were no taxes. He was able to buy a sofa and had enough promises to last a lifetime. But he had no idea when he could trade. That was three years ago. At twenty-one, he needed more.

"I need a new car," he muttered to himself, pouring another beer.

His eight year-old Cutlass required an overhaul that would cost more than what it was worth. Last night the ignition stuck and when the repair shop towed it in, they quoted five- hundred to fix it, more than he could afford. Certainly more than he wanted to put into such junk. If dealerships were open on Sunday, he'd go now. It was nearly noon. He threw away an empty can and poked around in the refrigerator looking for food, but there was only moldy cheese. Unread copies of the paper were strewn on the floor. He sifted through them to search the classifieds, but he was half-awake. Maybe he would make some calls later, but right now he just wanted to relax. Standing on his feet all day and running Oscar's errands was so tiring that he was too exhausted to go car shopping at night, and on Sundays he often stayed in bed all day.

A lousy two-hundred a week! He muddled through the mess in his apartment looking for the phone. Things were not working out. If only Oscar would give him a break. So far, Oscar's promises were worthless. Bills were mounting and his girlfriend, Rosa, was getting impatient.

Returning to New York was out of the question. What was there that would be any better than what he was doing here? He missed his mom; he talked to her every week. This minute he missed Rosa.

They had met six months ago in the neighborhood diner on the corner of the shady street where he lived. He ate there every night, figuring it was just as cheap as buying all the food to cook.

"Rosa Perkins," she announced, as she plopped a meatball sandwich in front of him.

"Joey Fortunato," he answered, looking her up and down. She had short black hair and big brown eyes that seemed to see right through him.

"Where do you live?" she asked, her hand on her hips.

"On Winona."

"That's right here, huh?" Her stare made him feel self-conscious. In Joey's world, women didn't come on to men.

"Around the corner," he answered.

A customer called and she stepped aside to get coffee, glancing back at Joey. He felt so uncomfortable that he left the restaurant without leaving a tip.

Once he was alone, he thought about her. A few days later, he wandered back to the diner to see if her lips were as full as he thought they were. He studied the way she smiled at the customers, strutting around to take an order, calling it out and bringing back food as if this were serious business.

"Here's the buck I owe you from last week," he said.

"Forget it. I'm worth more than a buck."

He laughed, "How about dinner?"

Joey was just about her size and smelled great. Good muscles. Nice-looking hands.

"Sure, honey. We can go for dinner."

"What time do you get off?"

"Seven. Pick me up here."

The distance separating them narrowed as they both discovered how much they had in common. Rosa had also left her family in search of a new life.

"Miami was a dead end," she explained, as they settled into a booth in a small Italian restaurant nearby. He guessed from her olive skin that she might be Hispanic. She explained that she had been born in Cuba and that her family left when Castro took over. "In Miami, you're either in or you're out," she told him. "And when you're not inside, there is no future. I thought I might catch a break here." Waitressing was temporary, she explained, to save money for beauty school because one of her friends told her she was making $500 a week in tips. Every week she tried to put a little away and every week something ate into the plan. With over $5,000 in credit card bills, it hurt when suckers like Joey didn't leave a tip.

Her story made him feel terrible. He would make it up to her. Standing in front of the mirror that hung over a dilapidated chest of drawers, Joey decided that Rosa would be the reason for his success. He would do it for her. As he dressed, he began to rehearse what he was going to say to Oscar Monday morning, a dialogue he practiced every Sunday.

"Three years ago you told me I'd be able to broker in the new pit. Three years! I'm not saying that that's a long time. I'm not saying I'm not grateful for what you've done for me." He combed his hair back hoping that would compel Oscar to pay attention to him. Then he struck a pose with his head tilted towards the ceiling, trying to emulate Zach, as if this might force the result he needed. The image staring back wasn't convincing. He slumped on the sofa and reached for a cigarette. Every week he practiced the speech and every week he lost his nerve.

Holly Rozner

It was Sunday. Rosa had to work the morning shift. She'd be back soon and she'd be madder than hell when she saw him drinking and smoking.

"Shit," he said, his legs on the coffee table, cigarette butts on the floor. The apartment was a mess. He flicked on the television. All the money he had saved to buy a ring would go into his broken-down car. The lure of big bucks hung in the air, close enough to smell, real enough to touch. It was a mirage. If he wanted a new car, how was it going to get financed? He had no credit. Oscar paid him in cash. There was no record of an income. When he had asked why they had this arrangement, Oscar said it would actually cost Joey money if they did it the other way. Eventually Joey figured out that Oscar simply didn't want to pay his Social Security taxes or cover his health insurance. Their setup had nothing to do with the money it would cost Joey. It was about the cash it would cost Oscar.

Oscar did whatever Oscar wanted. Joey watched the way he treated this new woman, Remy Masterman. It was awful. She was such a lady. But Oscar egged her on and Joey hated him for it.

It was a no-win situation. Without Oscar, all possibilities were gone. He didn't want to go back to selling shoes. But how much longer could he wait? Without power, you are nothing. He kicked the sofa, thinking about what it would be like to be starting out with no support like Remy. But this was terrible. Being owned pulls you way down, he thought, wishing he could find a way out.

Rosa knocked on the door. She waited a minute and then used her key. Joey didn't budge. She slung her purse over a chair and threw a kiss across the room. The apartment had a small bedroom off to the left. The living room was large enough to fit a round dining room table that Joey had found in the alley after the next door neighbors moved

Trade Secrets

out. The shades were down, the air thick with the odor of beer and smoke.

"Hey, babe. Let's get going. It's too pretty out to stick around here." She pranced across the room with a sassy walk. The dining room was piled high with a week's worth of dirty dishes and cans of beer.

"I'm beat, Rosa. I can't get moving." Joey threw his head back. His legs were spread out before him.

Rosa gave him a soft kick. She placed her hands on her waist as she surveyed the room. Rosa was five-one in stocking feet. Today she wore high-heeled boots and a short red leather skirt, dressed to go out and out she would go. But not without her Joey.

"Come on, you dumb jerk. We gotta get moving. You'll rot here."

"I can't. I'm beat."

"Joey, Joey, Joey. You gotta stop thinking about the things you can't do and do something about the things you can do. You can't just sit around here and mope."

"I need to be alone. You don't know hard it is to work every day and watch everyone else bringing home oodles of money. I have nothing. I hold those shitass cards. I do what they tell me to do. Why should those scumbags get what they get and I get zero?"

"It'll happen." She sat on his lap and pulled his arms around her. A black sweater clung to her. When she leaned against him, Joey could feel her luscious breasts. She guided his hands inside her sweater. No bra. No underpants either. She cuddled into him. For a minute he forgot how rattled he was. Rosa kissed him. He slid his tongue into her mouth. She bit him teasingly, unzipped his pants and took his limp penis into her hands. The blood rushed through his veins as he came to life, his cock hard and eager. He put one hand between her legs, thrusting his middle finger into the warm wet curve. She held his hardness in her hands, pumping him while her ebony eyes fixed on his face. He looked at her and felt nothing but fire. He ran his mouth against her breasts and licked her salty skin. She moaned and his hardness grew. She worked her fingers faster as he lost his senses and with one deep thrust he released his spasm.

"Baby, baby, baby," he whispered into her ear.

"You don't need more than this," she said, pulling his face to hers.

"Nothing, babe, nothing."

They held each other for a long time until Rosa pulled herself away and Joey collapsed on the couch. And then everything he had pushed aside for a few minutes came hurling back; the delight dimming as agony gripped him. If nothing changed, Rosa would remain a waitress and he a clerk. Real dummies were walking away with bails of money. He saw it every day. He had to do something to make things happen. And he had to do it fast or one day he'd sure as hell lose Rosa.

chapter 3

By December, wearing khakis and a white blouse under her red trading jacket, Remy looked like a pro, but she was terrified every time she walked onto the trading floor. She had no idea which product would be easiest to trade. Bonds, stocks, gold? She concentrated on the boards along the wall that flashed the prices. The neon lights were blinding. Pinned between traders twice her size, Remy struggled to be heard. One day she stood on the top level of the pit without knowing those spaces were reserved for brokers. She was elbowed out, jabbed in the ribs and even pushed to the floor. Eventually she learned which were the coveted spots and why Oscar stood on top. He ran the pit.

"A hundred at 5," Oscar Doheney screamed, but what did that mean?

Was that the right price? Disconcerted from the lights, deafened by the noise, Remy couldn't make sense of such disorder.

After several weeks of watching, she made a few trades only to find that she had made mistakes writing down her trades or recorded the wrong time bracket. Once she wrote her buys where the sells belonged, creating an out-trade, an error that cost her five hundred dollars. Without that, she would have made money that month. Rumor said that if a trader broke even by the end of the first year, he was on his way. Some who made it big their first year were generally out of business the next. To learn to trade you must lose and then figure out how to make back the loss. Those who counted on sheer luck discovered this was not a game of chance. Trading was a skill, one that Remy would have to master. She could not move forward with her personal investigation until she learned to trade.

The men avoided her, eagerly waiting to capitalize on her naiveté by selling to her at the highest price and buying it back at the lowest. She hadn't figured out what to do when the market went against her, which it seemed to do over and over.

Finally, it was Oscar's clerk, Joey Fortunato, who came to her rescue when the guys pummeled her. Joey's job as a clerk was to carry orders into the pit from the bank of telephones that lined the walls and handed them to his boss.

"Watch it, REMY," he shouted when he saw her writing her trade down on the wrong side of the card.

Oscar shouted, "A girl like you belongs in the beauty parlor. What are you doing here?" He broke into an audacious laugh. Others joined in.

Joey countered on her behalf. "She's just trying to make a living, Boss."

Once Oscar gave her a trade but for the most part, Remy was alone among a pack of animals whose sweat smelled and whose breath reeked of cigarettes. At times she felt faint. Aware of her uniqueness as a woman, she refused to be intimidated. She would not leave. She would find her niche.

One day Remy invited Joey to have lunch with her.

"You gotta know the players," he explained as they rode the escalator to the Club, a private restaurant for members and their guests.

"What difference does it make?" Remy asked as she carved her way through the crowd. Surrounded by multicolored jackets stuffed with trading cards and pencils, Remy looked like an insider.

"You gotta know who's got the paper, the orders," he continued.

"What paper?"

"Paper. It's short for orders of paper. The paper the orders are written on."

"Who cares who has the orders?"

"You can see who's buying and who's selling. You don't want to fight the paper. If the paper is buying, you buy. If you sell into it, you'll get licked. You'll get hurt," he said gently.

"If the major brokerage houses buy, the market goes up," she said trying to make the concept hers. "The trend is your friend. I hear people say that."

"It takes guts to survive in the pits. You are very strong to take a place among these wolves," he said.

The tables were situated on different levels in a long rectangular room with huge floor-to-ceiling windows overlooking the city. In the summer you could see the boats on Lake Michigan, but on this blustery day, the water was ice, the air gray.

"Why do some people make so much and others fail?" she asked when they sat at their table.

"No discipline," Joey answered. "You gotta have a system. Whatever it is. Buy and hold for ten minutes or ten points. Buy and sell in ten minutes or within ten points when the market gets away from you. But you gotta know when you're wrong. And get out. Trading is easy when you're right. I've seen guys make a little bit of money every day and then pouf, the whole thing goes up in smoke. They wait for a comeback and that's like trying to avoid a tornado headed towards you. You gotta run for cover when you're wrong."

Remy had a finite amount that she had inherited from her father's life insurance. She was too young to lose it. Remy listened attentively to Joey because she knew he saw a lot standing behind Oscar. Joey wore a yellow jacket to distinguish him from traders who wore red. Maybe he knew the secrets about this place, but it was too early to press him. To learn about her father, Remy needed to stick around and that meant figuring out a system. Until you understood a business, you couldn't find out if someone was mishandling it. Her father had once said that some traders stole money from the public, but when she probed for stories, his lips were sealed.

"Sometimes it looks as if the whole system could collapse. If one trader had a terrible error, it could affect another member and then another," Remy said.

"That's why members' accounts are guaranteed by a clearinghouse," Joey explained.

"Every trade is indemnified so no one can lose if one trader goes bankrupt. The system couldn't work without such guarantees. If there were nothing to insure a trader's debt, the next person's trade would be worthless. That's why the clearinghouses monitor their accounts so closely. If a trader loses more than the house allows, he will be hauled off the floor."

Remy understood all this, but she enjoyed hearing Joey tell her about it while he devoured his cheeseburger and fries. The Club had machines on every table so that Remy was able to watch the markets while she ate. They sat in a booth. There were so few women that it was hard to make friends and Remy's day was so frenetic that it was difficult to make a lunch date, even with Lara. Some days she stood on her feet from 8:30 until 3:00, grabbing only water and peanut butter crackers from a machine. Today she was glad Joey was with her.

"How does Oscar even get the orders?" she asked.

Joey felt important answering this. "Zach Silverman is his boss."

"I didn't know that," she said.

"That's what I mean, Remy. You need to know these things. You need to know who's who down here. Who's trading is just as important as what they're trading. Trust me."

Remy wondered how much Joey knew.

"How long have they worked together?" she asked, picking at her egg-white omelet.

She could see by the way Joey stopped talking that the question may have made him edgy. He didn't answer, continuing to chomp on his hamburger. "I don't know," he said finally. But Remy sensed that wasn't true.

She would have to be patient. If Joey needed to protect Oscar, she would find that out. Her father had talked about Oscar when she was young, but she was preoccupied with her own life and didn't pay much attention. By the time she was in college, her father's work seemed remote. She had her own love affairs, her own problems so that when he discussed work, she half-listened. Now she wished she had paid attention. Since there were no corporate records, there wasn't a place to look up who was who at the Exchange. She would learn what she could as she went along.

"Thanks for helping, Joey. Maybe someday I can help you".

"This is a great hamburger. I guess you're not too hungry?"

"My mind's on other things."

Holly Rozner

From the corner of her eye, Remy saw Jason Bramson standing at a nearby computer. Like many traders, he used the Club to follow the market and eat. He looked like a guy without a care in the world. His blond hair covered the nape of his neck. When he turned around, she could see the muscles in his hands and the dimple in his jaw that defined his face.

As if she had willed it, he looked directly at her. The blank expression on his face disclosed the truth that he hardly remembered her at all.

He saw Joey and walked towards the table.

"I remember. You're the girl whose name is not Honey," he said.

"Remy," she said.

"Yes, R-E-M-Y." He smiled.

"This is Joey Fortunato."

"Oscar's clerk," Jason replied.

"You know each other?" she asked.

Joey interrupted. "Jason knows everybody, Remy. That's why he makes so much money."

Jason turned as if to walk away.

Then he turned back, faced Remy and asked, "Hey, have you got a date for the Prom next month?"

"The Prom?"

Joey explained: "The Exchange dance. They call it the Prom 'cause everyone gets all dolled up."

"I didn't know about it."

"It's a fabulous party. Be my date. You will love it," said Jason, leaning over the table.

A little startled, Remy was also intrigued.

"How about it?" he insisted, his eyes fixed on hers.

"Sure," she replied as if the word had fallen out of someone else's mouth.

Jason smiled and glanced at his watch.

"Write your phone number here," he said, handing her a trading card. She did as he told her to do and gave it back to him. Then he was gone! She had accepted a date with a man she hardly knew. It happened so fast, Remy felt unsteady. Jason didn't know anything about her. He hadn't come into the Club to invite her. If she hadn't been sitting there at that very moment, would he have called her? He hadn't waited around long enough for her to say a word. After she had walked out on her marriage, Remy promised not to be so impulsive with men. She sat back and sipped her coffee, reminding herself that this was simply a dance, just one date. It didn't have to be anything more. And maybe she would learn something about her father.

"I'd better get back," she said to Joey. Remy signed the bill and considered asking Joey what he thought about all of this, but she could see from the expression on his face that he was pleased.

Only weeks ago she had vowed not to go out with Jason and now, in one second, she had accepted his invitation. Maybe she shouldn't have. This was not the time to let someone distract her. On her way into the trading room she considered what she could have said or what Jason might have said had he stuck around. Perhaps she should have said she was busy. Or that she was dating someone. Or maybe she would have said the wrong thing and let him know that she thought he was terribly handsome. Then she told herself that this would give her a chance to be in a social setting with people that she needed to meet. As the din of the trading floor enveloped her, she tried to concentrate on what she had learned today. Her mind began to wander until the complexities of trading faded into the background and she decided to stop at Neiman's after work to look for a new evening gown.

Holly Rozner

She would call Lara and ask her to go along. It will be fun, she thought. And it will be a change. If nothing else, the dance would be a place for her to view the community her father had kept so secret.

chapter 4

December 12, 1986

WHEN JASON CAME to pick up Remy, he smiled and reached around her bare shoulders to help with her coat. Then he took her hand and squeezed it, as if they had been going steady, guiding her into the back seat of a white limo. Securely tucked in, she tossed her hair back and her perfume infused the air as the car shot towards the Field Museum.

Remy knew nothing about Jason except that he made big markets. She asked questions about him in the pit—had he ever been married, whom did he date—but the guys didn't say much. When he called to make arrangements last night, he was all business.

Certainly this wildly handsome man didn't have trouble getting women. Where were they when he needed a date?

The dress Remy wore was ankle length. The very high heels of her black silk shoes were studded in rhinestones; the bustier of the dress was satin, the skirt chiffon, billowing in the wind as she strode onto the red carpet that lined the steps leading to the colossal entrance of the Museum.

Holly Rozner

Jason held one hand against her beaver coat to shield her from the icy wind that flapped against the white canopy.

The hall of the museum, famous for housing life-size animal skeletons, reverberated with noise. A dizzying display of red roses decorated silver cloths covering the tables. The enormous ceiling was draped with mounds of transparent white gauze speckled with tiny bulbs, hanging like clouds over the tables and transforming the room into a white, winter-wonderland. At the far end of the massive room, the Stanley Paul Orchestra dominated a neon dance floor that could have passed for an ice skating rink.

Remy tried hard not to show how impressed she was. No stranger to elaborate parties, Remy had accompanied her dad to fabulous affairs, especially after her mother died, when she was his escort. Hobnobbing with the rich and famous never fazed her. Remy had grown up among snobs, attending a private school in the Gold Coast before moving to the North Shore. Now, as she entered the splendid hall, she was reminded of the time she dressed in an accordion- pleated skirt and went to the Palmer House with her Dad. She pictured herself dancing with her father and the thought brought a tear to her eyes. Tonight she was determined not to let anyone know how anxious she was to be among people who knew her father. The truth was that fancy parties bored Remy. Silly conversation over appetizers, sitting through an evening all dressed up was an insipid way to spend time. But this affair was dazzling. For a while Remy forgot about her covert motive and concentrated on enjoying herself.

Exchange parties cost more than a $1,000 per couple. The dance was underwritten as a corporate expense to entertain bigwigs from Springfield and City Hall. The Governor and the Mayor, along with their wives, sat with Zachary and Oscar at the table with Remy and Jason.

Jason began by introducing them.

"Remy, Zach Silverman. You know Oscar, of course," Jason said as they took their places.

Zach looked at her and Remy tensed, worrying that he might figure out who she was, although she knew that was improbable. The teenager, Andrea Saks, who had visited his office years ago, looked very different from Remy Masterman. That girl wore braces and her hair in a ponytail, looking nothing like the woman she had become. Zach hardly noticed her when she was young. The two or three times they met, he was preoccupied with his quotron machines and telephone calls. If someone were to tell Zach that Remy was Harry Saks's daughter, he would probably laugh. The loud music kept her from hearing what he was saying, but when he leaned over to talk to Oscar, Remy guessed by the way he kept his eye on her, that he was talking about her.

Zachary's wife, a platinum blonde, accepted Jason's kiss and nodded to Remy. Kimberly Silverman had once been a model. Rumor had it that she had made a porno movie that Zachary paid dearly to have destroyed, though it was anyone's guess who had the copies. Remy presumed she was about thirty-five. She fluttered her false eyelashes and fingered a drop-dead oval diamond on her right hand and a gigantic diamond necklace around her throat. In each ear pave diamond and emerald earrings. Oscar hopped around the table like a nervous frog. He dropped his hands on Remy's back and she jerked away. His wife, Barbara, a lot younger than Oscar, wore thick pancake makeup that was smudged under her eye. Drenched in jewelry that didn't match her sequined gown, she looked if she had decided to wear everything that would show off her money.

Remy wondered what Jason thought about these people—dressed-up caricatures of success. Did he share her father's opinion? Had he ever been impressed with this society? So many envied traders for their stupendous wealth. But she didn't have time to wonder too much about how he fit in. His warm voice interrupted her thoughts.

"Want to see the stuffed animals?"

"Are we allowed to walk around the museum by ourselves?"

"Of course," he said with a sweeping motion.

"Mummies and dinosaurs, too?"

"This world is yours, lovely Remy, so let's get appetizers and drinks and then we can see the exhibits."

The Field Museum was immense. The most famous stuffed animal in the building was Bushman, a gorilla, dead for nearly forty years; there were exhibitions of American Indians and relics from ancient Egypt besides the celebrated mummy exhibit. As they headed up the stairs, Remy was careful not to slip on the stone floors. Walking in high heels was an art Remy had mastered, purposely overcoming a fear of falling she developed after breaking an ankle in college. Without realizing what she was doing, she leaned on Jason. At the upper landing, standing still to regain her footing, she found herself staring at him. He helped her find her balance and their eyes locked.

Waiters in white headgear passed Satay chicken skewers, vegetable pizza, tiny lamb chops and bite size hamburgers. On the upper corridor that overlooked the grand room were stations displaying food from all over the world: piles of shrimp and crab-legs, pasta bar, sushi bar, pizza bar and a whole table of vegetables. Each was decorated with a massive ice sculpture symbolizing different products traded at the Exchange.

"What do you think?" he asked, one leg against the railing. He peered over his half-empty glass of scotch.

"It's wonderful," Remy said, blushing under his powerful glance. Dressed in an expensive tuxedo, Jason was more than she had bargained for. She could feel his eyes undressing her and asked nervously, "Do you come every year?"

"If I can get a date."

Who was he kidding?

How do you rate a table with Zachary Silverman?"

"He likes me, I guess."

"Tell me about you," she said, accepting a glass of champagne from a waiter who was nearby.

"There's not much to the story. I got into this business pretty young, starting out clerking like Joey. Oscar taught me everything. The rest is history."

"You're being modest."

"Look, pretty Remy. I have no illusions about what I am. I make a living. More than others. But it's not any more romantic than that. Everybody wants to be a trader. They think they can make a killing. It's not that easy. I tried to tell you that at orientation."

"I see how hard it is."

"Once you make it, new traders think you are something you're not. I'm the same guy I was six years ago. Some people put me on a pedestal. I don't like being there. It's easy to fall."

"It's a hard business," she said.

"It's especially hard for a woman."

"The brokers can't hear me, the other traders seem to resent me, and I am just not as big or as loud as they are so everything takes an incredible effort."

"Don't give up. It takes time."

She had heard that so often, it was beginning to wear thin.

Jason put his drink down and slid his arm around her waist. They strolled through the musty hallways and then made their way downstairs to the dark room where the mummies were displayed. It was a part of the museum that Remy remembered the most and liked the least. It was dark and eerie and very quiet. Remy could feel Jason's eyes on her. She was waiting for the all the questions to come: How did she get to the Exchange? What made her decide to trade? Suddenly these questions that she didn't want to answer made her very tense. She was the one with questions. Had Jason known her father? Did he know anything about Zach and her Dad? But she couldn't go there now.

During trading Remy was so caught up in the frenzy that she forgot she was at the Exchange for another reason. Tonight she didn't want to dwell on any of it. The setting was terribly romantic.

They reentered the ballroom. "Let's dance," he suggested.

"Ok," she agreed.

Jason was easy to be near. Feeling like Cinderella, Remy tried to avoid his eyes, not wanting to reveal how quickly he had captivated her. The tips of her fingers were cold. He pulled her close. She could feel people staring at them. He whirled around the dance floor and melded into his step. She smiled as he hugged her to his chest. The sensation of his body against hers made her slightly flustered. When he suggested that they return to the table, it took her a moment to shake off the thrill of his touch.

During dinner Jason didn't take his eyes off of her as she visited with Oscar's wife. The conversation was stilted. This was a woman who had never worked, who filled her days shopping and working out, never having enough hours to spend her husband's money. Hunched together, the Mayor and Governor talked to one another while Zach sat back beaming.

Then, suddenly a woman in a bright red dress interrupted.

"Jason, I thought you didn't want to go to this dance." This striking brunette stood right behind Jason staring at Remy. She was five-feet two with silky dark hair that she wore shoulder length. Her piercing eyes fixed on Remy who found herself staring back. This vision in red carried herself with a sense of urgency that demanded attention.

"I didn't know you were here, Sarna," Jason said, standing to greet her.

"I'm sure you didn't. You found a date, so I found someone to bring me."

Sarna's eyes flashed to Jason, but Remy could see that she was interested in watching her too. Remy was caught up in the interplay, her own eyes jumping back and forth between the two. Suddenly Jason looked like a soupy-eyed dog. Remy put her hand out to greet her on her own, but before she had the chance, Sarna turned on her very high heels and walked away, swishing her taffeta dress.

"It's late," Remy said, wondering who this beauty was. The tenor of the evening had been transformed. To break the awkward silence, Remy said, "Maybe we should leave."

"I'm sorry for the interruption," Jason said. He looked amazingly handsome under the soft lighting. "I would like to get going," he agreed. "I'd like to be alone with you."

Remy felt herself tremble. She reached for the glass of wine on the table before her. It was still full. Searching for something to do, Remy took a sip and then replaced it, hardly tasting the liquor. Then she played with the goblet. Who was this woman? What was she to Jason? A half-hour earlier, dancing with him, Remy wondered what it would be like to feel Jason's hands on her flesh. Suddenly the moment had altered and Remy wasn't at all sure how to handle the shift.

Jason went to get their coats. Remy searched for Sarna in the huge crowd. She shifted her weight from one leg to the other. As she was rehashing this potent scene in her mind, Jason reappeared with their belongings slung over his arm. Before she had a chance to conclude her thoughts, they were back in the chauffeured car that had brought them there only hours before.

When Jason sank into the velvet seat next to her, he reached for a glass of scotch from a bar that was cradled in the side of the door. He offered Remy a drink, but she refused. He placed his head against the seat and pulled Remy towards him in an abrupt commanding gesture.

She wanted to ask about Sarna. But she didn't have to. His answers would have been all lies. Maybe if she had asked him point blank what he knew about her dad, he couldn't have been honest about that either. What she had witnessed was enough to tell the whole story. Jason had the eyes of an embarrassed child. This was an open and shut case of lost love. Remy removed his arms from her waist and placed them together in his lap. She kissed him on the cheek.

"Time out," she said.

"You got it wrong, Remy. I know what it looks like. Sarna and I go back a long way. We're not together any more. We once had a relationship, but it's been over for a long time." He pulled her towards him, nuzzling his lips against her neck. Sarna was history. He would concentrate on Remy today, not on the past.

But Remy wasn't convinced. Jason was incredibly attractive, but she'd been burned before and the last thing she wanted was more trouble. She held her head away.

"You may think it's over," said Remy. "But you're wrong."

She had only known Jason for a few hours, but he had gotten to her. Suddenly she felt sad. As the lights of the city punctuated the starry night, she realized how much she missed being in love. She hadn't really thought about Jason as a prospect until she was close to him. Still, she couldn't help but feel a little disappointment.

I've got the prince in my carriage, she mused, as the car sped down Lake Shore Drive, but someone else has his heart.

chapter 5

JASON DROPPED OFF Remy at her apartment building and slumped into the limo, quietly finishing off a bottle of scotch. She was some cool customer, saying thank you and a simple goodbye. Once he got home, he fell into bed, wearing socks and shoes. The telephone rang at 3:00 startling him. The voice on the other end was all too familiar. Not again, he told himself. Certainly not now.

"J-a-y-s-o-n," Sarna Richardson purred, drawing out his name as if it had five A's.

"I'm sleeping."

"So?"

"What do you want?" he asked, remembering Remy in his arms. Most women would have been in bed with him tonight. How the hell did she get away? He heard Sarna's voice, but what she said seemed dreamlike, as he wished himself back to sleep.

"I need to see you, Jay."

"It's over, Sarna."

"Don't be ridiculous, Jason."

He flicked on the light over his bed and checked the time.

"Where are you?"

"In front of your building."
"I'm going to sleep, Sarna."
"I'm on my way up. I'm giving my car to the doorman."
"Not tonight, Sarna."
"Yes, Jay, tonight."

Sarna was undaunted when she wanted something. Competition triggered her energy, starting her off like a horse let loose from a corral. Tonight nothing would deter her. It was the middle of the night, but she talked as if it were noon.

A bully in the pit, Jason was no match for this beauty. In fact, he had always been afraid of Sarna Richardson. They had met at the prom when Jason was eighteen and Sarna sixteen. On dates with other people, by the time the evening ended, Jason and Sarna were locked in the back seat of his father's BMW. He had never met anyone like her, more inventive than dames in porno flicks. Not that she was simply a stupid pretty girl. Sarna had more brains than most of girls at school, but, as soon as she started dating, she figured out that she didn't need to be smart to get what she wanted. While other girls feigned disinterest, Sarna made sex an occupation, perfecting her skills on one guy after another. Within a half-hour she was on her knees, letting him come into her mouth. No other woman had ever swallowed his sperm.

The following month Jason gave Sarna his high school fraternity pin. For the next year they talked incessantly about getting married when they were old enough. Jason was smitten with Sarna, but by the following summer, she had tired of him. Sarna needed a challenge. She jumped from guy to guy, turning each one away when he fell for her.

By the time Jason caught on to this pathology, he was hooked. Every time he tried to make love to someone, all he thought about was Sarna. No one else measured up.

Sarna knew that one day Jason would marry her, but she needed to see him find a career that would give her the lifestyle she dreamed about. His parents wanted him to go to Colgate and follow in his father's footsteps. Sarna couldn't have designed a better plan, but she knew Jason's limitations. She knew that the father's dream for his son was unrealistic and the father knew her need for material things would destroy Jason.

"She needs the kind of money that people talk about when they measure success, the kind that is a barometer against which others compare themselves. Thick wallets, hefty trust funds and important jewels." The warnings fell on deaf ears.

Jason finished college and went to law school, but Sarna felt it was the wrong path. He did not have the ability to become a lawyer. If he didn't have the brains to be a giant in his field, he would never acquire the treasure chest she desired. He finished law school at the bottom of his class and joined a firm chasing personal injury cases that might not be settled for a decade.

Unwilling to wait around for him to find himself, Sarna broke up with Jason and took a modeling job. Whenever they bumped into each other at a party or in a restaurant, she flirted with him, tormenting him with the lure of intimacy. She had learned early that her sexual charms could be used in many ways and though she had the capacity to do much more in her life, when she located this talent in herself, she was unable not to use it to her advantage. If she ever actually needed to outsmart someone, she'd find a way, but for now, this was her calling card and she loved pulling it out.

It didn't take Jason long to realize that he was on the wrong path—stuck in an office pushing pencils and waiting in court for judges to show up was not for him. His father begged him to stick it out. However, his mother could see that Jason would never make it as a lawyer and secretly loaned him forty thousand dollars to buy a seat at the Exchange. It was as if Sarna had willed it to be. She used to talk incessantly about the fortune traders made. Jason gambled that this was his chance to turn money into money, drive around in one of those Porsches with a license plate that advertised the Index he would trade: Bonds, Stocks, Ags. A mansion on the lake. Then Sarna would be his.

He took the loan, quit his job and met Oscar.

News of Jason's break reached Sarna. The time was right, but getting him back was tricky. She devised a scheme to make him jealous. They met for dinner and she told him she was going to marry Freddy Fields, heir to the shoe store chain. For weeks Jason couldn't sleep. He had trouble trading and the mistakes he made nearly cost him his career. Even though Oscar was feeding him winning trades, he got confused. Finally someone suggested a psychiatrist who specialized in trader's block.

"It's a psychological profession," Dr. Gruned said as he explained that loss in other aspects of someone's life can be mirrored on the trading floor. Unresolved grief causes people to lose money by turning the actual loss into a monetary one. Jason had trouble comprehending his mumbo jumbo. All he knew was that if he had Sarna, everything would be OK. How could she fall for someone else? And Freddy Fields? The thought made him want to puke.

Then out of the blue, immediately after he met Remy, Sarna called to say that she didn't want to marry Freddy, that she was going to break her engagement. She invited herself to the dance. Incredible! She had the guts to do anything, to walk up to a cosmetics counter, ask for a sample lipstick and actually get one. He vowed not to get involved. He told her that he already had a date, although he hadn't even entertained the idea of going to the dance. When he saw Remy in the Club that morning, he knew that there were other women who could fascinate him. Inviting her was a half-hearted attempt to validate his lie to Sarna and convince himself to move on.

Now Sarna was knocking on his door. He was half-asleep, wishing he were under the covers or smoking one of the cigarettes in his suit pocket. She knocked again and this time he pulled himself out of bed. This was the part of himself that he didn't like. He wouldn't let himself be manipulated. He pulled in his breath and vowed that he would insist she leave. In fact, he would ignore her. Show her that he was in control.

"The door's unlocked, Sarna," he yelled, wrapping the sheet around his waist and going to his bathroom. "Let yourself in." He looked at himself in the mirror. He needed a shower.

That Remy. Someday, he'd have her.

The huge bathroom housed a two-person Jacuzzi and a shower with criss-crossing shower heads. He felt the water to be sure it was hot and slipped into the center of the massive stall so the spray could hit him from all sides. He let the water run for five minutes as he imagined Remy's ivory skin against his. He lathered the soap and washed his hair. When he got out, he dried himself off, poured a drink from a mini bar that he had built into a corner of the white marble bathroom and splashed Boucheron on his chest. Would Sarna remember she had given that to him? He finished the drink, brushed his teeth and entered the bedroom with a green towel wrapped around him.

Sarna, her head tilted to one side, stood in the middle of the room in high heels and a full-length lunaraine mink.

Holly Rozner

Her brown hair brushed the collar of her coat. On her left hand was the diamond bracelet Jason had given her on Valentine's Day, just before she dumped him.

Jason stopped a few feet from Sarna. He could smell the familiar fragrance that defined her. Her arms wrapped the fur coat around her slim body. He wondered what she was wearing.

"What happened to Freddy?"

"I can't marry anyone but you."

"It's over, Sarna."

"It's not over, Jay."

Only a few feet separated them.

He didn't budge. "I'm tired, Sarna. It's been a long night."

She inched closer. "You used to say nights with me were too short".

She tossed her head and let her coat ripple to the floor.

Totally nude.

Utterly perfect.

Smiling at Jason, her almond-shaped eyes focused on him, she placed his hands on her breasts. His eyes followed her fingers.

There was a long, long silence, as his cock grew hard. He was dishwater in her presence and he knew that his vows to resist her would fail. He remembered the heartache and the confusion. He couldn't go back to that again. And yet, she was the most beautiful woman he had ever known and in so many ways the most interesting. Behind that seemingly empty head was a cunning mind that he had grown to respect and fear.

He reached out for her and his towel fell to the floor. His eyes locked on her face. Then he kissed her neck, his thumb grazing her nipples. All his promises melted away.

Sarna closed her eyes and let her arms fall. She pressed her body into his.

He licked the skin between her breasts. As he slid into her, his eyes burned, his arms clenching her body.

She smiled.

He was hers.

This time for good.

chapter 6

THE FOLLOWING MORNING Remy was awakened by the phone. She tried to retrieve a dream in which she was running away from a strange man. Though she didn't know who he was, she remembered his hand under her arm, as he escorted her through an amphitheatre surrounded by a mountain. The imaginary touch aroused her. As the dream evolved into a dream within a dream, Remy struggled to recall the first episode as the next one faded. In the dream she had hit a wall and when she turned to get out, she could not locate an exit. When the man leaned over her she couldn't identify him. The only distinguishable mark was the trading jacket he wore.

Remy's heart was pounding. She remembered dancing with Jason. Then, like an unexpected storm, the face of a woman sliced her thoughts and she heard the telephone. Wavering between melancholy and anger, she was happy to hear Lara's voice.

"It's nearly noon. How did it go? What's he like?"

Lara Spade had been Remy's best friend since fifth grade when the two of them tried to pull the chair out from under Miss Pickens who taught World History. Each student was required to re-write the outline Miss Pickens dictated in an elongated methodical drawl. The girls couldn't stop giggling in the back of the room. Lara devised a plan for one of them to ask for something while the other would come up a minute later. Then when Miss Pickens turned around, Lara told Remy to push the chair out. The trick had not been Remy's, but she went along with her friend's mischief. As she got older, Remy realized that people often choose friends who do what they wished to do, but were afraid to. At the last minute, Remy put the chair back and saved Miss Pickens from disgrace.

"It was an unsettling evening," said Remy glancing at the clock near her bed.

"So?"

Remy pictured Lara in her opulent apartment in the John Hancock building, the only sign of her wealth. Lara had been married for three years to a schoolteacher. Together they presented the facade of a struggling couple, hiding the fact that Lara was heiress to a restaurant dynasty. Her husband spent the money dribbling from trust funds and then complained about how they had to watch every penny. Lara had no illusions. She didn't interfere with her husband's pretense, but when she walked on Michigan Avenue, her charge cards were firmly in her hand. Occasionally she used her father's account to hide what she bought, though Rodney Spade didn't care what Lara did as long as he could do what he wanted. Eventually bored with simply being a wife and never wanting children, Lara became a lawyer.

"Jason is very handsome," said Remy.

"And?"

"Nothing happened, Lara. Nothing." She described the glittering evening, Sarna's entrance and the abrupt end.

"When we got home, he wanted to come upstairs, but I said no. I have to admit, he was hard to resist. Especially those eyes."

"Did he kiss you?"

"He tried to." What she didn't tell Lara was how hard it was to say no. Jason was a heartbreaker. With men, Lara and Remy were nothing alike. Lara broke beds when they were co-eds at Northwestern. But when Remy fell for a guy, it was not only about sex. She was afraid that Jason would be toxic. Trouble was written all over his face. Remy needed a man who wasn't in love with himself and certainly not in love with another woman. Maybe the right guy would never come along. Even if that were true, she would not settle again for the wrong one. A bad marriage was worse than being alone. Her parents had been devoted to one another and that was the relationship she wanted. Alan was safely in her past. Stuart Masterman, ancient history. She would not fall for anyone without recognizing the dangers.

"Now what?"

"Back to work. Forget it."

"Who's the woman?"

"I don't know. Last night was a date and that's all. I want to put it behind me."

Lara knew Remy better than that. She had been talking about Jason Bramson for weeks. What to wear. How to style her hair. When to kiss him. Remy might pretend to be a cool customer, but Lara knew the truth.

"If there is another woman in Jason's life, it is not worth the fight. Let's meet. Pancakes and a work out?"

"In that order?"

"Meet me at the Club. We can do an aerobics class and then head to Mitchell's."

"Great." Remy pulled herself out of bed and let the sunlight into her bedroom, the room she used to solve problems. Different from the rest of her apartment, it had a blue and white canopied bed and had become the enclave where she languished on long winter days. Lara was a perfect friend, who let her talk on and on. Remy grabbed a black leotard. She walked to the mirror. Without any lipstick she felt undressed.

Lara gave Remy a sense of family. This morning in particular, she felt lonely and missed her dad. She pictured Zachary Silverman and Oscar Doheney sitting together at the dance. With Jason she had lost sight of her goal. Finding out about her father needed to be her focus.

This morning Remy was glad she had someone in her life who really understood her. Someone with whom there were no ulterior motives, who cared about her the way she would have wished a sister would have cared, had she had one.

Lara Slade was, as always, the perfect friend.

chapter 7

February, 1987

THE SEASON SPUN quickly into winter. Gone was the holiday sparkle. In its place, a canvas of half tones coated the city. The sky was gray, the days short. Snow along the lake was knee deep, the temperatures below normal. Sundown moved up one minute a day so that by February, dusk didn't begin until 5:00 p.m. Trading picked up after the year-end as money managers made adjustments to their portfolios. This window-dressing created a flurry of trading activity followed by an eerie calm. The stock market accelerated with bigger swings and bigger risks. Remy had been on the trading floor for only a few months. In that time her confidence improved so she was willing to take on positions she would have previously avoided.

Remy saw Jason Bramson nearly every day in the pit or in the members' lunchroom off the trading floor. His place was in the middle of the pit. She stood off to one side. He always nodded and at times Remy wished they could speak. She had heard that he had become engaged to a woman named Sarna Richardson, presumably the woman at the dance. Today Remy sensed that Jason wanted to talk to her too.

After several months, Remy found a spot in the pit that she called her own, as much hers as it was anyone's. Here no one had an office. No chair to call yours. No cubby hole. No conference room. Wherever you laid your card marked your place. If someone beat you, it was his. An unwritten code of ethics dictated the place was yours if you claimed it first. Once you stood there for a steady amount of time—an unknown number of days, the boundaries were drawn. If someone threw a card on your space, you could try to reclaim it, but fights erupted and sometimes the pit committee had to have formal hearings to decide whose space belonged to whom. It was a phenomenon of this profession that was unlike others in many ways.

Remy's spot was not too far from Oscar. Because he held the orders coming in from customers, from this angle, it was easier to hear him and capture a good trade. It had become evident that Oscar favored certain traders. At times it looked as if he gave them trades. Remy watched him hand a trade to someone who then sold it to another at a quick profit. Sometimes this happened even if the market was not moving. Certain traders got these trades from Oscar over and over again. Occasionally he signaled to Jason on the other side of the pit. Then she would see Jason bid. Once in a while Remy wondered if she had imagined this. Then her days would get so busy that she didn't have time to pay attention to what looked like a fix.

"So now you think you are going to unearth some big mystery down there? You better behave yourself, Remy, or no one will trade with you." Lara warned when Remy told her what she witnessed.

Lara was right. If a trader made a fuss, he could be locked out of the trade. Was that what happened to her father? Was this what destroyed him? There was no rule requiring that someone trade with you, so it was important to stay on the good side of those who held the paper.

One day Oscar deliberately ignored Remy and gave a trade to someone else.

"That was my trade, Oscar," she insisted.

Oscar's permed hair framed his pockmarked skin. A hawkish nose accentuated a square face perched on a small neck.

"Who do you think you are, Remy, the Index police?" he quipped. He rubbed his hands together, a wild grin covering his face.

Then he walked away without saying a word.

When the same thing happened again, she announced from across the pit. "I was first, Oscar. You know I bid first. What's going on?"

Oscar tucked in his shirt. He acted as if he didn't hear her. Then he grabbed some papers from his clerk, Joey, and whispered something out of the corner of his mouth. But others had overheard the conversation.

"I'll get you next time, sweetie," he said, blowing her a kiss as he shuffled through the mess in his hands.

But he didn't. Instead he stuffed the papers into his trading jacket and he raised his arms into the air as if to begin a tribal dance. Remy felt weak. If she asked too many questions, he could put her out of business. Cross Oscar and you're finished. It wasn't in her nature to overlook things. Once, as an accountant, she told her supervisor that a client had deducted something he didn't deserve. The law was very clear, she explained. He instructed her to do the return with the deduction. To protect herself, she put a memo in the file regarding the incident. The following week she was removed from the account. Months later when everyone was at a conference, she peeked into the file. Her memo was missing; the return had been filed as the client had requested. She reminded herself that as long as she wasn't signing the return, it was not her problem, but she never forgot the incident or the client.

Oscar wasn't her business either. She wasn't sure if she was angry because she wasn't the one getting the trades she deserved, or because she had figured out their system. She thought about her father. One trade not properly executed could cause a bloodbath. The fierce look in her eyes disclosed her concern even as she tried to rein in her thoughts.

"Go get a woman's job," Oscar commanded. He arched his back, his paunchy stomach protruding.

"This is a woman's job," she retorted. "It's my job."

"Very cute, doll," he mocked.

She had riled him.

A few minutes later, a man she had never seen before entered the pit. He put his huge foot on Remy's card, his arms crossed like a policeman.

"That's my spot," she asserted.

"Prove it, lady." He was a new trader. Six feet tall, 240 pounds, smelling like a spoiled fish. Wearing a blue badge, PAT, he stood out in a magenta jacket.

"My card is there." She looked around for someone to validate her boundary. But others looked the other way.

"My card is there now," he proclaimed.

"I stand here every day."

"Not anymore."

"I've been standing here for weeks."

"Now I'll be standing here."

"No, damn it, you won't."

"Yes. Damn it. I will."

She could call the chairman of the pit committee, but if she did, she would look like a crybaby. If she held

Trade Secrets

her ground, she had a chance. If she stepped out, this guy would take her spot.

The prices flashing on the screen gave no clue about the direction of the market. It was 8:28. In two minutes the bell would ring. She would report the incident later. The opening bell sounded! A thunderous roar erupted in the pit as traders reached to ravage a trade from empty space.

"A hundred at 5," screamed Oscar. "A hundred at 5." A dozen taut bodies crept closer to him. She wouldn't let them beat her to the punch.

"Buy five," she screamed, reaching between the new boy and another trader.

"Sold," Oscar confirmed.

"A hundred at zero, At 95. At 90." He was jumping wildly. The market fell twenty-five points in an instant. PAT watched Remy. In twenty seconds, she had lost $1,000, more than she had made in the whole month.

"At 80. At 70." Oscar was jumping up and down, up and down.

There were no bids. You could hear a pin drop. No buyers. Calculating her losses, Remy froze. Her hands were clammy. She could feel the perspiration under her arms. Her head started to throb. The panic made her head swim. On the Boards she could see only red arrows signaling the market's freefall. PAT's smug face bore holes into her.

Maybe the market would reverse. If she sold, she would lock in her loss. Eventually the market would settle down. It would come back. A trader's plea—a cheap shot. It never worked. She had heard about calamities like this, but she never imagined herself in one.

Everything she had learned was eclipsed by the terror she felt. Take your losses the minute you were wrong, the cardinal rule of trading! She had lost her discipline. Cut your losses, let your profits run. The only way to beat the game. Everyone told her this. She knew it. If only she had gotten out the minute the market moved against her. She had let this idiot Patrick dislocate her. This is how fortunes were lost.

Finally a buy order came into the pit and there was a short rally. The market had fallen more than one hundred points before bouncing back fifty. Her losses exceeded $2,500, and it wasn't even 9:00. Why didn't anyone else buy? What had tipped them off?

As she reached over PAT's shoulder to confirm her trade, she felt his hands between her legs.

She jumped out of the pit. "You bastard, I'll report you."

"Go ahead, lady."

Her head was throbbing. She needed to sit down, to recalculate her losses. Maybe she hadn't figured correctly. Her hands were shaking and she needed water. The room smelled of sweat. She reached inside her jacket for an Advil and swallowed two without a drink. Her trading cards were stuffed in her jacket. She took one out and handed it to a clerk to turn in. If the card wasn't marked with the correct time bracket, she could be fined. Added to today's losses, it would be more than she could bear.

"Miss Remy," someone shouted. She tried to shove her way through the room.

It was Hank—the foreman of the pit. He was pushing into the crowd to find her. "Miss Remy, wait a minute please."

She stopped as he got near her.

"What is it, Hank?"

"We have a formal complaint against you."

"For what?"

"For hitting another trader".

"For what?" This was impossible. The room felt like a huge balloon ready to pop. The background noise felt like the clamor in a rock concert. She couldn't think straight.

"Patrick Sullen has accused you of puncturing his jacket with your pencil."

"Are you kidding?"

"No, Ma'am. It's written down here." He handed her the notice.

She glanced at the pit. The markets were still. Oscar was scowling at her, his beady eyes dancing. So this is how it worked. Oscar's way of getting even. She must remain composed. If she were logical, everything would work out. When the committee hears what happened, they will have to believe her.

She held the temples of her head, massaging the pain. She took the piece of paper Hank handed her. The hearing was set for that afternoon after the markets closed. She considered her options. It would be ridiculous to continue to trade today. She had time to go home and soak in a hot bathtub. Or she could stay downtown for the hearing. She stepped aside and took a deep breath. She would come back swinging. Instead of going home, she decided she'd go for lunch with Lara and then work out. That would give her all day to set up her rebuttal. By 3:30 she'd be ready for battle.

No way could they get away with this. No way.

chapter 8

REMY WAS ASSIGNED to a committee room on the third floor of the building. She needed to go downstairs into the corridor, past the food court and then up a bank of elevators situated in the East Tower. She arrived ten minutes early with time to use the members' washroom to freshen her face before she took her place at a long conference table in Committee Room B. On the sideboard was cola and ice and a big bowl of popcorn. The only other people in the room were Jordan Roberts, the pit committee chair, and Stanley Zuckerman, who sometimes stood near her in the pit. Within moments, Jason Bramson, wearing glasses, looking far more reserved than ever, sauntered in. She nodded and he motioned to her as he grabbed a chair at the other end of the room. His familiar face convinced her that this hearing would be over in a few minutes and that the outcome would be favorable.

Just before 3:30 Pat Sullen took a seat at the head of the table next to Remy. Behind him was a trader she had never seen before. Young, maybe two or three years younger than Remy, he wore the badge, MAX, her grandfather's name. She had never seen this boy before. Her concentration was broken when Jordan Roberts came over to shake her hand.

Holly Rozner

"Remy, I want to remind you that hearings are confidential. Nothing is to be repeated to other members or to outsiders. The Exchange expressly prohibits that. A member can be fined for disclosing anything more than the results of these meetings."

She hadn't realized that to be true. Very little leaked out of the committee rooms. Every week a newsletter in the mail summarized the outcome of such meetings. Most of the chatter involved trading infractions or occasionally a fight that had broken out in a pit. In almost every instance the summary ended with a statement that the defendant "neither admitted nor denied any wrongdoing." Then the verdict and maybe a fine. Remy never bothered to ask much because she never envisioned herself involved in a hearing. This, she knew, was a waste of time.

She nodded to Jordan Roberts that she understood his warnings. Then she folded her hands and waited.

To her astonishment, Joey Fortunato stood at the door. He looked at her, his eyes embarrassed as he took a seat. Joey wasn't a trader and didn't belong there. But he sat next to Jason, his hands folded like a goddamn judge.

At exactly 3:30, Jordan Roberts made the announcement that pursuant to federal regulations the meeting would begin and that it would be recorded. Then he asked Remy to take the microphone, to recite what had occurred that morning. She told her story slowly, staring at the eight men surrounding her. Remy had had years of speaking experience in college. Acting had taught her how to address an audience with ease. Poised, elegant, she chose her words well. During lunch, she had stopped at Marshall Field's to buy a new white shirt. The one she wore to work that morning was too casual, and she didn't want to take the time to go all the way home to change clothes. The others would be coming directly from the trading floor in their uniform:

khakis, a shirt, and gym shoes. Men were required to wear a tie. Women had no dress code, except that no one could wear denim. Generally, Remy chose the same outfit every day. A different pair of cotton slacks; in the dead of winter, corduroy and a cotton shirt. Sweaters were too hot and too thick under the red regulation-trading jacket. When she got to work, she changed into gym shoes. The rubber-soles helped prevent a torn disk from rupturing even more. Trading destroyed your body. Every morning she stretched, and worked out at least three times a week to stay in shape.

"I think that's it," Remy said, satisfied that she had summarized what had happened. She looked at Patrick Sullen. She nearly felt sorry for him bringing this ridiculous charge against her.

"Do you have any questions for Mr. Sullen, Miss Masterman, or for his witness?" asked Stan Dole.

So that's who this stranger was. Pat Sullen's witness. It was a set up. She had no one. She tried to think.

"As a matter of fact, I do."

"Go ahead then," he said, rolling his eyes.

"What's your name?" Remy asked, addressing the boy with the badge, Max.

"Max O'Hara."

"How long have you been at the Exchange?" she asked.

"Today is my first day," he answered.

"And you were watching the markets?"

"Yes."

"There's a lot of commotion on the trading floor."

"Sure is."

"Were you able to see the quote machines?"

"Sure."

"And were you able to see everything on them?"

"Well, it's confusing."

"But it must have been pretty clear to you."

"Not exactly. The room is noisy. It's hard to see."

"I think so. That's why I find it amazing that while you were watching the markets on your first day here, you had the time to watch me and Pat too."

"Yes, I did." He didn't flinch. He was just a kid, maybe eighteen, hardly shaven, a wannabee who would say anything to ingratiate himself with the guys.

Remy straightened her shoulders. " Then you saw that Pat forced me out of the pit."

"That's not true."

"Then what did happen?"

"You stepped on Pat's foot."

"The complaint says that I poked a hole in Pat's jacket."

"That's right, you did. With a pencil. That's why he pushed you."

"You saw this happen?"

"Of course," he glowered.

Her neck tightened as she felt the room close in on her. She cleared her throat. If her voice failed, she would show her fear. She needed to be strong. The voice was a dead giveaway. She faced Max.

"Do you want to tell me exactly what you saw?" she asked, expecting him to stammer.

But he did not. In a straightforward manner, he reiterated what he had just been asked, corroborated Patrick's claim, adding further that Remy had been angry because Pat was standing in what she claimed was her space.

Remy's knees buckled. She felt the chair behind her and sat in it.

So this was how it was played. She looked at Joey who returned her look with plaintive eyes. She wanted to ask what he had seen, for him to help her. But he had been sent as Oscar's messenger. If she questioned him, asked for his support and he failed to give it, it would make things worse.

He could be another obstacle in the inevitable catastrophe that was enfolding.

She thought about her training as an actor, how you have to zone out the audience to get into character. Drawing upon those years of training, she steeled herself. Show no emotion. She forced a smile, threw her head back, her gorgeous face posed as if she were in the center of a stage about to speak the line of a famous play. Let the committee do its work. Once they realized that these newcomers didn't fully understand the workings of the pit, her story would prevail. Her vulnerability must remain hidden. Fighting back tears, she struck a pose as if she were ready for a camera shoot. No doubt they were laughing at her, smirking in the men's room, thinking the whole thing was a joke. She wouldn't let them know how much it hurt her.

At 4:00 the meeting ended. Unless she had something more to say, both parties were told to leave.

Remy had hit a brick wall. To these men who wanted to wrap it up and go home, this was just another hearing. Left to decide Remy's future, they didn't care about her. They were glancing at their watches, anxious not to miss the trains that pulled out of the Loop in a halfhour. There was nothing to do, except to hope for a miracle.

Her career was on the line. And she was all alone.

chapter 9

WHEN REMY LEFT the Exchange at 4:30, it was freezing outside, but at least it wasn't pitch dark. The short winter days cast a grim light. At times like this the reality of not having a family made Remy feel alone. The time in her life when someone was home for her was remote. She plowed against the howling wind needing to talk to someone who cared about her. Bundling her coat around her, she charged towards Michigan Avenue to see Lara. She cut to Wacker Drive and then crossed the River. The alabaster Tribune Tower was lit by spotlights, but she was too cold to care.

The remaining eight blocks seemed impassable. Remy hailed a taxi and decided that if Lara weren't at home, she would stop at Bloomingdale's, grab a bite and then go home. But Lara was home and buzzed her up. Lara's apartment overlooked the city from the seventieth floor. The John Hancock building presided over Michigan Avenue as a beacon for the Magnificent Mile, the stretch from Oak Street to the Chicago River. From Lara's corner window lay the vast expanse of the high rent district. Across the street stood the 900 Building, its shopping mall and the Four Seasons Hotel. Beneath Lara's building was an ice skating rink and to the north, Water Tower and the Ritz Hotel.

Lara welcomed Remy into her apartment. It was furnished in black and red, punctuated with modern art.

"You look exhausted. What happened?"

"This day has been unbelievable."

"Shoot." Lara put a pot of tea on and sat down on the sofa, curling her legs, while Remy drifted into her story.

Lara listened, trying to analyze this as if it were a client's case. She studied Remy, searching for clues as to what triggered such a response.

"I'm not worried. They were dead wrong, but what do they want to accomplish? What was this about? Why was Joey there? What was Jason thinking? Where did this new kid come from?"

"Look, Remy. It's business. You haven't learned to play the game. These guys don't examine stuff the way we do. And they don't want a woman telling them what to do. You are neither mother nor the police. Fighting will get you nowhere."

"So Oscar can just give away trades?"

"I don't know what Oscar is allowed or is not allowed to do. But you won't have a friend in the pit and no one to trade with. Ignore them and work."

Lara was so perfectly calm. She would never be in a stew like this. But these hoodlums hadn't manhandled Lara's father as they had hers. Remy had no proof about what happened, but if she could be targeted like this, they could have done more to her dad. If only Lara could give her the right words to say. If only she could be like Lara who was able to make sense of a complicated universe.

"You're the best, Lara. "

Lara put her hands on Remy's shoulders, "Stop thinking everyone is out to get you. Just trade. Keep on working."

Lara was right. Silly things provoked Remy. Something wouldn't allow the sleuth in her to die. This time she could be forced out. To find out what she needed to know, she had to try to be one of them. She would be the actress she had once been trained to be, an astute observer of other people's behavior and keep her mouth shut.

A liar? No.

A fake? Maybe. If that's what acting was, yes. She would be a phony. A fraud. At one time in her life, such posturing would have seemed impossible. But she would live with it to get what she wanted.

If she didn't, she would not survive.

chapter 10

JOEY FOLLOWED JASON into Zach's office in the South Tower. It was 4:45. Zach was at his marble desk playing with his paperweight. The quotrons were silent and the room reeked of cigar smoke. Joey could feel his heart beating. Remy's hearing made him feel sick to his stomach. He had wanted to speak up, but he knew it would be his undoing. He grinned and reached across the desk to shake Zachary's hand.

"So, boy. Oscar tells me it's time for you to trade."

" I've been waiting a long time."

"We need to get to know our people. You will work for Jason, *indirectly* for Oscar and for me."

Zach leaned forward with his arms on the desk, folded as if he were going to teach a class.

"Sit down."

Joey took the chair in front of Zachary and Jason sat to the side.

"How much money do you have? To subsidize your trades?"

Joey's face whitened. He couldn't lie. If they asked him to put money to a trading account, they would find out fast what he had.

Holly Rozner

His armpits were sweaty. They had lured him into believing that they would hire him, but without a bank account, he had no chance.

He looked longingly at Jason.

"Joey will need to be financed." Jason said matter-of-factly.

"Ahhh. Zach leaned back in his chair. "Do you know what that means, son?"

"Not exactly."

"It's simple. We will agree to subsidize you." Zach waited for Joey's response. When he said nothing, Zach continued. "We put up the $50,000 the exchange requires you have in your trading account. Of course, we take what is known as a haircut."

Joey's expression was all questions.

"That means that once we put the cash into your account, we charge interest on the money. Two points over prime. And we take half your profits in addition to the interest. The rest is yours."

It sounded OK. A gift from heaven. He had heard people sponsored traders, but he never understood the mechanics. Now it made sense, though he didn't know why someone would *give* him fifty gees. Jason must really like him to get Zach to hand over a bundle like that. Of course, once he started making money he could pay the loan back and be free. If he made a quarter of what Jason made, he and Rosa could buy a condo with enough left over to go to the Caribbean.

"Mr. Silverman, I don't know what to say. No one has ever done anything like this for me. I can't thank you enough."

"You don't need to thank me. Just know the rules. We stick together." Zachary's jaw jutted forward. Joey thought that it could get stuck like that.

Jason interrupted. "You see what happens if someone gets in the way."

Joey winced. He remembered the hearing and the conference afterwards. Remy hadn't done anything wrong. Those guys wanted to stick her, to let her know she better not mess with them. But how could turn he down Zach's offer? This was the chance of a lifetime. His parents would do anything for him if he asked, but this was too much money. To them trading was gambling and he could lose. But Zach knew the ins and outs of this business. Now Joey would be part of their machine.

"You will stand next to Jason. Sometimes you will split trades. Keep your eyes on Oscar. He will let you know when he needs you. That way you can pay back your loan quickly."

Joey was too scared to ask any questions, too grateful to disturb their promise. The gold watch on Zachary's left arm glimmered across the desk. Joey had seen that watch advertised in a magazine. Twenty thou, easy. He had been to Jason's wedding. A quick hundred thou pissed away that night. What a blast. What a life. It could be his. Here on the table, the whole thing.

Joey Fortunato had a chance to be rich, a chance to get out of the hellhole he lived in and buy a real car, not some rebuilt jalopy, a chance to marry Rosa, have a kid, and send the kid to summer camp; go to Cubs games and set up a retirement fund. A chance to turn his life around. No one was going to stand in his way. From now on, it was Joey Fortunato that mattered.

To hell with everyone else.

chapter 11

AT 6:00 THE alarm rang. Remy slammed the buzzer to shut it off. Her head still ached. Yesterday's events came into focus as she realized she had to face the people from the pit. There was no message on her machine when she returned from Lara's last night. Hopefully the incident would be over and she could get on with her life.

Remy showered, threw on a pair of beige corduroys and a black cotton shirt. Getting dressed and out of the house in a half-hour enabled her to catch an extra fifteen minutes of sleep. A small amount of makeup was all she needed. With the flick of her wrist and a smidgen of mouse, her hair fell loose against her collar. Remy didn't linger over her looks the way some did. She didn't need to. When she emerged from her apartment building thirty-five minutes later wearing her cream shearling jacket and wool scarf, she could have posed for *Vogue*.

Remy lived in Lincoln Park, a mile north of the city's center. She considered purchasing her own condo, but she loved the building in which she rented. Interest rates were high, and she didn't want to be saddled with a mortgage. Perhaps in the spring. But she said that last year and then autumn turned to winter. Maybe this spring she would commit to a permanent place.

The day was cold but the sun strong. The gloom of winter got her down. Chicago was a Technicolor town part of the year and black and white the other half. Remy moved between the two like an actor, not knowing from day to day in what medium her story would be shot.

The blue sky painted a backdrop for today in vivid hues. Her path would take her straight down LaSalle Street into the Loop. Usually she got off her bus at Madison and walked the rest of the way across the river to the Exchange. But she was anxious to get there so she took a cab and was dropped off in front of the building.

She handed her coat to the coat checker and then rode the escalator to the trading floor. She felt herself getting jittery as she approached the turnstile. Then she bumped into Jason Bramson.

"Remy, I wanted to tell you how sorry I am."

"Sorry? About what?"

"Didn't anyone call you?"

"About what?"

Jason took her elbow and turned her around to face the wall where notices were posted. Remy had seen these from time to time, but never bothered to read them.

"You need to see this, Remy."

She pulled her arm away from him as she got close to decipher the words.

Remy Masterman had been "posted" and was found guilty of provoking another trader. For Patrick Sullen—no charges. Not true. Could not be true. What did this mean? She was guilty and he was not? She was the villain and he was exonerated? She was the target, not he? The summary of the meeting indicated that she would not be fined "this time," but there would be a record of "disobedience" in the pit and a warning that if it happened again, she would be penalized.

"You bastard," she flared turning to Jason. "You let them do this."

"Let me explain."

"There is nothing to explain. You know I didn't do anything wrong. I was set up. You fell for it. Either that or you put him there to snag me. You can't do that to me. Not to me. Maybe to some other woman, but not to me. I'll get you for this. If it takes my career, I will get you."

She was shaky and didn't know where the words were coming from or how she had strength to continue, but she spoke as if she were an advocate for someone else.

"Hey, hey, wait a minute. I wasn't in on this."

"You're just like rest of them," she shouted.

She didn't give him a chance to interrupt. By the time he took a breath to say another word, she was gone.

She fled into the members' ladies room. Inside, she stood against the metal wall, letting its cold exterior calm her. This must have been what her father had once faced, an impossible brick wall. The fire in her eyes was bright. They weren't going to lick her. She looked at her watch and saw that she had only fifteen minutes before the opening. She had to think fast. She wasn't going to let them get the best of her. She needed a guise, a trick as clever as theirs, something to disarm them. She couldn't afford to be their enemy. If there were an all-out war, she could never win.

All of a sudden, as if the memory of her father had given her an inner strength, what she had to do became clear. She would continue the performance she had begun yesterday. She would pretend. Just as they did. Instead of being a real person, she would create a persona to challenge them.

She examined her face to be sure there were no signs of weakness. No streaming mascara, no hair out of place. She pinched her cheek to revive the color. Then she marched out of the restroom across the gigantic space between the area she stood in and the pit. There in front of the pit, Jordan Roberts was the first man she saw.

"Jordan." He turned around expecting her to rant at him. Instead she extended her hand and smiled. "I'm so sorry you had to be bothered yesterday. That was such a silly incident. And I want to thank you for taking time to straighten it out."

His jaw dropped. He stared at her, taking in her incredible face. Before he had a chance to say anything, she walked towards Oscar.

"Oscar. You're right. Some women belong at home in the kitchen. But you know that I don't. I appreciate everything you did at the committee meeting yesterday. I don't know what we'd do here without you. Thank you."

Oscar's face betrayed no emotion. He looked at Joey, who couldn't look directly at Remy. Then she moved around the pit and shook each committee member's hand. Without flinching, she picked up her trading card, stared at the screen and announced that there were only three minutes before the opening bell. This time Pat Sullen stepped out of her way without saying a word.

Everyone was staring. All of them knew she had become stronger than they. They would no longer take advantage of her.

And she knew she would never be a victim again. Not ever.

"Let 'em roll," she yelled as she watched Oscar lift his arms into the air.

chapter 12

SARNA HAD PLANNED on furnishing her house and spending the summer in Europe, but by Spring she was pregnant and couldn't leave the country. The doctor ordered her to stay in bed five hours a day because she was spotting. No workouts, no tennis, no shopping.

"It is such a bore," she complained when she went into town to order dinner. Like others in Glencoe, Sarna never cooked. Aware of the population's dependence on ready-made meals, a gourmet shop accommodated the residents' need for fancy food without the fuss. Sarna stopped there three times a week, picking up Cornish hens or pre-cooked swordfish skewers, which she served as if they were her invention.

Sarna and Jason had bought their mansion shortly after they were married. Jason wanted to live in the city, but Sarna argued that the city was no place to raise a family. Jason had grown up in the northern suburbs. Glencoe was an extension of his childhood. She eyed a chance to live on the Lake. Sarna's family had lived in west Wilmette, a mile south but fortunes away in wealth. Her mother had promised her that moving up could change her future. Sarna's father had been a salesman, on the road most of the year.

Holly Rozner

He had missed the bull market and the opportunity to go into business with his brother-in-law. Eventually the products he sold fell out of fashion. Never able to find a niche that would make him rich, he dragged across the Midwest hauling goods in and out of an old Cadillac that his wife insisted they buy. Harriet Richardson's purpose in life to be sure that Sarna escape her fate. It was a necessity to marry well.

Harriet's taste became Sarna's. Both of them saw riparian rights as the ultimate trump card. Chicago's lakefront was the supreme location. People in the city might have a view of the lake, but homeowners on the North Shore could have their own border on the lake, sublimely private, reeking of status.

"It's too expensive," Jason countered.

But Sarna had done her homework. If Jason came up short, his parents would kick in. That was when Sarna invented her own trade. A child for the Lake. The Bramsons would agree to anything if they had a grandchild. Jason was their only hope. This baby would be the their first, maybe their only grandchild. Sarna sometimes threatened to move to California, knowing how this threat drove her in-laws nuts. They would do anything to keep their son nearby. Sarna would give them the baby they longed for and they would give Jason what he needed.

Sarna located the perfect home. Not far from town, walking distance to the train, smack on the Lake. Now she needed Jason's OK. She bought a can of whipping cream. That night, she put on a black lace negligee, opened a bottle of champagne and waited for Jason. After he had undressed, she followed him into the bathroom and put her arms around him, lathering his body with the white cream.

"Take me to bed," she commanded. She rolled on top of him and kissed his ear. Sarna held Jason's face, pressing him against her. Slowly she licked his neck, his chest, his stomach and slid her mouth over his penis. As he reached to enter her, she made him promise to see the house.

"I can't live without you, Sarna," he murmured, thrusting himself inside. Sarna knew that he would do what she asked. As long as she was in control, she would get her way. Jason would be putty in her hands. When they were done making love, Sarna curled herself under his arm and pulled out the picture of the house. He rubbed her nose and agreed to see it the next day.

The real estate agent met them in front of a stone structure built on a cliff overlooking the blue of Lake Michigan. Sarna didn't have to say much. She knew Jason. He wanted what she wanted. This house was a metaphor for the lavish lifestyle Jason tried to resist, thinking it was bad luck for traders to hunger for too much. But no one in his right mind could say no to this. Separated from Sheridan Road by a long driveway, the mansion had a tennis court and pool. Some traders had racing cars, private jets and brief encounters with cocaine. But this! Jason had learned not to display wealth. But Sarna needed a splash. If this was worth $3 million today, think what it would be worth later! A fabulous investment, she argued, knowing it would fulfill her grandiose dream.

She would stay in bed and have this baby! For her palace. She could call someone in to do her nails. Maybe even read a book. But the book had so many words. The Neiman Marcus catalogue sat on her bed stand. She would order something for AFTER the baby was born. Shopping from home would pass the time.

Shopping was one of the two things Sarna was really good at.

Fucking was the other.

chapter 13

Rosa's dress was black velvet. Her tiny fingers glittered with red polish and her usually curly hair, freshly cut that afternoon, fell to her shoulders. Rosa had never been to the world-famous Pump Room and it had taken the better part of the day to prepare for her grand entrance. The rhinestone necklace around her neck matched dangling earrings. She wore her sister's mink jacket and wrapped it tight so no one could tell that it did not fit.

"You are so hot!" Joey exclaimed when she turned to show off her legs. He grabbed her, but she stepped aside and let him know she wouldn't care if she got mussed after dinner. Right now she was going out on the town.

Joey had never been to the Pump Room either, but he had heard enough about it to imagine every detail of its elegance, especially the entrance with its gallery of celebrity-hung photos. Although he couldn't identify all the famous people, he wanted to see which movie star was with which at Table One. Hoping someone would pay attention as he waited for the maître d', he sucked in his stomach and straightened his yellow tie.

Holly Rozner

Every time Rosa looked at Joey, a silly grin covered her face and she looked like a kid dressed up in her mother's clothes.

It was Saturday night, the week of Valentine's Day. The room was ablaze in red. The tiny orchestra played "My Funny Valentine" on the upper landing, but only a handful danced to the music.

The host ushered Joey and Rosa down the small flight of stairs to their booth. When she sat down, Rosa caressed the white leather on the seat to test if it was real.

"It's all genuine, doll, " counseled Joey.

"I've never seen anything so gorgeous."

"Order whatever you want, baby."

"It's so expensive," she sighed.

"I can handle it."

"Last week you couldn't afford a tooth brush. Now this."

"Order and I'll explain."

Rosa studied the vast menu. Deciding between filet mignon and the signature duck, she settled on the latter. The waiter bowed and walked away with their order. Joey held up the glass of champagne. Then he began his story.

"Zachary Silverman called me into this office yesterday. You have never seen an office like this, doll, everything so perfect, down to the cigar holders. We talked for a while. His secretary brought in coffee and doughnuts. You should see how this guy lives!"

"What has this got to do with you?"

"Rosa," he announced holding up the champagne. "I'm gonna be a trader. I'm going to work with Jason Bramson and be a goddamn trader. And the world will be ours."

She put down the glass of champagne.

"You mean that you're going to do what Jason does?"

"I'll be working with him. Not for him. With him. Soon I'll be able to make all that money."

Rosa squeezed his hand, loving him more than ever.

"Who is letting you do this?"

"Oscar."

"I thought traders need money to trade."

"Zachary Silverman is financing me."

Rosa blinked. "I don't understand."

"Every trader needs to own a seat or lease one. If he rents one, which I will do, I have to put up what they call collateral against my trades so that if I lose money, the clearinghouse, in this case, Zach's clearinghouse, doesn't lose any money. It takes fifty thousand dollars."

"Where are you going to get that?" She pushed the champagne away as if it were poison.

"That's where the financing kicks in. Zach will *loan* me the money and I get to trade with it. Then I pay him back out of my profits."

"He must really like you, Joey. He must fucking love you."

"I guess so. It pays to be loyal. That's what I learned from this. Now this payoff." He shook his head in utter disbelief not quite able to digest the windfall himself.

"Joey, I love you." The waiter poured champagne first for her and then for him. They waved their glasses into the air. Joey waited for Rosa to take the first sip.

"What has Zachary Silverman to do with this?"

"We must be careful talking here. Someone may know him. All I can say is that I'm part of their gang. In like Flynn."

"Zach gives you fifty thousand dollars?" It made no sense but it didn't matter. She had decided to sip the champagne and it was taking effect. "Oh, Joey. I'm so happy," she purred. Her Joey knew everything. He would be a trader.

Holly Rozner

She couldn't let her mind leap ahead to the money she had always dreamed about, but for a split second she imagined curling into a plush sofa. Surely Joey understood the ins and outs of the business or they never would have chosen him.

"I love you, Rosie. Soon we'll be able to go to the Caribbean like I always promised. And then maybe…"

He looked so cute, all dressed up, his wide eyes ablaze with the future. The new black suit he bought fit his trim body and the wave in his black hair lay just right against his thick brow. They could get engaged even if he couldn't afford a ring. It would come.

They had made it through the bad times. Now they would be on easy street. With money in the bank, the ring, the trips, even a house could be theirs.

They each ordered a Caesar salad prepared on a cart near the table. Then duck `a l'orange, accompanied by fire under the domed platter. Finally Baked Alaska was marched across the room by the plumed waiters and Rosa held her head up the way she imagined a princess would. She swept her arm across the table. In one day, her life had turned around.

She had her man and he had the road to riches. What else was there?

chapter 14

LARA AND REMY left for Paris in July. Before Remy married Stuart, her father took her to France as part of an engagement gift. Harry Saks stopped at nothing to entertain his daughter: a suite at the Meurice, dinner at four-star restaurants and, of course, a lavish shopping spree.

Remy and Stuart spent their honeymoon in the Caribbean. The mark of Stuart's stinginess surfaced on the first day when Remy picked out an expensive bathing suit to replace one that had torn. When he balked at the price, Remy felt so diminished that she wanted to go home. Stuart was the first to impress friends with extravagant wines and lavish gifts, but when it came to her, he was stingy. Immersed in his work and his various collections, he locked her out materially and emotionally. Her mother had warned her that men who are cheap with money are stingy with their feelings. Soon Remy realized that Stuart's attitude about money and his inability to understand her grief were wrecking their marriage.

This time Remy would do Paris her way. She negotiated for a room with two canopied beds and a huge marble bathroom at the Grand Hotel behind the Opera, a perfect location near American Express and a straight shot to the Rue de la Paix.

They left their luggage at the hotel and rushed down the Rue Royale to the Place de la Concorde, making their way to Angelina's for hot chocolate.

"You need time to relish Paris," Remy said.

"We don't have much time," Lara said.

The waitress served a tray of rich petits-fours and small finger sandwiches. They poured over city maps to design a schedule that would keep them from having to double back to see all the sights.

"We must spend a day at Giverny," Remy announced.

They outlined the first two days. Then set off to the Picasso museum. They lunched at Joe Goldenberg's where they sampled French corned beef. In the Marais, the Jewish quarter, Remy thought about what Paris had been like when Hitler occupied it.

"That part of French history is incomprehensible," she told Lara. "They let him march into the country without even putting up a fight."

"It's hard to fight a tyrant," said Lara.

"But it's deadly if you don't."

They spent one full day near the Sorbonne going from one coffeehouse to another, then to Cafe' de Flore, inventing conversations Gertrude Stein might have had with Hemingway.

"Don't you wish you had been here when the great intellectuals presided over this city?" Lara asked, after she ordered cappuccino.

"I would have liked living here during that time. That reminds me. I know a great place where you can find old copies of Sartre and Stein." Remy took Lara's hand and led her to a bookstore she remembered visiting with her Dad.

Trade Secrets

The trip was not only a chance to be away from work, but a chance to be with Lara. Lara was the one who knew her history, who knew her parents. Lara had been there every day after her father died, knowing when to talk and when to be quiet. And she was the only person in the world who knew the real reason why she had come to the Exchange. Lara had warned her from the beginning that this would probably turn into a dead end.

"How can you infiltrate an entire corporation—you are one little person."

Even Lara could not deter Remy. Recently she had gotten so caught up in learning how to trade, in figuring out who was who and what products were what, that some days, even she herself forgot why she was there. She vowed to be more focused when she returned. She had only one chance. No one else in the world could find out what happened to Harry Saks.

Remy and her father were supposed to visit Giverny, but he had been called back to Chicago on business and they were forced to cut the vacation short. Monet was Remy's favorite artist and Giverny his home. She kept a book about Monet on the coffee table in her apartment, a birthday gift from her father.

On the third day when they took an early train to Giverny, Remy felt anxious. She would make this visit for her father too. When the train pulled into the tiny station and they located a shuttle that would take them to the gardens, they were still talking about work and men and all the things that made them friends.

"Go ahead," said Lara, when the cab dropped them off at the entrance to the gardens. "I'll get some literature from the front office."

Remy walked on alone. "It's the bridge," she whispered, her eyes tearing as she stood at the spot Monet had immortalized with his paint brush. There it was! The very scene, as if she had stepped into the painting itself.

Next to her a man with a large camera was busy taking pictures. "It's breathtaking," he said shooting from one angle and then another with an impressive, professional-looking lens.

"I wonder if a camera can capture it," she said.

"It depends on the cameraman," he replied.

"Are you a professional?"

"Not at all. Just having fun."

Remy turned around to look at him. He was tall with a ruddy complexion, sandy hair and strong hands. Remy noticed a scar on his chin and wondered what might have put it there. She guessed that he might have been in his early thirties though the creases around his eyes made him look older. As he turned to face her, his eyes displayed a distant stare.

"This doesn't seem real," Remy said. "It seems as if I'm looking at a picture."

"It's real. Let me prove it. Let me photograph you here," he insisted, guiding her with his arm towards the bridge. "There. This is a perfect shot."

"Oh, I don't think so," she said, stepping aside.

"It won't hurt. I promise," he said holding her with his eyes and placing her exactly where he wanted her to be. He moved back a few inches to frame the scene.

Remy followed his orders. His imposing camera clicked.

Remy forced a smile as the camera flashed.

"Do you always take pictures of complete strangers?"

"Only when they look like you."

Remy could feel herself flush.

"No scene is worth much without people in it," he added.

Trade Secrets

"Monet didn't paint any people in his landscapes."

"I'm not Monet," he answered as he tore out a fresh roll of film. "Hold on. I'm not done. You know the camera sees more in one shot than anyone can see in a lifetime."

"Did you make that up?"

"Of course I made it up," he said.

"What has your camera seen that's so important?"

"Someone I can't take my eyes off."

"I really can't stay," Remy said. He was easy to look at, but all this attention was unsettling. "I'm meeting someone and they won't know where I am."

"I should have guessed that you wouldn't be alone," he said. "Where is he?"

"Who?"

"The person you have to meet?"

Remy laughed.

"Let me introduce myself. I'm Ken Baldwin," he said, holding the camera in one hand and extending his hand towards her.

"Remy Masterman," she said, pushing her hair behind her ears.

"Remy. That's French."

"My mother's family was from France, but that goes back decades. My mom played around with names and named me Andrea. I changed it when my Aunt Remy died because I loved her so," Remy said, leaving out the part when she had imagined her name on a marquee.

"Where are you from, Remy Masterman?"

"Chicago."

"Al Capone territory."

"That was also a long time ago."

"Some reputations never die."

"That's ridiculous," she scoffed.

"It's part of your city's lore. Don't be insulted. It's history."

Remy looked around to see where Lara was. This man was taking up her time. They had only a few hours to spend in Giverny and she didn't want to waste it on Al Capone.

"I must get going," she said, but she didn't move.

"Can I send you a copy of the photo?"

"It's not necessary," she replied.

"But you'll be immortalized in my darkroom and no one will ever know who you are?"

"You will know. You will know that I'm Remy," she replied.

"Have you been to the Marmottan?" Ken asked.

"I don't know what it is."

"It's a tiny museum in Paris devoted to Monet."

"You know a lot about art."

"I just like beautiful things."

Remy fumbled in her purse for her sunglasses and put them on to block out the sun. That way she could see his face better. Ken had an angular face and well-defined lips, a warm smile and deep gray eyes. Nearly six feet tall, he wore an apricot cashmere sweater that didn't match his shirt. He looked as if he tried to put himself together perfectly and then lost interest. She watched him twist the camera lens and placed it into a cover. When he looked up at her, their eyes locked and Remy could feel her heart race.

"Where are you from?" she asked.

"New York."

"Is this the first time you've been to France?"

"I was at the airport years ago. It is my first time staying in the city," he answered.

"Then how do you know about the Marmotton?"

"I've done my homework."

His remark stung, making Remy feel that Lara and she had done only ordinary things, that Ken knew things she hadn't even considered. She liked a man who could help her discover things she didn't have in her own repertoire, someone who could show her a thing or two.

"We've seen the Louvre and the Marais district," she offered

"And the Picasso Museum?" he asked.

"Yes," she nodded as Lara reappeared.

"I went out the other side and wasn't able to find you," Lara said.

"This is my friend, Lara. Lara, this is Ken Baldwin."

"Hello," Lara said shaking his hand. "We better hurry. This is the most gorgeous spot I've ever seen. Did you see the bridge?"

"I did. It brought tears to my eyes," Remy said.

"I've got her on film standing on it."

Lara looked at Ken and then at Remy. She had been gone only five minutes and this amazing-looking guy was already taking pictures of Remy!

"Here. Use my camera, so we can have a photo too," Lara commanded.

Ken took the camera from her as the two women moved together, the bridge in the background.

"Aren't you with other people?" Ken asked. "Maybe we should wait for them."

"Just us," Lara said. "My husband's at home."

Ken looked at Remy and smiled. When he did, the wrinkle on the side of his eyes widened.

"It's just a simple camera," Lara apologized.

"It does the job," he replied. "A camera is only as good as its subject," he added as he held it to his eye, snapping them from different angles.

"This is great. Thanks a lot," Lara said.

"I was telling Remy about the Marmottan."

"The Monet museum!" Lara exclaimed.

"You know about it?" Remy asked.

"I don't *know* about it. I read about it in a guide book."

"If you are free tomorrow, let me take both of you there."

"I can't," Lara said. "I'm going to look for posters. There's a market outside of Paris I want to go to. But Remy should go with you."

This was not their agreement, Remy thought to herself. Not at all. They had promised not to even discuss men while they were in Paris.

"I'm going with you, Lara."

"I hate shopping with another person tagging along. I will get nervous having to make up my mind quickly so I don't keep you waiting."

There was a brief pause while Ken weighed his next move. Within seconds, he said, "Then it's a date, Remy. I'll meet you at your hotel .Then we can all have dinner tomorrow night and Lara can tell us what she bought."

Remy looked at Lara who simply grinned as Ken wrote down the name of their hotel.

"The front desk at 10:00," he said as he gathered his things.

"Who is this guy?" Lara asked as he walked off.

"I don't know. I don't know anything about him. He was standing here and started taking pictures of me."

"Well, if I weren't already married, I'd be all arms for him."

"He's too sure of himself. I know the type. I'm not interested." Remy forced her shoulders to relax so that even Lara wasn't able to see that he had reached her.

She had done it again, letting a guy make up her mind for her. It was like her date with Jason. Why hadn't she just said no? Now she had a date and she didn't even know how to call and cancel. She would either have to be at the front desk on time or stand him up and she wasn't the type not to show up for things. Maybe she would meet him and tell him then that she decided to join Lara after all. Yes. That was possible. She could still get out of it.

"He's OK," Remy said, thinking to herself that he might be a very sexy guy. Still there was something in his eyes she wasn't quite sure she could trust.

***

The following morning, Remy found Ken leaning against the Concierge desk waiting for her.

"You're even prettier than I remembered," he said as he held his arm out to greet her.

"I don't like compliments," she said, ready to suggest that they just have coffee and go their separate ways, but when she looked at him, his stare drew her in.

"Everyone likes compliments," he replied, guiding her with his arm against her back. He tipped the doorman and helped her into a taxi in front of the hotel. It was evident from the way he made decisions and the way he carried himself that he was a man who had been around, a man who was used to getting his way.

"I really don't like compliments," she said as she settled into the back seat, her hands on her lap. She didn't like to jostle words when she was on a date. She looked out the window at the busy streets trying to analyze her own motive for changing plans so quickly, trying to figure out if Lara had instigated this or if she had wanted it too.

"Paris takes time to appreciate," Ken said.

She stared at him. He had read her mind. Stolen her words. She turned toward him and studied his face. Ken had one leg crossed over another, relaxing against the stiff leather seats. Still she couldn't help but wonder what lay beneath that remote stare.

"You seem preoccupied."

"No. I've been told I look that way sometimes, but it's just that my mind is on a million things."

"What kind of things?"

"Stuff at work. This is a short vacation for me. I have to be in New York next week."

"For what?"

"A case I just took on."

His tone was cool, practiced. He didn't invite any more questions, so Remy didn't ask more and decided to concentrate on the leafy streets.

The Marmottan was set in an old house which made it feel intimate. Centered solely on Monet's art, it gave the viewer a close examination of the painter as if the art were part of a living room. Ken pointed out aspects of the paintings she would have overlooked on her own. As he talked, she looked at him, admiring him for being able to learn all of this while he was so busy with work.

"It's charming," she said after they had ambled through each room. When they left, Ken turned to her and asked her what else she wanted to do with their day. She shrugged her shoulders.

"Let's go to St. Germain and take a walk."

"I love this city," she said, as they strolled along the Quays near the Rue du Bac. They stopped at a small café and Ken ordered each of them café au lait. She watched him put a sugar cube into his and took a long moment to consider him more carefully. In some ways he reminded her of Alan. That had been all heartache, but he was not Alan. She was no longer in college and things didn't have to turn out badly this time.

"Do you work?" Ken asked.

"I'm a trader."

"On a trading floor?"

"Yes." People were always shocked to learn what she did for a living.

He asked questions about her work, pertinent ones that other people might not have thought to ask and she answered him, wondering if he knew anything about her insular, crooked world.

Ken began to talk about himself. He explained that his childhood had been a confused one. His father was away a lot in the army leaving his mother alone. After his father died on a secret mission, Ken considered a military career for himself, but his mother wouldn't hear of it. Educated in private schools, Ken was expected to go to Harvard. When Ken was accepted, his mother urged him to go to law school and establish a practice in New York. He followed her plan, but he wasn't happy sitting behind a desk all day. He needed more action and decided to enroll in an FBI program. His first assignment was in Las Vegas investigating Mafia involvement in the casinos.

His eyes hardened when he told her how he had been ordered to follow two men in the dark of night. Caught in an alleyway, Ken couldn't see clearly. He lost his footing and fell down a flight of stairs. When he stood up, he mistook an agent on his team for a mobster. The man he killed left a wife and two small children. The incident ended his career with the FBI and left him with a scar on his chin.

Remy listened quietly to his story. The far-off stare that she had noticed when she met him faded into a gentle look that summoned her. She felt so sorry for him, knowing how awful it must be to carry the burden of that for the rest of his life. Then he told her about his first marriage and how his wife had died and she could see from the look in his eyes that the distant stare she assumed was aloofness was actually pain. He leaned across the table and took her hand. If he had pulled her towards him, she would have let him kiss her. But he did not. Instead he paid the bill and stood up to help her out of her chair. His fingers grazed her neck. She was not yet ready for the unfamiliar sensation of his skin against her, yet she hoped he might touch her again.

***

"It was a wonderful, wonderful dinner," Remy said later when she and Lara were in the room that night.

Lara pinned back her hair and flung herself on the sofa in the anteroom. Remy was a rare beauty. It was easy for her to attract men, but she was too tough on them. She wanted things her way. She needed a man who would acquiesce to her, but when he did, she didn't want him anymore.

Tonight, excitement was written all over her face. The cool collected Remy Masterman was smitten .

"He speaks French," Remy said wiping off her makeup.

"Yes, I heard," said Lara trying to remain aloof. If she appeared anxious, Remy would withdraw. When someone actually agreed with her, Remy would change her position and argue to keep her distance.

"New Yorkers are more sophisticated," Remy said.

"Chicago is the boondocks?"

"No. I don't mean that. But it is a Midwestern city."

"You had your chance to live out East and you came back." If Lara took a critical position, it would give Remy something to defend, allowing her to think the crush was her own invention.

"You can't compare the two cities," Remy said finally and Lara dropped the subject.

"He wants to be with us tomorrow night," she continued.

With you, Lara thought, turning off the light and considering that she might pretend to be sick so the two could be alone.

"Now let's get some sleep."

"Nite, Lara," Remy said.

"Good night, Remy."

"Lara, you're a very good friend."

"I love you, Remy."

"He seems like a great guy, don't you think?" Remy asked, staring at the ceiling in the dark.

"A really great guy."

Remy lay awake for an hour reliving her conversation with Ken. She believed in instant romance. Her parents had married within just a few months after meeting each other. What could be more romantic than the garden Monet had painted?

She closed her eyes, but it was senseless. This would be a restless night. Even the pillow could not hide Ken Baldwin's face. She felt confused. This was happening too fast. She took a deep breath and wanted to turn on the light and stay awake for a few hours mulling over the day, but she couldn't wake Lara. Instead, she buried her head in the pillow, but it was no use. Ken Baldwin had gotten to her. She imagined what it would feel like to have his hands on her. She closed her eyes and tried to sleep as feelings she didn't want to lose raced through her mind. Finally when she did fall asleep, it was nearly dawn and, for a brief time, she dreamed about a man helping her out of a car who whisked her off into the moonlight his arm around her shoulder, hers around his waist, as if they had always been together.

***

Ken and Remy spent their final evening in Paris visiting the alabaster monuments, transversing the city from one end to the other, memorizing the bridges lit by frosted floodlights. Ken held her tight, knowing that weeks might pass before he saw her again.

He left early the following morning for the States. When his plane landed in New York, he found it hard to concentrate. As he opened the door to his brownstone and faced piles of work heaped on his desk, Ken wished he could stay up all night and get everything done so that he had time to be with Remy when she returned.

Ken sorted his mail before he reverted to his darkroom. There he could recapture the trip with photographs. Methodically he measured the chemicals. As he waited for them to work, he put on a Brahms concerto. In just a few minutes, Remy's face came into focus. Those intelligent, bold eyes. He removed the paper from the solution and watched as her features became clear. Then he hung the portrait up to dry.

At 3:30, he fell into bed and dreamed that Remy was lying next to him, her head tucked into his neck. When he awoke, she was on his mind. He decided to go for an early run before he tackled the reality of his job. Easing his way along the East River, he hummed to himself, realizing, as the sun came up, that this was the first time since his wife died that he had felt alive.

Ken Baldwin and Cathy Simms were married the year they graduated from college. Cathy accepted a job in Boston teaching school while he studied for the bar. Days after Ken passed the exam, Cathy began to hemorrhage. She died six months later from a virulent cancer. Her death devastated Ken. For one year he dragged himself to work and then home for a TV dinner, burying himself in work. As a child, Ken moved from city to city every time his father relocated. Ken learned to reinvent himself in each new community, where he was forced to make new friends. He took up photography because he needed something he could take with him from place to place. It provided an interior world, giving him a personal purpose to view every new location. He learned how to develop pictures, watching them evolve from a tarnished image in the dark into the scene he had envisioned when he first shot it. On summer nights, he followed police cars and fire engines to catch the human-interest story. At times, he slept on the floor of the fire station and woke up there the next morning.

He shot his scenes from different angles, delving beneath the surface, to the layer that exposed the hard truth. Ken saw what others overlooked, a skill he perfected from his training in the FBI.

This morning his mind was on Remy. He was ready for a woman in his life. But there was work to finish, an assignment he had taken before he left town that could complicate things. This was the perfect morning for a long run. Ken jogged past the apartment building where he once lived, picturing his mother the night she discovered his father's first infidelity when Ken was only ten. As he rounded the corner of 88th and Madison, his muscular legs slammed the sidewalk. His breath was steady, his ragged T-shirt dripping from the city heat, but he charged into Central Park, mulling over his past, considering the things about the city that he loved and hated. For Ken Baldwin, New York was a great contradiction, intriguing him as no other city ever had, a place that had had taught him that deception was a necessary tool.

The job he had accepted only weeks ago would take him to Chicago. As he shot past the pretzel stands and the carriages that graced the park, he wound his way back to York Avenue, struggling to figure out how to handle what was ahead and knowing that the situation in Chicago might become tense.

Holly Rozner

It was both ironic and disturbing that Remy was from Chicago. He couldn't change that, but he vowed not to let his job get in the way. He had a contract he must honor. The challenge would be securing Remy in his life without telling her what she would eventually have to know, and making sure his commitments didn't tear them apart.

chapter 15

Summer, 1987

"Oscar, you will throw trades to Joey. And get Jason out of the loop," Zach commanded, removing a cigar from his mouth.

Oscar thought this might happen. Zach was always jumping ahead of himself. It meant nothing if a guy got slammed along the way.

"I can't do that. It will make the trades easier to trace. That's why we hired Joey: to make the audit trail more difficult to follow. If you get rid of Jason, the whole thing goes up in smoke."

"You're scared of your shadow, Doheney," Zach bellowed, pounding his fist on the desk. "Who is he gonna squeal to? He blows the whistle and then we blow the whistle."

"And then we all go to jail."

"It's cleaner my way."

"You're nuts."

"Remember, Oscar. You were the one who hired Jason."

"Yes, and it's worked. You can't just get rid of him. You don't understand Jason. He's not like us. He loves money and that crazy wife of his can spend it faster than falling rain, but Jason is not like you and me. His mind is simple. To him Joey is a hungry kid who needs a break. He knows we use Joey to dilute the trades, but he doesn't know about the rest and you don't want Jason poking around. Remember what happened when Harry Saks started poking around."

"That's why he has to go," Zach insisted.

"If you cut him out, it will be all over our face. He will see that Joey gets trades that used to go to him. He thinks it's to protect us from regulatory problems. And to some extent he is right. Leave him alone, Zach."

From the corner window in Zach's office, Oscar could see the blue lake, shimmering like diamond studs under the August sky. He needed air. He was up to his eyeballs with Zachary Silverman. But they were joined at the hip, like Othello to Iago. Oscar's motives were more complicated than Zach's greed. He needed answers to a burning question.

Oscar Doheney grew up on the South Side of Chicago in an Irish neighborhood. When he was six years old, his father was drafted into the army. Three months later a telegram arrived saying that he was presumed dead. His body was never returned. His mother had to work in the local drugstore to support Oscar and his five brothers. Without help from the church, the family would have starved. When Oscar was ten, his mother remarried and after the ceremony, Oscar fell into a depression, insisting that his father was alive, off on a powerful journey. In eighth grade, when he was required to read a simplified version of the *Iliad* and the *Odyssey,* the myth struck him to the core. He allied himself with Telemachus, Odysseus's son, who had waited with his mother for twenty years until his father returned. Oscar plunged into the fable and eventually discovered that a modern Irish author had based a character on this legend. When he was fifteen, Oscar won a scholarship to travel to Dublin where he retraced the places that James Joyce's character had traveled on foot. Oscar never read the actual story of *Ulysses,* just the Cliff notes, but he was mesmerized by this modern day *Odyssey*. Last summer, he took his wife to the Mediterranean to visit places that Ulysses traveled when he wound his way back after the Trojan War.

Convinced that one day his father would return, he spent a month in Ireland browsing streets the fictional Bloom reputedly walked. There he could be Stephen Dedalus, Bloom's would-be son. Oscar's mission to locate his father was so intense that he could hardly acknowledge that he was visiting places fashioned after a fabricated hero. The search consumed him. Even to this day, the illusion remained alive. When he and Zach weren't stealing money, his mind drifted into these fantasies. Oscar's talent for fantasy helped him rationalize that he deserved the money he stole. His father had been taken away; therefore he could take what he wanted. He had no guilt when he pocketed a trade. Zach's inside information made it so easy. Every morning, Oscar knew exactly which way the market would go, even before the opening bell rang. With Jason as the front man, the ride had been glorious. After doing it for so many years, these deals didn't even feel unscrupulous.

By now Oscar was an expert dissembler. When he looked in the mirror and saw the heavy creases on his brow, he refused to acknowledge that liquor and food had taken a toll. Money didn't always keep his mind off his problems, but it kept his wife busy and she didn't ask what he did with his free time. Their marriage had been dead for years. Still he didn't want to break up his home and leave his kid the way his father had left him. He sought sexual pleasure wherever he could. Only on the trading floor did he come to life, his black eyes glinting as orders were passed among the crowd. His underhanded transactions with Zach were a thrill. He stood at the edge of the pit like a great emperor, forty-five years old, five ten, with thinning black hair, a straight nose and thick lips. Every now and then some clerk with big boobs came on to him and he was all hers. What the hell? His delight came from the titillation of the trade, his fingers on a rosy breast when he could grab one and these solitary moments when Ulysses and Leonard Bloom drifted into his mind.

"We brought Joey in to cause confusion if the regulators ever investigate us. It was a brilliant strategy, Oscar. That kid is money in the bank. Joey will owe us for the rest of his life. Even when he figures out what happened to him, he'll be putty in our hands."

Zach twirled the cigar between his fingers and then put it back into his mouth. He sucked on it as he spoke. "Maybe you're right. I guess Jason is different. We could never finance Jason. Still I think he is unnecessary now. When we took him in, we knew nothing about this business. Now we have it all wrapped up." Zach swallowed the smoke filtering from his cigar as he sang this part of their history. "Joey Fortunato is an ant. If we perfect this experiment on him, we can create a whole new enterprise, financing dozens like him. We'll find them in grocery stores or driving taxi cabs. They'll be begging us to help them."

The sun was shining on his desk. To stop the glare, he stood up and closed the blinds. He removed his jacket and reached for the cigar, caressed it and then put it down. He opened his drawer to get a stick of gum. "This is such shit," he said, pointing to the nicotine gum. "I hate this crap. But the doctor said I should try it."

"It's still nicotine."

"I know. At least it's not getting into my lungs. At least it won't keep my heart from beating."

What heart? Oscar reached for the package of gum and read the instructions.

"You were saying?" Zach asked.

"I was saying this." Oscar sat on the corner of the desk while Zach straightened some things in the room. It was late afternoon, Friday. Time to call it quits. Zach liked everything in order. "You're right. If this works with Joey, it will work with a dozen traders at a time. We'll have our own bank on the trading floor, a group we can control whether they succeed or fail."

"That's more like it. This is how I like to see you. Greedy and mean like me."

"Just be careful how you handle Jason. Joey is OK, Zachary. He's anxious to make it big. It took time to be sure Joey was the right one. It will take time with the others too. We can build an empire. Just don't screw it up with Jason."

Zach stepped close to Oscar, his nostrils widening as he breathed heavily into Oscar's face. Oscar could smell the nicotine.

"We can control the whole floor. What can anyone do? Sue us for helping a kid get started? If Joey owes us, he owes us. It's just a financial deal. Right, Oscar?"

"Right, Zach." The scheme was so smooth, it gave Oscar the jitters. So good that he wondered where the flaw was. So simple too. Oscar had invented it when he picked Joey out of a shoe store. Keep him starving with the promise of trading and then wham, one day keep the promise. Pass winning trades to him until he is completely dependent on you. And then, when the big out-trades occur, the one that will break him, you pass that over too. To any Joey that comes along. He'll owe you. And the debt will grow because the deal was half the profits and half the losses. The losses have to be made up in full before the profits start. Meantime, the kid pays back with financed money. He will never be able to pay back. The account will always run at a deficit.

"It's so brilliant, Oscar, I can't believe I didn't think of it," Zach repeated. "I've tried every which way to figure out how it could go wrong."

Oscar knew it pleased Zach to have him nearby. He always told people how alike they were. But Oscar could see the differences. Zach was a natural. He had done this in Wisconsin, but here it was even easier because he didn't have to buy anything first before he unloaded it. This set up was entirely riskless with kids breaking the doors down to get in.

Oscar had come to hate his dependence on Zach. When you lean on someone, there's always the chance that they can pull the rug out. Relying on a guy like Zach was like waiting to be pushed off a bridge. He knew that if Jason went, someday Zach could find a way to get rid of him too.

But right now, Zach owed Oscar.

One day he'd figure out how to collect.

chapter 16

REMY AND LARA stayed in Europe an extra week traveling by car to Normandy and Provence. They were anxious to spend the remainder of the summer in Chicago to enjoy the city when the beaches were full and the trees in bloom.

Once she was back, everything Remy did was interrupted with thoughts of Ken. He had moved in on her emotions so suddenly, so unexpectedly. Remy knew that vacation romances could fade once life got in the way. She didn't expect to hear from Ken immediately, though she hoped he would call. The day after she got home, a dozen red roses arrived! And two days later, Ken himself. He was on a business trip that had not been scheduled until that morning and was able to stay in Chicago only one night. He took a room at the Drake and invited her to meet him at the hotel.

"You look exactly like this fabulous woman I met in Paris," he exclaimed as he helped her out of a taxi on the Walton Street entrance.

"You didn't tell me to get dressed up," she said taking his hand and looking him over.

"I needed a suit for this meeting," he explained as he loosened his tie.

Holly Rozner

"I wish you had called me first so I could have planned something special," she said.

"You're what's special," he said stopping on the street corner, his arm against her back as if he were in charge of her life. They had dinner at a small restaurant on Rush Street and when the evening was over, Remy found herself greedy for his touch, wondering when it would come.

"I have to be back tomorrow," he explained when he took her to her apartment, "but I want you to come to New York next week."

Remy pushed back and looked him in the eye. This was so fast. Ken had stirred feelings within her that she thought were impossible to have again. If she went to New York, he might expect more than she was ready to give. He was smooth, very polished. If she weren't careful, she might lose control of her senses.

But she couldn't say no. They made plans for her to visit him in two weeks. During that time, Remy hoped to organize her feelings. She threw herself into work knowing that if she were busy, the two weeks would fly by. And they did. Trading had become very volatile. Certain days she was able to make a thousand dollars and then leave. She was proud of herself, confident that she had learned something about this profession that she could call her own. When she stepped off the plane at La Guardia and saw Ken's eyes smiling at her, her heart was throbbing. The Exchange didn't matter.

"I missed you," Ken said inching towards her. When he bent over to kiss her, she parted her lips. His touch made her feel light-headed. They stopped at the hotel to drop off her bags. Then he took her to his townhouse on the Upper East Side. It was a narrow space, decorated in gray and black. Obviously he had taken great care to make this his own. Every available space was filled with art he had collected, hung neatly next to photographs he had developed himself. In front of the window was a large black lacquered credenza. He clicked on Miles Davis, poured drinks and sat on the chair opposite Remy, his legs stretched on a leather ottoman.

"You've traveled so much," Remy said as she studied the myriad pictures on the walls. She sipped her drink and her anxiety eased as he began to talk about his life.

"I traveled when I was a kid because my folks moved around. Now I travel for work."

"Where next?" she asked.

"Chicago, of course."

Remy smiled and put the drink down.

"Tell me what you do."

"I am a lawyer, but I don't practice. I'm a consultant."

"About what?"

"Financial stuff," he said standing up and moving towards the window. Behind him the New York skyscrapers loomed in the background. It was obvious that Ken didn't want to talk about work. So many men were taken with themselves, in what they did, that they barely talked about anyone else. It was refreshing to meet someone who was not caught up in himself. Ken seemed interested in her life. Because he didn't live in Chicago, Remy felt relaxed talking about the Exchange.

"I'll take you on the trading floor one day," she offered. "There is no place like it. People can make unlimited amounts of money."

"Or lose it," he added.

"Some can't lose."

"Why?"

"Special trades are given to certain traders." She read the confused expression on his face. "They are riskless trades," she explained.

Holly Rozner

"You mean they're set up?"
"Yes."
"Isn't that illegal?"
"It doesn't seem to matter."
"How can it not matter?"
"No one cares."
"You are able to see it?"
"Anyone can see it if you're there."
"If everyone can see it, why doesn't someone stop it?"
"The people who run the Exchange are too powerful. Brokers pass out the trades and the orders come from upstairs. If you get in the way, that's it for you."
"You mean brokers do whatever they want?"
"Yes," she said, stating a simple fact.
"That's a serious accusation."
"It is serious." Her eyes filled with tears. Ken didn't know what he had said that would elicit this reaction, but he could see that there was something terribly wrong.
"What's the matter, Remy?" Her eyes burned and though she tried she couldn't hold back the tears.
"I have more than a passing interest in what happens in the pits, Ken," Remy said. She stood up and went over to the window where she could look out at the city. Then she turned towards him, knowing that she could not contain herself. "This will sound insane," she began apologetically.
"I've heard lot of insane things in my life," he said kindly.
"My father worked at the Exchange for many years. His name was Harry Saks."
"Then how are you Remy Masterman?" Remy told him about her brief marriage to Stuart Masterman, outlining how she kept his name to mask her identity.
"So you were born Remy Saks, but no one at the Exchange knows who your father was."

"I don't know what would happen if they did know. My father died in a car crash—it was assumed there had been an accident—but it never felt right to me. For weeks before he died, my father was very depressed about something he refused to discuss with me. I know it was about work because I heard some of the telephone calls."

"You are making a giant assumption."

"I know I'm right. I know I am."

"Are you afraid someone will find out who you are?"

"A little," she said. Her eyes stayed fixed on him as she continued. "It's better for no one to know. Once someone finds out who I am, I can never cover it up again."

"You are like a private investigator."

"I guess so," she admitted.

"That's a big job."

"Losing my father was a big blow," she said sadly. "Sometimes what happened overwhelms me. But it also makes me angry. I wonder if he took his own life or if something else happened. My dad and I were very close. He was consumed by what was bothering him. I worried that he might have been in danger. If he could have told me what was wrong, I know he would have."

"But that doesn't mean that he took his own life."

"You didn't know him, Ken. He was a changed man. Something had come over him, and it felt as if he had no way out."

Ken stood up and moved close to her.

"Maybe I can help," he said his arms on hers.

"You know nothing about these people." She stared at him wondering why she thought she could trust him. There was something in his powerful gaze that compelled her to divulge facts about her life she would share only with a close friend.

"I'll come with you and see myself," Ken offered with a comforting smile.

"Someday," she replied. She walked back to the sofa and sat down on it, her arms behind her head tossing her hair back wondering what Ken was really like. He had an honest face with piercing eyes and thick lashes. He displayed the self-assuredness of a man who was poised to make a power play. For a moment, Remy questioned her own judgment, going on like this with a near stranger, but it was obvious that a New Yorker had no interest in Chicago, so what she told him was perfectly safe.

He couldn't take his eyes off her sitting there like that, vulnerable, beautiful, and vibrantly mysterious. He wanted to take her in his arms, but he was afraid it would be too soon, that he would shatter her faith.

"You don't engage in any of these illegal trades?"

"Of course not."

"This is a treacherous game they are playing. Someday they'll get caught."

"They will never get caught," she said.

"Eventually one of them will make the wrong move."

Remy could feel herself getting apprehensive. "You will never discuss any of this, Ken, will you?"

"Of course not."

"It could be terrible for me if any of this got out. I could actually be fined for making insinuations."

"I don't discuss private business." He looked at his watch. "I'm getting hungry and I'm sure you are too. Let's go for dinner." He helped her up. She stood face to face with him, perfectly still. Her heart beat fast as he leaned in and nipped her lips. It felt good being near him and she hoped he would kiss her again. Ken had thrown her off balance with his deep voice and strong arms and eyes that could penetrate her soul. When he squeezed her hand, she searched his face for a clue about how he felt.

"Now let's eat," Ken suggested, controlling himself from taking her then and there.

They took a walk along Madison Avenue. The sun had set and the city was ablaze in light. With the shops closed, the busy street lost its usual stride. Remy wore a thin jersey that clung to her. The wind blew the fabric in such a way that the lace on her underwear could be seen through the sheer skirt. They wandered into the garden of a Bistro in the upper eighties, sharing stories about their past. At midnight Ken suggested that it was time to go back to the hotel. He let her off in front of the building, kissed her on the lips and then moved away.

Once she was alone in her room, Remy paused to listen to the silence, grateful for her own space. She knew how easy it was to miscalculate men. She had been wrong before and reasoned that it might be a good thing that they lived in different cities. The distance would give her time to examine the relationship and let it grow at a more even pace. Yet when she turned off the light and tried to sleep, she couldn't stop wishing for the touch that had come so near. Still, she was glad he hadn't insisted. She needed time.

Ken picked her up the following morning and led her on a whirlwind tour of New York. The crowded streets, the art galleries, the fashionable windows along Fifth Avenue all fascinated him and he passed that enchantment onto her. He held her hand as he showed off every neighborhood and told her stories to match each one. They took a subway to the Battery, crossed to Ellis Island and spent two hours browsing through the museum there.

"I would never have been brave enough to leave my country and move somewhere," she admitted.

"You seem pretty brave to me," he said, looking directly at her.

"Well, I'm not. I'm a real coward and I need my comforts. These people were daring, to come to a country where they knew no one, where they had to make their own way."

"You underestimate yourself, Remy. What you're doing is remarkable."

"It is hardly remarkable."

"You don't give yourself credit."

"It's just not that big a deal."

Over lunch Ken told her about his wife's death and Remy listened with serious concern. Then Remy talked about her father's car crash, about the dreadful call that came during the night and how she drove alone to the police station. The retelling was difficult. But when Ken squeezed her hand, she could feel the past softening. His arms were strong, unwavering and she accepted his embrace as if it were the most natural thing in the world. Ken kept his eyes fastened on her and suggested that they discard the tickets to see "Les Miserables." Instead they could go to his house, order a pizza and break open a bottle of Chianti. She fixed a salad in the kitchen for both of them while he dimmed the lights. Then he came near her and slipped his arms around her waist, turning her towards him. The rush of his hands on her made her quiver. She kissed him on the neck as he unbuttoned her blouse, reaching beneath to undo her bra, his tongue glazing her cheek, his warm breath against her. She pulled back just enough to look at him while he stroked her breasts. All she wanted was him.

The following morning they awoke to what would have been a shimmering New York day if only they didn't have to say goodbye. Ken drove her to the airport in the afternoon. Neither of them spoke much in the car, knowing how difficult parting would be.

Trade Secrets

On the plane, Remy forced herself back into the world she inhabited daily, knowing that she couldn't afford to let this weekend cloud her judgment. She would still have to make a living and that required concentration and a clear mind. As the plane made its quick descent and the city's familiar pattern came into view; she zeroed in on what she had to do when she got back to the pit. It was time to find out about her father. So far she had been so preoccupied with trading that she had learned nothing. She needed to focus.

Oscar was the first person Remy saw on Monday morning.

"I thought you quit, kid," he jeered.

Choking, she forced a smile.

"I was never going to quit, Oscar."

"How long were you gone, duchess?"

"Not long enough, Oscar. You were away when I got back from Paris."

"I bet you missed this stinking place," he quipped.

"I missed only you, Oscar."

"Welcome back, sweetheart."

"Welcome back, Oscar." That day, Oscar gave Remy a trade guaranteed to make money. While others in the pit were bidding, he simply ignored them and let her in a few points under the market. This was exactly what she had seen him do for Jason and recently for Joey. Maybe everyone got good trades if they stuck it out. Maybe it was just a matter of getting to know the right people. No doubt this was Oscar's way of saying he was sorry for the way she had been treated at the hearing.

She wondered if this made her as bad as the rest of them, pocketing a couple of hundred dollars she might not have if Oscar hadn't done her a favor. If she refused to take it, Oscar would simply give it to someone else. Ken was wrong. This was the way business was done. She'd use the trade to buy something new or maybe a ticket to see Ken again.

The two weeks would go by and soon they'd be together.

chapter 17

October, 1987

FALL CAME EARLY. The markets, like the seasons, had become increasingly unpredictable. Stocks could be way up one day, only to fall with a thud. The heightened volatility allowed Remy to make money more easily, but it came with increased risk. The quick up-and-down spurts were a result of inconsistencies in the market, as the Dow soared to new highs before sinking minutes later. In such an inefficient marketplace, professional traders had the edge, skimming profits from the wide range between the bid and offer. Floor traders locked in the profit within that spread, buying one side and selling the other, whipping investors who traded by phone. None of this was illegal. A disorderly market was a benefit to those on the trading floor. This inside advantage was the reason why seats at the Exchange had continued to climb in value. The seat Remy had bought, which gave her the right to trade the Index in the pit, had nearly doubled since she purchased it. Those who wanted to buy their own seat looked longingly at the prices that ticked up daily.

Joey had been locked out as seats got so expensive. In mid-October, when the seat market was jumping thousands a day, he approached Oscar with a plan that might allow him to buy a seat.

"They're awfully high, Joey," Oscar warned.

"They're going to the moon. I can feel it."

"You would have to add this to your financing."

"Can you do it for me?"

"It's a lot of money, Joey. A hundred and seventy-thousand dollars is not peanuts. I don't think you should."

"Look, this is how I figured it out. By the end of the year, I should be trading a hundred contracts a day. If I own a seat, I pay less in clearing fees. The money I save on fees will pay my interest charges every year."

"And if the seat goes down?"

"I still save that money. It goes down, it comes up," he said, singing the words as his shoulders moved up and down.

"Let me think about it."

The following week the seat soared another five thousand dollars. Joey pleaded with Oscar.

"I've never *owned* anything. I gotta have this, Oscar. I gotta be a member of this Exchange."

Oscar talked it over with Zach, and they agreed to lend the kid the money. They would simply add another one seventy-five to the bill he already owed them.

"At ten percent, it's another seventeen-five a year. The seat is collateral against the loan until Joey pays off. It will be good for his morale," Oscar argued.

Zach loved the idea. If they could find a dozen traders to do this, they would have another two hundred-thousand dollars in financing charges to pocket. A debt that would never be erased!

Before he could be approved, Joey would be required to go before the membership committee, but with Zach's endorsement and his guarantee, that would be a mere formality.

On October 13, 1987, Joey was an owner. As he stepped onto the trading floor that day, he felt as if he had been crowned. Now he could even join the Club and take Rosa there for lunch. No more mooching off of Remy, or having to use Oscar's account. He was a genuine big shot.

Jason showed Joey how to short the market, betting that it would go down, and that week Joey walked away with twenty-five hundred dollars. More money than he had made in three months. He began calculating how much he would have to make each day before he could buy the ring he had clipped from an ad in Sunday's paper. That would set him back fifteen grand. It was possible to make that in a week. Maybe he could afford an even bigger one.

"Hey, Joey, congratulations," said Remy when she saw him in the hallway. "I heard you bought a seat."

"I did. Now it's my turn to take you to lunch."

"You joined the Club?"

"Why not? Come on. It's my treat."

"OK, Joey, but just this once."

Joey escorted Remy to the Club and asked for a booth. The trees outside were ablaze with color, reminding Remy of the autumn day just a year ago when Jason had come by to ask her to the dance. She had learned so much since then. And she had met Ken.

Remy fiddled with the menu and then put it aside, sipping some water. She had her eye on one of the machines nearby and was glad that she didn't have any positions on in the market.

"How's the trading?" Remy asked.

"It's OK," Joey said. He didn't want to talk about trading. He didn't want Remy asking too many questions, though he presumed she saw Oscar throwing certain trades his way. He knew she was a smart woman and could figure out how things worked, but it was different when Jason had been the bagman. Now he was the one, front and center. It could make him very rich, but it could be dangerous.

Nor did he bring up Remy's hearing. Joey hoped to serve on that committee one day. As much as he liked Remy, she was a political outsider. Every now and then he had seen Oscar give her a winning trade. Oscar was at his best when he was working the crowd, dispensing trades in even amounts to keep everyone quiet, so no one would snitch on him. Joey could see how things operated; he was even beginning to talk like them, telling others when he made a thou, and flashing freshly manicured nails.

No matter how much he tried, he couldn't penetrate their personal lives. Once Joey suggested that he and Rosa go out for dinner with Jason and Sarna, but the proposal just hung there like dirty laundry no one wanted to touch. It was obvious that the lines were drawn. He was not an insider. Joey's tentacles didn't reach into their inner circle. He might look like one of them, but being their equal was as remote as the million dollars he longed for.

Joey wondered if Remy still liked him. Certainly she had not forgotten that hideous meeting. He pretended that it had never taken place, but there was something in the air that made him acutely aware that Remy remembered too well.

"How is Rosa?" Remy asked.

"She's great. I want to show you something." Joey took out his wallet and pulled out the photograph of the ring he had earmarked for Rosa.

"It's gorgeous," said Remy. Joey noticed her face flush, but he didn't know that she was feeling a little jealous, wondering if someday Ken would show someone a ring he had chosen for her.

"It's really beautiful," said Remy, putting down her cup of coffee. "Listen, Joey, I think I'd better get back. Let's take a rain check on lunch. I'm not that hungry. I have to run. These markets are so bumpy."

"I want to say something to you before you leave, Remy. I want you to know that I'm sorry about what happened last month. That was rotten. Those guys were cruel."

"They were," Remy agreed. "It's been on my mind. I didn't understand why you were there."

"Jason asked me."

"I don't get it."

Joey couldn't explain. His face got red and he fumbled with the menu. What had happened was wrong, but he couldn't risk his relationship with the top brass, nor could he explain why Jason had become increasingly important to his success.

"I don't know how to explain it, Remy. I know you were treated badly."

"Yes, I was treated very badly. Someday maybe you can make me understand. Right now I have to go. The experience taught me something," she continued as she stood up. "It taught me to be careful. I guess we all have to be careful."

Joey nodded good-bye, but he didn't agree. Once he would have said that she was right. Not anymore. With Oscar and Zach, his life was Teflon-coated. He was no longer vulnerable the way ordinary people were. He was part of the Silverman Empire. No one could harm him.

***

October 16, 1987

Remy kept herself busy so time moved fast. Every hour brought her closer to seeing Ken. By Friday, Remy was so preoccupied with Ken's visit she barely noticed that the market was unraveling.

Ken's plane was due in at 6:00. She called the airport to be sure it wasn't going to be delayed. She wanted to finish the day, run home to change and be ready to go out for dinner. She hadn't planned another thing for the weekend. They had stayed on the phone until one in the morning. Talking to Ken made the distance between them tolerable. Today, the lack of sleep took its toll. Her mind wasn't sharp and she had missed signs that a debacle was imminent. By noon, she had lost two thousand dollars and she still had positions in the market.

After the opening bell rang, an eerie tone had swept over the floor. Stocks began to slide. This dive was different from any other collapse she had witnessed. This time her losses didn't rattle her. She had learned that losing was an integral part of trading. She could recover from bad days and make money because she knew how to cut her losses. If she couldn't make money being long, betting that the market was going to go up, she could make it on the short side, betting that the market would go down.

Outsiders bought stocks banking that their investment would rise in value. Remy had learned that traders make most of their money when the market is going down. Or by trading the market as it moves from one spot to another within a trading range. That Friday, as the market began to tumble, Remy managed to get out of her long positions and go short, enabling her to make back her losses for that day. Then she could face the weekend without an open position.

She met Ken at O'Hare airport and they drove to a small Italian restaurant in Little Italy west of the Loop before retreating to her apartment. The following morning, Ken and Remy were sound asleep when a phone call awakened her.

Trade Secrets

"Remy, you have a serious out-trade." It was Michael, a young kid who ran the back room at her clearinghouse.

She jumped out of bed. It took a minute to realize that it was Saturday. How could she have an out-trade? Then she remembered that late Friday a notice had been passed around the floor calling for an emergency out-trade session the following morning. As a result of Friday's freefall, the Exchange wanted all disputes among traders settled before the market opened on Monday to ensure an orderly opening.

"Who's it with?" she asked getting out of bed and trying not to awaken Ken.

"Oscar."

"For how much?"

"Thirteen thousand. He says you bought ten and your card says five."

She tried to remember what trades she had made. It seemed very clear to her then and very clear to her now. It was five. This would not be a big deal. A year ago she would have panicked, but she knew these things happen. They would split it and that would be that. Oscar would pay her back over time. He would give her a winning trade to make up the difference. That was the advantage of trading against the paper that came into the pit. Ken was half awake. She smiled at him. As long as he was near her, what was going on at the Exchange was not so important. She would deal with Monday when she had to.

"Settle it," Remy said in a competent tone.

Ken overheard the conversation as he rolled out of bed, wrapping himself in a terry-cloth robe.

"Problems?"

"The Exchange had an out-trade session. I'm out with Oscar and it's going to cost me thirteen thousand dollars."

"That's a lot of money, Remy. Do you want me to drive you downtown?"

"Not necessary," she said, snuggling up to him.

He held her close. "I don't want you to lose money because I'm here."

"An out-trade is an out-trade. We each made a mistake. Oscar will make it up to me."

"What does that mean?"

"He'll pay me back. One day, when he has a bunch of orders, he'll see to it that I get my money back."

"Is that illegal?"

"It happens all the time. That's why it's better to have an out-trade with Oscar than with another trader. If it's just another trader on the other side, you never get your money back because neither of you holds any paper."

"But if you get your money back, someone has to lose."

"Yes. I suppose so. The customer usually gets the raw end of the deal. But now it's time for breakfast. No more, please," she said.

He took her face into his hands and studied her. "Remy, I want you to be careful. You're playing a dangerous game."

"I'm very careful, Ken. Don't worry about me."

She reached up to kiss him, but he pulled back gently. He needed to explain things, to warn her, to keep her safe.

"Didn't you tell me that you've seen Oscar giving Jason trades?"

"So what?"

"How is this different?"

"It's different. Trust me."

"I don't get it. Explain it to me."

She sat down on the bed and took the hairbrush from the end table. She began stroking her hair. Then she looked directly at Ken as she chose her words carefully.

"I suspect that Oscar and Jason have some deal going between them. I don't know what it is, but there are rumors about certain traders splitting their trades. I think when Oscar *gives* trades to Jason, Jason is making money he somehow gives back to Oscar."

"So?"

"They have an agreement. I suppose that they have formed some company and I don't know exactly how it's done, but I could pretty well guess that Jason's account is linked to Oscar's. I used to see things like this when I was an accountant. Layers of trusts, which fed into each other, devices to trick the Internal Revenue Service. This is different because I don't think it's any kind of a tax scheme. I think this is similar only in its complexity. When Jason hands in his cards, he can decide which account he wants his trades placed in. It's very likely that Jason and Oscar have an account established in which they both participate. I would bet profits go into a company account in which Oscar has a primary interest. It would be virtually impossible for anyone to untangle it unless they examined each trade on a given day and knew that the trades were then linked to Oscar through this company."

Ken listened very intently, his back against the wall.

"What makes you think this?"

"I just know."

"Then how is it different when Oscar pays you back?"

"I don't have any arrangement with Oscar. What he does for me is a professional courtesy to undo an out-trade."

"But he never pays personally."

"Right."

"So indirectly someone is paying for your error, and it's not you, Remy. When Oscar gives you a favorable trade like that, he has to be cheating someone."

"I suppose so."

"Where would the profit go if it didn't go to you?"

She thought about this for a minute as she replaced her hairbrush and pulled her robe tightly around her.

"It would go to someone else. That's why it doesn't matter."

"What if it would have gone to the customer?"

"Believe me, it would never go to the customer."

"For Christ's sake, Remy. Are you saying that the customer never gets a fair fill?"

Remy was silent. Ken was making her feel like a criminal. She knew what she was doing. She had never done anything illegal in her life. Once in high school, she tried to cheat on a French test, carrying a cheat sheet into the exam and throwing it in the wastebasket as she entered the auditorium. She didn't need to cheat, so why would she? This was the same thing. She didn't cheat. Why couldn't Ken see that? The whole problem with everything that she had seen on the trading floor was just that. Customers didn't get a fair fill. She knew it. Everyone knew it. That's why people were able to make so much money. She pitied anyone on the outside who put their faith in these markets. But that didn't make her a criminal.

Ken moved towards her.

"I'm not trying to imply anything, honey. I just don't want anyone to ever get the wrong impression of you."

She placed her head against his chest and then looked into his eyes.

"No one will ever get the wrong impression about me, Ken. I told you not to worry. You behave too much like a lawyer. Everyone is not that suspicious. Besides, there isn't any problem. No one even sees what goes on in any pit. It's a secret society. That's why Oscar and Zach are able to get away with everything they do get away with. They're impenetrable."

"The problem, Remy, is that sometimes innocent people get caught."

"Well, it won't be me. I haven't done anything", she insisted. "I think we should have something to eat. I already miss you and today hasn't even started."

That was what was wrong with living in different cities. As soon as their visits began, the inevitable parting seemed near. Every two weeks they took turns visiting the other. Either Ken would fly to Chicago or Remy to New York. Once they met in Pennsylvania near the Frank Lloyd Wright house, Fallingwater, and stayed in a romantic bed and breakfast; once they met at Gettysburg and, instead of going on the historical tours they had signed up for, they stayed in bed.

Remy wondered how they would ever be able to live in the same city. Ken needed to be in New York and Remy had her place in Chicago. Even if she wanted to trade at one of the New York exchanges, she would have to start all over. Carving out a place in a new pit in a strange city seemed impossible. During the time they were apart, Remy tried not to dwell on the distance between them, but life felt incomplete when Ken was not part of it.

He kissed her neck and face, his hands against her back. Her body pressed against him and the discussion about out-trades and Oscar and Zach were dropped, like disappearing rain when the sun hits the sidewalk on a hot summer day.

chapter 18

UNDONE FROM FRIDAY'S losses, Jason drove downtown on Saturday. His head ached; he was chilled. Even his chest felt tight. The freefall had cost him five hundred thousand dollars.

"You bastard," he yelled and grabbed Oscar, pulling him away from the session.

"Get your slimy hands off me," countered Oscar. He looked around to see who might have heard Jason and then he pushed Jason into the corridor outside the auditorium. Dozens of tables had been set up in the large room so the clearinghouses could centralize disputes. On a large table were doughnuts and coffee. Most traders wanted to clear their paper work and get the hell out.

It was 10:45.

"You gave those trades to Joey, Oscar."

Oscar raised his brow and spoke defiantly.

"What did you expect?"

"We never agreed that the money he made would be at my expense. You discovered that shit-head in a shoe store. Now you're going to bankrupt me."

"You're bent out of shape for nothing."

"Then explain it before I crack your head open."

"Watch what you say. I can bring charges against you."

"That would be some joke. What about the rules you've broken, Doheney?"

"Keep your mouth shut or I'll cut your tongue out." He took Jason by his sleeve and pressed him against the wall." Don't worry, kid. I'll take care of everything on Monday. When the market opens, there will be time to straighten it out."

"Let go of me, you moose."

Jason stared at Oscar. He was in no position to fight Oscar and Oscar knew that too. Jason had the dope—enough to put Oscar in jail. But if Oscar went to the clinker, he'd be dragged along with him.

His father had warned him this could happen years ago when he bragged about his highfalutin' schemes.

"One day you will be sorry," Jeremy Bramson warned, shaking his head. His monotone, coupled with that holier-than-Thou attitude, made Jason cringe. It was one reason why he never could work in his dad's business. Jeremy Bramson's story would be different. He would say that he never could rely on his son. Three years after Jason went to work in the headboard business Jeremy had built into a multi-million dollar empire, he could see Jason didn't have the talent to be his successor. Some days Jason showed up late for work; he couldn't handle the employees, and when there were meetings to launch a new product, Jason was never an idea man. When an offer came from a New York conglomerate, the old man sold the business and left Jason without a job.

Jason married Sarna and his father saw that she was after his money, so he tied up everything in trusts. She would never get her hands on it. The final wedge between father and son came when Jason took his wife's side in a family dispute. Indeed, Sarna had her eye on the family fortune, but Jason had no will to defy her, no way to calm her down when her anger burned out of control. Sarna played him like a violin, causing a permanent rift with his father.

Although Jason had never wanted to be part of Bramson's Furniture, he never imagined he would be disenfranchised. When his legal career reached a dead-end, he lost his footing. He had no skills, was not a good salesman and hated law. Then he met Oscar. Oscar assumed Jason had left a thriving career and wasn't desperate to make money the way other kids were. What Oscar didn't know and Jason would never tell him was that he had nowhere else to turn.

Now this huge out-trade squeezed Jason. Working for Oscar and Zach often made him feel like a child. Unable to direct his future made him feel powerless. Now he could see that he had traded tyrants: his father for Oscar. He had no ammunition against his father when his father dumped him. Here he had a weapon. If he were dispossessed, he would take Oscar with him.

The out-trade came on the heels of a personal tragedy. Sarna had miscarried in the seventh month of her pregnancy and was forced to carry to term. Once she surrendered to the prospect of motherhood, pregnancy had consumed her. She envisioned pushing a Perego carriage, strolling through town with other moms, sitting in the park, picking out adorable clothes for her child. Sarna concealed the truth, even from herself, that she could easily live the rest of her life without a child. But when the choice was taken away, she became so despondent, Jason didn't know how to help her.

Independence was her trademark. The femme fatale who had seduced him withered before his eyes under the weight of depression. She lost interest in sex and cared only about money, banking on it to give her something concrete when everything else was slipping away. With nothing to occupy her time, her spending habits became maniacal. It became obvious to Jason that without money, his marriage was doomed.

The doctor advised Sarna to wait six months for her body to rejuvenate before getting pregnant again. Bored and unfocused, she didn't know what to do with her time and didn't want to be with friends who were always talking about their kids. Finally, she had an idea.

"I want to trade, Jason, " she told him.

"Absolutely not."

"Why not? I'm as smart as that Remy Masterman. I just need someone to show me."

"I can't teach you, Sarna. You don't understand how dangerous it is there."

"It's not fair," she whined.

"A trader needs fifty thousand dollars to get on the floor, Sarna. If you lose money and you will, it could cost more. They will make me guarantee your trades."

"I have money of my own."

Sarna had managed to save twenty-five thousand dollars by skimming cash Jason had given her to furnish the house. It was easy when the interior decorator agreed to overbill and pass the excess back to her. It wasn't really stealing, she reasoned. It was *as if* it were hers.

"I need a career."

"Not this one."

She dropped the subject over the summer. But when Fall came and she couldn't occupy her days, her depression resurfaced. Jason couldn't stand to see her like this. She was a lost soul. She stopped working out and hardly ate. Shopping distracted her and she began to spend carelessly. As the bills mounted, Jason decided that it might be cheaper for Sarna to come on the trading floor. She would do paperwork while he traded. That way she could become familiar with the mechanics of trading. Eventually he let her place trades from the sidelines through a broker, because she wasn't allowed to stand in the pit. For several weeks, Sarna accompanied him into the city, never once complaining about the early hours or having to stay upstairs in an office. The excitement of work enlivened her. Sometimes she was awake all night waiting for the alarm to go off, anxious to return to the tumult. The floor gave her a new perspective. She wanted to figure out what others did and stayed alert for signals that would tell her which way the market might be going. Then she would plan her strategy, pretending she had placed a real trade and counting the imaginary profit she had made. More than anything, she wanted to wear a trading jacket.

One night she woke Jason up, took off her nightgown off and slid on top of him.

"Let me trade," she begged, her lovely breasts hanging over his face. " Do this for me," she purred, placing his hand on the curve of her stomach.

"Sarna, I need to sleep."

Her hand reached him and she stroked the skin around his penis until his cock was as hard as stone. She moved her body so his tongue could reach inside her and rode him until he pulled her into a position to enter her.

"You are so fabulous," he said gazing into her determined eyes. "Ok. Ok. "

The following day all he could picture was his mouth on her tits. When he told Oscar that Sarna would be trading, Jason ignored Oscar's ranting and raving. Jason had made up his mind. He promised Oscar that she would stand in a different quadrant of the pit and they could use Sarna to dilute transactions by giving certain trades to her.

"She better listen up, Jason, or she's out," Oscar warned.

Sarna studied meticulously for the test, one any dummy could pass. They could let anyone in as long as she was there. Consumed with the adventure of a career, her skin regained its dewy quality and her eyes their radiance. Sarna attended her orientation session on Friday, the one Jason had taught when Remy first came to the Exchange. She selected a purple trading jacket and an acronym, SB, etched in gold letters. Money was placed in an account under her name. Her first day trading was on Monday, October 19.

Jason was thinking about Sarna and the absurdity of these markets when Oscar's booming voice interrupted his thoughts.

"You're overworked," said Oscar. "You're nervous about Sarna."

"Don't analyze me, you shit. You squeezed me so Joey could make money. Don't put this on me, you grubby bastard. You squeezed me out."

Oscar considered Jason seriously. His angry look had intensified.

"Don't worry. I'll take care of you, Jason. With me you're always OK."

Jason would have thought that was true. But with Joey in the picture, everything looked edgy. After this out-trade, Jason didn't trust Oscar. The pre-market buzz called for a lower opening. If the market didn't open up higher, Oscar wouldn't be able to pay him back. When Sarna began parading around the pit, an already tricky situation was bound to get murkier. Sarna would beg for more in no time. In the meantime, the half million dollar out-trade hung over his head.

Oscar could take both of them down. He was a simple puppet. But he promised himself that if Oscar screwed him, revenge was a promising respite. The prospect of revenge would be his only option if things didn't go right.

***

Remy and Ken strolled to a coffee house on Sunday morning to buy a newspaper. The crash dominated the headlines, followed by a lead article reporting that an avalanche of sells had ravaged investors and ended a five year run up in stocks.

"Remy, did you see these statistics?" Ken asked. He handed her the paper. She studied it, glancing at the summary. Then she returned it to Ken.

"The Dow broke the October 6th record in a one day drop with nearly a hundred point plunge," Ken quoted from the front page.

"I know. It is one of the worst free-falls in history."

The article blamed the trade deficit, but Remy thought the falling dollar was the culprit.

"Look at this." She showed Ken an article that explained that the Reagan administration had decided not to intervene against the dollar's slide, in an effort to stop rising interest rates and ward off a recession.

"What does the dollar have to do with the stock market?" he asked.

"It relates to profits in terms of foreign exchange rates," she explained. "It's not so bad when the dollar falls a little against other currencies, but when it is out of line as it is now, everyone expects the government to step in and support it. Without that support, other countries stop pumping money into our market and this is what happens."

Ken stood back to admire Remy. He leaned over to kiss her.

"You're a financial dictionary."

"Trading 101. It's just basic stuff. But I don't want to think about any of this today. I just want to be with you. Put the paper down. The news will be there tomorrow. Let's go to the zoo. I can't stand to dwell on anything other than the fact that you are leaving."

He placed his arm around her waist and kissed her eyelids. She looked up at him with soulful eyes.

"I'll be back in a couple of weeks, honey."

She refrained from telling him what she was thinking. Everything depended upon his schedule, a schedule he didn't seem to be able to control. She didn't want to sound like a nag, but sometimes when Ken was gone, she had a hard time tolerating the separation.

"I'll call you every night."

"I may not be home," she warned.

"I know."

She waited for him to say something.

"He lost a woman once," Lara had told her over lunch last week, "and I'd bet money that he's afraid of the feelings he has for you. He probably never thought he would get deeply involved so quickly."

"I know he went through a rough time, but I would never hurt him."

"He doesn't know that."

"I don't think I've ever felt like this, Lara."

"I'm not saying that it's not real. But both people have to be ready at the same time to make a real commitment. You'll have to wait it out."

As usual, Lara was right. This time more than ever. Remy herself didn't want to rush anything. But without Ken the world had no luster. The rustle of falling leaves crushed beneath their feet as they walked towards the zoo. It was a sparkling day, though the sun cut through the trees in an angle that foretold the short days to follow when the clocks turned back and November's grey blanketed the city.

"Remy, I need to tell you something. I didn't want to bring this up, but you need to know something."

She looked him straight in the eye.

"I will be in Chicago for business soon for long stretches of time."

"Where will you be living?"

"My clients are renting an apartment for me."

"I thought that if you were here, you would consider..." Her voice trailed off. She hoped he couldn't hear her heart thumping or see the tears that were beginning to well in her eyes.

Ken lifted her chin with the forefinger of his right hand and moved her face to his.

"I need a place of my own, Remy. When a client goes to the expense of bringing me here, I can't tell him I'm going to move in with someone."

Remy pulled back. It sounded so businesslike, as if she were just any woman, rather than the only one. How typical, she thought, going over all the times she had heard things like this. Instead of joy, she felt anxious. Instead of love, she felt abandoned and she knew that she must withdraw, let him do whatever it was he needed to do. She turned away and tried to hold back tears. Let him have his space. She wouldn't let him know how disappointed she was.

It was so typical for a guy to make lopsided statements and leave a hole in the relationship. Maybe there was another woman in his life. That had never occurred to her before. The thought made her sick, but if it were true, it was better to find out now. Certainly, there was something he was concealing, something beneath that trademark stare that was hiding a secret. It's strange that people feel so close and sometimes say so little. It reminded her of the secrets her father kept. What were they and how was she ever going to find out how they hurt him? Now the man she loved had secrets too. By the time they reached that part of the Zoo where the animals roved in their natural habitat, Remy had lost interest in the exhibits. The conversation made her sad. She wanted continuity, the kind that comes with marriage.

Instead, she felt betrayed. Tonight he will be on a plane back to New York and he will be living here, but not with her? Would they be seeing each other every day or would she have to abide by some schedule then too? Her head began swirling. She had a million questions. Until this moment, the weekend had been so perfect. She looked at Ken and tried to figure out what he was thinking. If she said too much, she knew she would ruin the moment. She needed to penetrate his interior and, at the same time, stop herself from feeling so shaky.

Remy forced herself to unlock his gaze. She arched her back and held her head to see the Lake on the other side of the Outer Drive. She told herself to back off. But she could not let this happen.

If Ken could be so cavalier about their relationship and free to do what he wanted, then she could too.

This wasn't how she had planned it, but he gave her no choice. Lara and she had never rehearsed this part. And she didn't have the right words.

She would have to be strong and that meant pretending. It was not her style, not the relationship she hoped would turn into marriage. Ken had set new ground rules.

For the time being, it would be his way or no way and she didn't like it all.

chapter 19

Monday, October 19, 1987

AT 7:15 REMY entered the Exchange through the side entrance. She hadn't slept, tossing in her bed, unable to stop thinking about Ken. By 6:00 she gave up trying to sleep, showered and decided to have an early breakfast at the Club. She sat at a table near the quotron machines. Everyone wondered if Friday's debacle would carry over into today. As the waiter came by with a menu, she saw that the foreign currencies had already begun trading. The dollar continued its downward spin, just as yesterday's headline had predicted. The impact didn't register in Remy's mind as she picked at her toast. Her mind wandered and she stared out the window at the throngs, a colony of robots, rushing to their offices in khaki raincoats.

Everything that ever charmed her looked dreary. She could only think about Ken. She wondered if she might be better off at home.

She heard a voice from behind. "Remy, did you see where the Dow is going to open?" Joey shouted to her.

"I'm not paying attention. What's going on?"

"The futures are down 1,000."

Holly Rozner

That would mean a fifty percent drop. Could that happen? The Dow had closed on Friday at 2246. A gap like that was unthinkable. He must be wrong.

"Look at the screens."

Remy nudged her chair back and walked towards the quotron. "It's a computer glitch," she concluded.

Joey took her by the arm, to another computer.

"It's not. This is real."

The market wouldn't open for another forty-five minutes. The possibility that this was a computer error was fading. If the market continued to drop, seat prices would fall. Pandemonium would grip the floor. Remy rushed out of the Club. The hall was jammed with traders. Carving her way through the crowd, up the escalator and onto the trading floor, she didn't know if Joey was right even when she stepped into the pit.

"Man, did you see that?" someone shouted.

"In the toilet, buddy."

"These markets are dead."

Remy tried to shut the rumors out of her head. Then she thought about 1929.

"It's down a thou. And that ain't the end of it," said a trader next to her.

Calamity was written all over the face of men who were generally unfazed by commotion. Only those who were short the market were safe. Others feared for their financial survival. In such a freefall, mutual funds would liquidate, adding further pressure to the frenzy. Dozens of traders stood in the pit, mesmerized by the data jumping on the screens. European Exchanges traded before New York markets opened. There were no buyers in Europe; there would be none here.

Remy squeezed into the spot where she stood each day. She straightened her jacket, confirmed that she had an

Trade Secrets

ample supply of trading cards and several sharpened pencils. She swallowed an Advil. This would be a dangerous trading day, but it could also be lucrative. She had spent the past year learning to trade. She needed a clear head to take advantage of this moment.

When the bell rang, the Dow fell to a level not seen in years.

Oscar's jacket was stuffed with papers. There was a heap of trash at his feet. Rows of clerks were lined up behind him with customer orders. Phone lines were clogged, overflowing with sellers trying to unwind their positions. Remy looked up to the visitor's gallery where hundreds leaned into the glass to watch the traders below. The remaining pits were desolate. Everyone had crossed the room to watch the Index.

Jason ran to Oscar. "We're dead, Oscar. You can't make this out-trade good in a market like this."

Oscar didn't reply. He stacked a bunch of orders into his pocket, pretending that Jason didn't exist.

"Are you deaf, Doheney? I was down five-fifty on Saturday. Do you realize what this means? I could lose millions."

"Get out of my way, Bramson," Oscar shouted.

Remy stood nearby, her eyes bouncing from one to the other. The grave dispute between them erupted like a deadly volcano.

"You give me the next fifty trades and keep track of them, you sonofabitch. This could cost me my fortune!"

"If you don't shut up, Jason, I'll crucify you."

Jason lunged towards him. Joey intercepted.

"Jason, don't do this," shouted Joey.

"Get out of here, you little twit." He pushed Joey aside. Remy stood silently taking in the whole scene. Her heart began to pound. Did this happen to her father? He wasn't a trader, so they couldn't have hurt him like this, but as she watched Oscar and the intense anger in his eyes, she knew he was capable of anything.

The bell rang and Oscar screamed, "Listen up, Remy," he continued, "I bought ten from you at 05."

She scribbled the order down on her card and looked up at the screen.

She hadn't made a bid. Another gift. Oscar's payback for the out-trade Saturday morning. She could hear Ken's voice in her head warning her not to do this. But she reasoned that no one would see. These favors had been done for others; they were done every day. This is how business worked here.

She waited now to see how Jason's out-trade would be fixed. Oscar would take care of it. This well-oiled machine was always in gear. Inefficient markets like this made it easier to skim off the top. No one could keep up with the ticker tape. It jumped so fast, it was impossible to keep track of the prices. If a buy order was earmarked for one time bracket and was filled in another, no one could be blamed in such utter confusion. The "fast-market" signs went up on the boards along the wall relieving brokers from being held for trades they made. This rule was in place so brokers didn't go belly up in a market when it was impossible to keep pace with the volume.

"Ten at 05," Remy shouted, confirming the trade with Oscar. She counted the profit in her head and realized that he had doubled her price. Her three thousand dollar loss on Saturday had evolved into a six thousand dollar gain.

"Write it down," he whispered.

She did as she was told.

Jason watched. He said nothing.

"A hundred at 00," screamed Oscar.

No buyers.

The market continued its slide. The fast market signs were flashing. A license to steal was in gear.

Oscar signaled to Jason, who was now on the other side of the pit. Remy couldn't follow the signal, but she saw Jason write something down on his cards.

Down 500.

600.

700.

Oscar shouted across the pit to Jason to confirm his trade.

"A thousand at zero."

"Gotcha."

Remy watched. Oscar wanted to be sure that this part of their conversation had been overheard. He also wanted to be sure that it had been done from a distance, from across the pit to legitimatize the transaction. Jason had moved to the other side of the pit to facilitate the trade Oscar saved for him.

Remy thought Oscar had silently given Jason a trade and then covered up this loser to ensure that no one could accuse him of convoluting the system.

No one was paying attention to Jason and Oscar. The frenzy continued. Clerks couldn't move between the phone banks and the pit. By the time an order was relayed, the market was hundreds of points away from the price the customer thought it would be. Any price was a good price because no one could really tell at what the right price was. An order to sell a stock at fifty could easily be filled at twenty with the broker pocketing the difference for himself. There would be no way a customer could dispute it. Nothing would protect the public in this mess. Most investors couldn't get out at all. Remy's father had warned her years ago never to place a market order; it was like handing a profit to the brokers. The public didn't understand this, and most people placed their orders that way. Nor did people realize that a stop order could be filled at any price below the stop. Orders would be filled as the brokers found them, and if they weren't specific, they would be filled at prices below the customer's intent. Yes, there would be lawsuits and disputes, but this was a war zone and the remnants of battle were everywhere.

By ten o'clock, the tumult had subsided, enough so Remy could step out of the pit to hand in her orders. She was exhausted. Around her, traders scrambled to call their brokers trying to unwind their personal portfolios. A useless gesture. This was the first real crash since 1929. Like a capsized ship, the market was stuck.

In this pulverized condition, insiders and floor traders picked off the public, stealing trades that would otherwise be handled in a systematic fashion. The utter pandemonium presented an advantage to play with prices that were out of line. Remy decided that the past year had been a training ground for such a battle. This opportunity might never come again. She went to get some water and stepped back into the pit to make a small trade. And then another. By noon, she had counted her winnings at over sixty-thousand dollars.

She had never made that much money! Certainly not in one day, not even in one month. Huge risks. Huge rewards. That was why she had bought a seat. As long she didn't make any major errors, she could see how fortunes could be made on the trading floor. This day would be a turning point. She had worked hard to come this far, to get Oscar to recognize her, to have the nerve to take advantage of the inefficiencies that a fast market provided. After the awful hearing last month, she was still here. No longer the innocent who strode into the committee room expecting sympathy from such careless people, she had become a professional. This was a reckless universe. But she had survived. As long as she didn't have a fatal out-trade, she had crossed into a new zone. She reminded herself that she had to be particularly careful. So she double-checked everything.

She couldn't afford a mistake. An error on a day like this could wipe out a trader.

**

"How much did you make?" screamed Lara.

"Over sixty thousand ."

"In one day?"

"I can't believe it either. But I could lose that much tomorrow."

"Can't you do something?"

Remy cradled the phone in her neck and moved closer to her dresser where she had placed the copies of her trading cards. She looked them over as she spoke to Lara.

"It was amazing, Lara. Brokers were asking for *my* market. There were so few people willing to stay in the pit that I was actually dictating where the market was."

"I'm proud of you, Remy."

Remy was proud of herself too. She tried to reach Ken to share her excitement, but his answering machine clicked on and she remembered he had a political dinner tonight and wouldn't be home until very late. She was too tired to stay up so she left a brief message to call her tomorrow. She was glad when Lara answered her call. She could gossip with other women or share an intellectual discussion. Only Lara cared the way a mother or sister would, excited for her accomplishments as if they were her own.

"This was the only really great day I've ever had since I've been at the Exchange. Even Oscar treated me well."

"You're on your way!"

Holly Rozner

Remy was afraid to think ahead. It felt good not to have lost money.

Oscar's payback for the out-trade gave Remy confidence that she had crossed into a new territory. A new wave of assurance allowed her to make trades that day without worrying about how much she might lose. Tomorrow there would be more opportunity.

"I am totally exhausted," Remy said. She was stretched out on her floral sofa. The blinds in her living room were open and the city lights lit the living room. Her wood floors had just been polished and she admired the Oriental rug, filled with shades of blue, red and green, that she had bought last month.

"You should be exhausted, standing on your feet all day. I bet you didn't have time for lunch."

"I didn't think about eating."

"I envy you. When I'm at work, I wish the day would end. It's wonderful to find something so consuming."

"This is the first time in my life I don't look at the clock to see if the day is over. I'm not sure I could ever work in a normal job again. Trading is a challenge, but it has ruined my chance of ever working for someone again. It is a strange profession, if you can even call it that."

"Most people would give anything to change places with you."

"It hasn't been easy."

"Hopefully the bad stuff is in the past."

"I wonder."

Then, as if Lara had read her mind, she brought up Ken. "Give him space, Remy, if that's what he needs. "

"I know. I just don't understand why, if Ken needs to be in Chicago, we aren't living together. I'd love to meet for dinner."

"Sure."

"I'm worried about how the market will open. I can't even imagine what it will be like after today."

"I'll take you out. We'll celebrate."

"I'll call you after we close. We'll meet around six. I'll let you know where."

Remy placed the phone on the receiver. As much as she needed a career and the feeling of success that came with it, she also needed people in her life. Making money can get a person only so far.

Only people can make you feel real.

chapter 20

October 20, 1987

WHEN REMY STEPPED into the pit on Tuesday morning, she was greeted by a clerk representing the clearinghouse. All trades had to have a buyer and seller on each. Without a clearinghouse, if there were an imbalance in the system, someone could be left without a trader on the other side. Remy stood at the rim of the pit and watched the clerk leaf through bundles of paper.

"You're clear, Remy. No out-trades."

Yesterday's blitz had erased 508 points on the Dow in an avalanche that topped 604 million shares. The twenty-three percent drop, which was greater than the 1929 decline, heralded worldwide worries. Stories of million-dollar hits were front-page news. The Hong Kong stock market suspended trading after an eleven percent descent. The first hour of trading in Sydney had slashed twenty percent off American stocks. The Tokyo Stock Exchange, deluged with sell orders, posted a record three thousand point drop.

Remy took her sheets from Henry, folded them and put them in her jacket. It was a relief that there had been no discrepancies in her account. It was 8:15 and only a handful of traders stood in the pit. The space that Remy fought for every day was hers for the taking. Pat Sullen was gone, as were dozens of others, some driven out by losses or sheer fright. Droves of traders stared at the screens waiting for the opening. An eerie quiet enveloped the room. A bond had developed among those who remained, like one formed by troops in battle.

While she waited for the bell, Remy glanced at the morning paper. Maybe it would offer some explanation of what had happened. But even the experts didn't know. Merton Miller, a professor of finance at the University of Chicago said, "This is simply a panic, like a classic bank run."

Oscar stood on his platform, his eyes glazed. He looked up at the screens and then at the orders in his hands. Remy began to walk towards him to thank him for yesterday's trade and then decided not to. This professional favor need not be acknowledged. One day she would say thank you, but not today.

The market had been on a moon shot. This week's swoon was a hard lesson for those who never thought the bubble would burst. The eighties had been marked with the hope of trickle-down economics. Stockbrokers wore three thousand dollar suits, drove eighty thousand dollar cars, and hardly ever saved a buck. The Economic Recovery Act had introduced tax shelters, carving a highway to excess as the market took off like a rocket in 1982.

Remy saw Joey huddled in a corner with Jason Bramson. It wasn't clear how Joey fit into Jason's program, but they were linked in some clandestine way.

At 8:20, Remy noticed a beautiful woman standing near her in the pit. Her hair fell straight to her shoulders and framed a delicate face with piercing brown eyes. She wore a blue trading jacket and a badge engraved SB.

Trade Secrets

"Sarna Bramson," Oscar shouted. "You are just the doll we need to cheer this place up. What are you doing here?"

Remy turned around abruptly. It was the woman in the red dress who had snared Jason right before her eyes! Without her Christian LaCroix taffeta and four-inch heels, even at this hour of the morning, Sarna was a showstopper. Mint eye shadow accentuated the color of her eyes. Wearing a white shirt and khakis, Sarna hadn't overlooked a detail, as if she had been up all night primping for this debut.

Remy had grown protective of her singular rank as the only woman in the pit. Though she complained that there were not many women, secretively she enjoyed her unique standing. She smoothed out her jacket, and arched her back. She couldn't let herself be distracted. Not in this crazy market. She turned her back to Sarna to concentrate. This would not be an easy day.

"Listen up everyone. Two minutes till show time." Shouted Oscar.

Remy glanced at Sarna who seemed intent on following Oscar. He began his ritual, fussing with his orders and flailing his arms in the air. Remy pulled in her stomach, brushed her hair behind her ears, assuming the position of a soldier ready for combat. She felt Sarna's eyes digging into her. Remy lifted her head to show she was in control, reminding herself that she didn't own the pit, recognizing her only-child syndrome surfacing. The pit was not her personal domain. Even Jason's well-manicured wife could stand here if she paid for her membership. Still, it was upsetting to think that Sarna wouldn't have to go through the hoops she had to muddle through. With Jason's clout, Sarna's success was pretty well assured. It didn't seem fair that Sarna could just breeze in and get trades while she had to work so hard to learn the ropes.

Holly Rozner

The opening interrupted her thoughts, taking everyone by surprise. The next few minutes were a complete shock. The noisy din that usually marked the opening was replaced by dead silence. Oscar stood on his platform with orders stuffed in his hand, but he said nothing. As the second hand ticked on, traders looked at each other in dismay as they realized that there was no market to trade. Investors were sitting it out, waiting for the next guy to make a move. The pits were vehicles for locals to trade against the public but the public had quit. The market froze. Volatility spooked. The Index began jumping in hundred dollar increments, not the usual twenty dollar difference between the bid and ask.

At 10:30, Remy decided to go for breakfast. She walked across the street to a café on the river and sat down with a newspaper article about the crash of 1987 as it had been named. It seemed as if she were reading a novel about her own life. The past few days were so hectic that she had lost weight. She wanted to go home early and enjoy the money she made yesterday, but something told her she had better stick around. At 11:00 she took a final sip of coffee, paid her check and walked back into the Exchange.

Hoards of traders were huddled in the lobby.

"What happened?" she asked one of them.

"The pit closed."

"What!"

"They shut down the Index. And the New York Stock Exchange."

Remy blanched. Her hands were shaking. This wasn't a freeway that could shut down with traffic problems. She pushed through the bodies and ran to the escalator, scanned her badge and raced into the trading room.

The pit was empty. None of the machines were on. The New York Stock Exchange had shut down! She grabbed a nearby phone and dialed her clearinghouse. "This is Remy Masterman. Cut a check from my account for fifty thousand dollars. I'll be there in a half hour to pick it up."

Industry practice dictated that money from a trader's account was payable on demand. Today felt like a run on a bank. The woman at the other end explained that a check couldn't be ready until 2:30.

"I am coming over," Remy insisted.

"We can't handle the volume, Remy." Remy stood still staring at the neon numbers on the wall that were not flashing. Was this catastrophic? She bolted through the room and ran into Jason standing on the upper rim near the bond pit.

"What happened?"

"A trader from Taiwan stuck First Options with a $90 million dollar loss."

"Ninety million dollars!"

"Everyone wants out. One guy rolled a quarter of a million out of here in a portable wagon."

"What should we do?"

"I don't know," he admitted. "I don't think the system can collapse. Every brokerage house would go under. One trade guarantees the next."

Remy felt her throat close. Gone were the one-liners thrown across the pit like balls of popcorn. Real panic clutched even the biggest risk takers.

"One trade depends on another and then another," he explained as she half-listened. "A gap will impact a trade in a million other places. I just don't think the government can let it happen."

"The papers are comparing this to 1929."

"I think they're overreacting." He glanced at Sarna who stood near the phone bank. Remy followed his eyes.

"What a terrible day to start trading," Remy said kindly. "I remember when she stopped at our table."

"Yes. I remember that too," Jason said, his eyes trying to say more.

"I'd like to meet her."

Jason motioned for Sarna to come over. She carried three trading cards in her hand. Two were blank and one had a buy and a sell on each side. She showed them to Jason, not sure if she had written on the correct side of the cards.

"Sarna, this is Remy Masterman."

Remy put her hand out to greet Sarna.

Sarna nodded weakly, gave her cards to Jason and looked thoroughly bewildered.

"How on earth do you stand here all day?"

"If you want to keep track of the markets, you just have to be here," Remy answered.

"It's overwhelming!"

"It's not always like this. Maybe tomorrow, I can show you some things."

Sarna's eyes opened wide. "Would you?" She looked Remy over and Remy felt her putting the pieces together in her pretty head. "Didn't we meet before?"

"At the Exchange dance. I'm happy to do what I can for another woman," Remy continued. "There are not many of us. The markets are dead because of the crash. In a normal market, it's possible to know how to look for a good trade."

Sarna stared at Remy, but said nothing.

"I wish someone had done this for me," Remy continued as she silently acknowledged that Sarna must have expected some magic to carry her along.

Jason lowered his eyes.

"It's so quiet." Sarna remarked.

Remy looked at Jason and they both smiled.

"This is a very odd day, Sarna. Until the crash you couldn't think in this room. This quiet is temporary. I'll leave it to Jason to explain everything. I've got to pick something up. I'll see you tomorrow."

Remy dashed off to pick up her check at the clearinghouse at the other end of the Loop. Outside, the daylight surprised her. Like a Las Vegas casino, the trading floor had no windows. If not for the clock that kept track of the time brackets, no one would know the actual hour. It took a second for her eyes to adjust to the sun. She walked the six blocks across the Loop, proud of herself for toughing it out this week. When she reached the thirtieth floor of the Financial Center, there was a long line of traders waiting in line for checks. No one uttered a word. Remy signed in and sat in a sofa, trying to leaf through a magazine, but she wasn't able to concentrate. The wait made her tense. What if there wasn't enough cash to pay everyone? What if the markets actually closed for good? Had an exchange ever closed before? It was nearly 2:00 before she was handed a check and with it, some relief. She would deposit the check and go home.

Her accounts were at the First National Bank near City Hall. If the banking system were to fail as a result of the crash, she wanted her money in different banks. She passed the North Trust Bank on the corner of Madison and Dearborn and decided to open a new account. A middle-aged woman in a blue suit greeted her at the reception desk.

"I want to open an account," Remy said.

The lady told her to sit down at the desk and gave her a package of papers to fill out. Then she was told to endorse the back of the check. The woman accepted it and stamped the back with a ten-day hold.

"What are you doing?" Remy cried.

"We put a ten day hold on new funds."

"It takes two days to clear a check. This check was written on the Continental Bank. It's perfectly good."

"Our policy for new accounts is ten days." The woman looked Remy up and down. Remy felt self-conscious. Measured against the banker, she didn't look very professional. The uniform, khakis and white blouse, was what traders wore. She could feel the woman's disdain.

"Give the check back to me!" Remy commanded.

"One minute," said the lady, walking off with the check in her hand.

Remy stood up, her hands on her hips, as she tried to figure what she would do next. In less than a minute a well-dressed man introduced himself.

"Miss Masterman, I am Nigel Brown, one of the vice-presidents of the bank. Won't you come upstairs?"

"I want my check," Remy said.

"This won't take long, Miss Masterman."

Remy followed him into the elevator and up to the second floor where she was escorted past the trust department into the paneled waiting room of the corporate office. There she was offered a cup of coffee.

At first Remy was happy to be sitting down but when more than ten minutes elapsed, she lost her patience. She stood up to ask another receptionist where Mr. Brown had gone, but the new lady didn't seem to know.

"I need a telephone," Remy said. The woman escorted her to an adjacent office where there was a telephone. She felt as if she were being treated like a criminal. Hadn't these people ever seen a trader before? At that moment, she realized that she was being observed through a one-way mirror. Do they think I have stolen the check? She looked down at her wrinkled khakis and decided she had to call Lara.

"I will call the bank for you and let them know you are legit," Lara said.

Remy's head ached. This wouldn't have happened at her own bank.

Within a few minutes, Nigel Brown reappeared with the check in his hand.

"I am sorry, Miss Masterman. Your attorney explained who you were. Please accept my apology. We were only being cautious."

Remy's patience was gone. "Endorse the check to me, and I will have my bank call you if there is a problem depositing it there. Don't ever treat anyone like this."

"As I said, Miss Masterman, we were only doing our job.'

Remy placed the check into her purse and ran out of the bank. She hailed a cab and crossed the Loop to the white marble building that housed the First National Bank where she deposited the money in her existing account. Considering that her first instinct was correct, that the banks really could fail, she wrote a check for twenty thousand dollars payable to cash. The clerk watched as she counted out the hundred dollar bills. Without missing a beat, Remy stuffed the cash inside her jacket and ran to catch a cab home.

Then, if there were a complete breakdown, she'd have a few chips of her own.

chapter 21

"Don't tell me that it was my fault," Sarna screamed. She threw the mail on the granite counter. The newly remodeled kitchen had set them back one hundred thousand dollars. Jason was dazed. The blue lake outside the breakfast room window was usually a refreshing sight. Today the cliff on which the house was perched looked like a deadly precipice and the lake was foreboding. The landscaping was not yet complete, though the quarter million-dollar estimate sitting on the kitchen table was the first thing that drew their eyes. There it was, a remnant of the life they had been living.

"It was crazy for you to come to the floor. You have no experience and I have no time to teach you. No one learns to trade overnight. "

"There are women there, Jason. Remy Masterman for one. What about her? Or is she different because you fucked her?"

"To set the record straight, I did not fuck her. Not because I didn't want to, but because she's a genuine lady."

The minute he said this, the damage had been done. The implicit contrast hung in the air like putrid fish. Sarna might be tough, sexy, brash. But no one had ever called her a lady.

"So she gets special treatment because she wouldn't let you get into her pants."

"Sarna, I am not going to discuss the one date I had with Remy. We have more important problems. Do you get what has happened?"

Sarna flung her arms into the air and opened the door to the refrigerator. She poured orange juice into a crystal champagne glass and then turned around to face Jason.

"I know exactly what happened," she said in a raspy voice. "You lost $4 million dollars. $4 million. You are supposed to be the king of the pit. How could you lose $4 million dollars?

Jason let the water run in the sink and splashed cold water on his face. He wasn't sure how to answer. He didn't know exactly what had happened. Minutes after Remy left the pit, Oscar sent a signal across the room, but this time the signal didn't work. Jason bought a thousand contracts and within a split second, stocks tanked two hundred points. That accounted for the first million.

It seemed like a simple error. Then it got worse. Oscar had made a trade with him. Jason had been a buyer but Oscar told Jason to sell. A fatal misunderstanding.

Oscar announced another order. This time, Jason was sure Oscar had taken him out of the first trade, but again he was wrong. Oscar had added to his position and when the market continued down, the loss was a staggering $4 mil.

There was a tacit understanding among brokers that traders ate the error and waited for a payback. Jason had no reason to believe it wouldn't come, so his first reaction was calm. He had twenty-four hours to pay the clearinghouse before he would be hauled off the floor. Oscar knew the time limit. The deal was engraved in stone, though never discussed.

Jason moved to the center of the pit so Oscar could see him. He watched Oscar sort through his papers and saw a smile form on his lips. Jason had never seen Oscar smile before. But today, the first thing he noticed on Oscar's face was a smirk.

Then Oscar gave Joey a trade. It looked like two hundred gees. Jason took a deep breath and tried to suppress his jealously. OK, the kid needed a break. They had been awfully hard on him. An hour went by and nothing happened. Jason tensed. Something was wrong. His back was killing him, but he couldn't leave. There was hardly anything to trade. The loss grew like a malignant mole. Jason added the out-trade to the trading loss and calculated what he had lost.

When Sarna walked over to stand next to him, he broke out in a sweat. He watched her mimicking the other traders, offering to buy or sell. He grabbed her and she twirled around to face him.

"Sarna, you can't trade. You will lose more money."

"How do you know?" She turned her back like a two-year old. "Don't tell me what I can and cannot do," she said.

Oscar put his arms up as if he were invoking God. "A hundred at 50. A hundred at 50."

"I'll buy ten," said Sarna boldly.

"Sold," screamed Oscar. "A hundred at 40. Two hundred at 30."

Jason felt the room spin.

In five minutes, the market had plummeted a hundred points and Sarna was out $300,000.

She stood in her spot, unable to grasp what had gone wrong.

Jason snatched her cards and sold the ten lot to another trader. Then he grabbed Sarna's elbow and dragged her out of the pit.

"What happened?" she asked.

"You lost $300,000," he stammered.

"I couldn't have," she said meekly.

"But you did. You did, Sarna. You did." He began to cry. In front of everyone he began to shake. He couldn't stop tears from running down his cheek, like a little kid hurt on a playground. Then the weight of it all made him reel. He fell on his knees. No one moved. What bad luck, Joey thought, as he secretly eyed the chance to take Jason's trade.

Sarna knelt down to help Jason on to his feet. She had never seen anything like this since she witnessed her girlfriend crying at her mother's funeral. Sarna kept her arm around Jason's waist and guided him through the crowd out of the trading floor, down the escalator and into the elevators. Once they were in the elevator, Jason rested his head against the cool steel of the wall and closed his eyes, his hands hanging beside him. In the basement, Sarna gave the parking ticket to the valet. She held Jason's hand, but she could hardly bear the sight of him. With his nose running, he looked nothing like the sexy guy she had so carefully seduced.

It took a full five minutes for the Mercedes convertible to round the curve of the garage. The valet held the door and Sarna slipped into the driver's seat. The car, this black symbol of money, felt like a hearse. They exited onto Adams without exchanging a word and wound their way along Lake Shore Drive, past the fabulous homes on Sheridan Road. This neighborhood had been hers. Now what?

Trade Secrets

By the time they reached their house, Jason's agony had turned to anger and Sarna's disbelief to woe. Jason sat at the kitchen table while she ran her hands along the countertops so carefully chosen, so expensively custom made. The gesture bordered on a caress as reality became distressingly obvious.

What would she do if Jason lost all of his money? What if their swanky life evaporated? Fear washed over her as she envisioned Jason evolving into a poor drip, their life deteriorating like a crushed rock. In its place loomed a dingy future, hard work at its core, a gray notion, like the colorless lake before her.

Fear gripped her. As Sarna stood up, her knees weakened. All her life she had dreamed of riches. This pot of gold had been hers, real enough to sleep in, firm enough to touch. How could success be so ephemeral? And if this were to happen, if everything were taken away and she were left with nothing, what would she do with Jason?

chapter 22

"Go over the numbers again," Zach commanded.

"We've been over this ten times. Jason is out. It's done."

"You gave that kid a hundred gees, Oscar."

"A Christmas present."

"When did I give you permission to make decisions like this? I'm no charity." His eyes, angry as a tiger's, looked as if they could pop.

"Don't make a big deal out of this, Zach. Joey's into us for a fortune. Let him have his moment. You know damn well we did it to take the attention away from Jason."

"You ante up a hundred gees. I told you not to give my money away."

"The kid needed a break. Besides, Remy was watching."

"I suppose you helped her too."

"I made her whole."

"What does that mean?"

"We had an out-trade Saturday. I paid her back. Remy could be a threat."

"I could wipe her out in a second," taunted Zachary, piercing the air with his finger. "I'm not afraid of Remy. It's who she talks to. Remember this, Oscar. When two people know something, it's no longer a secret."

Oscar felt beads of perspiration on his brow. He wasn't sure why he had been so generous. All he could remember was walking into the pit, hungry for some kind of attention. The trade with Remy just spilled out of him, as if he were trying to seduce her, though he knew he never could. Still, that skin of hers would be something to touch. Zach was right. He had been careless, had lost his discipline. They had ambushed Jason, but he had to free himself from Zach's menacing threats. Giving Joey a boost was a small token to mitigate his guilt.

Oscar crossed his legs and put his hands behind his head as if he were holding himself to do sit-ups. Then he let go and leaned over, his hands clasped in front of him. He was beginning to hate himself. Who would be next? Zach could turn on him too. He thought about Harry Saks. After his car accident Zach never even talked about him. Nor did he go to the funeral, insisting that Oscar stay away too. If Oscar ever tried to break the cold-blooded bargain he had made with Zach Silverman, Zach would have him cremated. Once anxious to get into Zach's fraternity at any price, now it was too late. No one could question his power and certainly not his sanity.

"You must understand, Zach. After this crash, things aren't going to be the same. The flow of the paper has dried up. This market will become an institutional one. The show is over. You don't want to believe me, but if you would get your ass down on the floor you would see what I mean."

"You've gone berserk, Oscar. As long as there is paper to trade and pits to trade in, there will always be money to be made." Zach rubbed his two forefingers together with his thumb. "I control the paper. Nothing can come between my money and me. Not as long as I own this clearinghouse.

I run this building, for God's sake." His face was beet red. His words sputtered out with a tremor that Oscar had never heard before.

It was true that Zach ran the building. However, the crash had drawn a Maginot line. Oscar stared at the upper border of Zach's mouth which was red from a neurotic habit of licking his lips. Oscar covered his eyelids with his hands as his body sank into the chair. If he could grab a hot shower, get a massage and sleep for a few hours, maybe he'd be able to think clearly. He hadn't slept more than a couple of hours since Friday. He was jittery and hungry. But the thought of food made him nauseous. Oscar looked up and focused on the door. Zach's voice had reached such a menacing pitch Oscar thought the building might shake. He put his fingers to his mouth to suggest silence.

"Don't make rotten signals to me. Do you know who you are talking to?" Zach bellowed.

Oscar nodded. He had heard it all before.

"I built this building. Brick by brick. I built it first with my mind. Those pits were my idea. Without me, none of this would exist." He ran his fingers through the air as if he could make magic. "You would still be locked in an office shuffling files around if not for me. Where do you get off telling me to shut up? This is my palace. The rest of you are my guests. Jason. Joey. All of you. You are like this to me."

He snapped his fingers as if the rest of them were stardust. Then he turned to the window.

Zach loved this view, presiding like Zeus over the city. Had he been a god, he would have been an angry, vengeful one like the God of the Old Testament. Zach became a bar mitzvah for the second time a few years earlier, insisting that his early education was wasted on a "boy without a conscience." Religion, he explained to others, was inside him. When Zach met his wife, she went to the mikvah, to wash away germs she may have picked up from the dozens of men she had screwed. He contributed to local synagogues throughout the city where he would go to pray when the markets were not cooperating. When he began making big money, he made a pact with his Maker. For good fortune, he would become faithful. An even trade, a business deal, as good as a written contract. He kept his promise good by koshering his home and surrounded himself with people who agreed with his religious gibberish. For Oscar it was easy. Religion ran in his blood though his god was not the angry god. His god was a forgiving Catholic god.

Oscar envied Zachary Silverman for dreaming up such a cold-hearted deal. Oscar would have been afraid God would have turned on him. Zach had no such fears.

"You know, Oscar, sometimes I feel like I own the world. Sometimes I feel that I can actually make things materialize."

Oscar studied him. He got up out of the chair walked over to the window to share the view, to assimilate Zach's energy into his own. But he couldn't.

"We need to lay low for a while, Zach. The paper is so thin, anyone could follow our trail."

"You stupid bastard. There is no trail because all of the records are right here." Zach stammered, pointing to his brain as if it were a room of computers.

"Zach, there are records. They are in this office and they all point to us."

"To you. That's what you're scared of. You don't give a damn about me. You're only worried about your ass."

"I'm just trying to be cautious. We made millions this week. We can afford to lay low. The markets will pick up. In the meantime, give Fortunato a chance."

"You mean hand over money to this punk. Why him? Do you have a private deal with him Doheney?" He grabbed

Oscar by the throat and Oscar wondered if Zach didn't believe that he had hit on something.

Oscar had no such deal. How could he prove it? Would words calm this lunacy?

Zach had entered a realm of his own. For a brief moment this week Zach thought the whole system could topple with the $90 million dollar loss from a Taiwan trader. But the government could never let that happen. The pits were front and center. No clearinghouse could ever go under. Once Zach thought this through in his mind, he felt a new rush of strength. He could push the system to its brink. It could never fail. The swell of omnipotence was visible in the sneer on his face and the cockeyed look in his eyes.

Oscar plopped down on the chair. He had never been this close to insanity. Oscar thought about Nixon and Watergate. This must have been how Dean and Halderman felt watching their President unravel. The way Zach had scrunched up eyes reminded Oscar of the former President. But he didn't have the nerve to tell him that he thought he was nuts anymore than Nixon's staff had the guts to tell their boss. Oscar's silence merely signified approval when disapproval was written all over his face. If he tried to force Zach to face reality, Zach might crack and then what?

From where Oscar was sitting, Zach looked as crazy as King Lear.

**

October 23, 1987

On Friday the New York Stock Exchange announced it would close two hours early to ease the strain on its system. In Chicago the markets were at a standstill, with only a handful of orders coming across the phone lines. Without a public, spreads between the bids and offer widened. Board members of all the Exchanges discussed new price moves in order to compress volatility. Remy's pit was blamed as the culprit. It was hoped that new limits would let orders flow systematically and eliminate the fear that was paralyzing investors.

Brokerage houses would be open on Saturday to accommodate clients. The Big Board had processed 2.5 billion shares which was three and half times its normal volume. On Thursday the S&P had lost one quarter of its value in just seconds and its total trading was down to half the previous sessions.

Deposits at banks leapt as investors sold stocks to park money in federally insured accounts. One psychiatrist was quoted in the morning paper for calling the panic a "disorder" of broken confidence. He explained that investors believed that no one was in control of the financial markets, not even the White House, and warned that the psychological chaos would continue unless there was substantive action to calm the public.

Added to the alarm were confirmed stories about the infamous Taiwan trader, Hwalin Lee, who was held responsible for the $90 million dollar loss at First Options. Fortunately, First Options was owned by the Continental Bank. According to a lawsuit filed by Merrill Lynch, Lee's assets were insufficient to pay his debt, and the firm insisted that his assets be frozen so it could recoup money it was owed in an unrelated dispute.

Remy was exhausted. As she took her place in the pit, she realized that she needed a break or she would make simple mistakes and lose money. She called Ken, cashed in a free ticket and flew to New York.

Bursting with stories, Remy talked non-stop through dinner, filling Ken in on every detail, including the Hwalin Lee drama.

"It was incredible," she explained, cleaning up the dinner dishes.

"You look so tired, honey."

"I couldn't eat or sleep."

Ken brought her near to him.

"Not less sexy, I hope," she said, unbuttoning her blouse.

"Never," he said, kissing her neck.

They made love to Paul McCartney's songs, but Remy's mind was fixated on events at the Exchange. Even Ken's touch couldn't completely distract her.

"You need sleep," he said.

"I'm not sure I can sleep. Everything keeps going over and over in my mind. It was like a war zone, Ken. I've never been through anything like it. When they closed the Exchange, I thought that the financial world had collapsed. I took twenty thousand dollars home in cash because I was afraid that no one would be able to get to their money."

Ken smiled, loving her even more in her disorientation. Remy was an organized woman with a methodical mind. Today she seemed so vulnerable. As she revealed her fears, he could see how much she needed him.

"I told you that Sarna began trading this week. She looked like a lost soul. I felt sorry for her."

"Jason can take care of her and from what you've told me, Jason is well taken care of."

"Oscar nearly destroyed him this week."

"Maybe he wants to get Jason out of their deal."

"Now it looks as if Joey is part of their scheme."

"I didn't know he was trading. I thought a trader needed to cover his losses. How can the clearinghouse let him trade without money?"

Remy sat up in bed and slipped on a nightgown. "Joey is financed."

"Financed?"

"I hear Zach finances him. There is a rumor that that Zach is looking for others to finance, kids with no connections."

"You mean a stranger guarantees their trades?"

"Yes. If the trader makes money, the financier takes a cut. If the trader loses, the financier gets a high rate of interest on the outstanding debt. Not only must the trader pay back the principal, but also interest charges that can run twenty percent."

"So the trader is indebted for years?"

Remy nodded.

"Why would someone do that?"

"It's their only break. There are kids who could never save up enough to buy a seat or have enough to collateralize their trades. The Exchange is a place to make tons of money."

"Or," Ken intervened, "get into debt."

"No one puts a gun to their head," she reminded him.

"It's a scandal."

Remy considered Ken's take on this. It wasn't exactly how she thought about it. But she had to admit that Oscar and Zach had a retinue of servants. She wondered if there were contracts or if the agreements were more subtle.

"What if I tried to get financing?"

"It wouldn't work. They choose kids out of college or people who never went to college, kids with hopeful eyes who yearn for big bucks."

"What was Joey doing before he came to the Exchange?"

"Working in a shoe store."

"And Jason?"

"I don't know how he started, but when I got there he was bagging Oscar's trades," Remy said, wrapping herself in a terry-cloth robe and talking as she applied toothpaste to her toothbrush.

"What does that mean?"

"I've told you this Ken. When Oscar bids, he lets Jason in the trade first and then splits the profits with him." She wiped the toothpaste off her mouth and washed her face hastily.

She slipped into bed next to Ken. He brushed her hair back before he kissed her on the forehead. She leaned against him. They were together and for now, the trading floor felt very far away.

"How does Oscar know which trades will be profitable?"

"Oscar holds all the paper, the orders, from Zach's clearinghouse. Before the market opens, he knows which way it will go. It's known as dual trading. He uses the customer's orders for himself. Then he fills it for the customer. He trades with Jason. If the market goes against him, he can get Jason out with the orders he knows he has. So there is hardly ever a loss."

"Give me an example."

"Ok. Let's make it simple. Say there is a market order, which means that the customer doesn't set a price to buy something and most people use market orders. The people in the pit make the market, so if something is selling at 20, Oscar has Jason buy it at 17 and then he sells it to the customer at 20."

"So Jason buys it three points lower? Isn't there some way to trace this?"

"Not really, because Oscar can let Jason know beforehand to start the bidding at 17 and the OFFER at 20. Those three points can be thousands of dollars on the opening."

"Or, there could be a time when the traders in the pit want to buy at 15 and sell at 20."

Ken nodded. Mentally he made a note to himself understanding that the pit wanted to buy at 15 and sell at 20.

"Oscar bids 15. Jason now knows that Oscar has a bid in his pocket. Jason buys up any offer close to 15 because he knows that if Oscar is bidding 15, that means he has orders in his pocket to buy at 15. Until the orders in Oscar's pocket are absorbed, the market won't go below 15. If the market goes up after Jason makes his trade, it's money in the bank. If he has to bail, he can use Oscar's bid as an exit."

"So he trades before anyone else, before any public customer can trade."

"Yes, that's right. But instead of doing the trade himself, Oscar has Jason do it for him. Jason knows Oscar will save him, so his trades are riskless."

"Then what?"

"Jason waits. Generally the market goes up a few ticks. Because he has a safety net, he can trade huge quantities. Then he sells. On a thousand lot trade, he can capture twenty-five thousand dollars in a matter of minutes. Later he splits with Oscar."

"How do you know this?"

"If you are there, you can just see that they are two sides of the same trade, like a pillow and a mattress. They just go together," she shrugged.

"But you've never actually seen them split money."

"Of course not," she said. "You'd need the FBI to figure the rest out."

"You better go to sleep," Ken said.

"I really am tired. I'll tell you more about it tomorrow." Then she suddenly jumped up in bed. "A funny thing happened last week. Oscar stuck Jason with a big loss, enough to break him. He tried to pay him back, but the market was so volatile I'm not sure he was able to. I never saw that happen before."

"Maybe he was trying to disguise their relationship."

"I heard that Jason broke down and cried. And that Sarna had to help him leave. I felt sorry for both of them. At first I was critical of all of this, but I don't see what the big deal is. Maybe the bagman stuff is wrong if customers get hurt, and I'm sure they do. They can never get the trade before the bagman does because he's the right arm of the broker. The broker gives it to him so they can split later. This is just how business is done in the pits. It will always be that way."

The conversation made Remy wonder if her father had seen this. Had he done something illegal? She couldn't imagine that. Then she tensed. How could she even let it cross her mind that her father was a criminal?

"Go to sleep, honey," Ken said leaning over to kiss her as she eyes closed her eyes. He quietly pulled himself up and walked into the other room. There was a pad of paper on his desk. He jotted down some notes, glad that his thoughts couldn't be heard. All of this was exactly what Ken had surmised, but hearing it from Remy made a difference. It was hard to fathom that no one in the pit cared how things worked, because he certainly did.

Tonight Remy had told him precisely what he needed to know. Now he could proceed.

chapter 23

December 15, 1987

ZACH SILVERMAN'S ANNIVERSARY party had been arranged long before the October 19th crash. With plans underway to honor him for his twenty-five years at the Exchange, no one could have anticipated that the mood would have shifted from euphoric to dismal in one short week. Life before the crash and life after it separated into two distinct worlds. Even those who came away with a profit faced a profession that had been altered. The market had evolved from an inefficient one into an institutional one marked with increased risk. Spreads between bids and asking prices shrank or expanded with such intense volatility that only traders with very deep pockets could handle the swings. For those who had lost their fortunes, the pits were a mere memory. Newcomers, recognizing that trading had become a gamble, had to reconsider their goals.

Tolerating risk was a characteristic necessary if someone wanted to survive in the pits. When the odds were fifty-fifty, traders could break even. When the odds fell as they had, it was hard to assess if any trade was worth the bet.

Holly Rozner

Spending came to a grinding halt as traders saw their bank balances dwindle. Real estate flooded the market and pricey items at Saks Fifth Avenue sat on the shelves.

One of the houses on sale was the four-acre Bramson mansion on the Lake in Glencoe. Built for $3 million dollars with a still unfinished swimming pool and unpaved tennis courts, when it was finally listed in early December, it carried the bargain price of $1.8 million. In six short years, Jason had made over $10 million and consumed every cent. Now the value of his over-priced art collection had collapsed along with the stocks he owned. His home was mortgaged to the hilt; his cars were worth a small percentage of what he had paid and the million-dollar boat with gold faucets wouldn't sell for half that. While the money was rolling in, caution seemed superfluous. Now, without savings to fall back on, he was caught empty-handed.

Sarna had widened the hole in his wallet with her wholesale fervor for fashion. The custom dining room table was inlaid with mother-of pearl, setting them back fifty thousand dollars. Sixteen matching chairs, covered in chintz, had retailed for fifty-five hundred dollars apiece. Their gold silk tassels had not yet been cut, but the non-refundable down payment had been cashed. Despite Jason's pleas to the Oriental rug dealer, the piece could not be returned. When the appraisal was done, Jason was dismayed to learn that he had lost half on every item. Sarna had spent $600,000. On furniture! Added to the two million-dollar mortgage, even if they got their asking price, they would not have enough to pay Zach. Jason had violated the cardinal rule of traders: not paying cash for his house.

Their undoing nearly broke Sarna. She blamed Jason. He had needed a gorgeous woman to screw in the middle of the night, and she desired a fat checkbook. All the time she was overspending, Jason had done nothing to stop her.

Trade Secrets

Chicago traders bid up the price of houses and cars, paying premium dollars for tickets to Bulls games, front and center to see Michael Jordan. They gave glamorous parties, took first- class vacations and marquised the pits they inhabited on their vanity plates: BONDBUYER, SELLEMHI, and BUYEMLO. That was the life she married. Watching it hemorrhage cut the heart out of her.

On Saturday morning a real estate agent came to discuss a selling price for their house. Sarna shut herself in the bedroom wondering what her former sorority sister would think. To depend on Marcia Becker, who had grown up in a small house, was more than she could bear. She had known people who had lost money, had heard about bankruptcies, but for her own life to capsize! When Jason told her they would have to sell the house, she stared at him for the longest time, until finally, as the truth sunk in, she had difficulty breathing.

Jason could see the transformation in his wife's vacant stare. When Sarna emerged from the bedroom, she was shivering. He looked into her bloodshot eyes. Where was the girl he knew, the one who fucked him like a whore? He held her and her tiny bones seemed so frail. He remembered the moment just a few months before when the doctor told him their baby had died. He was sure she was thinking about that too.

He might be able to console her, but who could console him? His father would disown him when he saw the mess he had made. He could hear his savage voice: "That's why I couldn't take you into business with me. I had to sell the business before I let you take it over. You've always been careless. Now you'll have to live with the consequences."

He could recite his father's invectives without hearing them. His father was right. Jason had lost the money his parents had given them as a wedding gift. At thirty, he had lost more than most earn in an entire lifetime. From the moment he stepped into the pit, easy money had gained him power, embellished his stride, altered the way he ordered in a restaurant, even the way he doled out dollar bills. Success had obliterated his fear. After a while, he thought he could never lose, and as long as Oscar and Zach were with him, he could not.

Now he wished he were dead.

He had no plan. Only Zach could save him. He would meet with him, beg him. But what leverage did he have? He had never been more than a puppet in Zach's personal army. Joey could take his place and no one would give a damn. He was as dispensable as an unmatched sock. The lopsidedness of it shook him to the quick.

He shuddered to think he could actually end up on the street. Would his father let that happen? Would he let his father help him? Could he ask his father? What if his father refused? There was nothing substantive for him to hold onto, a reality that filled him with horror.

Then he convinced himself that Zach would have to finance him. If he financed kids out of college with no experience, certainly he would bail him out. And if he didn't, he would snitch on him. Why hadn't he thought of that before? His armpits were soaked. The frown on his forehead had wrinkled his skin. His thoughts turned from his imaginary revenge to reality.

The meeting with the agent took less than an hour. Sarna and Jason sat in the sunroom overlooking the blue waters of Lake Michigan only yards below, while Marcia inventoried the house, suggesting little details that would help them sell quicker: move the credenza into the corner to make the room look larger, put the office papers in storage so that there was an appearance of more space, make sure the garage was immaculate.

Sarna returned to the bedroom, while Jason signed the papers. Zach's party was that night and she desperately wanted to go.

"We still live here," she told Jason when Marcia left."The car, the furnishings, and the jewelry aren't gone. Let's go. Maybe there will be some whispers but no one can be sure what really happened. Someone might think you had spread off the loss against another market at another exchange. Only Zach and Oscar know the truth. The others will just be guessing."

Jason weighed her words. No one did know. If they showed up at the party, maybe they could fix things with Zach and Oscar.

The outline of optimism on Sarna's face gave him hope. Her eyes lit up as she allowed herself to believe that life wouldn't be so bad after all. She loved parties. And then, as if nothing had gone wrong, she jumped up from bed and began searching her closet for a dress. Three hundred square feet of carefully organized shelves, a small antique desk and velvet- covered chair where she could muse over her choices. There were dozens of options, but she settled on two: the sequined St. John or the satin Chanel. First she would take a long hot bath in the deep bathtub. She telephoned her masseuse to be there at 3:00. What was another hundred and fifty dollars? Then they would get all dolled up and face the world as if they didn't have a care!

Perhaps for the last time.

***

With Ken by her side, Remy felt complete. She looked at him and smiled, grateful that he was in her life. She felt deeply connected to him, relying on his advice and sharing her life the way she did with Lara. She had fallen in love and she had trusted Ken with her deepest secret—her reason for coming to the Exchange. When she told him what she was undertaking, he had warned her that the task might not be possible. Zach was completely isolated, a fact she learned was true. Ken knew about corporate America and how certain people were insulated because no one outside was allowed into their inner world. She hoped tonight at Zach's party she might pick up some clue about her father. She was sure Zach didn't know who she was. If he ever found out that she was Harry Saks' daughter, she would be stopped dead in her tracks.

Remy wore a turquoise and black satin dress, pulled tightly around her waist. Her hair fell against her bare shoulders emphasizing her ivory skin. The lipstick, a muted mauve, highlighted the shadow that outlined her eyes.

Zach's party was markedly different from the gala last December. Gone was the tinsel. Gone with the bubble that had burst. The opulent excesses of the past had been eliminated. There was not even a dance floor. As committee members haggled about what kind of band should play and as recommendations evolved into arguments, the chairman of the committee put an end to the debate and decided that there should be no dancing at all. As it turned out, music would have been out of place in an atmosphere crackling with doom.

On each table sat two dozen yellow roses. Gold tableware had been ordered from a New York designer who had dressed each chair in cream sateen to match the clothes. The room looked distinguished, thought Remy, as she folded her fingers into Ken's hand.

"That's Oscar," she whispered, as she took Ken to the corner of the room.

"You described him perfectly. His nose does look like a hawk's."

"You cannot know the real Oscar without standing next to him in the pit."

"Handing out trades."

"You can't ever mention that, Ken." She looked around to be sure no one had heard.

"Do you want to introduce him to me?"

"Maybe later," she said. "Ken, I need to talk to you." He turned to her as she continued. "I'm worried that Zach might figure out who I am. I never introduced myself to him. It would seem so strange. My father and he were partners for years. What if he knew me?"

He looked at her intently, staring into her blue, blue eyes.

"Why would he come to any conclusion about you, Remy? You don't know if what happened had anything to do with Zach and even if it did, why would he think you came to stake out this place?"

"I need your help," she pleaded.

He put his arm around her. "I will do anything I can. But not tonight. Tonight point out the people you've told me about. You can even talk to Zach, congratulate him, test him out."

"And if he did recognize me?"

"Tell him you didn't want any favors. You didn't want to bother him. You wanted to learn how to trade on your own."

She looked around the room at the ensemble before her who suddenly looked like characters from a play.

"There's Zach," she said, pointing to the stocky man who was huddled with Oscar.

"I didn't think he was so short."

Remy stared at this mighty little man. A kaleidoscope of ambiguity, controlling a secret society that had no regard for anything, Zach ran the Exchange like a tyrant. How had he treated her father? While it was true that they had grown up together, she didn't really know what kind of a man Zach Silverman was.

Zach's exaggerated toupee didn't match his graying eyebrows. Surrounded by his usual entourage: Oscar and his wife, the Governor, the Mayor and finally, Jason and Sarna, Zach scanned his fingers along his red tie. Everyone was pretending to listen, even if they were not.

"The younger couple over there are Jason and Sarna Bramson."

"Your date last year."

"That was a lifetime ago," she said, smiling.

"It does seem as if we have always known each other, Remy," Ken said.

"I wish we had. I wish you had been in my life all of my life." All of a sudden, Remy saw Sarna waving for them to come across. Before Remy could turn the other way, Sarna started walking in their direction. Remy pulled Ken away.

"I don't know what she would want with us," Remy said.

"We can leave if you're uncomfortable. This is your party, Remy."

"She knows I saw her," said Remy, waving back. "I don't want to be rude. Let's make it brief."

Sarna snatched Jason from his conversation and led him across the room. When they approached, Jason extended his hand to Ken.

"Remy has told me about you, Jason."

"Ken, this is Jason's wife, Sarna," said Remy interrupting.

Sarna greeted Ken with a big smile, her voice rising as if she were very nervous. Her big brown eyes looked him over carefully.

"Remy has been helping me. She's teaching me the ropes. These guys don't want women around," she explained, as if Ken had asked, making it sound as if she would return to the trading floor soon.

"Sarna needs experience."

"You have offered to do what no one else would do, Remy," Jason interjected.

"Let's not discuss business tonight," Remy suggested.

"There's no band," Sarna remarked, twirling in her own space.

"Someone wanted to keep this subdued," explained Jason, "as if that were possible in this crowd."

"I'm sure it will be a lovely evening," said Ken, touching Remy's elbow and guiding her away.

Before Ken and Remy could exit, Sarna took Remy's hands into hers. "I really do want to thank you."

"You don't need to, Sarna."

"I do."

"Then you have. No more is necessary." Remy could see tears in Sarna's eyes. Word of Jason's loss had spread. Remy knew Jason had taken a big hit and that he might never recover. She tried to think of something to say that might be comforting, but before she had a chance, Sid Keller interrupted. Sid was a newcomer to the pit, trading for only two months before the crash. He was reputed to have made a killing during his very short career. For a few days last month he stood next to Remy, but most of the time, his spot was near Jason. Right after the markets caved, he disappeared.

"Sid Keller. My wife, Sarna. You remember Remy Masterman. Her friend, Ken Baldwin."

Ken shook Sid's hand.

"Sarna, you look ravishing," Sid said.

Sarna's eyes opened wide. She fluttered her thick lashes. His compliment brought her to life like a baby waking from a long afternoon nap. She tilted her head to one side, swept her hair off her face and looked him straight in the eye.

Ken and Remy exchanged an awkward glance.

"Let me get drinks for everyone," offered Sid.

"None for me," said Remy. "In fact, if you will excuse me, I'm going to freshen up."

"You're perfect as you are, "said Ken, letting go of her arm.

"She is perfect," said Jason. As he watched Remy disappear into the crowd, he wondered what his life would have been like if Sarna hadn't seduced him back. Would he have faced such an utter mess if Remy had been at his side?

"Let's let Jason and Ken get acquainted," said Sid. "Come help me carry the drinks." Obediently, Sarna darted off with Sid, her arm in his as if they were old friends.

Jason and Ken stood alone during a long pause.

"Your wife is beautiful," said Ken, breaking the silence.

"Yes. She is," Jason said, his eyes following her as she pranced across the room. "Maybe Sid will entertain her. I'm not much in a mood for a party. Where do you live, Ken?"

"New York."

"What do you do?"

"Legal consulting."

"With a firm?"

"I was with a firm for a few years, but I don't practice anymore."

"Long distance romance is tricky."

"It is."

"This is our coldest month."

"We get our share of cold too, but Chicago winters are worse."

"Yes. I guess so." Jason's voice had trailed off. He could sense that Ken wasn't interested in this conversation and neither was he. His eyes followed Sarna. "My wife is certainly busy," Jason said as he watched Sarna and Sid talking. Her right arm rested on Sid's shoulder as she leaned into him. Jason hadn't been jealous of his wife since they had dated when she would shamelessly throw herself at another guy. Tonight he couldn't prevent the familiar pang from tugging at him. He knew Sarna too well. If another man could save her life, she'd be gone.

"Sid works with us," Jason explained. "He hasn't been there for that long. He told someone that he traded in London before coming to Chicago, that that was where he learned how to trade. He seems to do quite well. Even has an apartment at the Ritz."

"He's made it big."

"Seems like it," Jason concurred. He rubbed his hand along the rim of his now- empty glass. Then he tilted his head to the left to bring his wife into closer focus.

Ken noticed Jason's eyes glued to the bar across the room. From where they stood, it was impossible to miss Sarna's flirtatious gyrations. She threw her head back laughing as her hands billowed in mid-air. Jason fumbled with his drink and Ken, wanting to find something to say that might break up the tension watched him. Finally Ken excused himself and left Jason standing alone against the wall.

As Ken approached the bar, Sarna put her arm out and insisted he join them.

"It's lovely here, boys. Nothing is more fun than a good party!"

"This is certainly some party," Sid remarked when Ken settled on a stool near them.

"These parties are the talk of the town."

Sarna kept her hand laced in Sid's. Then she turned the other way to speak to one of the wives who was ordering a martini.

"How's your place?" Ken asked Sid quietly, while Sarna returned to her drink.

"What a setup!" Sid spoke through the side of his mouth.

"I won't be back for a couple of weeks."

"We'll be ready soon."

"There is no hurry," said Ken, his head straight ahead as if he were talking about something in the room. Then he turned into the bar.

Sarna saw the two men talking to each other.

"Do you two know each another?" she asked.

We met in New York a long time ago," Ken said.

"Do you live at the Ritz too, Ken?"

"No, I'm not in Sid's league."

Sarna laughed. Sid slipped his hands into his pockets. She slid her arm into his, smiled up at him and caressed the sleeve of his jacket with her other hand. The despair that had nearly overcome her this morning was gone.

"Are you alone tonight, Sid?" asked Sarna, staring directly into his face.

"Strictly solo," he replied, his eyes searching hers.

She met his gaze. He had broad shoulders, a straight nose, dark brown hair and beautiful eyes. About thirty-five, maybe slightly little older. Not that age mattered much. What mattered was that he was alone and obviously keenly interested in her. And he lived at the Ritz. An infusion of power overtook her as she arched her neck. Maybe she wouldn't have to be poor. Maybe she wouldn't have to sell the house. With a guy like Sid, life could be a joy ride. Who wouldn't want to get laid at the Ritz? Before the thought could fully develop, Jason was at her side.

"It's time for dinner," he said, grabbing her hand.

"Sid's by himself, Jason. Let's invite him to sit with us."

Trade Secrets

"We are seated with Zach and Oscar. I don't think there's room at the table."

"What about with Ken and Remy? Sid doesn't have a date," Sarna persisted.

"Sid can take care of himself," Jason insisted, turning his back. He pulled his wife towards Table One.

"You are making a fool of yourself."

"You have made us into fools, Jason, not me."

"Have you forgotten what we're going through?"

She shot Jason an irritated glance.

"I didn't get us into this mess, Jason. I've been on the trading floor for only one week. So don't go and blame me for the trouble you're in. This is your torment, not mine."

"Sarna," he warned, his voice deepening. "I have to get through this evening. It's important to our future so shut up and act like a lady."

She batted her eyes and held back tears not wanting to smear her mascara. She stopped short in the middle of the room and recomposed her thoughts. She felt the silk of her dress and glanced at the five-karat stone on her left hand. She needed these things and she would find a way to keep them. She would do what was necessary, even run as fast as she could, to escape the disaster looming before them.

The tension between the Bramsons was taut, discernible even to Ken. When Sid went to the men's room, Ken followed him.

"Be careful with Jason's wife, Sid," Ken warned when he had a moment alone with Sid. "You're playing with fire."

"I can take care of myself, buddy. Don't worry about me."

"She's trouble, Sid."

"I imagine that she is," said Sid laughing. "That will be the adventure."

"You're out of line, Keller."

"Mind your business, Ken."

When Remy returned to the ballroom, she noticed Sid and Ken talking before Sid was able to shoot away like a kid caught with candy he was forbidden to take to school.

"What were you talking to Sid Keller about?" asked Remy.

"About how pretty you are."

"It looked like you two had something to say to each other."

"Except for the fact that he's sorry that he's not with you tonight, we have nothing to say to each other," quipped Ken.

"Ok. So don't tell me," she replied. "But I'm not that stupid."

"You could never be accused of being stupid, Remy," Ken said. Then he led her towards the appetizers and suggested they might find the table they would be sitting at. Ken knew he would have to be more careful. Remy was smarter than any woman he had ever met. Her extraordinary mind was one of the many things he loved about her. He watched her eyes follow Sid Keller as he walked across the room. For the first time since they had met, Ken couldn't help but wonder if the fact that she was so smart might become a liability as things heated up.

chapter 24

SARNA COULDN'T GET Sid out of her mind. On Monday she called him to tell him she would be in the city on Wednesday.

"Come to my apartment," he said.

His response had been so immediate, it confirmed Sid had been thinking about her too, so it was a total surprise when he opened the front door and stayed on the phone, motioning for her to put her coat in the closet. When he hung up, instead of reaching for her, he sat on a chair behind a huge mahogany desk. Sarna wasn't sure where to put herself.

The two-bedroom suite at the Ritz was furnished in yellow and green chintz. Sarna dissected the décor, comparing it to hers. Sid was the only person she had ever met who lived in a hotel. She wondered if he ordered meals from room service as she imagined how divine it would be to have maid service all day long.

There was a long silence. Sarna fumbled with her purse and even considered leaving, when Sid finally stood up and walked over to her. There was a long awkward moment. She expected him to kiss her. Instead, he began talking about Jason.

Holly Rozner

"This has been an awful time in my life," she admitted. Sid's stone expression exhibited an indifference that panicked her.

"I heard Jason had a bad out- trade," he said matter of factly.

"Enough to bankrupt us."

"He'll work something out," Sid remarked. He stood up and walked to the sofa.

"That's unlikely," she said, not sure if she should follow him."But he is still allowed to trade."

Then Sid launched into stories about what it had been like to trade in Europe—how different the markets were.

"Why did you come here?"

"I was bored. I find myself easily bored," he said, locking his gaze into hers.

Sarna felt his eyes undressing her. Men were always attracted to her, so it was no surprise that Sid was too. But his expression was difficult to penetrate.

The doorbell rang. Sid had ordered lunch: smoked salmon, caviar and champagne. Sarna wasn't hungry, but she enjoyed watching the waiter fuss with the silver service. She sat on the sofa and crossed her leg. Then she kicked off one shoe and extended her foot, pretending to stretch as she watched Sid watching her. He made a sandwich of salmon and capers. Then he clicked on the TV to a station that had a stock tape.

He poured two glasses of champagne. The telephone rang. Sid rushed into the bedroom to take the call and Sarna walked to the window. From this suite the sixteenth floor, Sarna could see Lake Shore Drive, bounded by the gray waters of Lake Michigan. Winter had chilled the city to its core. The beach was deserted. Sarna could see pedestrians bundled in fur, racing for shelter. She hugged her arms around her body as she envisioned her house on Sheridan

Road and the small walkway down to the water. She pressed her head against the window as if she might find an escape in the cold glass.

Within a few minutes Sid came into the room. Her back was to him. Without saying a word, he stood behind her and slipped his hands beneath her silk blouse. She wore no bra. She let her head fall onto his shoulder. He stroked her nipples, his mouth buried in her neck. She tried to turn around, but his grip was firm. His right leg held her still as he undid her blouse and loosened her skirt until it fell to the floor. He cupped her breasts and ran one hand along her stomach. His mouth followed the curves of her back with light kisses.

As she reached for him, he turned her towards him. She opened her eyes and looked into his. Something heavy and unspoken hung in the air. She tilted her head back. He pulled her into him and helped her down on the floor until she was kneeling. He held her face and skimmed his penis over her eyes until he found her mouth. Then he thrust himself into her, rocking to his own rhythm until he came.

"Swallow it," he commanded. And she did.

Like a marionette, Sarna obeyed him. No man had ever taken her like this. Sarna loved playing with men, watching them lose their senses. When Jason made love to her, it was her inventiveness that created the magic. Beneath his handsome face was a man without cunning. No doubt that was why Oscar and Zach had hired him. It was also why he now bored her.

Sid Keller was a mystery. The puzzled expression made him terribly desirable. It wouldn't be easy to mold him. With one touch he had made her his instrument. She had actually swallowed his semen, something that had always disgusted her. He pulled her up and studied her perfect body, tracing a line from her neck to her stomach with the forefinger of his right hand. As he teased her breast, she felt nearly faint. He examined her with his hands as she waited for him to take her. He helped her up and cemented her against the wall, running his tongue along her neck and down her chest. Then he pulled her down and sucked her with his tongue.

Then without a word, he pulled away and stood up. He grabbed the robe that he had discarded earlier.

"What are you doing?" she murmured.

He looked her in the eye and spoke in a distanced tone: "I have an appointment. I have to run, Sarna."

Sarna was half-dressed, her nipples swollen, her body wet with desire. Suddenly she felt foolish, self-conscious. She stared at him, but Sid didn't invite any questions. She could see that he was struggling with himself. She had raced to the Ritz as fast as her Prada shoes could carry her because this escapade offered an escape from her misery. Maybe he had sized her up. Could he guess how much she coveted money? Yet, in his presence, the money didn't matter. It was Sid, not the Ritz, that captivated her. She didn't think this could ever be true, but she would desire him, even if he lived in a bungalow.

Sid stared at her. She had reached him. It would have been easy for him to take her again, but he did not. Her soft, supple skin was so ready.

"Get dressed, Sarna," he said.

She walked to him and held her right hand up to touch his face, but he clenched her fingers. Staring straight into his eyes, she flashed a fiery glance that revealed a range of emotions, but she said nothing.

All at once, she felt betrayed. No one could do this to her! She would have him and on her terms. He could not get away with this. She couldn't stop her heart from beating. She didn't want to leave, but staying would disclose how much this meant to her. She felt vulnerable.

Again the phone rang. This time Sid didn't answer it.

"Let me know when you'll be downtown again," he said, as he led to the door.

"Come to my house," she said, staring into his eyes.

"What about Jason?"

"He'll be gone all day tomorrow."

If he would drive all that way, she would know he had feelings for her.

Her hands grazed his legs, but Sid didn't respond.

"Sarna, Sarna, you do have a way about you. Ok, love, I'll drive out tomorrow."

He had said love. And he would come to her house! She would make lunch, and they would spend hours making love in the bedroom that had recently become a morgue. Sidney would bring it back to life. Sid stood at the entrance holding the door. The only touch was his finger on her chin as he lifted it and planted a quick kiss on her cheek.

As she drove north on the Drive, she ruminated over every innuendo of his touch, recalling each word, hoping that, in memory, the experience would become comprehensible. At home, she went into her bathroom to run hot water for a bath. Sid would come tomorrow! She had that to hold onto. Tomorrow was only hours away.

She placed one foot in the steamy water and then immersed herself in the huge tub, imagining what it would be like to have him in her house. Everything would be different tomorrow when he came to her.

Sarna creamed her face with expensive lotion and studied her body in the large mirror that hung over the sink. Her dark hair was pinned off her face. Her skin was flawless, her body firm from endless hours of training, her breasts like a teenager's. It was a silhouette that thrilled men. She concluded that Sid Keller's restraint had nothing to do with her. He had calls to make so he was distracted. That was all there was to that. The important thing was that he would be here tomorrow and if it took every last ounce of creativity, she would make Sid Keller hers.

***

Ken moved to Chicago without much fanfare. Remy tried to convince herself it was ok that he was taking his own apartment, but when she saw the place, a wave of sadness washed over her.

"Why can't you tell me what you will be doing here?"

"Remy, one of the reasons we can't live together is because I can't tell anyone about my work. I have been hired for a highly confidential job. No one will know I'm here or what I'm here for."

"But that's ridiculous. I'll know you're here. People will see you."

"I don't mean it like that. If someone knows me, they know me, but what I will be doing can't be discussed."

"Even with me?"

"Even with you."

The secrecy was more than Remy had bargained for. A wide corridor divided them—one she could not cross. It made no sense that Ken locked her out. Could she discuss her predicament with Lara? What was this dark secret he hid? She stared at him with hardness in her eyes, wondering if this mystery would drive an irreparable wedge between them.

"You can't even tell anyone about this conversation, Remy."

The gulf was widening. His orders struck a nerve, even made her angry. "You want me to keep your secret when I don't even know what the secret is."

"You'll have to trust me."

"Why? You can't trust me," she retorted.

"This has nothing to do with trusting you," he said, his hands on her arms.

Remy stood still for a long moment and looked at Ken's face in the soft light of the room. She didn't want to fight. A needless argument would only make things worse. But his restriction seemed ridiculous and impossible to live with.

"Why tell me anything, if you can't tell me something?"

"This is confidential. That's it. I have no control over the situation and I can't discuss it. You'll have to be satisfied with that."

"And if I can't?" she asked, her eyes now burning.

He said nothing. The tension between them made her sick to her stomach. She didn't want to plead. She wanted him to kiss her, tell her that he loved her and everything she needed to know. What she said was coming out all wrong. She hadn't expected a confrontation like this. A compelling mix of feelings clouded her judgment and she didn't know what to do with the contradiction.

What if they were married? Would this still be a secret? She didn't have the nerve to ask. It was perfectly clear that as long as Ken Baldwin had a hidden life, he couldn't get married.

She had fallen in love with someone whose life was a riddle. Suddenly he seemed like a stranger. She felt herself getting nauseous. She pushed her chair back and ran to the bathroom.

Ken didn't try to stop her.

She plopped on the stool in front of the vanity and put her face in her hands. She sat there like that until the feelings passed and when she finally let herself look into the mirror, she saw that the glow in her cheeks was gone. In its place was a shadow under her eyes and lines along her mouth. She touched her face. Her skin felt dry. She ran her fingers along her cheeks but her image made her feel as if she were looking in on someone else's life.

Everything had been perfect, so what had happened? Or did she invent that happiness because nothing had ever tested the relationship? Was she to blame for not asking questions? Or was she expecting too much now? She envisioned their relationship as an intensely meaningful one. Maybe she had created an imaginary bond. The one thing she knew was that she could not pretend it didn't matter when it mattered a lot. She needed to share her life and someone to share a life with her. With this secrecy hanging over them it would be impossible to go on dating. Remy's emotions showed on her face. She was not the kind of woman who could dissemble, pretending to be someone she was not. Living a lie would compromise her integrity.

Did this mean that they would have to break up? She brushed her hair away from her face and looked in the mirror, telling herself not to be stubborn. But this wasn't about obstinacy. It was about trust, even if Ken denied that. It was about having a genuine relationship.

When Ken told her that he would be in Chicago for some time, this was the last thing she had expected. Suddenly she felt helplessly confused, isolated like a child lost in a store who can't find her mother. Her balance was gone. She faced an uneven dilemma: to insist Ken tell her more or just ignore it. Remy was too curious, too straightforward to pretend something was right when it was not. What would happen now? Looking back on the past months, she saw that their conversations revolved around her problems, about events at the Exchange, but nothing about him. She hadn't pressed him about his job because he seemed to be off-handed about it. Until today, what he did at work hadn't mattered.

Now the very thing that didn't seem to matter was the most important part of their relationship, the very thing that could tip the balance of their love and turn them away from one another.

She emerged from the bathroom still not sure what she would do.

When she opened the door she heard the telephone ring. Ken was in the bedroom and she answered it.

"Is Ken there?"

"Who's calling?" she asked.

"Sidney Keller."

"Sid, this is Remy Masterman."

There was dead silence.

Then she said, "How do you know Ken? I mean, didn't you both just meet each other at Zach's party or I am imagining that?"

"Ken can explain. Tell him to call me. I can be reached at (312) 299-7395."

Then he hung up.

"Who was that?" asked Ken.

"Sid Keller," she said, her heart racing.

There was a long silence and then in a steady voice Ken said, "I have to call him back, Remy. This is why I need my privacy."

"That was the Sidney Keller I know from the pit. I recognized his voice." She reached for a chair and fell into it. "What's going on, Ken? Just what is going on?"

"I told you that I couldn't discuss anything and I mean it. If you care about me, you cannot say anything about this phone call and you must not ask any more questions." He came over to where she was sitting and looked directly into her eyes. "It's very important, Remy."

"Obviously, more important than me."

"That's not true. If you wouldn't have picked up the phone, you would not have known anything."

"What do I know? I don't even know what I know. But you do. You somehow know a man I work with whom I've introduced you to at a party and you both pretended not to know each other. What am I supposed to make of this? What the hell am I supposed to do?"

"Calm down, honey," he said, pulling her up and drawing her to him.

She could smell his body and she wanted to stay in his arms. But she could not. She looked up at him and then closed her eyes before she broke away.

When she picked up her purse and slammed the door behind her, Remy had no idea where she was going or what she would do now that it looked as if she had run into a brick wall.

***

Sarna Bramson studied her eyes in the lacquered mirror hanging over her bedroom dresser. Battles with insomnia had taken a toll. She didn't want her looks, which she valued as much as her checkbook, to slip away. Sarna had grown up poor. This was more painful. Watching her status and fortune dissolve cut the heart out of her. She pinched her cheek to bring color back. Sid consumed her thoughts. His presence had added such distress to her life that she couldn't concentrate. Here was a man who compelled her attention so much that he impinged on her will. In the meantime her world was collapsing. It wasn't fair, she thought, pacing through the hallways of the mansion which would soon be gone.

Sid had aroused her so that when she got home yesterday, she let Jason make love to her, in order to satisfy the insatiable desire Sid provoked. But as she drifted deep into her beguiling fantasy, Jason's mere appearance became an intrusion.

Now Sid was at the front gate. Sarna ran to the door, but when she opened it, Sid kissed her cheek and strolled in, his hands tucked into his pockets. He sauntered from room to room as if he owned the place, scrutinizing the furniture, as if he were taking inventory for a report. Without asking, he walked into the den as if Sarna were the last thing he cared about. Then suddenly he faced her, removed his glasses and tucked them into his shirt pocket.

"This is some palace," he said finally.

Sarna wasn't interested in what he thought of her house. She knew it was gorgeous. She also knew that it would not be hers very long. She wanted Sid Keller and she wanted him now.

"Come here," he commanded.

Happily, Sarna slid into his arms.

Sarna laid her head against him. Then she looked up, searching his face for some clue as to how he felt about being here, but he seemed intent on the setting rather than her.

Sid Keller was no stranger to money. Raised in a Detroit suburb, his father had owned a plastics plant that it was assumed Sid would take over when he graduated from Wharton. Unfortunately, high interest rates drove the business into the ground. Sid was never interested in going into business with his father and once his father paid off his creditors, there wasn't anything left. Sid joined the FBI because it was a chance to get out of Detroit. An economics background helped him land an assignment in the fraud division. Within a short time, he was investigating financial scandals on Wall Street.

He was determined never to marry. Watching his parents' marriage wither, he vowed never to end up like that.

Holly Rozner

Should a woman come into this life, he wouldn't say no, but he wasn't looking for love. Sex was fine, but a house and kids were not.

"Maybe you'd like something to eat?" Sarna asked when it was clear that Sid was not ready to make love. "I could put coffee on."

"Fine." Sid followed her into the kitchen. He stared out the window at the turquoise waters of Lake Michigan while Sarna fussed with the cups and saucers.

"The lake is intriguing," he said.

"It looks different every day. I fell in love with this view," she said. "Now the house is for sale."

"That must be tough."

He walked towards her while she fiddled with the coffee pot and he slipped his arm around her. He kissed her gently, his hands easily cupping her breasts.

"Let's go to the bedroom."

"Later." Without another word, he undid her shirt, loosened her bra and jostled her pants. She yanked at the zipper on his slacks, clutching him tight.

With his eyes riveted on hers, he probed his finger into her. His breath was warm. She pulled him close. Shivering under his touch, she closed her eyes. Finally he slid into her as she dug her fingers into his back.

Sarna had always manipulated men. But sex with Sid was different. She opened her eyes to search his face for a hint of feeling, but she saw cool detachment.

For a long while, they lay on the rug in the kitchen, the very rug Sarna had chosen to match the draperies. Finally, Sid pulled her up and led her to the sofa in the living room. His blue oxford shirt was opened to his waist. Sarna cuddled into him, hoping that a physical lock would be as emotional for him as it was for her. The balcony door was shut as the wind slammed against the pane. She held him tight.

"How big is this place?" he asked.

"Seven thousand square feet. We were supposed to add on more for a guest house."

"Before things changed."

"What do you know about me, Sid?"

"I don't pay much attention."

"Have you heard that Jason may not be able to come back to the floor."

"Oscar and Jason aren't getting along anymore?"

Sarna stared at him.

"How long have you been trading?"

"Less than a year."

"Then you see that Jason needs Oscar."

"Oscar's the broker. All trades come from him."

"It's more than that."

"He's been giving trades to Joey, the kid who used to clerk for Jason."

"The trades that went to Jason are going to Joey," she blurted out. "I don't know why it changed like that. All I know is that we can no longer afford this house and it has something to do with Oscar and Joey."

"You make it sound as if Oscar is supposed to give trades to Jason."

Sarna felt her stomach tighten. She didn't want to sound stupid, didn't want it to appear as if she didn't understand the system, but she didn't want to say too much more. She kissed Sid's chin, hoping to divert his attention.

"Why did you come on the floor, Sarna?"

Sarna pulled away to speak to him.

"I had a miscarriage. I don't know if I can have children."

"So you thought you could come to the pit and Oscar would give you trades?"

"Oscar doesn't pay attention to me, even when he comes here."

"He comes here? To this house?"

"Jason and he have some business together. I've seen papers but I don't understand it."

"Maybe trading statements."

"I don't think so."

Sarna felt Sid's body stiffen. Maybe she had said something she shouldn't have said. She certainly didn't want to get Jason into trouble, but she was so grateful to have Sid lingering with her, she would have given him the house if he had asked for it.

"It's legal stuff," she said, showing off what she knew.

Sidney stroked her hair.

"You're very smart, Sarna," he said, pulling up her chin with his index finger and peering into her eyes.

Sarna knew she was smart. But she loved hearing it. She also liked to prove how smart she was.

"Everything is piled up in our office."

"How often do they meet?"

"Oscar was here a few weeks ago. It's a tax thing. Everything goes to their lawyer, Ivan Bloch. He's due here next week." He followed her eyes to the library. "All I know is that every time Marcia shows the house, everything must be spotless, so I have to keep the papers looking neat."

"Let's make love," he said suddenly. He kissed her face, his hands skimming her body. This time, he took her with great force and she felt she had triumphed in some incremental way, that the distance separating them had diminished.

"Let's take a shower."

"I'm hungry," he said, sitting up.

"We can eat afterwards."

He followed her into the master suite, outfitted in gold and beige with shantung draperies that matched a custom spread. The four-poster bed in the center of the room was very high because of an extra thick mattress Sarna had ordered from a showroom in Palm Springs. On either side of the room were marble bathrooms with separate dressing rooms, Sarna's brimming with shoes and matching purses.

The dressing area centered on a red laminate vanity where Sarna's cosmetics were carefully displayed. In front of the dressing table was a plush velvet bench where she could sit to apply her make-up.

Sid didn't comment on the size of the suite or its opulence and Sarna assumed that someone who lived at the Ritz would not be impressed. All of these riches would soon be gone, unless she did something, so it made no difference if Sid was taken in by the grandeur. As soon as a buyer materialized, it would not be hers.

If only she could find a way to make the millions others made on the trading floor. Then she could keep this house. It was she who had located the house, who had selected each delicious item. Although she never admired women who were defined by the homes they lived in, once she lived here, she understood how much the house characterized her. Its majesty had made her consequential. Once it vanished, she would disappear from the social circle that acknowledged her for what it gave them.

She stepped into the glass-enclosed shower to turn on the sprays that spouted from three separate angles. The glass door was left open. Sid slid in. She arched her back and let him touch her. When he entered her, she held him and timed her climax to his. She felt a sense of calm as she confused their sexual rhythm with reciprocal feelings she assumed they held for each other.

Sid turned off the water and held her in his arms. When he finally pulled away, she reached over his shoulder and located an oversized towel.

"You're a goddamn goddess, Sarna," he said, straightening his hair.

She accepted his words as a sign that he had responded to her in a substantial way. Sarna watched him comb his hair trying to figure out some way to prolong his stay. She trembled to think that they might not see each other for days, or worse, that she might not know when they would see one another.

"I'll wait in the other room while you dress," he said.

"There is a TV in the study."

"I'll catch up on the markets."

Sarna sat down on the divan in her dressing room and rubbed her legs with vanilla lotion. Then she dabbed oil on her breasts and dotted perfume between her legs. She opened the door to her walk-in closet to try to figure out what to wear, what Sid might like. Surrounded by the most expensive wardrobe money could buy, she selected a pair of tight jeans and a white shirt because he didn't really seem to care about clothes.

Sid dashed into the library. He started searching the room. An unsealed envelope from Bloch and Levin, Attorneys at Law sat on the desk.

He perched on the desk facing the door. Then he pulled out the stapled sheets.

"This document between Jason Bramson and Oscar Doheney...The parties hereby agree to the dissolution of their partnership heretofore named B.O.D. Inc..."

There was no time to absorb this. Only that it was important. He had not expected to get this much information. He reached into his pocket for a tiny camera, photographed the pages and managed to put everything in order and reach the couch before Sarna entered the room. He looked straight at her, wishing he could touch her once again but feigning indifference. She sat down and laced her fingers into his, hoping to feel him inside her one more time, but she could see from the expression on his face that he had locked her out.

He kissed her gently on the nose.

"I better scoot," he said.

"What about lunch?"

"You were lunch, doll."

"You said you were hungry."

"It's nearly 1:30."

"When will I see you?" she pleaded, her voice faltering.

"I'll be in touch."

He pulled away. She was perfumed and ready for him. Her gaze pleaded for him to stay. She touched him arm and placed his hand on her breast.

"I'll call you later," he said, pulling away and grabbing his jacket. Then he slammed the door behind him without looking back.

Sarna Bramson stood alone in the quiet of the huge house. She was shaking. This feeling of dependence was unfamiliar and unsettling. It was not like her to lose control. She ran to the window and watched Sid get into his car.

Sid didn't look up. Nor did he wave. The red Porsche spun out of the driveway and down the Ravines.

Sarna went into the kitchen and turned off the coffee.

Sid pulled down the visor and grabbed his phone. As he sped back to the city, Sid pressed an automatic button that dialed its only pre-programmed number.

Then he waited for Ken Baldwin to answer.

chapter 25

Monday

LIKE THE WEATHER, the markets were frozen. The cold temperature kept people home and the illiquid market did not invite much trading. Quiet markets meant traders took long breaks, so the Club was bustling with traders who were afraid to trade. Reeling from her conversation with Ken, Remy took refuge in the jam-packed restaurant.

She knew Ken loved her. Was she making a big deal about nothing? This time even Lara couldn't provide an answer.

"Many men with a career in government or in the army can't talk to their wives about their job," Lara said.

"But he's not in the army. It feels clandestine," Remy said.

"Can't you treat it as if he worked for the CIA or the FBI."

"Absolutely not. Maybe if he told me from the start, I would have expected this restriction. It makes me feel insignificant as if I were a mistress."

"Is it worth breaking up?"

"I don't know. I feel so isolated. Imagine if I told you that I couldn't talk about my work?"

Any reasonable person would concede Remy was right. The circumstances had made her so shaky she could neither sleep nor eat. Her back ached. Her head was pounding. The dreary weather added to her internal torment.

Instead of finding a peaceful spot for coffee, there were no tables at all. Remy decided to go across the street when she heard someone calling her name. Jason Bramson was waving to her.

"Sit down, Remy. I need company," he said, standing to greet her.

She took the chair across from him.

"Are you OK?"

"Does it show?"

"Did you have an error trading?"

"Not that simple. Some personal stuff. I haven't been trading that much."

"Can I help?"

"It's about a guy."

"And?"

Remy launched into the story about Ken and how his secret was tearing them apart.

"Sometimes a fellow needs space."

Naturally Jason wouldn't understand. He was a guy and guys need breathing room women don't crave.

"Doesn't Sarna know what you do?"

Jason thought about that and then replied sadly. "She knows too much."

"That's marriage," Remy said. "That's part of the deal."

"Being married doesn't mean that every detail has to be disclosed."

"I'm not talking about every single detail."

Remy felt misunderstood and even more confused. It was difficult to get this straight in her own mind. Trying to clarify it and not being able to talk about it made it worse. Ken had specifically forbidden her to discuss this with anyone. And here she was telling Jason.

But that was the point. Ken had asked her to do something unnatural. He had no right to demand that she not share her feelings with other people. Had she betrayed Ken? She didn't even know enough facts to betray him. It came down to trust. If Ken loved her, this would not be happening.

"Let's not talk about me anymore, Jason. Talk about something else."

"Order something, Remy."

"I'm not hungry, "she said. "Just coffee, please," she told the waiter as he brought Jason his food. He plunged into a cheeseburger while Remy sank into her chair.

"I feel guilty eating like this."

"I'm really not hungry. I wouldn't be shy if I were. Is Sarna still trading?"

Jason put down his sandwich. "Not if I can help it. I can't lose a nickel."

"I'm sorry."

"You've heard?" he asked, reading her face.

"Some things."

"It's true."

Jason pushed his food away. "One thing I've learned is that you have to acquire a skill and stick to it. I didn't do that. Short cuts work for a while and then they dry up and you've got nothing. I grew up hearing my father brag about his connections, so I looked for my own. But he never told me what to do when the connections fail."

Jason was like a rubber band ready to snap. Watching him made Remy nervous.

"You know how to trade, Jason."

"I've never traded in small quantities. I've never needed to. I always had an advantage. I was a real big shot. Now I can't figure out how to make a living."

"Do you have any positions on now?"

"Of course. And my positions are turning into losers."

Here was the legend. Remy had watched Jason trade, always taking on huge risk but she had no idea how he was able to do that. Did all big traders have connections like him? Was this a profession or just a guessing game unless you were inside someone's pocket? Did her father know this? How could he have lived with that?

"Can't you cut back?"

"I don't know how."

"That is ridiculous. Just cut down your size."

Remy saw him glance at the screen and wince.

"Are you long now?"

She studied it too.

"Do you have a stop in?"

"I was just stopped out."

"You lost more money?"

"Right on."

"How much?"

"A hundred."

"A hundred thousand dollars?"

That was more than she made in a year, and he had lost it in an hour. Of course he would go bankrupt.

"You must stop, Jason."

"I start with one and end up with a thousand. It happens all the time."

"I don't get it."

"It's a very long story, Remy. It would bore you."

It was none of her business. Nor could she help him. She could barely help herself. Her mind drifted to Ken and the paradox of their dispute. Yesterday they were a perfect couple. Today, the fantasy was up in flames. The past had dissolved. She was hanging on for dear life.

"I better go, "she said standing up. "I hope things work out for you, Jason. I really do. You were the first guy to show me the ropes. It wouldn't be fair for you to be shut out."

She said goodbye and rushed through the hallway reworking the dialogue with Ken, wracking her brains to try to put the pieces of the puzzle together. Jason's troubles faded into the background as she concentrated on figuring what Sid Keller had to do with Ken.

That night as Remy sat home alone, she went over everything in her mind and tried to guess what her father would have advised. He was always so logical. It was evident that he had to know about Zach and Oscar, and looked the other way. Would he tell her to ignore what she was suspecting now? The telephone near her bed stand rang, but she did not answer. It must be Ken. Nothing could change her feelings and nothing would alter his position. They were locked in an impossible conflict. Once trust is shattered, what's next? She was jittery, nearly panicked. Maybe she was being too headstrong. Ken had locked her out but she still loved him.

On the fifth ring she picked up, but there was silence. She stood still staring at the telephone, waiting for it to ring again. But it did not. She struggled with her desire to talk to Ken and her determination not to compromise herself. She paced back and forth, sat on the chair in front of her desk, did a load of laundry and drank a glass of Diet Coke. Eventually she reached for the phone. She would tell Ken she loved him. They would both be able to see how ridiculous it was to argue like this.

As she waited for an answer, she knew that the slightest jar would undo her. Everything that seemed so perfect just seventy-two hours ago had evaporated as a gaping chasm cut her dreams short.

She didn't want to endure a long conversation that might end badly. When Ken didn't answer, Remy decided to go to sleep. Tomorrow he would explain everything. As she got ready for bed, she convinced herself that he would have to tell her his secret. And when he did, everything would be all right again.

chapter 26

"Come over here, baby," Joey commanded.

Joey carried a pina colada in one hand and a bamboo hat in the other. He sat nude on his verandah, waiting for Rosa to get out of the shower. The sun in St. Lucia was bright and the view overlooking the Bay spectacular. He could hear the waves hitting the shore and his thoughts drifted to last night when the two of them had spent hours making love.

Rosa reappeared wrapped in a terry-cloth towel, sat down next to him, her dark breasts dangling. He put his drink down and as he bent over her, his mouth grazed the skin around her nipples.

"Joey, you drive me crazy."

"I am crazy, baby."

"We're so lucky, Joey. Look at this life we are living."

"I love you, Rosie. I love you." He licked the skin between her breasts and then cupped her, his finger finding the spot that made her writhe.

"Give me more, Joey."

"You are such a doll."

"And you are my Joey," she cooed, covering him with her mouth.

Holly Rozner

He came again, the third time that morning, his cock sore from burrowing into her. Then she lay on top of him, the sun on her back, his fingers on her hips.

"Let's stay here. Let's just fuck our brains out in the sun without a care in the world."

"And not make any more money?" she asked.

The money. Ah, the money. The money was rolling in and Joey and Rosa had set a wedding date. They would be married in the Rosewood Hall on June 14 in front of a huge crowd. They didn't want an intimate wedding. They wanted the whole shebang with liquor flowing all night. Rosa had picked out a dress at SAKS as she now called it. The same lady who had helped her dress for Zach's party helped locate a wedding gown, by a woman named Vera Wang. The name was odd, and Rosa wondered if this Wang was an American or an Asian. It was a simple style and made her look taller than she was. A staggering $5,000. But Joey said he could make that in a week and sometimes in a day.

The money was rolling in and soon they would be able to buy the house they had been eyeing—the one that was more than ten times what her cousin Bobby had paid for his house. The money was rolling in and it was fun to shop when any price was OK, because with money, you could buy what you wanted. All her life Rosa dreaded going into a store because that meant that she had to leave things she drooled over and get something practical she didn't really want. Her mother said " that was life." That you had to learn to compromise. She had a wardrobe she hated because none of the things she wanted were affordable.

"That is just how it goes," her mother said.

But her mother was wrong. Because when the money was rolling in, life really was different. You could buy what you liked and stroll in and out of stores grabbing designer

Trade Secrets

dresses and handbags, looking like the women in fashion magazines.

Never to be poor again. Oh, please G-D, never let me be poor again, she prayed while Joey's sticky semen floated inside of her.

She pressed her body against Joey's. It wasn't because of the money that she loved him. She had fallen for Joey Fortunato when he was a poor schlep. But the money made him sooooooooo sexy. The money made her different and it made Joey different and here they were in St. Lucia, three thousand miles away from Chicago where it was freezing and lying naked on a verandah, making love in the sunlight and it was so sublime, it didn't even seem real. And what could possibly happen to ever bring them back to the life they had left far, far behind? Nothing. Not as long as the money kept rolling in. With the money came power and with the power, cocky optimism: a glimpse into another day and another week with money rippling from the money pit. That's what Rosa and Joey called the pit. It wasn't just a pit anymore; it was a money pit.

Joey seemed a little sexier now. He walked different. He smelled different. He spoke different. They were different. Tied to each other and to the dough. The cash and what it could buy. The money had made a difference. Her mother was wrong. Dead wrong. Money talked. It talked loud and clear, getting them corner tables in restaurants and a suite in the hotel, front row tickets to the Bulls and first-class seats to St. Lucia.

Don't kid yourself, she thought, dreamily eyeing the three-karat stone on her left hand. Money was a second language, but it was the only one that mattered if you didn't have it.

***

Holly Rozner

Remy spent most of the night flinging off her duvet, pulling the pillows and then hurling them onto the floor, trying to diminish the panic that seized her. Sleep she needed eluded her. Why hadn't Ken answered his phone? At 6:30 when the sun filtered through the window, she got out of bed, poured herself some orange juice and a hot cup of black coffee. As the city awakened, she decided to face this head on.

"Did I wake you?" she asked when Ken answered.

"Remy, I tried to reach you last night."

" Ken, I must know what's going on."

"I miss you," he said.

"I miss you, too" She tried to read the tone in his voice. "This is just a terrible misunderstanding."

"But I can't budge."

Her heart sank. She was grateful there was a chair nearby. She sat down. "I don't understand. You make this sound like some mystery. Why are you doing this?"

"I told you that I can't explain it. You simply need to trust me. No questions. Believe me, Remy, I'm not doing anything wrong, but there are other people involved and I'm accountable to them."

"Spoken like a true lawyer," she retorted.

"None of this has anything to do with us."

But Remy felt that it was all about them and the distance that had come between them. They weren't a couple anymore. The bond between them was dangerously frayed.

"Ken. I don't get any of this. And I don't see how you aren't able to see my position. You expect to cut out everything from your life that is about your work. You claim you can't discuss it and you expect me to accept it."

"I do expect that."

"I don't know any woman in the world who would buy into this. You know how much I need to be involved in things. What made us so special together was that we could be partners. This is a one-way decision you have made, setting up impossible terms and not even trying to compromise."

"Remy, stop doing this. You and I are special together. Don't spoil that."

"You are telling me not to spoil it. Don't you think you've got the wrong person spoiling the wrong thing here? All I'm asking for is equal time and all you give me is bullshit about how important your work is. Well, I don't seem to fit into your little scheme. This is all about what's missing between us. This is about you seeing us a certain way and about me seeing us a different way."

"What can I say?"

"Tell me what you're doing!"

"Remy, I can't."

She began to cry. "I've shared everything with you. I've told you about the people I work with because I thought you were interested in what I do. I've even told you my biggest secret—why I came to this Exchange in the first place. I've told you about my father. You know what that means to me."

There was a long, long silence. So long that it seemed as if Ken wasn't even on the line anymore.

"Remy. I love you."

"That doesn't help."

There was another punctuated silence and then Ken said slowly, "I can't say anything else right now."

She didn't feel the phone drop but she heard the click, not realizing that she had hung it up. Then she pulled the blanket over her head and sobbed quietly until exhaustion overcame her and she fell asleep.

chapter 27

SID DIDN'T NOTICE the white-capped trees or magnificent mansions on either side of Sheridan. Holding the phone to his ear, he spoke rapidly to Ken Baldwin.

Sarna stayed in her house looking out the window. Sid's touch had distracted her so that the problems she and Jason faced faded temporarily into the background. The real-estate agent left a message on the answering machine about an offer that had to be accepted by 5:00. Sarna had no interest in these negotiations. Sex was on her mind. Her huge eyes outlined the marquis home she would have to relinquish. Bile rose in her throat at the thought of losing it.

She kept on the jeans she had worn with Sid. Jason would never notice anything about her. His oblivion drove her mad. Surely Oscar and Zachary had discovered this characteristic and knew how easily he could be pushed aside to make room for Joey. Sarna hadn't identified Jason's passivity until years after they married. Banking on the money he made trading, Sarna invented him as she wanted him to be. Now she would have to be smart enough for both of them. She must learn to trade. None of those punks in the pit were smarter than she. If Remy could do it, so could she.

Holly Rozner

    The minute hand on the clock barely moved. She considered climbing into bed, pretending that it would be Sid's hand, not hers, that could satisfy her, but it was getting late and she hadn't thought about dinner. She would prepare a candlelight dinner, make a big fuss, flowers and all. Later, she might even fool around with Jason, making believe he was Sid.

    At a quarter to six, Jason came in through the mudroom. Sarna greeted him, escorted him into the library and snuggled on the armchair. Perfunctorily she asked about his day. He answered her questions, omitting his lunch with Remy, concealing any feelings she may have stirred. Remy on the other side of the small table! Would his life be different if she were in it? He focused on Sarna's face, those delicate features that had enchanted him. No doubt that she would leave him. The life he had once taken for granted had been surrendered in the pits. Ambition had contaminated his honor, mutilated his soul. Any particle of morality his father had taught him had been forfeited to Oscar and Zach. He had misused his wealth, choreographing schemes to make more. He had submitted to Sarna's sexual tricks instead of searching for a woman like Remy, and he had lost the battle for his own integrity.

    Remy never would have settled for him. He wondered what kind of a guy Baldwin was. He had better cherish her, or someone else will grab her, Jason thought as he watched Sarna hug a pillow that had set them back a thousand dollars. She sensed his distraction and moved to the sofa, rubbing her toes on his slacks. Her touch still moved him but there was no passion. In a rote, disinterested manner, he responded to her. She took off her shirt. The vision of her pink breasts, those breasts that had always inflamed him, failed to ignite him. He took her mechanically, imagining she was Remy. When Sarna clutched her legs around his torso, he felt a momentary tinge of authentic pleasure, only to realize that it was his imagination triggering desire, rather than the woman he rode.

Afterwards they lay together in silence, neither prepared to fill the air with questions they needed to ask. What would happen once this house was sold? Where would they live? Hoping to avoid the dreadful reality beating down upon their once- perfect lives, Sarna rolled onto her side. Things were coming apart and neither had the energy to fight it.

Silently Jason left the room to take a long steam in the huge bathroom he called his own. Bit by bit his life was disintegrating. Standing in front of the mirror, combing his curly hair, he looked for an answer. The reflection gave no clues. The legend was gone. In the privacy of his own dressing area where he could shave, shifting between the steam and sauna, occasionally dipping into the Jacuzzi before slipping into the indoor pool near the gymnasium, he remembered when, merely a year ago, they systematically studied the blueprints to ease from the workout area to the pool and onto the beach without having to step outside. Tonight the snow had stopped, but the frigid temperatures locked the air. It felt marvelous to be inside in such luxury, steeped in the hot liquid of a bubbling tub, welcomed then by crisp, clean Pratesi linens. How carefully these luxuries had been chosen, now dissolving into thin air.

Wordlessly Sarna had slipped under the blanket. When Jason emerged from the bathroom, he took his place next to her. She said nothing, her head tilted back on the pillow, shuffling through a recent copy of Vogue. Jason flipped on the radio, welcoming the sound of soft jazz that he hoped could calm him. He envied those who could find solace in a bottle of scotch. Occasionally a touch of marijuana would do the trick, but he had to go to work tomorrow. If only there were some pill that would put him to sleep for several days so that he could wake up with space between this life and another, the distance offering a possible bridge from his turmoil.

Sarna was wrapped in a short pink silk negligee paging through the articles about New York's most fashionable designers, eyeing items she could no longer buy. Determined not to let this glorious lifestyle slip out of her hands, she crinkled the paper while Jason drifted into his own reverie, half-sleeping as he recalled his childhood and that time in his life when he wasn't yet aware of the toll his father's demands would take.

Then as if a storm had leveled the house, there was a startling clamor at the front door.

Sarna jumped out of bed. An extensive alarm system surrounded the property. No one could penetrate it without being buzzed in. Who could it be? Jason's father? Her mother? Even they would have to go through a security system. Could she have forgotten to turn the mechanism on? Could it be a burglar?

Burglars don't ring doorbells, she reminded herself. She shook Jason and threw on a robe that hung inside the bedroom door. Jason grabbed a pair of slacks and followed Sarna through the long hallway down the stairs to the foyer.

The bell rang again.

Sarna spoke through the intercom.

"Who is it?"

"The FBI. Open up."

She looked at Jason, he at her. Gazing at the space in front of them, neither knew what to do.

Responding to the threat of authority, Sarna swung open the door.

Before her stood two strange men. One was short and wore a blue nylon jacket and a heavy scarf around his neck.

The other wore a lined raincoat with a brown hat. Without an introduction, they each flashed an identification card. She pulled it away from the short man.

"What do you want?"

The tall man glanced at Jason.

"Are you Jason Bramson?"

"What is this about?" asked Jason.

"Are you Jason Bramson?"

"I'm calling my lawyer," Jason retorted.

"You might prefer to talk to us first."

Sarna began to tremble. "Jason, talk to him. Do what he wants."

"Not without a lawyer."

"You don't need a lawyer right now, Jason," the short one said.

" We have some preliminary questions to ask you."

"Am I under arrest?"

"Not yet."

Jason looked from one to the other. Sarna jumped into his arms.

"We need cooperation, Mr. Bramson. You may be able to save yourself."

He stared at them. What was he to do? If he said the wrong thing, he could get himself into a worse jam. What did they want?

"You're standing in my house," he said finally. "I have a right to know what you are doing here."

"Can we sit down?" asked the short one.

"Yes," Sarna said, offering them space to enter.

The short man strode past them and looked around, soaking in the opulence. Sarna could read his cash-register eyes.

"Would you like something to drink?" she offered.

"For Christ's sake, Sarna," Jason screamed. "It's nearly midnight. They come barging in here and you are offering a drink."

"If you have coffee, I'll take some," the tall man said.

So this would take a while, Jason surmised, still not sure if he should call his father, or Oscar, or his lawyer, Ivan Bloch.

"What is this about?" he asked calmly enough to give Sarna a chance to release her grasp on him. Off she went to make coffee.

"Get me a robe," he called to her.

RICO charges will be leveled against you if you don't cooperate."

"What is that?"

"The right to seize your property."

"For what?"

"Conspiring to fix trades."

Where was Oscar? Why didn't they go after him? Didn't they know who was guilty? What did they know? Jason's head swelled with questions.

"I did not," he said firmly.

"Look buddy," said the short man with his hands stuffed into his pockets. "Let me make this easy on you. Then you can decide what you want to do. Let's sit down, huh?"

Jason led them through the foyer into the library that smelled of English leather.

The short one sat behind the leather desk, while the tall one took a seat in a plaid chair that he guessed was from Great Britain.

"We know that you've been complicit with Oscar Doheney. We also know that Joey Fortunato has stepped into your shoes. Rest assured, your future is in jail if you don't talk turkey."

Jason could feel his throat close. He coughed nervously, something he did when he couldn't think of something to say.

"If I cooperate?"

He didn't really know if that was an admission. He had heard his father warn him time again never to talk to anyone without a lawyer. This seemed like one of those times when you had to think on your feet.

"I made instant decaf," Sarna said when she reappeared. She had heard Jason utter the word immunity as she entered the room, but she didn't know what that meant or what the implications would be.

"What is immunity?"

"Immunity protects people from prosecution. It gives protection to someone who cooperates with the government in bringing charges against other people." The tall man spoke clearly to make a point.

"You need to do what he asks," she urged. In fact Sarna still had no idea exactly Jason did on the trading floor or how he had made so much money. It looked like genius to her, but like many other wives of successful traders, she had not been privy to the innuendo of pit trading, did not understand what a bagman was or that illegal trades were customary. Even though she had spent some time in the pit, she had not yet discovered the layers that had allowed Jason to make all that money.

"Shut up, Sarna." She curled up on the couch like a wounded kitten.

Jason walked around the room touching his possessions. *RICO* would confiscate everything. He wondered if the FBI had a right to do something like this. It was the middle of the night. But his father had warned him that the government could do whatever it wanted to do and strangle helpless people. Irwin Bramson liked to tell the story of a woman who owned a trucking company who was forced to give fictitious testimony in court for fear of losing her license. His father repeated these stories to demonstrate that you can't buck the government. Its pockets are deep enough to break you, he warned.

Jason felt paralyzed. He hadn't admitted to anything. Surely his silence was a dead giveaway. They took him by surprise. And at this hour of the night. Oh, God, how would this end?

His eyes smarted as if he were blinded by smoke. He rubbed them with the palm of his hands. The room was spinning. He fell into a chair, his head down. Sarna put her arms around him. With as much dignity as she could muster, she turned to the two men.

"You must leave now."

"We can't do that, ma'am," said the short man.

"Can't you see he's not feeling well?"

"I'm sure he's not feeling well," the short man said.

Sarna tried to hold back the tears streaking her face. These bastards! She wiped her cheeks with a Kleenex pulled from the pocket of her robe. This was not how she wanted to be seen. Not in public. But she was not in public. She was in her library, the one she had furnished article by article, following the interior designer in and out of antique shops trying to get it just right. And now, nothing was right. Nothing was even the slightest bit right.

Then as if another person had entered the room, Sarna straightened herself up and took charge. "I insist that you leave us alone to talk," she said. "This is not fair. You barged into my house making wild accusations and haven't given us a chance to think. Even if you think my husband is guilty and I know he is not, you have not given him a chance to defend himself. If we go to court, I will report you." She sneered at the short man who eyed his companion with a wary look.

"Sarna, you need to stop," Jason said.

"I will not stop. This is the United States of America," she announced. "These things just don't happen. We have rights. My husband has a right to consult an attorney. You cannot say another word, Jason. These men are dangerous."

She didn't know where her energy was coming from or how she had found the words, but what was happening just didn't make any sense. She would figure this out. She just needed time.

"Without a statement, we will have to arrest your husband."

She looked the other way as if the walls had an answer for her.

"You cannot do that without him talking to his lawyer."

"He has the right to talk to his lawyer, but then the deal is off."

"What do you mean?"

"We don't have to make a deal here, Mrs. Bramson. It's up to you and your husband. You can fight, but we will win. If you want to talk to us, we can work together and mitigate the punishment your husband is facing."

Were they bluffing? What should she do? Who could guarantee that they would keep a deal?

"My husband will talk to his lawyer."

"From jail, lady."

He had her, pinned against the wall like a dead ant.

She began to gag. Jason caught her arm. But the short man had his arm and turned him away. Sarna collapsed onto the chair. She wasn't sure when she awoke the next morning if she had actually seen them handcuff Jason or if she had imagined the whole thing. But she did know one thing.

Holly Rozner

Nothing had ever matched the terror that gripped her.

***

Following an afternoon shower that sprinkled St. Lucia with a soft covering of moisture, Rosa and Joey got ready to take a spin on a catamaran that circled the bay at dusk. It was scheduled to leave from the dock of their hotel nestled between the Pinions and would travel for two hours into the sunset while gallons of rum drinks were passed out to the thirsty travelers. Then they would go to the top of a mountain where they were promised a gourmet Creole dinner.

While Joey shaved, Rosa flipped on the international news. How amazing to be in such a remote part of the world, miles away from Chicago and still stay in touch with events in the US. She didn't understand globalization when Joey talked about it in terms of the stock market, but as she lay with the warm breeze wafting into their stucco room and watched news of the blustery weather still covering the Midwest, she saw how small the world had become. Technology made it impossible to keep secrets. No one could escape being seen.

"It is marvelous, this new technology," she chirped last night to some New Yorkers they had met on the beach. "We're like one big family."

And though they agreed by nodding their heads, Rosa knew she was uninformed when she started a discussion of world events or modern trends. Politics and economics were out of her league. She had learned how to dress more appropriately since Joey was in the green, but she knew, especially when she was with total strangers, that her knowledge was severely limited. She vowed that when they got married, she would take classes to catch up. She didn't think of herself as stupid, just uninformed. And if she could study current events, maybe she would never be caught off-guard when someone brought up an unfamiliar subject.

She heard the shower click on and at the very moment that Joey actually stepped into it, she caught a story that stunned her. The setting was Chicago and through the slush melting on the street, she saw cameras in front of the Exchange. It was something about the FBI and the Exchange and a bunch of traders that had been caught doing something.

She had been polishing her fingernails when the story began and she missed the gist of it. But she was pretty sure she had seen a photo of Jason Bramson flashed on the screen.

She would feel dumb repeating half a story. It had nothing to do with the two of them, she reasoned. News about the markets, no doubt. "Silly information" Joey would say, letting her in on the real truth that the reporters knew nothing anyway. Anyone who had to depend on television for insight into the market was a real jerk, he told her. Joey knew so much. And he was making a bundle. She finished off her manicure with a coat of quick-dry.

To get away from what she clearly didn't want to understand, she flipped the channel to the movie station where one of her all time favorites was being shown. *A Letter to Three Wives*, with Ann Southern and Jeanne Crain. She had seen the film dozens of times and could never remember whose husband had pulled out and who had written the letter. So instead of concentrating on what was current and possibly painful, she curled up to watch the movie one more time. Maybe next time she would remember who the adulterer was. In a minute Joey would be done in the bathroom and she could have it to herself to get dolled up for their night out. Chicago was a million miles away. And she reasoned that if anything were wrong, there was nothing Joey could do. Certainly not from here. Certainly not tonight.

chapter 28

ALTHOUGH THE SHADES in Zachary's office were wide open, the residue of ice on the windows clouded his view of the lake. This view, his life were being demolished.

Sitting behind his desk, Zach played with the paperweight that had been presented to him at last month's party. Configured from dollar bills, INDEX engraved in the center, the globe represented the universe over which he had presided. Now it was a mere sculpture, the symbol of a distant past, like Hermes perched on its top. He placed it back on the stand and nervously tapped his keyboard.

"Stop doing that, Zach. I can't stand the noise," bellowed Oscar from his chair on the other side of the desk. Oscar had slipped into Zach's office when news of the break-in was announced on the radio. He had heard only one sentence, enough to make him nearly puke on the scrambled eggs he had been eating.

"Who's holding your deck?" Zach asked.

"I gave it to one of the guys. I had to get off the floor. God knows who's swarming around."

"Damn it, Oscar! We cannot cave. Cannot." Zach's face was red, his brow damp with sweat. "I was afraid of something like this. I've always thought that someone might go to the Feds. But I can't actually believe they did. We had such a setup. How did they get in?"

"Maybe an insider."

"Who? Who?" Zach barked. "Tell me who and I'll twist him into a pretzel."

"Dunno." Oscar slumped into the chair, his hands on his head, his legs stretched out.

Zach rang for his secretary. "Get me the late edition of the newspapers. Both papers. Anything you can get your hands on."

"What are we going to do?" Oscar asked after Zach had clicked off the intercom.

"Nothing yet. All we know is that Jason has been arrested. We need to talk to him."

"Did you call Ivan?"

"I left a message."

"Maybe he's with Jason."

"No one else can handle this. Ivan put the goddamn plan together. And he's taken a pretty good cut over the years. He'll have to protect us."

"Try him again."

Zach pushed the auto-dial button but Ivan Bloch was still out of the office. He would return the call the minute he got back, the secretary promised. Zach began to shake. He needed Ivan Bloch the way a kid needs his mother after a fistfight. He clenched his knuckles as if he could will Ivan into his office. Ivan Bloch was his lawyer and confidante, the one who had thought of using a bagman to steal good trades, the one who helped hide the shadowy network that kept Zach's machine in motion. Zach was the monarch, the one everyone saw, but Ivan was never more than a phone call away.

Only Zach knew how much he owed his career to Ivan. He and Harry Saks met Ivan when they came to Chicago.

Ivan was addicted to betting: horses, roulette, the Stocks, but nothing captured his attention like the pits. He loved them the way a man loves a mistress, desiring her even more when they are apart, risking his reputation for another touch. As a trader he lost a fortune, calling the change in direction too early, identifying the end of a bull market months before it fell and getting whipsawed as it moved against him. He bet too much and eventually lost more than he made, so he escaped to law, using his experience as an IRS agent to help clients figure out how far they could push the system. The design was perfect until Harry Saks figured out what was happening and refused to endorse the lawless schemes Ivan devised. The telephone buzzed. Zach put Ivan on speakerphone.

"I'm returning your call."

"What's going on?"

"Meet me for dinner. "

Zach understood. His line could be tapped.

"My house. 6:00." Zach hung up and stared at Oscar. "Where's Fortunato?"

"Somewhere in the Caribbean."

"When does he get home?"

"The day after tomorrow."

"No more trades with him, Oscar. Not a one."

"You can't just cut him off."

"You want to go to jail, Oscar, or do you want to feed that kid?"

Oscar held his head. The pipeline was shutting down. Poor Joey. The schmuck was just getting started and POW, the ship sinks.

"No bagman?"

"You got it, Doheney. Just fill the paper, nice and easy. You hear me?" Zach shook his finger. Then he ran his hand along his scruffy face.

Holly Rozner

Oscar felt a deepening sense of horror. No bagman, NO MORE MONEY. The Exchange paid two bucks to fill an order. There would always be out-trades, and two bucks an order would never offset the losses. You could never break even without someone in your pocket.

The curtain had fallen. Out front was an empty house. All these years he had wondered how it would end, but he never dreamed it would be such an abrupt finale. They were such tricksters, had been so impervious. Oscar wiped his eyelids. He hadn't cried since he was a kid when a car hit his brother on the front lawn. He felt like crying now. If Bramson started to blab, they'd all be in the can. Unless he could think of some way to shift the burden away from himself.

Oscar placed the palm of his hands on his forehead and made a circular motion to try to erase his thoughts. He had no more ideas. Only fear. Unable to stop trembling, he felt like a kid afraid to tell his mother that he had wet his bed. No one knew the truth because he hid it from the world with his bravado, but the underside of Oscar Doheney was mere putty. He took orders and bowed to Zach's power because he had found the American Dream. Now the Feds made it impossible to have an accomplice and Oscar knew there was no way to operate alone.

He studied Zach. Would he cave? Would Ivan protect them? What if Ivan had to choose? Ivan owed Zach. Oscar stood up and thought about this. Maybe he would have to cooperate to get protection. He didn't know how to do that. He had seen it done on T.V., but that was make-believe. He had no script. If he asked Ivan, Ivan would tell Zach and he'd be chopped liver.

He could have cried, all right. Right there in Zach's office.

Trade Secrets

They had the whole thing so neatly sewn up. Their world was impenetrable. Now he could see it was nothing but a glass house. A single well-placed BB gun could implode the whole scheme and he'd be crushed in the rubble.

Oscar arched his brows. An involuntary smirk wiped over his face as he realized that there might still be a trade left. Maybe it didn't have to be over. At least not for him. If he could turn the tables, maybe he didn't have to be buried alive.

Perhaps when the ship went down, the Feds would need someone to squeal and he was in the most perfect position. Oscar thought about that as he began pacing around the room. It had never occurred to him that he could be a star witness, the only witness who knew the whole thing and hadn't actually written the original script. He was an actor in this drama, after all, and actors were not responsible when the show closed, were they? The producers took the hit, and Zach was the executive producer.

chapter 29

REMY CURLED UP on her suede sofa watching television. The image on the screen flashed by so fast it would have been hard to identify the subject had she not already heard the story. In living color and handcuffed, Jason Bramson was being pushed into a car by an FBI agent. The short sequence in front of the Federal Building was followed by an elaborate interview with someone who was introduced as the key person in the government's investigation into trading infractions at the Chicago exchanges. Remy's eyes widened as she focused on Ken Baldwin. Poised behind the microphone, wearing a khaki raincoat, his eyes showed signs of exhaustion. Ken oozed a stoic elegance as he stared directly into the camera explaining in simple terms that, yes, the investigation had brought him to Chicago, but no, he would not be a witness during the trial. "That job had been reserved for another man who had served as a mole during a twelve month period in which agents infiltrated the floor of three Chicago Exchanges. By trading in the pits and befriending the traders, Sid Keller had obtained hands-on information," Ken explained to the interviewer.

The morning paper repeated the same news. The lead article explained that the FBI was so convincing in penetrating the social scene at the Exchange that certain agents had been invited to dinner parties and even accompanied traders to baseball games with their families. The papers explained that the blitz had been swift because of such personal contact. The idea, Baldwin explained in the article, was his invention. Once hired to bring the criminals to their knees, he knew it would be easier if they had inside access.

"These guys held a stacked deck," he said solemnly.

"How did you get your leads?" the interviewer asked.

"Rumors. Speculation. What I suspected was affirmed from various sources over a period of time."

"Why were you brought in?"

"The Justice Department decided that the investigation would go more smoothly if the investigators weren't from Chicago, so we wouldn't be recognized."

"Did you go into the pit?"

"No. I directed traffic. I did most of my work from New York. I moved to Chicago recently and kept a low profile."

Remy was dazed. When the news broke, she called Lara, but she was in court and couldn't be reached. There was no one else to talk to. To be in love with the man who conceived this blueprint left her breathless. Her eyes stayed on the screen as her temper grew.

Had she missed a clue? Had Ken ever disclosed what he was actually doing? Had she been stupid? Overlooked the obvious because she loved him?

How much did Ken learn from her? Did she provide evidence that was then used by the government? Had she told him too much about her father?

The phone rang. She didn't answer. If it were Lara, she would leave a message. Remy waited until the clanging stopped.

When the silence finally came, she felt more alone. She touched the phone. Maybe Ken was trying to reach her. She guessed that this interview had been taped. It was dark outside, but the camera had photographed Ken in front in broad daylight.

Remy's thoughts drifted to Sarna Bramson. She wondered what Sarna was doing and almost wished she could call her. For a minute it crossed her mind that she would like to talk to Jason, but then she realized that she would be an intruder. None of her friends except for Lara could understand any of this so she was stranded with her thoughts.

Now it was clear why Ken wouldn't tell her what he was doing in Chicago. How ridiculous she must have sounded begging him to let her into his life! Everything about him had been a disguise. His life was a lie, and her life was now smashed like a broken dish.

Only a week ago she dreamt about marrying Ken. How childish to have thought that he was in love with her.

She stood up and straightened her slacks. She moved about the room trying to size up her errors. She wasn't a dumb woman. It was odd that she had let this happen. Remy sat down on the sofa, this time with her head in her hands. She refused to believe that she had been set up. Meeting Ken was a sheer accident. No one could have planted him in Giverny. He was already working on the investigation when they met. Their encounter was a coincidence. And once they began to share their histories, it was only natural that she shared her concerns about work.

She couldn't imagine at what point it became an obvious conflict for Ken, nor could she pinpoint the time that he should have ended the relationship and disclosed that his work might come between them. If she thought about it carefully, she didn't know what he could have told her. If he said he was working with those who were spying on the pit, that the people she worked with were targets of his investigation, he would have revealed his cover. She knew all of this, knew it in a logical, academic way. She also knew that even though they became caught up in each other's lives, Ken could never have shared his secret.

Still everything that happened had played out right before her eyes, a few feet away from where she stood every day, inches away from her place in the pit.

Questions reeled through her mind. Why did they target Jason who was just another bagman when they should get Oscar? If Oscar was feeding Jason trades, why didn't they arrest him? How could Sid Keller not know who was important? What about Zach? What about Zach and her father?

How close she had come, she thought, wincing at the idea that the government could have arrested her. She mulled over the conversation Ken and she had had and she wondered if his admonitions had kept her safe. Maybe she had done things she shouldn't have done. The trades Oscar gave her were silly favors. Or was that a rationalization? His favors could have been misconstrued. To an untrained eye, she could have been identified as a bagman.

Maybe Ken had saved her from that humiliation. The more she thought about it, the more puzzling the plot. Suddenly she felt immense despair. As she stared at the phone, the fear of losing Ken Baldwin forever was becoming a terrible reality.

***

Sarna Bramson surprised even herself. Instead of triggering fear, Jason's arrest filled her with anger.

"How dare they do this?" she ranted as Ivan Bloch escorted her to put up the million-dollar bond required to get Jason out of jail. It would be weeks, maybe even months before the trial.

Trade Secrets

"He's just one of a ton of people there who do bad things. I've seen it. That trading floor is swarming with rats."

"Hush, Sarna." Ivan admonished. He leaned into her and she could smell the liquor on his breath. A stocky man with a protruding stomach, Ivan wore custom-made suits to hide a bulging torso. His shirts were extra large around the neck with short sleeves. His beard was speckled with gray and his thinning hair made him look much older than fifty. He wore horn-rimmed glasses and stared out of them from the bottom because his sight had deteriorated from straining to see the screens during the years he tried to trade. Now he needed trifocals. His heavy brow rose as he spoke.

"Listen to me, young lady. You are a member of the Exchange, Sarna, and the rules forbid you to make insinuating statements against anyone else on the floor."

"You are a simple coward," she retorted. "They're trying to put my husband away, strip us of our life and you think I'm afraid of a fine? These animals don't scare me, Ivan. I hear the guys hush hush all the time, scared shitless of this and that. They keep their lips zipped because they are afraid of being shut out of a trade. That's how Jason got into trouble. He was scared. Well, I've got news for them."

"As your attorney, I'm telling you to shut up."

"You listen to me, Ivan. You are Jason's lawyer and you can tell him what to do. They've all been telling him what to do for years and that's why he's in this pickle. You can't tell me what to do, and they can't tell me what to do." She pointed backwards as if the whole exchange was behind her, as if she could ooze their guilt out of them like pus from a sore.

"Don't come running to me when you get in trouble."

"Don't worry, Ivan. I can take care of myself." She placed a pair of sunglasses on her hair, turned on her high heels and stomped off.

Holly Rozner

As the elevator swished down the thirteen floors from Ivan's office, she began to plot her revenge. How dare they terrorize people? They couldn't scare her. She had seen trades directed to specific traders. She knew Oscar was the ringleader. So why didn't they nab him?

She stepped out into the frigid cold and wrapped a shearling coat around her. She had forgotten something. Turning around, she ran back into the building. As the elevator climbed to the thirteenth floor, she ruminated about how to proceed. When she reached Ivan's office, she didn't wait for his secretary to buzz her in. She strode into Ivan's office unannounced as if it were hers.

The shocked expression on his face blazed with consternation. His trademark smirk was replaced with a serious frown. Sarna frightened him more than the FBI. You could bargain with the government. He had done that before. There were legal remedies to prevent things from spinning out of control. Sarna was a different matter. She had the guts to take on an army.

"Tell me something, Ivan. How does Doheney get off without a mark? How can that be?"

Ivan stood up. He ordered her to sit down. She opened her coat, her breasts heaving beneath a tight cashmere sweater. Her sunglasses were perched on top of her head like a headband and her gorgeous eyes sparkled. He spoke very firmly. "I'm telling you for the last time. You cannot go around and name names like that. If you don't shut up, you will end up at the bottom of the Chicago River."

She burst out laughing. "Come on, Ivan. Do you actually think that they are going to do something to ME? You've read too many mystery novels. They're not going to touch me and you know why? Because I could screw up their whole plan. In fact, if you know any of these morons, you might want to tell them to be careful because I've got the goods on them. And they can't kill all of us. There are too many people who know their secrets. These trade secrets that they think can't get out are a whisper away from being headlines. This FBI investigation will expose them like Pandora's Box. You wait and see."

She posed for a minute with her legs crossed and her hands draped over the chair.

"Don't look at me like that. I will bring this Exchange to its knees, if I have to. They are not going to wreck my life without my sinking the whole ship."

She said this as if she knew what she was talking about. Ivan believed that she had it in her to make a mess of things. And if it got really dirty, he could be involved too, a thought that was beginning to make him nervous. It had been two years since Harry Saks had died. If Sarna went too far, someone might figure out how that happened. Ivan felt surrounded. He liked his anonymity, having a back office and out of the way in his legal cubbyhole where no one could ever think about him.

Sarna knew only a fraction of what there was to know, but she spoke with total conviction. This beauty, who seemed like a simple broad who needed her Neiman Marcus charge card more than food, could outwit any man, Ivan thought. Her accusations were filled with bitter truth. He returned her fabulous stare like a teacher trying to figure out if the student had cheated on the term paper.

Suddenly Sarna stood up, pulled her coat around her and swung her Botega bag over her shoulder. She had no idea where these theories were coming from or how she had managed to speak so articulately. As she watched the sweat form on Ivan's hairline, it was obvious that she had touched a chord. He looked scared. For a split second Sarna imagined Ivan in the nude, wondering what he would be like to touch, but the thought was so repulsive, she erased the picture from her mind and decided to put on fresh lipstick.

Struggling for a solution to his predicament, Ivan watched her retrieve a gold compact from her purse that she raised into the dim light as she applied lip liner. He followed every move.

"Sarna," he admonished. "The Feds can take away everything you own. Under the *RICO* statute, they can confiscate your property."

There was a long pause as Sarna watched him swallow involuntarily like a child caught sneaking out of school.

"You mean this compact, Ivan." She flung it at him and he caught it as if it were a baseball. "You didn't hear me, Ivan. I'm not scared. There is nothing more they can take from me. Jason has lost everything. Some jewelry? My gold faucets? It's over Ivan. They can have all that. What I have now they cannot take away. They can have Jason. My marriage is dead. His reputation is ruined. Your warnings don't shake me up. I've always been stronger than my husband. I will save myself, Ivan, if it's the only thing I do. Even if it means putting every one of those sonofabitches behind bars. They can take everything away, but they can't stop me from knowing what I know."

Then she turned and strutted off without even looking back.

Ivan stayed behind his desk, his mouth wide open. He had always been good at dealing with an angry man, but a woman was different. They name hurricanes after women, he thought. And this one was a holy terror.

***

Once out of the building Sarna tried to reach Sid. She was unable to understand how he had dismissed her after the incredible moments they had shared. She had left a message for him yesterday, but he had not returned her call.

First she called the Exchange and when she couldn't reach him there, she tried the hotel. When he answered, she hung up the phone. Fresh from her tirade with Ivan, she hailed a taxi to the Ritz and marched straight up to Sid's room.

He answered on the second knock.

"Sarna. I can't talk to you," he said. But Sarna was not convinced. It was easy for her to see him fight his impulse to grab her.

"What does that mean, you can't talk to me?" She held her coat in one hand, the other on her hip.

"I can't be disturbed."

"You can't treat me like this. I've never been treated like this." She walked past him and threw her purse on the foyer shelf. As she entered the living room of the hotel suite, she eyed the furniture from a new perspective. It wasn't her taste, but she could see why the hotel chose dark mahogany. The drapes were elegant, yellow and blue, perfect for a Duke's mansion. This was how she would design her next home. She walked around the room as if she could purchase the items, registering in her mind how they had decorated this luxurious suite.

Sid wore a monogrammed shirt and a light blue cashmere sweater. A Mozart piano concerto played in the background. On the coffee table lay the *New York Times* and a Scott Turow novel.

Sid walked towards her, anxious to quell the fire in her eyes. Her anger made her look delicious. Sid kept his hands in his pockets. The struggle between being a man and being on duty tore him apart. All he wanted was to put his arms around her, but he couldn't. Not now. Someday when this was over, perhaps they could have a life together, but his first obligation was the investigation and they had come too far to lose their footing.

He sat down on the sofa, put one leg on the coffee table and leaned over to talk to her. "Sarna. I can't explain anything to you. If I could talk to you now, I would. I simply can't."

Her body showed no sign of defeat, but her eyes filled with tears. She stared at him silently, wondering what words might reach him.

"I don't understand," she said sitting up straight. "How can you treat me like this?"

"Let me help you understand," he said in a deep tone that was more than she could stand.

"What has this been about?" she asked.

"It's not about you, Sarna. I think you're spectacular. I did from the first minute I set eyes on you. But we're on colliding paths."

"What about that time at my house? Here in this room? We had something, Sid. Don't pretend we didn't."

How could he explain this? He hadn't meant to use her. He had no designs on her when they met. Nor did he plan on the dynamic shift in emotions he now felt. He had never intended to fall like this. He thought he knew himself better. When this started, he was sure he could simply rummage through her house to make his case and then forget about her. That wasn't what was happening. How could he tell her how callous he wanted to be?

And how could he explain how his feelings had changed without compromising his work?

"It was inappropriate for us to get involved."

"You are working with the government against my husband, aren't you?"

Now he was all business.

"Let me make you understand," he said. "I was working on the investigation before you and I had anything to do with each other. If we hadn't met at Zach's party, none of this would have started. I shouldn't have let this happen."

She waited for him to say more, to tell her that she meant something to him. She wanted him to hold her, tell her he cared about her, maybe that he loved her. But he didn't move.

"What did our time together mean to you?"

"More than it should have," he said. She knew he meant it.

"I don't know what to say. I should hate you. I should be throwing things at you for deceiving me, but I can't," she cried as her voice faltered. "I never felt this way about someone."

She had touched the very part of him he had tried to hide even from himself. Sid Keller was a cool, detached man who had never fallen for any of the women he had seduced. Now this. It was the wrong time. The wrong place. The right woman, but the wrong moment.

"I'm sorry, Sarna. I never meant to hurt you. It started as a fling. For both of us. I never dreamed that either of us would feel this way." He paused and waited for her expression to change. "Or that I would."

"But you do. Admit you do."

She reached her arm out and he took her hand. But when she started to move towards him, he stepped back.

"We can't, Sarna. I can't. Not now."

"Are you responsible for Jason's case?"

"It's very complicated. It has nothing to do with us."

He had said it. Us. It was all she needed.

"Now what?" she asked.

"Now you have to leave. We cannot see each other again. If you ever need something from me, I will try to do what I can for you, but you must not rely on me. I can't be there for you right now. You must protect your husband."

It was his sense of duty that was resisting her. His eyes told her that he wished to touch her as much as she wished to be touched. She was trembling. Sid Keller's job was not finished. And she would not plead with him. She had her own job to do. She accepted his reassuring glance as a promise that someday things would be different.

Then as bravely as she could, she stood up and twirled gracefully towards the door. When it slammed, Sid put his head in his hands. Sarna remained outside the door trying to catch her breath before she slowly walked the necessary distance to the elevator.

***

At 6:00 Ivan arrived at Zach's house, a sprawling manor off Hibbard Road in a section known simply as Woodley Road. Zach let him in and led him into the den. Ivan nodded to Oscar who was hunched forward in a chair his hands twined together. He had been there all day trying to make sense of the world collapsing around him.

Zach had known Ivan for over twenty years. When they met in the gold pit, they both discovered quickly how to steal from customers. They shared the same instincts, smelled the money and decided to do whatever was necessary to get it. Within a year they made enough to form their own clearinghouse. When Zach invented a vehicle to trade currencies, Ivan handled the legal work and the rest became history.

Once banks realized they could hedge against foreign currency fluctuations, ten thousand dollar seats were selling for thirty thousand dollars. Ten years later for one hundred and fifty thousand dollars.

Zach controlled the new pits like a nurse taking care of a baby. For the first three years he stood on the top step directing trades, pocketing the best for himself. With only a handful of traders and an unregulated environment, every trade was a winner. As word got out that this was where the action was, hordes converged on the pits like Okies during the gold rush, stampeding the building in the Loop that quickly outgrew its space.

Zach was elected chairman of the Exchange in 1975. Ivan moved to another building to become the legal consultant. After Harry started complaining about how things were being handled, Zach put him in charge of a mutual fund, newly bankrolled by investors who wanted a piece of the Midas touch. In one short year the fund quadrupled its profits.

"What do we do now?" Zach asked when he closed the door to his den.

"We need a criminal lawyer for Jason."

"Why can't you handle it?"

"It's not my field. I need Anthony Brooks."

"What about these other guys? They got forty-five others besides Jason," Zach stammered.

"Each one is on his own."

Zach gnashed his teeth and finally he threw his arms up.

"You have a leak out there. Sarna Bramson is on a rampage," Ivan said.

Zach jumped out of his chair and hovered over Ivan's desk. "You get that cunt under control, do you hear?"

"It's not that simple. You will have to do something."

"What can I do?"

"She will be watching every move Oscar makes. You need to make it easy for her to trade so she is distracted."

"What are you talking about?"

Ivan straightened his floral tie and smoothed out the cuffs on his shirt.

Ivan had to protect himself. If the government clawed through everything, they could find their way to him. Sarna was a deflection. "Jason is easy, but she's a terror. You can negotiate with Jason, tell him what to do. Not her. All she knows is that her mansion is gone and she has nothing more to lose. You will have to give her a piece of the action. It's your only hope."

Zach glared at him. "I'll make mincemeat of her."

"I don't think so. You better play along. She does not want to go to jail. I can assure you of that. She wants her manicures and expensive haircuts. Let her be Jason's replacement. But you have to be careful."

"What about the Feds?"

"They're concentrating on their case. They've got the guys they want. Sarna is a baby to them. Besides, she doesn't look the part. You forget, Zach, that there is much more to hide here. If the Feds get really interested, they could find out what happened to Harry Saks."

Zach's face turned white. He crunched his shoulders and his neck seemed to disappear. "They could never figure that out."

"They could subpoena records—examine the sham mutual fund we set up and then look into your bank statements—It wouldn't take a genius to figure out what was happening—putting losing trades into the fund and winning trades into your account."

"Traders do it all the time," Zach responded. "Guys who are getting divorced do it with their wives' accounts—pension plans are loaded with winners and the individual accounts are loaded with losers. What we did is iron tight."

"No, Zach, you're wrong. Not everyone ends up dead."

Trade Secrets

Ivan was right. "If we help Sarna, you think Jason won't get in our way. He'll understand this?"

Ivan nodded.

"Consider it done," announced Zach as if he had just made a trade.

Oscar listened closely. He was squeezed between two rocks. He was the one who had actually siphoned off the trades, moving the winning ones into Zach's account and losing ones into the fund until the fund went belly up. And he knew that if only one of them survived, it would be Zach. Oscar felt sick. It had been a good ride, but he could see it toppling. And so fast. How could he not have seen this coming? Why would he think he would be more important than Harry? Once the shit started to fly, he would be a gonner. He needed to think of something, do something so all of this didn't just evaporate into thin air. He needed to hold on to the one small hope that when they tried to bury him, he'd have some way to get even.

chapter 30

REMY SAT ALONE in her apartment not sure of what to do. Her hand settled on the phone as she struggled with whether to call Ken or wait until later. She needed to think this through, to analyze if Jason's indictment may have been her fault. According to the newspapers, the sting operation had been planned for months. She went over everything in her mind, trying to piece events together to confirm that Ken had begun the investigation before they met.

The French windows in her bedroom were open, but the fresh air did little to allay her anxiety. February offered some relief to the terrible cold that had paralyzed Chicago. The days were longer and the sun hit the city from a slightly different angle. As the months ticked on, a few minutes were added to every day. Spring was imminent, though it would be weeks before the air warmed.

On her dressing table was a Philip Roth novel she wanted to read, but she could not concentrate. Not even the *Vanity Fair* that had just arrived could engross her. A tear fell as she touched her blanket thinking back to just a few weeks ago when she had considered redecorating the room and decided not to in case she and Ken got engaged. She hugged a pillow without much comfort.

Holly Rozner

The light over her bedstand remained on as she drifted into sleep. Within a few moments she was lost in a dream. She was in college on her way to a huge amphitheater that resembled a coliseum. As she entered the gigantic arena, she realized she was undressed. She ran through the open space searching for shelter. She explored every corridor looking for a safe spot to hide when suddenly a man placed his hand around her waist and pulled her into a hollow section of the stone edifice. She turned around to see him but could not make out his features. He held her firmly. She didn't resist, submitting to his touch without knowing who he was. She felt protected, even cherished, as he took her into his arms.

At 2:00, Remy awoke with a sudden start, disoriented. Who was this man? As its creator, only she could identify him. As the minutes ticked on, she couldn't hold on to the dream and soon the context faded.

If only she could go back to sleep where she heard Ken's warm voice. The dream itself was an ocean of unfinished clues, an oasis from the shipwreck of her current reality.

Remy sat up in her bed. Then she pushed the covers away and stepped onto the carpet. She paced back and forth, sat back on the down comforter and stared intensely at the telephone. A sinking feeling overwhelmed her. Trying to retrieve her reverie, she pulled the coverlet around her. Soon she fell back to sleep. When she awoke it was 6:30. Apprehension gripped her.

Instead of solving the dilemma, the dream had re-opened a struggle. The faceless stranger must be Ken Baldwin—the only one who could protect her. Yet it was he who had put everyone in harm's way.

She sat up in bed wondering if she were being unreasonable. The traders had been targeted long before Ken stepped into her life. And if it weren't Ken who had unmasked the corruption, someone else would have. She, of all people, wanted the improprieties unearthed.

She tried to dissect the dream: the faceless stranger with strong sexual undertones. Remy looked out the window. The sun was barely up. Only a shadow of light fell on the leafless trees.

Perhaps it was wrong to judge Ken so harshly. She reached for the phone and called his apartment. When the answering machine clicked on, she felt lost, as if she were running naked through an ancient building in a dream from long ago.

Remy got out of bed and dressed quickly. She brushed her hair back to show off a pair of small pearl earrings Ken had bought for her in New York. Then she grabbed a fresh white cotton shirt and corduroys. She tied a black cashmere sweater around her shoulder and put on a gray alpaca coat.

She would have breakfast downtown and then call Ken. She felt better. The dream would lead her in the right direction and put her on the path that would provide answers about her father's death.

***

Joey and Rosa had left St. Lucia as soon as the news about Jason broke on CNN. When Joey saw Jason on TV in handcuffs, he let out a scream. Then Rosa confessed that she had seen a blip about this before, but had kept the news to herself because she didn't want to ruin their vacation.

"Ruin my vacation? How do you think I'm paying for this gig? Rosa , don't you realize that I'm one of these guys?"

Her blank stare told him she didn't know what he was talking about. All Rosa knew about her Joey was that he was parading around in expensive silk shirts and handing out hundred dollar tips to waiters he would never see again. She watched him strut along the beach snapping his fingers to get service the way rich people do, handling himself as if he had been born with a silver spoon in his mouth. But she had no idea how he had made this fortune. When she visited the Exchange, clerks swarmed around him—kids who wanted to be like him.

Now Joey was back, worried about Jason's fate and how it would affect him. Joey brushed past Remy on the escalator and ran into the trading room. He leapt into the pit. Oscar was on the top step shuffling through papers. The daily numbers flashed along the screens. Everyone was in place. Same traders. Same smirks. Same shit.

Thank God. He had worried for nothing. He had left a Caribbean paradise and everything was the same. Jason's arrest had nothing to do with Oscar and certainly had nothing to do with him.

"Oscar, how ya doing?" Joey asked as Oscar glanced his way.

Oscar waved to his clerk, giving him verbal instructions while Joey stood on the side, his heart pounding so hard he could feel it in his head. Oscar didn't respond, so Joey waited for him to finish his business. It wasn't unusual for Oscar to be preoccupied. The markets would open in twenty minutes. Then everything would return to normal. Soon he and Rosa would get married. He had an appointment with a jeweler that week to pick out a diamond necklace to match the hulking ring she wore. Everything he dreamed about was happening. His life was perfect. This thing with Jason was nothing. He smoothed his trading jacket with his hand, stacked pencils in his pocket and stood there ready for action. This mess, like a vapor, would blow over.

Oscar would have time before the opening. And if he was busy, Joey would talk to him at lunch. They would catch up in the Club. He loved lunching with Oscar, being a member of this private fraternity.

Joey edged to his regular spot. No sense in pushing Oscar who had told him never to interrupt. Joey winked from across the pit. When Oscar didn't return even a nod, Joey's throat tightened. Must be really busy. Joey wore his fresh suntan the way a woman wears a new mink coat as he continued to tell himself that everything was fine.

Finally, someone asked where he had been.

"St. Lucia," he responded, as if it were just down the street.

"Welcome back."

"What's going on?"

"Jason Bramson was arrested."

"I saw it on CNN."

"Oscar has shut down."

"What does that mean?"

"Life has changed."

This guy didn't know what he was talking about. He didn't know that he and Oscar had an arrangement. Like politics. It was all in who you knew. That's what Zach told him, and Zach was the most powerful man he ever met. Everything was going to be just fine. These other guys didn't get it.

As long as Zach ran trading heaven, Joey and Oscar went together like vanilla ice cream and apple pie.

chapter 31

JASON'S LAWYER WAS intensely serious and never afraid to use legal tricks defending a client. Anthony Brooks dealt with an impenetrable expression on his face and usually got his way.

Jason warmed to him slowly. He had not slept in two days. The skin around his eyes was blue and his hands were shaky. He had been asked to summarize everything he could remember about the past six years. As he put the history into his own words, he could hardly believe it himself. His had been a Hollywood story: fade out, as it all falls down.

As he revealed hidden truths about the trading community to Brooks, Jason began to see that the insidious plan that Zach devised was filled with gaping holes. They were as vulnerable as kids on stolen bikes. Now the promises Zach had made were worthless after the lawyer made it perfectly clear the Feds had the goods. Jason, the lawyer explained, was the first layer. They wanted to dig further to decipher how the trades wound their way, if they did, to Zachary Silverman's checkbook. It was his bank account they were after, and Brooks assumed they would find it.

"You're small potatoes," the lawyer said bluntly.

"So what do I do?"

"We have to strike a deal."

"What kind of deal?"

"The government put a lot of money into this. They need a case. We have to give up something to make it easier for them."

"Are you nuts? There are dozens of guys involved in this shit. Why me?"

"You're better looking," quipped Brooks.

Jason couldn't decide if he liked this guy. Ivan chose him without giving Jason a chance to say much. Anthony Brooks held all the necessary credentials and certainly looked the part, the epitome of refinement, a Harvard grad with rimless glasses and a pompous-looking briefcase. His hair was slick, his face carefully shaven. His skin was smooth and dark with certain features that belied his African American heritage. He wore heavy cologne that made Jason cough and spoke to the floor as if Jason wasn't even in the room.

Jason searched for some way to warm up to him.

"Mr. Brooks. Should I call you Anthony?"

"Anthony is fine."

"I don't get this. How can they barge into someone's house like that?"

"The Judge granted them a warrant. It looks like an illegal entry, but it is not".

"What judge?"

"Look, Jason. We don't have time for a lesson in politics. You are out on a million-dollar bond. We have to get to work."

"Why didn't they lock me up?"

"Ivan put up a bond."

"Does a lawyer usually post a bond for a client?"

"Yes." Brooks finally stared into Jason's eyes. He didn't invite too many questions. Ivan Bloch was a colleague. Anthony Brooks guessed that Ivan had been involved in designing Zach's network. If Jason asked too many questions, he would eventually realize that Ivan had picked him out of the ten thousand lawyers in Chicago because he would protect the right people. The lawyer let Jason's question drop like a speck of dirt.

"Ivan is not on trial here. We need to concentrate on you."

"But there are so many…."

The lawyer interrupted. "I don't need to know this. I only need to know what you can tell me that will help defend your position."

"Isn't that your job?"

"I can't build a case without information."

"How can I protect myself?"

"Look Jason. I told you we need to make a deal. You need to cooperate or you won't ever get out of jail. We will give them enough to make their investigation worthwhile. If you squeal too much, you'll be forced out of Chicago."

"Leave Chicago? My house?"

"Your house won't be yours very long," Brooks reminded him.

Jason knew that. The throbbing of his heart beat through his shirt. Where was Sarna? How much had they told her?

"What's next?"

"Cooperate. Hopefully they will pay attention to the other traders they've arrested."

"How many did they get?"

"Forty-five in addition to you."

"Are all the charges the same?"

"Basically. Everything is open to interpretation, you know. One person sees you make a trade, but can they really prove it is illegal? They have to prove it."

Any idiot could see through it, thought Jason. It was all bogus.

"If I help, will they let me go?"

"Maybe."

"If they do?"

"Then you will sign a contract."

Jason always wondered how such deals were made. He had been fascinated by articles he read about Mafia members who snitched and then lived their lives in seclusion.

"Do I tell them about Oscar and Zach?"

Brooks stood up and walked around the desk. "That is out of the question."

Jason broke into a sweat. Wasn't that what this was about? They had started this. Brooks had said so himself. "I don't get it," Jason said.

"Try to understand this, Jason," Brooks said speaking very slowly. "If you turn them in and get off, you won't live to talk about it. Your testimony needs to be very carefully worded, artfully stated. You cannot blab about everything you know."

"Isn't that what they want?"

"That may be what they want. But that will not be what we give them."

"Then I will go to jail?"

"I'm afraid that is likely."

"So this is hopeless."

"I think we can work out something so your sentence could be lightened. If they like you, that is. And we need to make a deal with Oscar and Zach."

Jason looked perplexed.

"Listen, Jason. You are in a no-exit zone. If you squeal, you will be crucified. Zach runs this kingdom." He paused for a very long time, walked around the room, and then put both hands on Jason's shoulders. "It will be best if you make it easy for the Feds. Then we will strike an inside deal so that you are properly compensated."

Jason sat back in his chair trying to digest the irony. The newspaper said they had taped conversations. Those would have been made months ago before Oscar stopped trading with him. His head was in a noose, Joey is free, and Zach and Oscar get to go on stealing.

"If I save Zach's ass, what do I get?"

"A couple of years in jail and some money."

"If I don't?'

"A longer time in jail and no money."

He had stolen plenty. But why should he be the one to pay? Anthony Brooks in his black silk suit and a red tie didn't look the least bit concerned. Alone in his agony, forced to give up a racket that had already deserted him, Jason had a feeling that he was being dealt a very bad hand. He stood up and looked Brooks straight in the eye. He didn't say anything. Even if they could strike the deal with Zach, what would he be saving, after all?

They've already passed his legacy on to Joey. Jason could picture him strutting into Gibson's ordering shrimp cocktail and a thick steak. Something else was going on, but he couldn't yet figure it out. All Jason knew was that he had nowhere to turn. If he tried to get another lawyer and told him the story, who would believe him? Brooks had the city all tied up.

This time he wouldn't let them make a fool out of him. They thought he was stupid, but he wasn't that dumb.

Jason took a long deep breath and let the air out slowly. It was obvious that Anthony Brooks would do very little to protect him. He would go on trial all right, but like everything else in this nasty universe, it would be tainted. He was disposable. To get out of this mess, he would have to stand on his own. The house. The money. That was history. And even if he made a deal with Zach, how could he make him pay? He'd be in jail and Zach would never deliver. Jason steadied himself. This time around, he would stay one step in front of them. They thought they could read him like a book but he was more complicated than that. As their duplicity became increasingly transparent, Jason realized he would have to be on guard every step of the way. And if he could no longer relish the gold, he'd be damn sure no one else would. That would be his payoff, all right.

If it was over, it was over. For all of them.

***

Sarna had not been at the Exchange for weeks, but her trading privileges remained active until the lease on the seat ran out. When she began losing money, Jason tried to get her out of the contract but it was impossible. The Exchange required a lessee to pay the full term even if that person left the trading floor. However, as long as there was money in her account to cover her trades, Sarna was not prevented from trading, so she decided to try again.

While Jason met with Anthony Brooks, Sarna stopped at the bank to get a ten thousand dollar cashier's check with money she had saved. She handed the check to Duchess Clearing across the floor from Zachary Silverman's Crestwood office. Once deposited, the money would operate as an advance, and she could draw on it to meet margin requirements.

Sarna marched into the pit in black gabardine slacks and a white silk blouse. They had screwed around with Jason. But they wouldn't screw with her!

Remy looked up from the newspaper she was reading. She was surprised to see Sarna back on the floor.

"Hello, Remy," Sarna said, taking her spot.

Remy turned to face her. Nearby Joey waited nervously for the market to open. He held his jacket in such a way that anyone nearby could see the gold Rolex he had bought in the duty- free shop. He and Oscar had still not spoken. Once the markets got going, everything would be smooth, he told himself.

"Hi, ladies," he chimed.

"Sarna, this is Joey."

Sarna wasn't interested in introductions. Hoping he would notice her, she waved at Oscar. Being acknowledged was as important to her today as it had been when she was a kid. She had to overcome Jason's stigma. She had done nothing wrong! She counted on others gravitating to her because of her looks. She had learned early to use that asset. It had to work now.

As the clock ticked towards 8:30, Sarna concentrated.

"A hundred at 95," Oscar bellowed, as the quiet of the pre-market trading floor erupted into a tumultuous din.

He leapt up into the air, his hands reaching for the sky.

"A hundred at 90," he ranted hoping to ram the order down someone's throat.

"Why isn't anyone buying, Remy?" Sarna asked.

"At 80," Oscar screamed.

Remy watched Oscar. Her eyes darted to Joey who was hopping up and down in his spot.

"75 bid," Joey shouted.

Remy watched the monitor and then looked at Joey who was so intent that he wasn't paying attention. IBM ticked down three points. What was Joey thinking? Sarna moved close to Oscar, her eyes burning.

"75 on one," she announced in a small voice.

"Get out of here, Sarna," Oscar shouted. "Go back to the manicurist and get another polish change. We don't trade in one lots."

The men began to laugh. Remy winced. Feeling the bruise intended for Sarna, she kept her eye on Oscar.

Sarna moved closer to him. "You and I can fuck later, Oscar. Right now, I want to trade." Even Joey was stunned. Oscar grimaced. Remy's jaw dropped.

Oscar poked his chin up and began to roar again, "Listen up folks. She wants some good sex. We'll show her what that means." His eyes were laced with contempt.

"A thousand at 50."

"Buy 50, boss," shouted Joey.

Oscar didn't acknowledge the trade. The market ticked up. "Five hundred at 60."

Joey cleared his throat and shouted across the pit. "Bought 50."

Oscar was mute. Remy was aghast. Joey thought he had bought fifty contracts from Oscar, but Oscar wouldn't confirm the trade. It was hard to tell from where she was standing whether his silence was deliberate. Her thoughts were suddenly interrupted.

"Buy 5," Sarna shouted across the room.

"Buy 5," Oscar said, his hand on his hips, imitating her.

Remy could see tears in Sarna's eyes.

"Sold, darling. Sold," Oscar retorted. "Five hundred at 50," he screamed into the crowd. "At 45," he jeered, his eyes on Sarna who had stepped back into the crowd.

Trade Secrets

The market continued its descent. Sarna didn't know what to do. This was exactly what had happened two months ago. She thought she had learned her lesson. The pit was silent, everyone's eyes bouncing from Sarna to Oscar.

Remy moved near Sarna. If she didn't cut her losses, she would suffer a brutal blow.

Remy grabbed her and hauled Sarna to the side.

"Get out of your trade, Sarna. Now."

"No. The market will come back."

"There are no prayers in a pit. Scratch your trade."

Sarna looked perplexed.

"Your loss is not so terrible. Just get out. Scratch it. Try not to lose any more."

"I can't," said Sarna.

Sarna was paralyzed.

"Can I do it for you?"

"Yes. Please."

Remy stepped up and hit a bid across the pit. She carded the trade carefully and walked over to the trader to tell him that the trade belonged to Sarna. When Remy was finished, she handed the card back to Sarna and asked her to initial it. Sarna had lost five hundred dollars.

Remy pushed Sarna to the side of the semi-circle, taking her arm to lead her through the crowd. They stopped outside the trader's break room, Sarna half in a trance. Remy remained controlled, determined to make her point.

"You haven't traded for weeks, Sarna."

"Over a month."

"How is Jason?"

"He has a new lawyer."

"Are you OK?"

"I guess so."

"It takes nerve for you to come back."

Sarna studied Remy who carried herself with such grace. Jason warned her that no one could be trusted and she needed to be careful.

"I need to understand what mistakes I made so I can avoid them now. I need to make a living, Remy," Sarna admitted.

Remy could feel herself drawn in. Fate had hurled them into the same lion's den. Two totally different women with divergent impulses: Remy who needed to carve her own destiny; Sarna, her silky dark hair tied at the nape of her neck, dedicated to the great god, money, desperate to salvage her life. Remy's sympathy kicked in, and she saw herself as Sarna's mentor.

"Trading is a tough game, Sarna. You need to learn how to make small amounts of money incrementally. Then if you don't lose a lot, you will be OK."

"My husband had no system."

"Jason didn't want to learn the system."

"I suppose he didn't have to." She said this without any guilt, knowing full well that Remy knew the truth. Once the FBI wrecked their lives, she realized that all that money had been given to him.

"Can someone actually learn how to trade legally?"

"Trading is a skill just like any other profession. You need to acquire a rhythm. Success doesn't come overnight."

"It seemed to for Jason."

"And look what happened."

A deafening silence filled the space between them as the din swelled while traders responded to another flash about corporate earnings. More traders nudged their way into the pit.

Remy kept her eyes on Sarna. "I can learn," she whispered.

"I'm sure you can."

The instant rapport between these women was visible in the expression on their faces. From opposing vantage points, they had each witnessed the under-side of the pits. For Sarna, trading had been a quick route to lake-front mansions and five-carat diamonds. For Remy it was an avenue to unlock the story behind her father's death.

"How much you earn will be in direct relationship with how much you risk. The more size you trade, the more likely you are to make or lose a lot of money."

"I can't afford to lose any more money."

"Then you must trade small quantities. And you must scratch every trade that looks like a loser."

"Scratch?"

"Erase. Get out of the trade. Break even. Don't wish for it to go your way. People lose fortunes waiting for markets to come back. That's for amateurs. You want to be a pro."

Sarna smiled at the notion of being a professional. She admired Remy and wanted to be like her. The road to riches had been paved with disappointment. Even Sid couldn't give her everything she needed. If she were to survive, it would have to be on her own. Wasn't that real life?

"Try to ignore the other traders. Most of them are men, and men treat this as a game. Women are cerebral. We don't recover from losses easily. Men are not afraid of losing because they know how to come back. They go after trades that I would never chase. And they get them. Before you can be a successful trader, you have to know your limits; you have to know who you are. It takes time. And you need to know how much money you can risk. Take it slow. Take it easy."

Sarna listened intently as she looked at Remy. Remy would never have a married a guy like Jason. She would not have been able to put up with his weaknesses. Remy was a strong woman, but so was she. She could do this! Ultimately, it was inner strength that counted. She saw it in herself the night the FBI clamored their way into her house. Now she was dead set on surviving. She would extract what she needed from the very place that had ravaged her husband.

"Show me how," she begged.

"I'll do what I can," Remy promised. "Let's go for coffee," she suggested, as she rummaged through her own thoughts to figure out where best to begin illuminating Sarna. If she could teach her a few hard-core tricks, then all she had learned would be that much more worthwhile. Her investigation into her father's death had been severely sidetracked. And with all that had happened on the trading floor, she wondered if she would never discover the truth.

As a trader, Remy enjoyed the money she had been able to make, and she enjoyed being able to learn a skill. If she could share her insight with Sarna, she would have a new purpose, a new focal point since Ken was no longer in the picture.

chapter 32

To the amateur investor, the day looked uneventful with the Dow inching up a few points. Outsiders did not know that these listless days could make or break a professional trader. There had been wild gyrations and the traders were weary, their hopes buoyed one moment and then dashed with a bad earning's report.

By 3:00 Joey was wiped out. Coming back from vacation was like climbing a mountain barefoot.

His back ached and his brain felt like crepe paper. Oscar was finishing with his clerk when Joey finally interrupted him.

"Boss, how ya been?"

Oscar winced, brushed his hair back and turned away, jaunting down the steps as if Joey were invisible.

"Just want to confirm that 50 lot from this morning, Oscar."

"We did nothing," Oscar mumbled.

"I bought 50 from you Oscar. Early on. At about 8:38."

"Check with my clerk," Oscar said coldly. "I don't remember the trade."

"That's not possible. Even Remy saw it."

Oscar turned his face to Joey who stood no taller than his chest. He laid his hands on Joey's shoulder and shook him hard.

"I said that I didn't remember the trade. That's that. I don't care what that cunt saw. Do you hear me?"

Joey stepped back. Oscar must be putting on an act because other traders were around. Joey looked up at the screen. That trade was made hours ago. The market had rallied a hundred points since then. He had sold the contracts and bought them back from Oscar all in a few minutes' time. If Oscar refused to make the trade good, he would be out a quarter mil.

"I'll work it out with your clerk. You never make a mistake, Boss, I know that."

Joey moved aside to let Oscar pass. He began to quiver. Oscar had no reason to hurt him, but he had no power to challenge his authority.

Oscar moved forward and hovered over Joey's nose. He spoke out of the side of his mouth, his spit misting Joey's cheek.

"Listen, you idiot. Stop calling me boss."

Joey's mind jumped to his charge account and to the ten thousand dollars he had spent last week—massages every afternoon on a private terrace overlooking the mountains, two hundred dollar bottles of wine, filet mignon dinners. He felt faint. If Oscar cut him out, what would he do? He had seen what happened to guys who went belly up. Until this morning, he had been the one they envied and there had been plenty to envy. These past months had been a dream. This morning he had laid Rosa. At 5 a.m. she wrapped her suntanned legs around him, holding on to her lifeline to riches.

What if he had to go back and stuff smelly feet into cheap leather loafers? He had tasted the good life, and he couldn't let it slip away. He studied the terrible expression on Oscar's face and realized that Oscar looked frightened too. More powerful, but scared. Perhaps more vulnerable. Without Zach, Oscar was nothing. In a way he and Oscar led parallel lives, just groveling to different people. The necklace of dependence reached around this huge building, to the highest floors, right into Silverman's well-furnished office.

Zach needed Oscar and Oscar needed Joey. If Oscar disappeared, there would be no one to route trades to the right people. Joey was necessary to pocket the buckets of money. He felt better knowing this. Their whole operation depended on a bagman, and Jason was gone. If they didn't give him what he needed now, he'd snitch. If they deserted him in outfield, he'd be sure no one survived. As soon as he could, he would tell this to Zachary Silverman and put an end to his fear.

***

Oscar could smell his own sweat. He needed a shower and he needed a lay. It wouldn't matter who she was—any broad would do. But he smelled so bad, no dame would let him into her pants. At 3:30 he stopped at the Club and sat at the bar. He rummaged through the newspaper, downed two scotches and ordered a hamburger and fries. He piled on a layer of mustard and topped it off with a hot house tomato and a raw onion. Then, like a man released from prison, he washed the food down with a cold beer and splashed some water on his face before leaving the waitress a ten dollar tip. Oscar Doheney was no cheapskate. He remembered the days when money was tight. He always felt sorry for waitresses who made a living catering to others. Though he took a lot for granted, he knew luck could turn on a dime.

He rode the elevator to Zachary's office thinking about Joey, the little tweet. He got him good, that ass kisser.

Holly Rozner

Good and done for, he thought, counting up the quarter of a mil he had nailed on him. A waitress was one thing. Ten bucks was just ten bucks. And there was always the off chance that he could buy himself some skirt. But this Joey had an attitude. Oscar didn't like it one bit.

Goodbye, Joey. You little toad. Back with a sun tan, thinking you could take over. Jason and Joey, gone in a flash. Like little ants on a wall. He laughed to himself thinking about Sarna Bramson and her big mouth. Some beauty. So was that Masterman woman. But at least she didn't make a fool out of herself. Knew where to draw the line. Suddenly he imagined himself with Remy licking her breasts and brushing away her auburn hair while he slid into her. Maybe someday he'd get his hands on that doll. She would be quite a treat.

***

He strolled to Zach's office, but the door was locked. When he tried to jostle it, he heard Joey's voice through the walls.

That bastard. Oscar let himself into Zach's ante-room and opened up the bottle of Vodka Zach had bought in Russia. Some private label he had never heard of. He waited a minute and then he knocked. Still no response. Maybe Zach was on the telephone. He glanced over to the desk in the outer office, but the telephone lights were not flashing. Maybe they had a girl in there. Maybe the two of them were banging one of the short-skirted clerks who ran around the trading floor hoping to nab a rich hunk.

He fell on the sofa and crossed his legs, his arms over his head stretching his back. Perspiration drenched his armpit.

Imagining Joey and Zach locked up in that room, he felt like a jealous school kid. What did they have to talk about? Didn't Zach know that they were done with Joey? There was no one left but the two of them. They had started together and they would end together. For twenty years they had been in bed together. Did that kid actually think he could come between a relationship cemented in stone? What happened to Harry could happen to Joey, Oscar thought smiling to himself. Finally he left a note for Zach and rode the elevator down to the Club to shower.

Oscar got a key from the attendant to unlock one of the showers. As he stood at the desk waiting for her to find the key, he let out a fart. He took the key and locked himself in the locker room to undress. He let the water run for a while so that the room could heat up while he examined his face in the mirror. Forty-five years old. He looked older. This job had robbed him of his youth. He hadn't been bad looking in his thirties. Life was going fast. What was it worth? $6, maybe $7 million dollars—a wife he didn't really love and two kids who barely spoke to him. He had been so immersed in amassing money that he had paid little or no attention to his family. Tired of their endless requests, he had nothing of his own, and no one who valued him.

He turned the water temperature up so high that it nearly scalded him when he slid into the small compartment. Still it was soothing. Not much else in his life was. Lots of love affairs, but never anyone he loved. He hardly saw his wife except at a dinner party or out with friends. When they screwed they didn't even look at each other. At least Jason had that beauty to go home to. Maybe someday he could have her too.

Sarna Bramson. He hadn't meant to give her that bad trade. He'd make it up to her. She was so pretty. He loved the way she came back at him. Maybe if he cleaned himself up good, she'd let him touch her. First he'd take her out for an expensive dinner. Jason wouldn't be able to do that for her anymore. Maybe he'd even buy her a piece of jewelry. What the hell. Suddenly, he pictured her in the shower with him, her thin body pressed against his, her hair dripping wet while he got down on his knees and sucked her pussy until she begged him to take her. The image gave him an erection and while the water splashed his body, he pumped himself with his hands hard, until he spewed his own liquid all over walls.

Then he started to laugh. He would leave his mess: an imprint to the next person. His mark. His insides. But not his blood.

***

The minute Joey walked into Zach's office, all of his courage evaporated. He let out a despairing cry before he launched into the drama of what had happened that morning, about the 50 lot and Oscar's refusal to acknowledge the trade or even to discuss it with him. Then he went on and on about Jason being arrested and how he saw it on CNN in St. Lucia and didn't know what to do or who to call. As he carried on, Zach sat in his leather chair watching the boy crack.

"Joey, you're a big boy," Zach finally said in his most charming manner. "You know the risks. You win some and lose some. That's just how it goes. "

Joey shivered. His mouth puckered and his thick eyebrows creased his tanned forehead.

"I know I made that trade, Zach. Remy Masterman saw it."

"So? You'll take it to arbitration. They will decide who was right."

Zach refused to let this pipsqueak get to him. It was obvious from the kid's hysteria that they had to get rid of him; break all relationships cold. That was Ivan's advice yesterday after he put up Jason's bond.

"Someone will take the brunt of this," Ivan warned.

"It won't be me," Zach assured him.

Too bad that this kid is caught in such a nasty web, Zach thought as he watched Joey shrivel. He wasn't a bad kid. Oscar and he could have made even more money with him than they had made with Jason. Joey never would have demanded an escalation clause like the one that precipitated cutting Jason out. Now Jason was dried toast.

The game was up.

He heard Oscar knocking on the door. It was important to finish with Joey. They would have to lay low for a long time, run their business solely for brokerage commissions. Though those were sizable amounts, it didn't compare to what they could steal. Ten or twenty gees a week seemed like pennies. Once they got rid of Joey, the spotlight would dim. They would trade quietly without a stir while Ivan worked on Jason and kept the Feds off their back. In a year Jason would be in jail and they could resume their golden plan.

"No one in this city can put me out of business," Zach told Ivan. "Give me Jason on a platter and I will serve him back to you well done."

Ivan knew that Zach was serious. He took his orders like a soldier. The deed would be done. Ivan would be the messenger. Zach could count on that. Jason would listen. But that wife of his was another story.

Zach looked Joey in the eye. He felt a little sorry for the kid. But what could he do? Throw away his whole career for one kid who dreamed too big?

"Look, Joey. We'll let you pay it back," he said in his nicest tone.

"Mr. Silverman," Joey muttered. "For me to pay this back plus the rest of what I owe you will take a lifetime. The only way I can get out of this is if Oscar continues to give me trades. Instead, he's sinking me."

Zach clenched his teeth. He would have growled if he thought that it would scare Joey out of the chair. Instead he controlled his anger and walked behind his desk. He stopped there and spoke in a very low voice as if he were sharing a secret.

"Oscar doesn't give away trades, Joey."

Joey began to say something. If he insisted that he was Oscar's bagman, he would so infuriate this tiny tyrant that his life wouldn't be worth a dime. If he apologized, Zach would pretend he didn't hear him. There was really no way to reason with Zach.

Joey looked around the lavish office he had coveted, dreaming that someday he'd have one like this. Now he was nothing, less than a shoe salesman who at least had the chance for a few minutes of dignity when the sales sheets came out. Joey had seen clerks transformed into princes. Now the fairy tale had turned upside down.

"Will you close my account?" Joey asked.

"We can't absorb losses like that."

"But it wasn't my fault."

"I know, Joey. Unfortunately my backroom has no heart. It hurts me to see this happen to you, kid. I know how much this place means to you."

Joey buried his face in his hands. "Please don't do this," he pleaded.

Zach watched him. "We will try to work with you, son. Maybe cut the interest rate."

Joey looked up into Zach's eyes searching for a sign of genuine sympathy. What he saw from the intent look in Zach's eye that nothing would move him. Zach didn't see him as a breathing person, nor did he understand anything about the life he had led. All Joey needed was money to trade and he had none anymore. This gig was up. It was all over.

chapter 33

THE FOLLOWING MORNING Joey was at the Exchange by 6:30, hoping an early start might deliver a miracle. Maybe Oscar was kidding. Maybe he had carded the trade.

On the way downtown, he tried to reconstruct the moments just before and after he had made the trade. He should have known immediately that something was wrong. Known it the second Oscar refused to look at him. Once the trade was made, he was stuck. If he pretended it hadn't taken place, he might have won in arbitration, but if he refused to eat it, Oscar would never trade with him again. Under normal circumstances, Oscar would pay him back over the time, but not now, not with the Feds crawling all over the place.

If only he hadn't spent so much. The trip, the jewelry. He had pissed money away, his intentions to be prudent fading daily as he promised he would save the following month, and then the next.

Now he had fallen on his ass.

He thought about Jason. No one even mentioned his name. As if he had just disappeared. He could see what this world was really like. As the crowd began to congregate, Joey looked for Oscar's clerk. Then he saw Remy. He knew she had seen the trade. She might be able to help him. He ran to her with his sheets in his hand.

"Remy, I need to ask something."

"Sure, Joey."

He stood in front of her, her cologne filling the air. She looked so clean, so unruffled amidst a chorus of smelly rats.

"Did you see my trade with Oscar yesterday?"

"Sure. A 50 lot."

"Do you remember the price or the time?"

"It was around 8:40. I remember the time because I took an early break. I'm not sure about the price."

"Did you see him confirm the trade?"

"You asked him to, but he never did."

"Did you think it was valid?"

"Absolutely. You made the trade with him."

"Would you testify to that?"

"Sure."

He stood quietly.

"Is he trying to stiff you?"

Before he could answer, she continued, "How much?"

"Two hundred and fifty gees."

She shot Oscar a venomous stare.

"Let me talk to him. If he knows you have a witness, he might back off."

"You would do that?"

Without answering, she walked to Oscar who was busy talking to his clerk. Oscar folded his arms as she approached.

"Doll, what can I do for you?"

"Straighten out the trade with Joey."

"I never made a trade with Joey."

"I saw him make a trade with you."

"Did you see me confirm it?"

"That seems to be the problem."

"The problem seems to be that you have your nose in business that is not yours. This trade is not your business, Masterwoman. Nor is it your problem."

"What happens in these pits is as much my business as yours."

"This is not about the pit. This is an out-trade."

"An out-trade that shouldn't have happened, Oscar. Let him out of it. I don't know what you're trying to pull, but you won't get away with it."

His face reddened.

"Listen, sweetheart. If you know what's good for you, you and your friend Sarna will take out your charge cards and march over to Saks Fifth Avenue. Go argue with some salesperson. Get out of my way."

Remy moved closer. Oscar took a Kleenex out of his pocket to wipe his forehead. Remy didn't budge. Her blue eyes punctured him. He studied her. Her reserve, her unmitigated determination was staggering.

Who did she think she was? He stomped his foot on the rubber floor to remove a wad of gum that was stuck underneath. "Don't bother me with this shit, Remy. I've got a clerk. Joey's got a clerk. Let them settle this. If they can't, we'll meet in arbitration."

"I'll be a witness, Oscar."

No one spoke to him like that.

"You do what you need to do, and I'll do what I need to do."

Remy felt the heat swell around her. She didn't want to lose her confidence in front of this villain, but she could feel her breath shorten. She was getting light headed. Remy never avoided confrontation, but facing Oscar created enough stress to make her wish she could hide from this beast.

Holly Rozner

Their eyes met. A stream of tension like a billowing fire rose between them. Suddenly a small group of traders surrounded them. One guy whispered to another that if he were Oscar, he'd sock her.

Oscar wished that he could hit her. But that would get him suspended. If Remy were a guy, this wouldn't be happening. No man would be stupid enough to alienate the person who held the orders.

"Call the trading police, Remy." Oscar taunted.

"I may not have to. The FBI is here Oscar. Unfortunately, they picked the wrong person."

Sarna stood nearby. Her eyes widened as she watched Remy and Oscar slug it out.

"Look, lady, I think you should shut up. One more word and I will bring charges against you."

"I'm not afraid of you, Oscar. You think you can dictate what goes on here because you're Zach Silverman's patsy. I'm not afraid of you, and I'm not afraid of him."

Oscar stood very still. Zach would have to take her side, would even have to support her or the whole damn building could be sued for discrimination. That was one reason why Oscar hated working with women. They didn't stand on their own two feet because they had special protection under the law.

"This sexual discrimination thing was getting entirely out of hand. Some employers didn't even want to hire women anymore," Ivan told him just last week. Well, this Masterman woman might have great tits and big balls but he would never let her stroll in and take over. He would get her, make her squirm. He would stick her with a trade. Then he would watch her wriggle. He could imagine her crying. He wished it could be his shoulder. He really wished he could stick his hand up her pants.

***

By 9:00 the whole floor was talking about Joey's out-trade. At 9:30 Zach's clearing house hauled him off the floor. He was asked to return his badge: his precious badge, the emblem that had given him an insider's edge, that identified him as a member, that opened roads to riches.

Being part of this frenzy had changed his life. The transformation from poor to rich had been an easy ride. Going down was catastrophic.

Remy ran into the hall as the security department was piling Joey's belongings into a bag. Like a prisoner, he was stripped of his identity, a hostage like Jason. Each was restricted from going on the trading floor. Both could be bankrupt.

Joey watched Oscar riding up the escalator towards the Club. That stinking sonofabitch. His presence blackened the air. Him and Zeus on his goddamn throne.

If only they could be stopped! Who was he? What could he do? They had taken away his living, seized his honor. They had cut him out. He imagined the twin ringmasters testifying.

Remy found him at the membership desk where he was signing a release.

"Joey, let me help you fight this."

"There will be a hearing tomorrow. You know how those turn out."

"The odds are stacked against you. You were there when they nearly creamed me."

"Oscar is immune."

"Not this time, Joey. I know someone involved in this federal investigation. I think I can put pressure on him to mitigate this."

"Mitigate?"

"Lessen the impact on you. Maybe someone will step up and..."

"Make the whole thing go away?" he laughed.

"Well. I don't know about that."

"You better not mess with these guys, Remy. They're tough."

"So am I."

"They're bigger and stronger."

"You know an awful lot, Joey."

He was getting shaky. He did know a lot, but how could he be sure he could trust Remy? She could have been planted. Anyone could be with the Feds. Anyone could be Zach's toad. It was important to be careful. Still, Remy didn't seem like the kind to betray him. Of course, he had known Sid Keller too. Had stood right next to him. He shuddered to think how easy it would have been for Sid to have zeroed in on him and not Jason.

"I'm going to go to arbitration. I want a record of this dispute."

"I will be your witness," Remy said. "Maybe he will split the trade. That'd better than eating the whole thing."

"It's still more than I can handle." He looked Remy straight in the eye with a forlorn stare. "Why are you going out on a limb for me?"

"Because Oscar must be stopped. Everyone is afraid of his power. He can run anyone out of business. I wish I could go to a newspaper with the story."

"But you can't."

"I can't because we live under the constant threat that Oscar will refuse to trade with us. Sooner or later that will change."

"Why would you think that?"

"Nothing stays the same."

Joey admired her intensity. Her glamour in no way diminished her intellect.

"Can you help me, Remy?"

"You have to promise me something. If I do make a deal, it would be by contract and you must agree to work with me."

"Who do you know?"

"I can't say yet. Give me your phone number. It may take a couple of days."

Jason had warned him never to give his number out. Had told him that the only reason someone would want to contact him wouldn't be a good reason. He had also told him never to talk on the telephone with anyone about Exchange stuff. You would never know who was taping a conversation that could later be used against you. But it was impossible to refuse Remy. He wrote the number down on a trading card, and as he held the cardboard in his hand, he almost caressed it, realizing how much he was going to miss this place. The noise, the action, the excitement was in his blood now. He would have to find some way to come back.

He looked into Remy's warm eyes. "I'll do whatever you ask me to do. If you can save this for me, I'm all yours."

She returned the glance. Until she had been preoccupied with her own goals—her desire to make a living, her struggle to unravel her father's death and solve the conflict with Ken.

Perhaps she could do something worthwhile and, at the same time, rid the Exchange of its corruption. Maybe she could crack the puzzle of her father's death and figure out the intricate network that let traders engage in daily crime sprees. Then perhaps she would understand what Ken was doing and everything that had torn them apart could be mended.

***

Remy used a public phone in the main hallway to call Ken. As she waited for him to answer, she could barely catch her breath, but when she heard his voice, her defenses collapsed. Her hands began to shake and she couldn't think of the right words to say. As much as she wanted Ken to help Joey, she also knew that this call was very personal.

"How are you, Remy?" Ken asked sincerely.

"I'm OK."

"It's so good to hear from you. I've missed you. You have no idea how much I've missed you."

Remy cradled the phone as if she could bring him near to her. All these wasted days! She had been so stubborn.

"I've missed you too," she murmured.

"I need to see you," he insisted.

"Tomorrow."

"Tonight."

She had been up since dawn and needed to think.

"Let's make it tomorrow."

"6:00 at the Italian Village."

"Ken, I need a favor."

"Shoot."

"It's about Joey Fortunato. He's the one who took Jason's spot in the pit as bagman for Oscar Doheney."

"You shouldn't say that on a telephone, Remy. You don't know who's listening."

"Don't be ridiculous. Do you think my phone calls are being taped?"

"You can get in trouble. And I can't discuss any of these people with you. You know that."

Her heart sank. What was he saying? That he missed her, but he still couldn't discuss what was important to her. Again he was silencing her. She began to tremble. They had gone over this. This is precisely why they couldn't see one another. How naïve to think anything would change because they had been separated. It would never be different. Nothing could bring them together.

Trade Secrets

"Remy, are you there?"

"No," she said weakly. "Not if you can't help someone I know you have the power to help. I have misjudged you. How stupid to bother you with such trivia. You just keep to yourself. Just think of that notoriety you will get while you lynch the people I know."

"You've got this all wrong, Remy."

"All I know is that you continue to lock me out of your life."

"Let me explain."

"There is nothing to explain."

She hung up the telephone and began to sob. The tears streaked her makeup and she used her hands to clear her vision just as Sarna Bramson walked by.

"Only a guy can make a woman cry like that," Sarna said gently.

"You don't understand, Sarna. I need to be alone."

"Oh no. You think you are made of steel. Well, no one is. Come with me. You think you've got problems. My husband is going to jail, I've lost everything, and I still don't know how to make money."

Sarna took her hand, and Remy followed her up the escalator. The hordes of traders rushing through the building were simply irritating now. All Remy felt was utter loss as they walked quickly through the marble foyer and into blazing daylight.

chapter 34

JOEY DECIDED TO call Jason. There was no one else to turn to, and he couldn't let his world dissolve without trying something.

"Joey wants to talk," Jason told Sarna. "The kid sounded desperate so I told him he could come over."

"He is desperate because Oscar won't trade with him," said Sarna as she set the table.

"I don't know what he thinks I can do. I don't owe Joey."

Jason stood next to Sarna while she prepared pasta. Thinking about the life they had once lived, he tossed the salad. That world seemed so remote, as if it had belonged to someone else.

Sarna was exhausted. She needed a hot bath. She watched Jason across the custom- built island that separated the sink from the refrigerator. The cloud hanging over their lives had brought them closer. Sarna had quieted her initial impulse to divorce when she realized she had nowhere to go. There would be nothing for her on her own, certainly not a settlement. She hadn't decided what to do next. Ivan explained that the Feds would strike a deal if Jason cooperated. Both of them were forbidden to discuss

Jason's case with any outsider and everyone was considered an outsider. "Everyone," Ivan emphasized.

Concentrating on her next move, Sarna concluded that the only way out was work. If others could trade, so could she. If she stuck around and Zach agreed to a payoff, she might get a share.

Sarna sat down at the table, poking at her food. The $500 she lost on the trade with Oscar had shaken her confidence. From now on she would trade so she could get back her life. The Exchange was a money machine. The guys on the floor were plain dummies. There must be some way to figure out how to do this. She stared at Jason and wondered how he got through the day waiting for the trial, mulling around the house with nothing to do.

At 7:00, Joey rang the bell. His eyes ablaze, he followed Jason into the kitchen. What a place! He had never seen such a house, certainly no crystal chandelier that size. The handles on the cabinets matched the crystal dangling from the fixture. Off to one side was a glass-enclosed breakfast area overlooking a patio that jutted out to the lake. The view was breathtaking. A genuine palace.

"Sit down, Joey," Jason said, directing him into the den. He put his feet on the stone coffee table.

"I need to talk to you, Jason. I need to explain something."

"OK."

"You know that Oscar manipulated it so I would take your place."

"It wasn't your fault, kid. I know how everything works."

"I want to help you," said Joey.

Jason smiled. Touching, but hopeless. "You better take care of yourself."

"I got nothing to take care of. I had another awful out-trade with Oscar. I'll owe them for the rest of my life."

Trade Secrets

Jason looked at Joey and smiled. He had fallen into a lion's den.

"I want to go to the Feds, tell them what I know."

Jason's throat tightened. If Joey did that, it could mean the end of his defense. If anyone were going to go to the Feds, he needed to be the one. Joey would just make a mess of things. It would get out of control and then no one would trade with Sarna.

"You'll get in trouble," Jason said.

"It doesn't matter."

"You'll need a lawyer."

"I have no money." Joey leaned forward as if he were going to whisper. Then he continued in a strong voice. "This is how I figured it. You will need a witness. If the government knows you got a witness, they'll go easier on you. If the Exchange knows that I'm testifying on your side, wouldn't that help you?"

Jason's back straightened. No one else was on his side.

"Sid Keller knows the story. He's been there on the trading floor while all of this was going on. If I help you, it'll help him and his boss, Ken Baldwin," Joey continued.

Jason's eyes lit up. "Who is that? How do I know that name? Where the hell did I meet him?" He stood up and walked over to the refrigerator for a can of pop.

"Want some?" he asked.

"Sure."

"Oh yes. It was at Zach's party. Remy was with Ken Baldwin. He's from New York. What's he got to do with this?"

"He's the consultant for the Feds," Joey began. "You don't think that Remy is in with them?"

"Not a chance. She's not an agent. She may not have even known that he was working with the investigation. I would trust Remy with anything"

"Remy's in trouble too," Sarna said as she came in from the kitchen and caught the last part of the conversation. "She made a fuss about Joey's out-trade. Now they're trying to implicate her. After she insisted that Oscar had made a trade with Joey, he gave her a trade. I am sure it was a setup. Then the Exchange called in compliance. Now she'll have to have to have a hearing and those don't usually go well."

"She's accused of trading illegally," Joey offered.

Jason sat back in his chair. These bastards would stop at nothing.

"It all happened so fast," Sarna said. "Oscar mumbled something and then they made a trade. It did look like a fix."

"Who would believe Oscar would fix a trade with her?"

"Someone who wanted to shut her up."

Jason jumped up. "Remy was never involved with Oscar. Ken Baldwin will straighten this out. He wouldn't want anything to happen to Remy," Jason said, ignoring Anthony Brooks' warning not to talk to anyone.

Joey interrupted, "We must get to Oscar, get him to talk."

"Oscar will never talk," Jason said.

"Look Jason, I didn't grow up in a mansion like this. I grew up on the street. I learned how to get people to talk," Joey said.

"You'll get yourself killed," Jason warned.

"I can take care of myself."

Sarna and Jason looked at the each other. At that moment Sarna's mind shifted into gear. In one second flat, she envisioned the whole thing, the scene in which she could reach Oscar the only way she had ever known how to get a man.

"I have an idea," Sarna interrupted. "I need to talk to Sid Keller."

Trade Secrets

"That's absurd. He's a mole," Jason shouted.

"He can help us," she insisted.

Jason stared at his wife. It was pointless to argue with her.

"First I have to figure out how to find him," she said thinking out loud. Her mind was racing a million miles a minute, thrilled by the sheer notion that she had a reason to contact Sid.

Jason had no idea what his wife had up her sleeve, but he could see the wheels in motion.

Sarna smiled. Jason's fate might not be sealed. With Sid's help, she could get to Oscar with the one trick that might work. Her incredible imagination had already outlined a script that would make Oscar deliver. This wouldn't be easy, but it had to be done.

What they needed was a spy. And Sarna Bramson knew just who that should be.

chapter 35

"Remy, you can't afford to mess around with these people," Lara said emphatically. She stood by the treadmill that Remy was using and spoke in a very deliberate manner.

"I won't let them destroy me."

"They can and they will."

"What am I supposed to do? Exchange rules prevent me from going to the newspapers. I could be fined if it ever gets out that I leaked a story. The rules are clear: a member who brings disgrace on the Exchange can be fined. And I can't hire a lawyer. The Exchange doesn't permit representation in a hearing."

"Listen, Remy. And listen hard."

Remy wiped herself off with a fresh towel and followed Lara into the café so they could speak privately. Lara leaned into her so no one could overhear their conversation.

"You have to call Ken Baldwin," she said.

"I will not."

"You need the government on your side, Remy. You've been set up. It looks as if you've done something wrong."

"What will they gain?"

"Plenty. The government doesn't know who is guilty and who is innocent. If the Feds can be convinced that the Exchange is policing itself and can land a big catch, that makes their investigation a success. By implicating you while they are completing their investigation, the Feds and the Exchange each get a payoff."

"I just don't see how." Remy had ordered a fruit smoothy and one for Lara too. As rattled as she was, she hadn't lost her appetite or her energy. She had spent the past hour working out and planning a defense. So far she had come up empty.

"You're in the middle of it so you don't see their tricks. They are using you to deflect attention away from Jason. He moves out of the line of fire while you become the star target. The two of them will walk away. Oscar should be the prime suspect, but it's easier for them to go to the weakest link. That's why you could evolve into an unlikely victim."

"And what could Ken do?"

"Ken knows you are not part of this. He can reach the right people and make them understand that this is a set-up."

"Why can't I just call the US Attorney myself?" asked Remy.

"That's just not done. And they have absolutely no reason to believe you."

Remy had never been in trouble. She was always the first to be sure no one else was in a tight spot. In that way she was a lot like her father. Had he been in her position, she wondered what he would have done. What did he do, in fact, surrounded by these criminals? Why didn't he stop them? Why didn't he ever discuss the things he saw? He must have known as much as she did. How on earth did he get along with Zach Silverman, or was that the point? He couldn't; he had to leave and that's what caused his problems. None of this explained the car crash.

Remy was too nervous to eat. If she asked Ken for help, it would be like acknowledging that his involvement had been OK. Now that she was a possible target, she saw that his work was necessary. Ken's role was more important than she wanted to admit. She could hear Lara's advice without having to say anything. She sipped a fresh cup of coffee. The bitter taste hurt her mouth. She put the cup down on the plastic tray and leaned over to touch Lara's arm.

"What would I do without you, Lara?"

"Get a good kick in the ass. Now get out of here and tell him what's going on. I've got a brief to write and I'll be up all night if I don't get started."

As she walked away, Remy's eyes followed her. Such different lives. Lara, the rebel, fastidiously cautious as an adult. Now Remy was forced to admit how flawed her idealism was. All the harsh words she had leveled at Ken seemed weak. Remy knew the danger inside the spidery web Oscar and Zach had spun. Without Ken nothing would have been uncovered. The realization brought a shattering reality and a terrible sense of loss. Now it was perfectly clear. Ken had been right after all.

***

Joey left Jason's house at 8:30, his foot tight on the pedal. Now he was an insider, plotting a way to bring justice to this reckless universe.

When he got home, Rosa was in bed. He looked at her, finally allowing himself to feel the depth of the crisis he faced. Maybe he could be a hero with Jason, but in his own home, he was a flop. He had made a gigantic step forward and then slipped like a kid on a sheet of ice.

Rosa saw Joey come in. She kept her eyes shut while he sat down on the bed and began to tell her about his meeting at Jason's.

"So this is over?" She screamed sitting up.

Holly Rozner

"Yes. Of course this is over. But I have a plan."

"When do we have to move out of here?" she asked, not hearing the rest of what he was saying.

"Next month."

"And I will be a waitress again?"

He slipped his arm around her waist but she kept him at a distance.

"I'm sorry, Rosa. It's not my fault. These guys are sharks. "

"I am not going back to that shit," she said, intent on her own thoughts.

"It'll only be for a little while."

"Then what? You gonna be President of the bank? Who are you kidding, Joey? We ain't never gonna have a chance like that again. There are no second chances for us. Can't you see that?"

"It won't be so bad. We still have each other."

"For me it will be hell."

She got out of bed and walked to the closet. She grabbed a new outfit she had bought.

"You see this, Joey. I never in my life even looked at clothes like this in magazines. Now you're telling me it won't be so bad. You know what? It will be the end of my life. Cause I'm not going to wipe up tables some slob dirties. I'm not going back to that apartment you and me lived in. No."

"We're gonna be OK."

She sat down on the new velvet sofa that had been delivered from Marshall Field's yesterday. She ran her hand over it and felt the plumpness of the pillow underneath.

"They're gonna take this away, Joey. We won't even have a couch. We're not gonna be OK. You just can't face the truth."

Everything Rosa said was true. He looked at her and still loved her, though he also knew that didn't matter. The fortune he had made was gone. The money. Ah, the money. That was the only thing that mattered.

He confronted her icy glare with harsh eyes, trying to assess her words. Her expression showed despair. But not for him. He rounded his shoulder and rocked back and forth as he began to understand what was distressingly obvious.

Without another word, he stood up, grabbed the dress and pulled off the Saks Fifth Avenue tags. He threw them on the floor and spit on the dress.

"I guess I botched it up, Rosa. When we started out, I was more than a dollar sign. You don't give a damn about me. So go back to whatever life you want. 'Cause I was wrong about you. You're nothing to me."

As he slammed the door behind him, he could taste the bile in his throat. He had fallen in love with a woman who loved a mirage.

The conversation with Jason had given him hope. He may be a meathead to Rosa, but he was back in action. If he couldn't have the life they cherished, he could at least do something right. Like a soldier, Joey stood up and straightened his shoulders. No one could beat him into the ground.

Not even Rosa.

***

Sarna met Sid Keller in his office. Doused in expensive perfume, she had spent an hour making sure every hair was in place. This meeting carried a double motive. While Sarna needed Sid for her plan, she also longed to be near him. Smoothing her skirt, she knew she couldn't afford to confuse these dual messages. She must stick to business.

His deep voice penetrated and her steadiness waned. She tried to read between the lines, looking for something in his cadence that would reveal if he ignored her because of his job, at the same time trying to sense if he wanted her as much as she wanted him. She held a firm gaze, but when she began to speak, her voice wavered.

Sid listened without saying a word. Beneath that layer of clothes were those luscious breasts. His eyes followed his desire as he imagined her, supple and needing him too. He fumbled with a pencil as he forced himself to remain aloof. He spoke as if they had barely met.

"We need to understand what this would mean for Jason," she said.

"And that would be?" he asked.

"Immunity."

She gave nothing away. If sex was on her mind, she hid it. Sid closed his eyes and then opened them again wondering how that pretty head of hers could fill with such machinations.

"I have to talk to Ken Baldwin," he said, regaining his balance. He wished he could say more, tell her how he had never meant to hurt her. He had been trained to hide his feelings, even from himself. But this vision, her arms hanging to her side, her legs crossed at just the right angle, moved him.

"Do you know who Ken Baldwin is?" he asked, realizing that she could not.

But she had done her homework. "Yes," she replied.

Sid called Ken on the intercom as Sarna repositioned herself. Sid spun his chair pretending to be busy with some papers. The air was tinged with fever, and if Ken hadn't appeared as quickly as he did, Sid may have said too much.

Ken entered the room and recognized Sarna immediately.

"You shouldn't be talking to us without a lawyer," he said.

"That's out of the question. I have an idea and we have no time."

Trade Secrets

"And this will do what?"

"It will help everyone. Remy. Joey. My husband."

"What has Remy got to do with this?"

"Oscar put her in a bad trade. She could get in a lot of trouble."

"Are you saying Oscar invented a trade, or that Remy did something wrong?"

"She did nothing wrong. It's Oscar and his crazy schemes." Sarna sat up very straight and launched into the stories of what she knew about the pit and what had happened when Oscar got mad at Remy. "It was a setup to punish her and make it look as if she is part of their shady network."

"And this was done to deflect attention from himself," Ken said out loud, putting the puzzle together as he understood immediately that everything Remy had told him about the pits was true.

He stood up and walked around the room. He couldn't get involved in this if it created any conflict of interest. His job was to find a way to prosecute Jason. No, that wasn't all true, he told himself. The goal was to bring down the system. He could do something to help Remy as long as it enhanced his case.

"Can I talk to you alone?" Sarna asked.

Ken looked at Sid. "I'm outta here," he said, leaving the room.

Sarna straightened out her suit. A string of deep sea pearls hung around her neck. Her eyes opened wide as she laid out the elaborate design. Ken calculated the odds of success as he listened to her electrifying melodrama.

It was unorthodox, he thought, but worth a try.

"You know this is risky. And very dicey."

"My life is on the line. People make fun of me. I am materialistic. So what? My passion for money is just as real as some intellectual's passion for literature. Is theirs elevated because it's heady? There is no difference, you know. Some people put themselves on a pedestal because they don't focus on material objects. I'm as greedy as they, or they as greedy as I, but the world gives them slack."

Maybe Sarna was right. What she said made sense, and what she was willing to do to preserve her life was a lot more than anyone else would do.

"Ok, Sarna. But be careful."

"You must promise my husband immunity."

"I can't promise that, but I will try to get his situation mitigated."

"Jason knows about this, but I don't think he has digested the gory details."

"I would think not."

Ken stood up and walked around the desk. Up close, Sarna looked fragile. Her small frame next to his made her look defenseless, and when he pictured her in the dramatic episode she had invented, he wondered if it might be a mistake to continue. Yet she seemed so determined, and she was correct—it was their only shot at Oscar.

Before he had time to change his mind, she rose to leave. She opened the door and had just about stepped into the corridor when she peeked back. Holding the knob with one hand she commanded, "No photos."

chapter 36

JOEY KNEW OSCAR'S daily habits so it was easy to decide when to start. The Club was the logical setting because it was there that Oscar would retreat after a frantic day.

The plan was set for 3:30 the following Tuesday. It took all day Saturday, each with a different task, to gather what they needed and most of Sunday to complete the setup. Sarna was in charge of the furniture. Her natural eye for color made shopping easy and with a single visit to three stores, she streamlined the décor, opting to keep costs down, marveling at the selection of goods that were ready-made. She found a rug with a burnt orange and green Indian design and worked the rest of the living room around that: Rattan sofas, plump, but inexpensive, a laminate coffee table, built-in TV cabinet and small pine dining room table with bright colored fabric on the chairs that picked up shades from the rug. The bedroom was done in white, and the den needed only a desk, a computer and a chaise lounge. It would have to do, she sighed, recognizing how temporary this gig would be.

Jason was in charge of obtaining the three- month lease on a two-bedroom with a fabulous view. When the escapade was over, they would ditch the apartment and try to sublet it. Joey picked up electronic equipment: television, radio, clock, tape recorder, computer and lamps. By Sunday evening they had everything but the big pieces. Sarna stopped at Fields for bedding and towels. When she added the last touches, the place looked inviting enough to live in.

Joey had mulled over the story so many times that the fantasy seemed real. Sarna would tell everyone that she rented a place near the Exchange to make it easy to get to work since she was leaving Jason. Ken tried to isolate any holes in the story, but Sarna was so precise in completing the lavish plot, there was little for his staff to do.

As Joey predicted, Oscar was finishing his second drink at the bar in the Club when Sarna sauntered in. Perfectly made up, she perched on a stool next to him and watched him order a third scotch. As she got ready that Monday morning, she told herself this was an acting experiment. If she pretended to be a whore, it wouldn't feel real.

"I'll buy drinks, doll. What do you want?" Oscar asked swirling the dark liquid in his glass as he spotted Sarna.

"Diet Coke."

"I would have thought you liked champagne, Sarna," he said looking her over. Up close she was some beauty.

"Not today."

She tilted her head and stared out at the city. It was a clear day. The last remnants of winter had faded into spring. She leaned across to get a napkin, and her breasts grazed Oscar's arm. He pushed his hand to squeeze her and then stopped, not wanting to cause her to retreat.

"Not yet," she said.

"When, Sarna?"

"Oh, Oscar, you are so bad." She looked him straight in the eye. His breath stank. This would not be easy. She threw her head back, her brown hair swinging, her silk blouse tightening around her breasts. She watched him swell as his eyes followed the outline of her nipples.

"You look tired," she said.

"Tough day," he said, his eyes on her. Such tits.

"You need a rest."

"That would be nice. Maybe we could lie down."

"I am tired, Oscar."

He studied her deep eyes and wondered what would make a dame like this tired.

"This ordeal with Jason has done me in," she said.

"It is a mess," he agreed.

"I need to make money, Oscar, so I can pay the bills that just don't stop."

He considered her plea. Maybe if he helped her out, she'd let him suck those tits.

"Stand near me tomorrow, Sarna. I'll see what I can do."

Her arm fell on his. "I don't know what will happen to me."

He held his hand in hers, looking to see if anyone was in the room. The bartender was in the back. The crowd that usually inhabited the Club late in the afternoon hadn't come in.

She fluttered her lashes. "I'd be so grateful," she whispered.

He looked into her eyes. His glance found the crevice where her blouse loosened slightly. Her skin looked so soft. The fragrance she wore made him light-headed.

"Maybe you and me could have a little fling." He winked.

"What would your wife say?"

"Don't worry about my wife. I take care of myself." He nudged closer, the air teeming with his foul breath.

He slid his arm around her waist, this time stroking her breast with his thumb. Sarna didn't budge. Her nipple hardened. He pressed against her and closed his eyes.

When she didn't move, he asked, "You want to go somewhere?"

"You're too quick for me, Oscar."

"I need another drink." Oscar sipped on the ice in his glass. Oscar had never considered Sarna more than a woman interested in gold bracelets. With his hand on her, his eyes danced. Such wicked lips. He could imagine them on his dick. Maybe Sarna didn't go in for down- and-dirty sex. She might be one of those who needed a guy to fall in love with her before she would suck him.

He reached his fingers towards her long neck. Her white shirt creased, and he could see a hint of her breasts. He wondered what kind of boobs she had: rosy bubble gum or dark and sumptuous.

"What makes you tick, Sarna?" he asked softly.

"I'm a complex person."

"I bet you are."

She smiled. "And you, Oscar. What makes you tick?"

"I'm more complicated than you think, Sarna Bramson."

"You sure know how to make money."

"That's not all I'm good at." He placed one hand on her thigh and pinched her gently. Most broads were easy. Give them a thousand bucks and they'd crawl all over you, but this babe was a challenge. If he could screw her, he'd never ask for another thing.

His hand inched its way up her leg as he pondered whether or not she was wearing underpants.

Unable to decide whether she should tell him to move his hand or let it stay where it was, Sarna stared back at him.

Trade Secrets

They sat like that for nearly a minute until Oscar spoke. "I'll rent a room at the Four Seasons. Dinner in bed."

"We'll see," she said, knowing she had clinched the deal. As she slid off the stool and stood near the bar, Oscar grabbed her arm.

"I could make a woman like you scream."

"I'll bet you could," she said.

"We could make music together." His insides hurt. He tried to stand. He had never been this close to such a good lay and not known how to snag it. He had been so preoccupied in the pit, he never noticed how beautiful she was. Long legs. Great hips, tantalizing boobies. He loved titties. He would give a bundle to touch them. He looked into her eyes hoping for some confirmation that she might want him too.

Oscar placed his hands on her hips. She didn't stir. There was a long, long silence. Finally she said, "I have an apartment."

He nudged towards her.

"Let's get outta here."

When she nodded, he couldn't tell if she was kidding. Up until now the only women who came onto him were fat clerks who couldn't get a lay with anyone else. Recently when he bothered to look in the mirror, he could see signs of aging. His beginning-to-be bald spot made him look older than forty-five. All his life he had searched for dames like this. He'd have to be careful not to push too hard. He didn't want to lose this chance.

Sarna breathed deeply. "We'll go to my place," she suggested.

"With Jason?"

"I live alone, Oscar."

"Where is he?" Oscar asked anxiously.

"I left him."

Holly Rozner

"You must be lonely."

"Yes."

Suddenly he could picture her beneath him. He wondered how she liked her sex, how he could please her. He didn't want to make any mistakes. If he did it right, he could have her again. And again.

"I wondered how you would hold up under this pressure."

"It's been ghastly," she whimpered.

"I feel responsible for what happened."

"Jason is his own worst enemy."

"He's a fool."

"He isn't as smart as you, Oscar."

"Let's talk about this later," he said softly.

He took her arm and continued talking as if he were her father. "No one will blame you for leaving. He's in a terrible situation."

All at once he saw himself as her savior. If he could get her to lean on him, he'd be able to hold her, dig deep into her, while he helped her though this difficult time. As they entered the hallway outside of the Club, he kept on talking. "Do you still have that mansion? On Sheridan?"

"It's up for sale."

"You need a lot of money for the lawyers. It's a mess."

"I can't deal with it, Oscar," she said, her eyes pleading.

She had taken him into her confidence. This new perspective aroused him so profoundly that he couldn't control himself. Without any warning he pulled her into the corridor and kissed her, resting one hand on her face. "You'll need someone to get through this. Let me help you."

She didn't answer. She moved her face to one side and licked his finger.

"Let's go." He seized her hand and led her down the escalator and out of the building where a bank of yellow taxis were lined up. He stood with one hand around Sarna and the other extended hailing a cab. As soon as one pulled up to the curb, he slithered next to her. As the taxi pulled away, Oscar held his hand between her leg, gently inching under her pants, working to find that sweet spot. Sarna looked over his shoulders at the oncoming traffic. It was only six blocks to her building, but she felt lightheaded. The cab bounced along the pock-marked streets, finally finding its way into the driveway of Presidential Towers. As it jerked to a stop, Sarna pushed Oscar away.

"We're here," she squealed.

He threw a twenty to the cabby.

His arm remained at her waist, his eyes never letting go. As she fumbled with her keys, his hands brushed against her skirt. He felt like a fire burning out of control. If he couldn't relieve himself soon, he would burst. Inside the elevator, he rubbed against her, grasping her hands into his, his brittle beard grazing her cheek.

"Take it easy," Sarna said, but reason had no hold on him. When they were in front of her apartment and she jostled the keys to unlock the door, he unzipped his slacks and held himself, hard as a rock. With the door slightly ajar, Oscar pushed Sarna against the wall of the foyer, tearing at her clothes. He hiked up her skirt and fell down on his knees, yanking her underpants. He began to lick the skin between her legs as she gasped for breath. Then he pulled her on the carpeting, his mouth on hers and plunged into her.

Sarna hadn't bargained for this. She had planned on getting her information before Oscar got to her. Now she was utterly helpless. Jason was with his lawyer. She knew Joey was in the other bedroom, but if she called for him, the drama would end.

"I need a drink," she said finally crawling out from Oscar's sweaty clasp.

Everything had happened so fast. Her body was weak, her mind cluttered with things she must do. Oscar had satisfied himself, but she didn't have anything she needed.

"I'll be back," she said as she stood up. Sarna ran into the bathroom and washed her mouth out with toothpaste. She felt nauseated. She wanted to talk to Joey, but she couldn't risk it. She splashed her face with water and downed two Tylenol. She couldn't afford to let this opportunity slip away. She girded herself as a real actress might, trying to remember what she had ever learned in the one acting class she had taken at the University of Illinois. She would do what famous movie stars do when they have to get through difficult love scenes with co-stars they abhor. She envisioned herself as Kathleen Turner with Danny DeVito's hands mauling her.

Oscar flopped on the sofa, his eyes taking in the newly-furnished room. The view was great, overlooking the city towards the east. The location ideal. But the quarters were cramped. His shirt was hanging out, his pants half on, half off. He closed his eyes while Sarna pulled herself together. Sarna dabbed cologne behind her ears. On her way into the living room, she grabbed a bottle of wine. Then she sat down on the sofa next to Oscar.

"I've always wanted you, Sarna," he said running his arm down her back when she sat next to him.

"You never acted that way," she said, prying open the wine.

"I never thought you would want me."

"You're not a bashful man, Oscar."

"I can't let on to what I feel when I'm in the pit, doll. The guys would make mush of me."

Trade Secrets

"I'm sure they wouldn't care," she said, as he kissed her ear. She pulled the cork out of the bottle.

"You're the most beautiful woman I've ever seen, Sarna. How did you ever end up with Jason?" he asked.

"What do you mean?"

"You're too smart for him."

"I was young," she said. "I fell in love, Oscar."

"And now?"

"I'm not in love with him anymore." She poured a glass of wine and handed it to Oscar. He was glad to hear this. It opened up the possibility that she could be interested in him. He wondered if he could hold onto a woman like Sarna, calculating what it would take to make her his mistress. He felt dazzled at the prospect of doing this again. He would do anything just to have her skin near him night after night. He might even share his money with her. God, she was gorgeous.

"Let's go into the bedroom," he said.

"Let's talk, Oscar. I want to get to know you. Then we can screw."

Just as he thought. Next she would want to know if he cared for her. Broads were all the same. He would go along because he wanted her so. He would agree to talk if that's what she wanted. Dames like to talk. As long as he could screw her, touch those tits, suck that pussy. It would be worth a five million dollar settlement with his wife to wake up next to Sarna. To run his finger down her stomach to that thick dark bush! He placed one hand on her belly.

"So what do you want to talk about?" he asked.

"Tell me all about you," she said. Her long legs were dangling, her legs slightly parted. "Tell me how you started out in this business. How you ended up with such power."

"My story is very simple and boring."

She sat up. "I need to know," she pleaded.

"You're lonely, sweetie, aren't you?"

"I am," she said, her eyelashes fluttering.

He was quiet for a moment trying to figure out how he could sum this up fast. "I was an Irish kid who met a Jew. The rest is history. Zach and I became a team. We knew how to make it big."

"How did you end up with him?"

"What do you mean?"

"You know. As partners," she purred.

"We were neighbors, we trusted each other. That's all. You are one sexy broad," he murmured snuggling into her neck.

"Let's lie down," she commanded, abruptly cutting off the conversation. When she put her arms out for him, he just grinned and followed her into the unspoiled bedroom with its delicate fresh linens. She lay down and slowly unbuttoned her shirt. If he'd had a camera, he would have taken a picture and kept it in the pocket of his trading jacket so he could peek at it when he wanted to. Sarna nude, her velvety skin exposed, was more than he could bear. She reached up for him and he knelt over her as if she were a wax figure. For a quick second a strange mixture of desire overtook her as she closed her eyes and tried to imagine that Oscar Doheney was Sid Keller. The minute Oscar's head hit the pillow, she reached behind the bed and fumbled with a box she had placed there. Inside were five perfectly formed marijuana cigarettes.

"For us," she announced as she took one out and lit it.

Sarna handed the joint to Oscar. He took it with his right hand and puffed. Then he handed it back to her.

"Take another," she insisted. After three shots of scotch and a glass of wine, it took only minutes for Oscar's head to spin. As soon as she could safely confirm that he was off balance, Sarna reached behind to verify that the microphone was in the right place. Then she curled up on top of Oscar. With detached calculation she placed his hands on her breasts. Thrilled with what he thought she wanted of him, he began to stroke her, but she held his hand steady.

"When did you make Jason your bagman?" she asked.

"Don't you love that? Zach made up the term. Or maybe it was that lawyer, Ivan Bloch. I forget. But once we had someone to steal the trades, it was so easy. The bagman just stood there and the good trades went to him. Then the profit was split. The Feds want us, but we will never get caught. No one can prove who gets the first trade off the customer orders. No one can actually prove it, you know." He cupped her breasts. The nipples were dark and sumptuous. "I know it hurt you when we had to can Jason, but we had to. He took too much. Zach got cheap. Out goes one and another comes in, someone who won't ask for so much." The tape recorder over Oscar's head made no sound. "I was the one who discovered Jason. We had to cut him out and give the trades to Joey, but at least we didn't have to kill him. We had to get rid of him; it's not like Harry Saks." As he said this, he ran his thumb over her nipples.

"Who is Harry Saks?"

"Harry was Zach's partner. Long before you got there. Jason didn't know him. Good man. But no guts. Zach and he started together as kids, but after a while, it didn't work out. When Zach set up a mutual fund to collect the bad trades, Harry got upset and he threatened to expose the whole thing. Zach couldn't let that happen. It would have closed us up. Destroyed the Exchange. Zach hired me. I was the one ordered to follow him down a slippery ravine with bright lights shining in his rear-view mirror. Anyone would have been blinded."

"What are you talking about, Oscar?"

"You should have seen it when his car hit the tree. I burst out laughing. I didn't really think I could pull it off. But I did. I did it. God, my head aches. What is in those cigarettes?"

"Why did Joey take Jason's place."

"That little prick was easy pickings," Oscar said. "No backbone." He held her tight and smiled at her. "You've got more backbone than that dago." His hands played with her as he spread her legs apart. "Harry Saks, that was different."

Sarna clutched his head and stared into his eyes.

"You stuck Remy with that awful trade."

"I only follow orders, doll." Oscar could hardly speak as he slid his finger into her.

Sarna glanced at her watch. She needed to hurry this. She took his penis in her right hand. Oscar swelled to her stroke. All at once he couldn't remember what he had been talking about. Then it came back as he saw the image of blood that had spilled on the road when Harry Saks' car was crushed. He didn't know until the following day if Harry Saks had actually died.

"Poor Harry. It simplified things that he couldn't testify. There was the outside chance that he had seen me, but once he was buried, it didn't matter," Oscar said as if he were talking to himself.

Oscar was wasting her time talking about some man she never heard of. She had to get on track. Oscar was lost in his own reverie picturing them together on a trip in the Caribbean, Sarna nude, drinking daiquiris. They would make love all day. And at night, she would sleep on top of him.

"Did Zach make you do it?"

"Kill Harry Saks?"

"No, no. Oscar. I was talking about Remy. Did Zach make you stick her with a bad trade?"

"Of course. Zach hates her. She's a cunt. She wants to get us, but she'll never succeed. We'll get her first." His head fell against the sheets. "She thinks she can protect Joey. Now she needs to get out of this mess she's in. There won't be any more Joeys or Jasons, not anymore." Oscar's voice began to trail off as he lost his equilibrium.

"How many others have there been?"

Oscar motioned for Sarna to lie next to him. "Those stupid kids. They want to be traders in the worst way. Think that then they'll have the world in the palm of their hands. They are all so fucking greedy. You've seen them. They start out as clerks, like chorus girls lined up in front of a Broadway producer. We pick 'em as we see them. The hungrier, the better. We learned our lesson from Jason. We can't do it without them. Someone has to bag the trades or the inside info we have is useless. Then they're on our payroll forever."

"What payroll?"

His eyes rolled into his head. "Crestwood Trading. Zach owns it. The biggest clearinghouse in Chicago and all the brokerage houses use us. We got a scheme that no one will ever figure out. Zach created it. Well, actually Ivan Bloch did. The whole thing is so brilliantly complicated. Ha. How we did this, Sarna, how we did this will never be unraveled. On top of everything else Ivan figured out a way for us to do it all tax-free. We haven't paid taxes in years. The mutual fund got to Harry. He didn't have guts."

She let him hold her. She laid her head on his chest as she took his hands into hers.

"So Zach does none of the dirty work?"

Oscar opened his eyes as he contemplated this thought. "He's a goddamn Greek god sitting behind his desk. There was a time when he worked the floor, but it's been years. Years. I bet if you added it up, we've stolen $30 million dollars," he crowed. "You think people can make a living like

Jason did without knowing where the orders are? Well, they can't. And that's why our plan works. We know before the world knows which direction the market is going. It's all in the orders and they're stuffed in my pocket at the opening."

"Some people can," Sarna pressed.

"Name one."

"Remy Masterman."

"Remy Masterman is history." Oscar straightened himself up and tried to fight the dual effects of pot and liquor. "Let me tell you something. Remy is one inch away from going to jail."

"What did she do?"

"It doesn't matter. Zach can make it look like she did. He'll invent something. He needs the Feds to concentrate on someone else. He will get them to go after her."

Sarna listened quietly knowing that Oscar had lost his focus.

"It's his word against hers. And who is anyone gonna believe? That two bit broad? Or Zach Silverman?"

"But it's all untrue."

"That's what makes it so delicious," Oscar raved as he looked right into Sarna's brown eyes.

"You would try to destroy her because she doesn't do what you tell her to do?"

"I don't want to talk anymore, Sarna. I just want to eat you up." He lunged towards her, pulling her down and burying himself in her breasts.

When he looked up to kiss her, his smell made her feel faint. But she needed to know one more thing.

"Do you hate women, Oscar, or just Remy?"

"Does it look like I hate women? Jason was lucky to have this every night," he said, stroking her thighs. "What would he say about it if he could see us?"

"You would destroy one woman just to save yourself?" she continued. "One innocent person."

"The world loves a devil," he bellowed.

"Yes." As she said this, Oscar collapsed on top of her, into a deep sleep.

Sarna sat still until she could feel a tear fall on her cheek. Carefully she moved herself out from under him, pulled a chenille blanket over her body and reached over to click off the tape recorder. Then she undid the tape.

When the recorder clicked, Joey appeared from the second bedroom.

"That was some performance," he said.

She put her hand to her lips to quiet him. Then she handed him the tape. He could see tears brimming in her eyes.

"That was real Academy Award stuff," he whispered. Only this scene was for real, she thought as Joey took the tape from her hands. "Are you OK?" he asked.

She wanted to wail against a world that had let this happen to her; she wanted to strike out at Jason for allowing her to be mauled by Oscar, this devil-who-should-be dead. But it was important for Joey to get going. She signaled for him to leave. If he didn't get out of there fast, the whole plan would go up in smoke.

Sarna wrapped a silk robe around her trembling body as Joey Fortunato took the tape and ran like a bat out of hell.

chapter 37

OSCAR WAS ASLEEP on Sarna's bed—the one Joey and Jason had helped her buy over the weekend. Sarna began to shake. She got out of the bed and went to the mirror. Pale and even thinner than usual, the image in the mirror was the face of a stranger. A hooker? A whore? Was she that? She had done this because her husband couldn't find his way out of a paper bag. The past week confirmed what she had always known: women are stronger than men. On his own, Jason would be in jail and she would never secure their financial footing. This escapade had been a last ditch effort to stop the hemorrhage.

Oscar's scent lingered in the air. She had to get rid of his smell. She took a hot shower and then selected a red dress from the closet so she could leave before Oscar awoke. Her mischievous plan would make Zach the centerpiece of the investigation, a fact that helped overcome her anguish.

Jason wouldn't ask many questions. His inertia had been the plague of their marriage. It certainly allowed Oscar to manipulate him. At least he wouldn't delve into her life like a critical parent. Still, the responsibility of handling everything took its toll. It actually stung to think that Jason had let her do this and now she felt a pang of depression.

Holly Rozner

The deed had been done and she had done it successfully, but how could he have let her?

While the money was pouring in, it was easy for her to overlook Jason's weakness. Falling for Sid let her push Jason into the background. What would Jason do if he found out about Sid? He would never confront her. Now he had let her go too far. Even if he didn't know the bloody details about what she and Oscar were doing, what could he possibly be thinking? He knew enough to obtain the lease. He knew too much. He expected her to have no feelings. But she did.

Before she left the apartment, she looked around and, for the first time, realized how much of her life she had wasted collecting expensive things. In the future she would focus on perfecting a skill so she could be free. The favors Jason had accepted from Zach and Oscar exacted a hefty price. As she applied her lipstick, Sarna determined to take control of her life and never be in Jason's shoes.

The beguiling drama with Oscar had been a gamble, landing her a starring role in real-life theater. Basking in her success at finessing him, Sarna smiled bitterly at her reflection and closed the drawer.

She might not be Remy Masterman, but in her own devious way, she was unstoppable.

***

While Sarna and Oscar were locked in the apartment, Jason met with his lawyer, Anthony Brooks, who listened quietly as Jason narrated the seedy scheme that Joey and Sarna had cooked up. He had never heard anything like it. And he felt a genuine sense of dread that indictments could materialize to derail the Exchange for not policing itself.

"Who will deliver the tapes?" Brooks asked.

"Joey."

The willingness of all the parties to go through with something so outrageous fascinated him. He retained a cool demeanor and tried to figure out how to pass a signal to Ivan without jeopardizing his client privilege. Prohibited from discussing anything with outsiders that a client told him, he could make Ivan co-counsel and then be free to tell him everything. He must protect himself. Like everyone else, Anthony Brooks was indebted to Zach and equally reliant on Ivan Bloch for his meteoric rise. If he didn't stop this ludicrous plot from unfolding, he would lose his credibility with both men and that would not help his run for Governor. The state needed a candidate from the African American community. He was first in line to fill that niche. Zach wielded such power in Chicago. If Anthony double-crossed him, his career would be compromised and all hell would break loose.

It was 4:15. Sarna would still be in the apartment with Oscar and there was time to intercept the plan if he could reach Ivan and get someone to block Joey before he got to Ken Baldwin's office.

He stood up abruptly. "Excuse me, Jason, I need to make a phone call."

Jason slouched into the plush leather chair. During those few minutes alone he examined the awards on the wall—citations that Anthony Brooks had framed and positioned next to his *summa cum laude* diploma from Harvard Law School. On paper Brooks looked great, but Jason had his doubts. Ivan raved about how important it was to have Brooks as the lead lawyer, but the deal was not clinched.

Immersed in his own worries, not once did he dwell on the fact that his wife was two miles across the Loop with Oscar. He never actually envisioned Sarna doing what she would have to do, driving the image so far into the back of his mind that when he pictured them together, he imagined her sitting at a desk while Oscar spewed out his secrets.

He rationalized that Sarna was doing whatever she was doing as much for herself as for him. She was an avenue to refashion this disaster into a happy ending. By denying the actual version, Jason leapt to the next level—nabbing Oscar and Zach.

Then he would finally be the man his father wanted him to be, forgetting that Sarna was the brains. He felt a surge of power he imagined the rescue as his own. His mind transposed him from victim into savior, a man who could set things straight.

Jason didn't notice that Anthony Brooks had been gone for a very long time. He picked up a newspaper from the desk and glanced at the headlines, but his mind wandered. The clock touched 4:30. Joey had been instructed to call Jason's answering machine when he got to Ken's office. He grabbed the phone to dial home. There were no messages.

Jason was afraid that Ken Baldwin might be gone before Joey got to his office. That would delay things until tomorrow. Ken Baldwin was the only one in a position to turn things around.

***

Once he heard from Brooks that Sarna would be taping Oscar, Ivan hung up and called Zach. He told him to find the thugs who dwelled in the inner crevices of the Exchange, tucked away just for situations like this.

"The apartment is just ten blocks away so it will be easy to cut Joey off."

In less than five minutes, two men knocked on the office door. Zach led them into the conference room, trying to remember their names. The two look-alikes had been around for a long time. Now his fate was in their hands.

"No fingerprints," he commanded. "Get whatever tape he has and bring it here. I don't care what you do with the kid. Don't make it messy. If Joey disappears, the newspapers will be asking questions."

The two nodded. They both had paunchy stomachs and thick hair. From a distance they could pass as twins, but up close Zach saw that one had a round face and small black eyes, while the other, a bit thinner, had thick lips and bushy eyebrows. They wore turtlenecks and light ski jackets.

Zach got right to the point. He handed them a photo of Joey. Then he instructed them to grab Joey as he exited Sarna's building. Zach glanced at the clock. It was 4:29. If Joey were to reach Ken Baldwin's office by 5:00 o'clock, timing was critical.

They caught the next elevator and exited the building. A car was waiting outside. They were told to wait in front of Presidential Towers until Joey came out. One decided to stand in the lobby while the other stayed in the car across the street. If everything went right, the tape would be in Zach's office by 5:00.

That way, as soon as they captured Joey, they could dispose of him.

chapter 38

As soon as Remy called, Ken rushed across the Loop. He was visibly upset. He knew that if she were in danger, it could have been his fault. That she was targeted reinforced what he suspected: anyone who messed with Zach was a mark.

As the cab wound through traffic, Ken calculated his next move. Zach could hold up the investigation by scaring innocent people like Remy. The situation had to be dealt with gingerly. At this moment, Ken had no idea how to block Zach, but he had to prevent Remy from being the ultimate casualty.

He paid the driver and bolted into the River Club where Remy was leaning against the front counter. She looked so delicate. Her eyes latched on to his as he rushed towards her. When he touched her hand, he could feel her shaking. He held her against him, her familiar scent igniting all the feelings he had forced himself to push aside during this past painful month. She laid her head on his shoulder and he could feel her quiver as she fell against his body.

He took her face into his hands.

"I never dreamed anything like this could happen. You shouldn't be involved..."

She didn't let him finish. "It's not your fault," she said. "At first I thought it was. I thought you had no business barging in and digging into something that wasn't your business. But you're right. This proves it. I'm the one who has been wrong."

He kissed her on the lips and when he pulled back, he saw a smile wash across her face. Never would he let that smile slip away.

"I've missed you so," he whispered.

"I was afraid I lost you, Ken."

"You can't lose me," he said.

"I've behaved badly."

"I love you, Remy."

"I love you, Ken. I understand what you were trying to do. I was horrible. I didn't mean to be. I just couldn't stand being locked out. "

"You won't be from now on," he said, pulling up her chin with his forefinger, his eyes locked on hers.

"I want us to be together."

"We will be."

"No more secrets?"

"No more. But you must let me get you out of this mess. You are in a vulnerable position. These men are animals."

"I'm safe with you," she said, hugging him.

Her trust was an almost childlike dependence that made him feel powerful when he was not. Her reliance on him made him worry. He wanted to make her world secure, to look after her for the rest of his life. As he looked back on his career, there was no other time he had been at such a loss. He was always able to think on his feet, even in the tightest situations. His analytical ability to mete out a problem had defined his career. It was the very reason why the government had hired him for this investigation. But at this moment, as he nestled Remy's face into his and kissed her lips again, he had no idea what his next step would be.

***

As he waited for the elevator, Joey paced up and down the hallway, figuring out how he was going to make it to Ken's before the office closed. The past hour, locked in Sarna's bedroom, he had nearly gone crazy. Now it was time to pin down his enemy. He lay on the call button as if he could will the elevator onto the twentieth floor. Then he began scuffling in small circles, his hands in his pockets as the pressure mounted. If this plan worked, he'd have his revenge.

He looked at his watch. It was 4:40. Ken's office closed in twenty minutes. Ken didn't know he was on the way. He pressed the button again, standing with his hands folded, his eyes searching the lights above the elevator shaft to find out what floor the elevator was on. The tape was safely tucked in his breast pocket. He located an exit and contemplated taking the stairs. Then he moved down the hall like a baseball player stealing a base when at last, after what felt like an hour, the elevator door opened.

Two women were standing inside when Joey got on. He tried not to appear nervous as they chattered on about where they were going for dinner. 4:44. At best, it would take ten minutes to cross the Loop and then only if there was no traffic. As he considered the fastest route, he realized that he would never make it on time. Even if he got across the Loop quickly, it would take another five minutes to get to Ken's office.

When the elevator landed on the ground floor, Joey pushed in front of the ladies. The short, pudgy man who worked for Zach was standing there but the ladies clicked their heels close behind Joey and the goon had to wait for them to leave. He grunted, stepped aside and figured that if he failed to snatch Joey, his partner could get him outside.

At the last minute, Joey turned around abruptly and followed the exit sign to the back. That would be a shorter route across the crowded streets.

When Joey disappeared, Zach's assistant was stunned. As soon as he realized what had happened, he ran outside and hustled into the car.

"He went out the other side," he stammered, closing the car door.

"You let him go?" the other one exploded.

"Two women were in the way. I couldn't do anything. Step on it."

"If we lose him, Zach will cut us into pieces."

"He went out the back door."

"We have to find him."

The thinner guy slammed on the gas, and the car swerved around the building.

They turned north. From a few hundred yards away, the fat one spotted Joey walking east.

To follow him, they would have to go around three blocks because the street Joey had chosen was one-way.

"I'll get out and run after him," he offered.

"You can't grab him in broad daylight."

The stooge thought about it and realized that he was stuck. In the driveway of Sarna's building, they could have easily captured Joey, but here, near the train station, there were hoards of pedestrians and hundreds of cars. They couldn't even park. Between 4:00 and 6:00, cars were not allowed to stop on streets in the Loop. If they waited at another corner, they would be shooed away by the police.

The car missed a squad car as they shot past the Chicago and Northwestern train station.

"Does Zach know where Joey's headed?"

"He must."

"Should we call him?"

"When he finds out we screwed this up, he'll go bonkers."

But they had no other option. Zach answered immediately and started screaming. The short guy held the phone away from his face. Zach's voice was loud enough to set off a bomb. If they didn't figure something out fast, they could kiss this job goodbye.

"We couldn't help it," he explained, emphasizing the detail of how the one way traffic intercepted their plans. But Zach simply wailed.

"We'll get him, Mr. Silverman," he promised without any idea how he would keep that promise. "Do you know where is he headed?"

"The Federal Building, you moron." Zach snarled. "Wait for him there."

The thinner guy hit the gas. Now they would have to go around the station, turn left, take Randolph over the expressway to turn south again. It was 4:46. The Federal building certainly closed by 5:00. Traffic was gridlocked. Knowing that this was a futile chase, they stared at each other. Joey on foot was much more agile than they were, encumbered in this sprawling Cadillac. Joey's route to Ken's office would take him south, but by the time they got there, they would never be able to find him. The streets were flooded with pedestrians rushing to their trains.

"Zach's nuts, you know," one of the men said to the other.

"Yea, that's what scares me. He's crazy enough to kill us if we lose this toad."

Silently, they bore through the dense traffic. The ten-block ride had taken fifteen minutes. It was 5:15. They looked at each other and moaned.

"I'm starving," said the fat one.
"We might as well get a sandwich," said the driver.
"Mitchell's still open?"
"Don't they stop serving after lunch?"
"I dunno. I could eat a horse."
"We have to call Zach."
"And tell him the truth?"
"Zach Silverman doesn't like the truth."

The pudgy guy started to shake. The light changed. Traffic was crawling. They needed a miracle, they needed Joey to come strolling by.

"We'll wait five minutes and then…"
"Then what?"
"I don't know what. You got any ideas?"

The other one shook his head.

At 5:30 they began rehearsing what they would tell Zach.

Joey was on his way home. He had abandoned his plan after he called Ken's office. When no one answered, he decided to take the tapes to his apartment to make a copy. He would deliver them to Ken tomorrow.

Then he hopped on the bus that went north on LaSalle Street.

***

It was dusk when Oscar awoke. The sun had moved behind the skyscrapers. When Oscar first opened his eyes, he couldn't remember where he was. He glanced at his Rolex. 5:25. Whose apartment was this?

He stared at the newly furnished bedroom and could smell perfume. He sat up and dangled his legs over the bed. Nothing looked familiar, but Sarna's sweet smell lingered in the air. As he rubbed his eyes, everything came into focus. He had had the lay of his life.

He reached across the bed and felt panic when he realized it was empty. His head was heavy and he thought he might pass out. He called out Sarna's name, but there was no response. Then he fumbled on the bed stand for the TV clicker. As soon as he located it, he lay back and closed his eyes. The news droned in the background as he dozed off once more, retracing their chance meeting at the bar. All he could remember was Sarna beneath him. His cock stiffened. Everything else was a blur. When he opened his eyes again and stared at the empty glass of scotch beside the joint he had so happily inhaled, he felt woozy.

Then the sexual encounter engulfed him and he couldn't control himself. His hand smoothed his stomach and he reached between his legs. His own touch made him spew his liquid on his hands. Where was she, that gorgeous doll? He wanted her so.

A few minutes went by before he hoisted himself up and struggled into the bathroom. It was late. He usually called his wife by 4:30 to tell her what he was doing, but in his ecstasy, he had forgotten. The excuse he used on most occasions was pretty simple, a handy alibi that he had gone to the River Club to work out and taken a massage. If he took her out for a fancy dinner, she might not ask questions. Maybe she would be glad that he got it somewhere else. She hardly touched him anymore. Sometimes he had to pay one of the clerks on the floor, but more often than not, the excitement of making it with an honest-to-god trader turned dames in his direction. None of them compared with Sarna. His hand brushed the afternoon stubble on his face. He wondered if he might have scratched her, though she certainly hadn't complained. In fact, he thought she had been downright charmed.

Holly Rozner

Once he found his balance, he searched each room and noted to himself that Sarna kept everything in perfect order. Then he decided he had to dress and get out. He took a shower, wrapped a towel around his waist, and telephoned his wife. They agreed to meet at the Rose restaurant. She asked routinely about his day. As he answered, he smelled his clothes. His shirt stank, but he had no fresh clothing. He would have to go home a mess.

"It was a frantic day," he said as he stuffed his wallet and keys into his pocket. The telephone rested on his shoulder, his head cocked to one side.

"I was so tired I stopped for a massage. I'll catch the 6:30," he said as he zipped up his pants and sat down on the edge of the bed to put on his socks and shoes.

When he hung up, he searched the bathroom for some men's cologne. There was none, of course, because this place was Sarna's. Along the bathroom sink he reveled in the trinkets that were signs of her. Fresh flowers in a vase. A large bar of green and pink soap. He picked it up, trying to find her in the scent.

He stopped to scribble a note. He felt in his pocket and found a trading card, a hard cardboard paper four by six. On it he wrote "thanks." He threw the card into the bed, that bed he knew she would sleep in by herself. He would be up all night imagining that pale body. He stood still for a very long minute to set the image of her clearly in his mind so that he could draw on it as the evening passed, and the physical reality of the afternoon faded into a dream.

Then he finished dressing and checked to see if he had left anything. He closed the lights and slammed the door. Tomorrow he would ask her for a key. They could see each other next week. Maybe this weekend. He would sneak away. He must have her.

Trade Secrets

Once outside in the cool air, Oscar drew a long, deep breath. Just last week he had thought about fucking Sarna Bramson, and now he had. You never know what life has in store, he thought, as he wondered how long it would be before he could suck those tits.

He began walking quickly to catch the northbound train. The distance to the station was less than a half-mile. A taxi in this god-awful traffic would be useless. He felt slightly shaky, but he trudged on, taking long strides, now and then strutting like a peacock, thinking about how well he had performed. He had screwed the hell out of her. Now he couldn't get her out of his mind. As he moved closer to the station, he promised that he would call her tomorrow morning and then realized that he didn't have her phone number. Why hadn't he written down her phone number? Across from the station at the corner of Madison and Canal, distracted at having forgotten this, he looked to the left before he stepped off the curb to see if a car was coming. Everything was clear. Then he stepped down.

What he never considered was that the real danger would be coming from the other direction.

***

Sarna left Oscar in the apartment and drove to Glencoe, ruminating over what she had done. Jason greeted her in the front hall. Afraid to ask about her afternoon, he tried not to catch her eye. Sarna shot past him and went straight into the kitchen to get a Diet Coke. There was a salad in the refrigerator left over from last night. She sat down at the breakfast table and picked at the vegetables. She had done everything possible to salvage their lives, but she knew now it was over. Jason had let her go too far, and if she stayed in the marriage, it would always be that way. A wave of disgust washed over her, a sadness that verged on depression. After a few bites, she was too tired and disappointed to eat. She threw out the salad and stared at the lake in a daze. Although the plan had been hers, Jason's passivity was a brick wall. For all these years, she had hidden this side of Jason, choosing to invent him as she had needed him to be: a man who made markets, whose clerks followed him around like a god. The thought of Oscar's clammy hands on her skin made her cringe. That indelible touch would always be there, and Jason had let her do it!

Replaying the scene with Oscar in her mind, she reminded herself that it had only been an act, no different from a nude love scene in a movie. But this wasn't Hollywood, and she was no movie star. It was impossible to shake off the messy, personal dilemma confronting her. She may have saved Jason, but the marriage was dead. Her ingenuity and his inertia would be a continuing theme she could no longer accept.

She would be the first to admit she had chosen Jason for all the wrong reasons. The lifestyle she coveted was gone, but that was not the central issue. No amount of money could compensate for this! Had he protected her, refused to let her go through with this, it might be different. Now she had lost all respect for him. What he had let her do proved that he didn't really care about anyone but himself. She watched him from across the table and decided that she couldn't love him anymore. If she had saved him, which she very well may have done, it would be for another woman. Her eyes surveyed the Italian tile behind the sink, custom-made imports that once filled her time as she dashed from store to store making this house into a colossal palace. Today, it felt like a mausoleum.

Sarna left the kitchen without saying a word and walked into her bedroom, lush with expensive tassels hanging from the slightly- parted draperies, the bed heaped with tiny pillows. She placed her head on one of the pillows and cried. She closed her eyes and when he came into the room she refused to talk. She wondered how he felt. Sarna could never figure out if Jason was plagued by those issues he refused to discuss. He could avoid issues for weeks, even months at a time. If Jason were able to confront the truth--that he had actually let Sarna's body be used to free himself, could he go on with his life as if nothing had happened? Even if he could conceal the truth from himself, this episode would haunt her for the rest of her life. She could never wash away the reality of Oscar's touch.

Stranded with her feelings, like someone on a platform during a raging fire, if she kept these feelings to herself, she might burst. If she exposed them and Jason didn't acknowledge them, she would feel more isolated. They had reached the end of the road.

The T.V. was on. Sarna wiped her eyes and tried to focus on the evening news hoping that by watching someone else's problems, hers might not seem so heavy. A ghastly image caught her attention, and she jumped up. She turned up the sound.

Like all dreadful events that fill a television screen, what she saw stretched her capacity for reason. She blinked her huge brown eyes to be sure that was she was watching was real. There it was!

The newscaster in a gray suit and yellow tie announced that a trader from the Exchange had been killed, hit by one of the buses that had been re-routed to go against traffic. It was an experiment of the Mayor's and had killed a pedestrian last month. Chicagoans were not accustomed to looking to the right when they stepped off the curb. The peril in crossing a street was that traffic streamed from the left.

Holly Rozner

"The death was the second in the city's trial run within a short period and would more than likely prompt the Mayor to reconsider this plan," the newscaster emphasized while Sarna tried to digest what she saw. There was a picture of the victim on the screen for nearly a minute. How did they manage to get these pictures so quickly, Sarna wondered, as she stared straight into the face of Oscar Doheney?

chapter 39

KEN LAY NEXT to Remy, fumbling with the buttons on her blouse, his body searching hers. Their favorite jazz filled the room as Remy let him slide into her. He brushed her hair from her face and kissed her. A tiny slice of the moon slipped through the bedroom window and hit his eyes from an angle, shadowing the scar on his right cheek. His remote stare had been replaced with intense longing. Nothing would separate them, not even her instinctive impulse to insist she was right when, in fact, it was Ken who had been right all along.

When they unlocked themselves, it was nearly 9:00, and they hadn't eaten dinner. Ken's arm around Remy, his gray eyes locked in hers. "I am crazy about you, Remy Masterman, but I am starving."

She leaned over to kiss him and smoothed his hair from his forehead. Then she sat up and threw her legs over the side of the bed, picked up the phone, dialed her favorite Chinese restaurant and announced her order: vegetable moo shoo, hot and sour soup and garlic chicken.

"I'm going to clean up," said Ken, slipping out from under the covers.

Holly Rozner

Remy curled her legs on the bed and wrapped the pink satin sheet around her, basking in the happiness that was now hers. A new episode in her love affair with Ken had begun. The past had steeled her to expect things would not work out as they did for other people. Life could turn on a dime. Now it was turning in her direction. Still plagued by the uncertainty of not yet unraveling the facts surrounding her father's death, for the first time in a very long time, Remy didn't feel the throbbing anxiety of trying to hold Alan's attention or the tension of having been married to Stuart Masterman who tried to control her.

Ken had been absent too long. She got out of the bed, went into the bathroom and opened the shower door. The water splashed against the glass as Ken pulled her in. When he reached between her legs, she trembled with desire.

Afterwards, she stepped onto the white rug on the marble floor, wrapped in the terry cloth robe she had bought for Ken's birthday a few months ago. The bathroom had been configured to double as a dressing room, with a vanity and a row of lights along the mirror where she could do her make-up. Ken emerged from the shower and leaned over to kiss her neck. Then he stood near her, his weight on one leg, his arms crossed, watching her, as if he were discovering her for the first time. He took her face in his and pushed her damp hair behind her ears, softly kissing her cheeks. Then he knelt down next to her.

"I don't like the name," Ken said, as if he were thinking out loud.

"What name?"

"Masterman. It's too sharp."

"Oh?"

"It has the wrong ring," he said, locking his gaze in hers.

"And what should it be?"

She put the hairbrush down and ran her fingers along his face.

"Baldwin," he said.

She was afraid to move, afraid that this moment would dissolve.

Ken looked directly into her eyes.

"Marry me, Remy."

This was the moment she had been waiting for. Now it scared her.

"What's the matter, Remy?" he asked.

"Ken, there's been so much back and forth. We're together, and then we're apart. It changes so fast."

"We were never apart because I wanted us to be. I've loved you since I first saw you."

She rested her head on his chest and clung to him. He wrapped his arms around her, and she could feel his heart beating against her skin. Remy had rehearsed this moment in her mind and always let it fade. There had been such a mess to clean up, so many things left unsaid during those months when she felt locked out. Now here he was, saying the words she wanted to hear.

"Of course I will marry you," she said looking up and laughing.

"I thought you were going to walk out on me."

"I will never walk out on you, Ken."

"Does that mean we have a deal here?"

"Yes. Of course."

"I haven't bought a ring," he said.

"You know I don't care about that. I care only about us."

"I am so in love with you, Remy."

"Kiss me, Ken."

She parted her lips and he pressed his to her, pulling her close.

"I've got to call Lara," she whispered as his face grazed hers.

"Not just yet," he commanded.

She reached for him with her tongue.

"I want dozens of kids," he said, breaking loose and smiling into her smile.

"Just two," she said, nipping at his lips.

His arm steadied her. They held each other with their hands, with their eyes, hungry for the exact touch that would satisfy their passion, only to find that once they met that desire, they wanted each other again and then again.

It was nearly 10:00 when the doorbell rang.

"The food," Remy announced.

Ken jumped out of bed and threw on a shirt so he could open the door for the deliveryman. Remy tousled her hair and put on a silk robe.

"Let's eat in bed," she said.

"We'll spend our life in bed, honey."

Remy kissed Ken and walked to the kitchen to get a yellow laminate tray and some dishes. When she came back into the bedroom, she sat on the bed, her face flushed. Ken unpacked the cartons of food while Remy made space for them to eat.

"We will pick out a ring next week. Then you can plan the wedding," he said as he searched for the TV control.

"When I was a kid, I wanted the whole package, and when I married Stuart, that's what we had. Maybe it should be just a few people."

"Your choice."

"Let's just have something small and private," she said.

"As long as you're there, it doesn't matter. Now let's eat." Remy had bought dishes on trips she had taken with her parents, adding to a collection begun by her mother. She handed Ken two she had bought in France last year. As

Trade Secrets

she watched him empty the containers onto the porcelain, Ken turned on the television set.

When Remy glanced up, she couldn't believe what was on the screen. "Ken, look. That's Oscar Doheney," she shouted. "There was a picture of him on TV, and it looked as if he had been booked for something. I didn't catch the words."

"Can't be."

"Watch." She caught a glimpse of the photo on another station just as a commercial interrupted. Again she had missed the content.

Remy grabbed the remote and flashed from one station to another. There was a snatch about a new elevated station the city was building, followed by another story of a hit- and- run murder on the South Side. Then a brief story that a bus, routed to go against traffic on a Loop street, had accidentally killed a pedestrian.

She had seen Oscar's face. She was sure of it.

Frantically, she searched for another channel. Finally, she located news. It was just starting.

Ken stood near the bed. As the incredible report unfolded, Ken Baldwin stood silent, digesting the story before he grabbed the phone. He listened to the TV report with one ear, as he dialed the U.S. Attorney at home. The announcer rambled on while Ken Baldwin came face to face with a profound truth. Remy was right. It was Oscar, and he was dead. A photo of him was followed by a short story about the Mayor's controversial plan about buses traveling against traffic on Madison Street.

Remy looked at Ken whose face was covered in disbelief.

"Doheny has been killed," Ken announced into the phone.

Holly Rozner

There was a long pause while Ken held the receiver to his ear hardly able to digest what was happening. "Do you think it was an accident?" Ken asked.

Remy sat still, her heart racing. She thought about her father. Had Oscar been killed? Had her father been killed? She searched Ken's face. She needed him to calm her down. But she could see from the look in his eyes that he was visibly shaken. All at once she realized that they were thinking the same thing. Oscar could have been the victim of a dirty plot and if that were the case...

"Whoever was after Oscar might be looking for Jason Bramson or Remy Masterman," Ken said into the mouthpiece, finishing the terrifying thought for her.

Once Ken had validated her fears, each of them knew that if Zach had killed Oscar, he would not stop until he had them all.

***

Eventually Zach's men had to tell him they had lost track of Joey. With surprising calm, Zach told them to drive to Joey's apartment and wait for him. "Stay there until you find him. Then call me."

The two men picked up sandwiches and potato chips and drove to the north side. Then they holed up in a van on the street where Joey lived, taking turns sleeping. This time they had a gun. Very few cars traveled down this street so it would be easy to grab Joey, get the tapes and follow Zach's orders.

As soon as he got home Joey made three copies of the tapes, one for himself, one for Ken and one just in case. He fixed a sandwich and decided to go to bed early so he could get to Ken's office as quickly as possible tomorrow. It would be his day of reckoning. The following morning when he awoke, he dressed quickly: white shirt, blue suit and yellow tie, everything selected to make a good impression on Ken.

Trade Secrets

It was time to wrap up the adventure, to stop Zach from infecting more lives. At 8:40 a.m. he stuffed one copy of the tape into his pocket and called Ken's office.

"I've got what you need to clinch your case. It's about Oscar Doheney," Joey blurted out.

"Oscar?"

"I have a tape about the schemes that he and Zach Silverman cooked up. I tried to deliver them last night, but it was too late. I can be there within the hour."

"Oscar's dead," Ken interrupted.

"He will be after you hear this."

"He was killed last night by a bus."

What was Ken talking about? Just hours ago, Oscar was banging Sarna. How could he be dead?

Joey launched into the story, his big brown eyes stinging as he insisted that the evidence in his breast pocket could help Remy, ignoring Ken Baldwin when he said the tape was meaningless now that Oscar was dead.

"This is important," Joey insisted.

"The testimony of a dead man cannot be used as evidence."

"It exposes their setup. He even admits that Remy was used as a ploy."

"I'm sorry, Joey."

"It can't be over," Joey screamed. "It can't be. We worked so hard. You have to hear the tape. You have to."

"It's a blind alley." Ken said.

"Just listen to them," Joey insisted.

Ken thought to himself. Maybe there was some clue they could use. Maybe a thread that could link Zach to something tangible.

"Bring it over. But you don't have to hurry."

Joey let the phone drop. He paced around his apartment. There was no way he could let go of this. He would deliver the tape to Ken, but he wouldn't stop there, not after all this! Something more daring had to be done. He would go to face Zach. He imagined the mighty Zach Silverman squirming when he heard this confession!

He grabbed the extra tape he had made, put it into his pocket and telephoned Zach Silverman's office.

"Joey, what's up?" Zach asked, accepting the call.

"I have something for you," said Joey.

"Sure, kid."

"About Oscar."

"Oscar's dead." Zach said.

"I'll be there in an hour." Joey said in a businesslike manner. Zach hadn't refused and that was the first hurdle. Joey patted his breast pocket to be sure both tapes were secure and opened the front door. Outside of his apartment was the *Trib*. He picked it up. There, on the front page, was a picture of Oscar Doheney with an expose' about the failed bus plan. He took the paper, shut the door, and walked down three flights of stairs to the street, never noticing the van across the street where Zach's men sat. Only seconds before Joey had exited the building, Zach had ordered his men to let the kid alone.

Joey's plan was to drop a set of tapes at Ken's office. Joey sauntered past the bungalows toward the L station, basking in his new role, relishing the company he was about to keep. This appointment with Zach would put him eye to eye with the most consequential person he had ever known. No longer a clerk, he was in control. Once Zach heard Oscar's confession, this towering icon would cave.

The ride from Ravenswood carried Joey through the guts of Chicago. As the train wound its way downtown, he rehearsed his monologue in his head. Once the train pulled into the Chicago and Northwestern Station, he hurried towards Ken's office. Ken wasn't there, but that didn't matter. He left one tape with his secretary knowing that anyone who worked for Ken Baldwin was trustworthy. Then he ran to the fabulous glass building where his career began and ended, his stride becoming a dance of revenge. While he waited in Zach's anteroom, he picked up the *Wall Street Journal* and skimmed the lead article. His right foot stomped nervously on the floor and he fidgeted in his seat. His mind was on one thing. He couldn't wait for the little Napoleon to open the door. When Zach finally swept him into his office, Joey was ready to roll.

The marble desk, the complex machines, none of it impressed Joey today. This heartless czar had money and power, but Joey had the goods. Maybe the government couldn't use the tape as hard evidence, but he knew Oscar's confession would squeeze Zach. Joey took the same chair he had sat in when Zach first hired him. Then their eyes met as he was about to ambush his victim.

Zach forced a weak smile and sat behind his desk. He could see from the wildly fierce stare in Joey's eyes that Joey could be trouble. This little shrimp made him jumpy. He presumed Joey had the tapes. This visit saved him the messy job of having to steal them and maybe even having to do something nasty in the process. Another murder would complicate an already snarled plot. He had to remain calm and find out what Joey wanted.

The small talk ended quickly. Joey pulled the tape out from his pocket, took a recorder out of the bag he carried and placed it on the desk so that they could both listen. As the tape rolled, their eyes remained glued to the machine, each man visualizing the scene. The high pitched sounds of Sarna's voice made it obvious that Oscar had been manipulated. As they listened to Oscar explain the intricate web Zach had concocted, Joey's eyes were riveted on Zach.

When they got to the part about Harry Saks, sweat formed on Zach's brow.

Zach twisted in his chair like a caged animal. Zach had called Ivan as soon as Joey telephoned him and Ivan assured him that the kid had no legal grounds, but the Internal Revenue Service would be interested in this. Zach didn't want them snooping around, unleashing a new set of problems. Even that would be chickenfeed if anyone got wind of the Harry Saks story. In the intricacy of this master plot were glaring holes. Zach knew that this tape couldn't be allowed to get into the wrong hands. If anyone delved into the mutual fund, it would be a landmine. An idiot could figure out how they had stolen the winners, bankrupting the fund with losing trades. A derivative shareholder suit would bankrupt Zach. Zach's eyes burned as he acknowledged that this liability would be in addition to what was owed IRS for unlawful under-reporting. With Oscar dead, Zach would be responsible for the whole thing. Then it dawned on him that Sarna Bramson was strutting around with this information too.

Zach Silverman was in a stinging face-off with Joey Fortunato. This runt had him by the balls. Electricity charged the air as Zach tried to figure out how to outsmart this Brooklyn dago.

Zach grabbed a cigar and began chewing on it while Joey crossed his legs and sat back in the chair. Zach couldn't remember when he had been in a position like this. It was extortion, the kind he might have used if he had been Joey. He swirled around to face the window to take in the view he always used to solve his problems. Skyscrapers loomed over the Loop. He reasoned with himself that even the Mayor and Governor had profited from his schemes. Zach had funded their campaigns with the millions he had stolen. But the SEC was a different animal. Ivan would shit when he heard Joey's threats. He could be disbarred if anyone found out how much he had skimmed for himself in these sweet deals. So far Ivan had kept the IRS off of their backs, but it would be different if someone sniffed a homicide. A fine was one thing, but jail was another.

"Exactly what are you looking for?" Zach asked Joey.

"Get out of Remy's way," Joey said. "She never did anything wrong."

"And then?"

"Let Sarna make a living."

"What do you mean?"

"You know what I mean. She needs to work without anyone standing in her way."

"And Jason?"

"Jason will cooperate with you if you leave Sarna alone. He needs her to get them out of their financial mess. Jason's testimony will make the investigation valid. He can be convinced to place the blame on Oscar. It makes no difference now. Oscar can't go to jail, but you can. Go along with my plan and you walk away."

Zach let the room fill with cigar smoke. He watched it make small curls as he held on to a deadpan expression. He didn't want the kid to know how much he liked the idea. The heavy gold ring on his finger caught the sun and glinted in Joey's eye. Zach turned it around so that the enormous diamond was folded into his palm. Joey hadn't said a word about Harry Saks. The kid never knew Harry. Maybe he hadn't understood what Oscar had said, couldn't know how he made sure that Harry couldn't get in their way. That was Zach's trade secret. One favor for another. As always. *A quid pro quo.* Wasn't that what trading was, after all?

Somewhere there was evidence that could link him to Harry's accident. And a note in Zach's handwriting with a diagram of the ravines. The day after the accident, Oscar couldn't find that piece of paper. Maybe Oscar had hidden it. Now a natural set of events erased the deed; it was doubtful that anyone would ever discover that scribble.

Zach reached over his desk for the Baccarat paperweight given to him last year after his party. Perched on it was a picture of Hermes, a replica of the image that graced the entrance of the Exchange. Zach loved the Greek gods, loved them for their conquests, their deceit and their disguises. He wished one of them could materialize and tell him how to proceed. Joey offered him an out. The plan was simple, an easy solution. Oscar would be remembered as the author of this fiasco and it would stop there. As long as the tapes were concealed, Zach would be safe. Joey was right. Sarna would keep her mouth shut as long as she was guaranteed a living; Ken Baldwin's investigation wouldn't be a complete failure and he would be satisfied because Remy would be protected. Jason would go to jail, eventually getting off for good behavior. The Feds would find someone else to taunt. More important, Zach's power would not be diminished. Only Oscar's reputation would be ignominiously ruined and who gives a shit about Oscar? He was dead.

Zach turned towards the window. He could have Joey killed, but that was a terrible risk. There was probably a copy of the tape in Joey's apartment and if that was searched, they could trace everything.

This kid had it down pat. It was a bitter pill. But it would be OK. Under this plan, someone would take Oscar's place and there would be no shake-up. A wild grin covered Zach's face as he slammed his fist down on the fifteen thousand dollar table.

Joey's plan was perfect.

chapter 40

KEN LISTENED CAREFULLY to the recording before deciding he had to let Remy hear it. Explaining this would be so difficult. How could she comprehend that her father had been killed by a friend and partner, and that the murderer was free?

Ken had told her to meet him at his office. When she came in, he took her in his arms not knowing how to warn her that what she would be hearing would be disturbing. Then he removed the tape from his pocket. "Remy, sit down. You need to be calm." He pulled out a small machine and watched her listen to the incredible confession of the man, who only days ago, had tried to implicate her in a trading scandal.

Her stare became blank. She began to quiver.

"They killed him," she said. "They killed him to hide their schemes. That was how my father died. It all makes sense. My father trusted him, so when he discovered that Zach was stealing customer money, he either had to turn on his lifelong friend or condone his behavior. No wonder he was depressed and wouldn't discuss anything with me."

"Remy, I know how hard this is."

Holly Rozner

"It's worse than I ever imagined. I suspected wrongdoing, but never this. My father was an innocent man. He tried to do the right thing, and he got in their way. They're ruthless, Ken. They always will be. Tell me, tell me in plain English, how Zach can get away with this?"

"It's how the law works. There is no one to testify. The tapes are worthless. They can give you some information—hopefully some closure on what happened to your father, but they can never be used in a courtroom. The prosecutor would be laughed out of court. Murder requires evidence. The evidence is gone because, at the time of the accident, no one surmised anything intentional."

"I lost my father, Ken. Do you understand?"

"Of course."

"Then you know I can't let Zach get off."

Ken reached out for Remy and pulled her towards him. "I know this is unbearable for you. When this investigation began, no one thought we would end up with a murder suspect. We knew there were secrets on the trading floor. We uncovered them. We had no idea how complicated Zach's web was, or what he was concealing."

Remy held her arms around herself trying to let the news digest.

Then she turned towards the door.

"I need time alone. This is business for you. But this was my family."

"What about us?" he asked.

"We have to wait," she said, grabbing a sweater.

It was one of those perfect Chicago days when the lake was as blue as the sky. Remy walked a long distance to Lincoln Park and then to the lakefront where she often found solace. She knew what her father would say. He would tell her to go on with her life. "When there is nothing you can do, don't try to do it. Put it behind you and move on."

Tears welled as she imagined this conversation with him, one that she had many times growing up: when Alan ditched her, when she knew she had to leave Stuart. Moving on was always tough, she thought, remembering problems she had faced as a young girl after her mother died, when she had only her father to rely on. When you are dealt bad cards, you have to be tough. The good days are easy, her father warned, but it's the hard ones that make us strong.

And he was right. But her father been murdered and the murderer would be free. If what Ken said was true and there was nothing she could do, how could she go on?

Her mind drifted to Sarna. How brave she was, Remy thought, trying to consider what she must have gone through to think up this audacious plan. And for what? Only to have that filthy Oscar die. An ironic death that would exonerate Zach.

Remy walked along the lake for an hour until she came to the corner of Oak and Michigan. There she crossed the street and walked two blocks south to the 900 Building where she rode the escalator to the mezzanine where a musician was playing Gershwin on a grand piano. Remy listened to the melodies as she calculated her next move. She thought about calling Lara, but what was there to say? No one could assuage this awful experience.

She could never live with this without doing something. Not even Ken could make it right.

She sat for an hour listening to the familiar melodies that she remembered as a young girl when her world was innocent. Then as if she had known all along what she had to do, she figured out how she would have to proceed. Even if she put herself in danger.

***

Joey answered the phone in his apartment. He had been watching TV and finishing up a pizza he had picked up on the way home from the gym. The future didn't scare him anymore. Someday he would find another career. He had witnessed the insides of the financial world, and certainly he would be able to use this knowledge.

He didn't feel like talking, but the clanging reverberated through the small apartment.

On the tenth ring, he grabbed it.

"It's me, honey."

He put down the beer he was drinking and collapsed onto the easy chair.

"I need to talk to you, Joey."

He had dreamed about this moment over the past few weeks. He missed Rosa's body next to him when he went to sleep, and when he reached for her during the night, the empty bed rattled him. He missed the sex, the fun, her cute little nose and he missed her smile. At times during this past week he missed her so much that he didn't know how he would go on. But not after this morning. Facing Zach Silverman had changed him.

He was no longer the Joey Fortunato she had fallen for—the one who threw money around and bought her expensive bracelets. No longer the silhouette of his own dashed dreams.

He was a guy on the street again. He had no more illusions. Rosa had fallen for some guy and he wasn't that person anymore. If he ever could retrieve his lifestyle, he wanted no part of her.

"It's over, Rosa."

"I miss you, Joey."

"I miss you too, but it's finished."

"Joey, this is your Rosa."

Joey felt his pulse quicken. It would have been so easy to let her back into his life. To let her come over and screw her in the dark on the living room carpet where they could go at it for hours at a time. That life was no more.

"The Joey you are looking for doesn't live here anymore."

He hung up. When the phone rang again, he took it off the hook. After a while, he fell asleep dreaming about New York and how much he missed that too. He had come to Chicago and had learned a lot. He could never go back to the Exchange. The people in his inner circle were gone. He thought about his family and how much he missed them, even his father's stinking barber shop. He thought about what he could do on Wall Street now that he knew about the markets and how down and dirty the financial world actually was. He didn't need Chicago anymore.

It was time to go back.

***

Remy walked from North Michigan Avenue into the LaSalle Street canyon and across the bridge. There, on the other side of the River, was the rubble of her past. She walked up the stairs to the coat room where she housed her trading jacket. She reached across the counter and placed it on her, fingering the badge that was embossed with her initials. Then she picked up the telephone and asked for Zach Silverman's office. She identified herself as Remy Masterman and the secretary said she could see Zach Silverman in a half hour.

She walked around the building to the North Tower and rode the exclusive elevator in the interior of the building to the fortieth floor. As she got off, she held her hand against her stomach and took a deep breath, wondering how the words she had rehearsed on the way over would sound when she spoke them.

Holly Rozner

The wait in the ante-room was short and she hardly had time to leaf through the magazines strewn on the counter when a woman with glasses and short red hair called for her to come in.

"Mr. Silverman," Remy said.

"Sit down, Remy. I don't think we've ever met."

"Thank you for seeing me on such short notice."

"I always try to see traders who have questions about the Exchange."

"But I have no questions," she said coldly.

"Ah, my dear, I am sure you have something to say."

She studied his thick body and held his gaze as she readied herself for what would be the biggest role she ever played.

"I have plenty to say, Zach. But there are no questions. I had a lot of questions at one time, but I got the answers. Now you might have some questions."

"Whatever you say, dear."

"You call your traders 'dear'?" she asked.

Remy examined Zach, the would-be Titan. His crisp white shirt and red tie. Slick hair. Bulging eyes. She saw him clench his fist.

His eyes fell on her blouse. Was she here on some insinuation of discrimination, he wondered, thinking he may have walked into a trap.

"Just making a joke, Remy. What do you want?"

"I am here to talk about Harry Saks."

He blanched. "What about Harry Saks?"

"You tell me," she shot back.

"I don't answer questions," Zach said.

"I told you, I don't have any questions to ask."

She saw his brow tighten. She maintained a neutral expression as she kept her eyes on him. The muscles in his throat tightened and his skin became ashen. For a moment, he looked like a dead man.

"What do you want, Remy?" he asked, as he turned to face the city.

"I want you to look at me," she demanded.

He swirled his chair to face her.

"I am Harry Saks' daughter."

"Don't be ridiculous," he bellowed.

"I was Andrea Saks. I changed my name to Remy before college. Then I married Stuart Masterman. You were invited to the wedding, but you couldn't come. I met you in my teens when I visited your office with my father. I was here the year the Exchange gave you that crystal globe."

Zach removed his hand from the globe. He was accustomed to rolling it around in his hand when he got nervous. He stared at her, looking for some familiar feature in her gorgeous face. Oscar had told him about Remy. Everyone at the Exchange knew about this glamorous doll who tried to keep things straight in the pit. But Harry Saks' kid? It was preposterous. Not this dame. Impossible.

"As I was saying," she continued in an even tone. "I am Harry Saks' daughter. I came here two years ago to find out what happened to my father."

"He died in an automobile accident."

"He was killed," she said.

Zach reached for the phone. He could have her removed from his office. He had plenty of people who could do that. He needed Ivan. What was she saying? *She could be killed too.*

"I know everything, Zach. I even know about the mutual funds and how you moved winning trades into your account and bankrupted your clients. I know about Oscar and the kids you have financed. I know about every filthy scheme."

Holly Rozner

He didn't answer. He just sat there thinking about what he could do next and whom he could talk to before he said too much. How did she get this information? And the balls to confront him? No one treated him like this. Who did she think she was? His mind was spinning with options, but none of them made any sense. If he called for her to be removed and if she had a plan, she would walk away and execute it. He needed to find out more, see if he couldn't charm her. After all, he was the lord of this kingdom and who was she anyway?

But she didn't give him time to say a word.

"Here's what you are going to do, Zach, so I don't put you in jail."

He sat quietly. She knew too much. Too much for a broad. Her father's daughter, all right. He had the manpower to get rid of her, but if someone found out she was in his office, his hands would be tied.

"I don't know what you are talking about," Zach said, straightening his tie.

"No one will go to jail if you cooperate."

"You think you are going to tell me what to do."

"Absolutely," she replied, and she knew he would listen. She never even blinked as she launched into the scenario she had rehearsed. The plan was much like the one Ivan and he had discussed. Remy told Zach that she was leaving the Exchange that day, selling her seat, giving up her badge, but that Sarna would stay in the pit.

"She doesn't deserve to suffer," Remy commanded.

"She's...." but he stopped when he saw the venom in Remy's eyes. He wasn't sure how far she would go or what she was willing to do next, but he wasn't taking any chances.

He turned his back to her again, taking the glass globe with him in his hand as he mulled through the possible outcome.

"What else?" he asked without looking at her.

"You will leave."

"Leave? Leave what?" he screamed standing up and hovering over the desk. He thought he might faint, or throw the globe at her.

"You will leave the Exchange. If you stay I will expose your secrets to your children. This tape might not be good in court, but do you want your family to hear it? Oscar is dead, but he left behind a whole narrative of your deeds, and I will take them to the newspapers, or even write a book, but I will not let you stay here for the rest of your life."

This is my life. What else is there? A wife he no longer loved. A daughter who didn't return his phone calls. How would he see his grand kids, the only people that he cared about? This Masterwoman knew too much, enough to ruin what was left of his life. Even if she left him alone, could the machine ever run the way it once had? With the Feds around the corner, nothing would ever be the same. At least she hadn't threatened to go to the IRS. Maybe she hadn't figured out the tax ramifications of their plot, how the winning trades were taxed at a special break, making the millions they stole worth even more. The prospect of exposure was indeed untenable. Still, he wasn't going to be told what to do.

"You can't make me leave."

"I don't have to, Zach." She stood up. "I am going downstairs to sell my seat. In thirty minutes, I will not be a member of this Exchange, and I will no longer come under the rules of the Exchange, rules that try to keep people from speaking about what they see on the floor. Once I turn in my badge, I am no longer bound by your internal regulations. I can say what I want to whomever I want."

"But you can be sued for libel."

"Not if I speak the truth."

"Then why warn me. Why not just leave and do that."

"You and I both know that leaving is the worst punishment anyone could give you."

He began to twitch. This was a dream. It had to be. She was right, of course. Without this building, this universe, these people to boss around, he was just a middle- aged man. But such arrogance. He looked into her eyes trying to find Harry's eyes in hers. Instead he saw Harry's delicate mouth-that mouth that was constantly telling him how they were going to end up behind bars if they didn't stop their crap. He clenched his fist and stopped himself from banging it on the table. It would do no good. She had him. This child. When did she say they had met? He couldn't think while room began to spin. He could feel himself getting nauseous and the crevices under his arm getting wet.

"You have one week, Zach. One week. Then I go to the papers. In one week, you need to be gone, not just hiding in a corner office, but gone. And trust me, whoever takes your place had better have clean hands, because I am going to be sure that Sarna knows exactly what he is doing. The only person who is to benefit from any of this will be her. No more bagmen. Just some rich trades for her. So help me, Zach, if it kills me, I will close up the whole goddamn place."

She meant it. If he ran to Ivan or Anthony, they would make him listen to her to save their own goddamn asses. He made them all millionaires, and what did it get him?

He put the globe on the desk and stared at her. She stood up. Without speaking she turned her back to open the door. Then she walked into the hallway where she waited for a minute. On the elevator, Remy began to cry, not for her father but for the woman who had once been. Full of hope, now full of experience and truth. Her innocence had been stolen. Without hesitation Remy walked to the membership office and removed her badge. She cradled it as she had the first day it was handed her. So much had happened since that day. So much had been discovered. It was difficult to even recall how she felt when she first walked into the Exchange now that she knew everything.

On the board before her the bids and offers on the seat she had bought two years ago. Fifty-thousand dollars then. Now it was one hundred and twenty-five thousand dollars. She asked for a form and on it she wrote her offer. She hit the bid and in less than five minutes, her seat was sold to another trader, a young kid who would be anxious to place his bets. Remy wouldn't be here tomorrow or any day after that. No longer would she have to rush downtown to hold a spot or fight for a trade. The markets would rise and fall as they had for decades and there would be more crashes and no doubt, more investigations into trading infractions. She knew there was no regulation that could prevent criminals from stealing money from public customers, but she also knew she had done something significant to stop the crime spree in this building. In the future she might never even look at a newspaper to see what how markets were doing. These years had taught her a lot. She would always know more than those who never dwelled in these pits. At dinner parties when people talked about the market, she would be the one who knew the secrets, secrets she would never forget and could never tell.

Epilogue

July 15, 1989
  Crete, Greece
  Dear Remy:

I am writing from Greece, the one place I always wanted to visit. It is glorious here. Every night I read the stories about the Gods who presided over this war and that love affair. What a world that was!

This is the first time I have been away since Jason went to jail. I went to visit him, but the visits are very painful. It is so strange and the conversations are awkward. It's already been one year since Zach left the Exchange. Without him there are no Oscars doing their dance. Traders make real markets and there are rumors that eventually the floor will become electronic, though that is probably some years away. Wouldn't it be amazing if traders were no longer needed in the pits and the markets could become efficient?

No one really knows why Zach left. It happened very quickly, just a week or two after you gave up your seat. There were all kinds of rumors, even that he had killed a man. You know how people talk.

Thanks to you, I have learned to trade, and every now and then, one of the brokers does me a small favor. I managed to pay off Jason's legal bills and was able to sell the house. I sold it for less than it would have gotten before the '87 crash, but none of that seems important any more. I have grown up.

Jason has served nearly six months of his five year term. I hope he will find something to do when he gets out. Our marriage was over a long time ago. I filed for divorce in February. Sid and I are getting married. I want you to be the first to know.

He is here with me. I have never felt like this about anyone. He makes me laugh and makes me feel good about myself. I imagine it is how it is for you with Ken.

We will be living in Washington, so we won't be too far from you now that you and Ken are in New York. I will miss Chicago. It is where I grew up and where my family is. But I do not think I will miss the Exchange—that frenzy—the adrenalin rush, trying to catch the trade on the way up and smash it on the way down—it taught me a lot, but it is time to move on.

Even time to have a family.

When is your baby due? I hope it is girl, as lovely as you are, Remy. I do owe the Exchange one important debt. I had the chance to meet you. You changed my life. I am no longer the woman you met at the gala when we both had our eyes on Jason. I hope someday I can inspire someone, as you have inspired me.

In the meantime, mark your calendar for October 24th. I would like you to be the matron of honor and sit at the head table. The wedding will be in New York. Don't tell Ken yet, but I know that Sid will be calling him to be the best man.

I miss you, Remy. I hope we both have wonderful lives we can share with one another and remain good friends.

I love you,
Sarna

Made in the USA
Lexington, KY
27 January 2013